I0526181

MAN ADVANTAGE

L.A. WITT

MAN ADVANTAGE

Trev Allen and his ex-husband had an amicable joint custody arrangement. During the hockey season, his ex took the twins whenever Trev's team was on the road. Easy peasy.

But now, just two weeks before training camp, Trev's ex gives him an ultimatum—lock down reliable, full-time childcare for Trev's custody weeks before the start of the season, or his ex is pursuing full custody.

Trev's in a panic to keep his kids, but as luck would have it, an old friend—and old flame—is also in a jam.

Cam Wright's ex didn't just cheat, he kicked Cam out *and* got him fired. Cam's desperate and flailing... until he receives a message from a man he hasn't seen in years. Now he has hope of getting back on his feet, not to mention reconnecting with his friend and first love.

Cam's not prepared for how much Trev has glowed up. Trev is stunned by how kind time and a fitness career have been to Cam. The intense attraction is both instantaneous and hotter than ever; living together, it's only a matter of time before passion ignites.

But Cam is depending on Trev for stability. Trev is depending on Cam to keep joint custody of his kids. Like it or not, they *need* each other.

Which means if they stop *wanting* each other, their lives could come unraveled.

Man Advantage is a 95,000-word standalone Trans M/M hockey romance.

Copyright Information

CHAPTER 1

TREV

"What the fuck?" Standing in in my kitchen, I stared at my ex-husband's face on my phone screen. "You can't just... drop that on me!"

Bryan gave a sharp shrug. "And you can't just expect me to live my entire life around your schedule anymore. Enough is enough."

I raked a hand through my hair and exhaled. "For fuck's sake..."

"If you want partial custody," he declared, "then you need to step up. It's been long enough."

"Step up?" I glared at him. "I'm doing the best I can. It isn't like I can ask the League to lighten up my schedule so I—"

"You can figure it out," he snapped. "Either lock down some consistent, reliable, in-home childcare while you're on the road, or I'm petitioning for primary custody."

And child support, he didn't say.

"I..." My head was spinning with everything he'd just thrown at me. "You know training camp is in two weeks, right?"

He smirked, adding to the fiery ball of rage in my chest. "Of course I know that."

Yeah. Of course he fucking did. Since his new piece of ass would *also* be going to training camp.

I gritted my teeth. "Okay, so you know two weeks isn't really enough time to find someone, vet them, get them started, make sure—"

"Figure it out," he said, "and let me know what you come up with."

Before I could answer, the call ended.

I very, very nearly hurled my phone across the kitchen, not giving a damn in that moment if it shattered into a thousand pieces. Instead, I dropped it beside the sink and, with a groan, I pressed my elbows into the granite countertop.

I was done. Just so, so goddamned done.

Our divorce had been messy, co-parenting had been a bear, and at every turn it seemed like he wanted to make things worse. Like he got some thrill out of trying to make me regret divorcing him. Right, because the divorce was my fault. Sure, I'd been the one to initiate it, but I wasn't the one to put my dick where it didn't belong, take photos and videos, and "accidentally" sync them with the shared cloud.

"Jesus fucking Christ on a Zamboni," I muttered into the stillness.

I cringed inwardly, fully expecting one of my six-year-olds to pipe up and say, *"You said a swear, Dad!"*

Neither of them did, though. Because they weren't here. They were with Bryan this week, and my house would be painfully empty until I picked them up on Tuesday per our custody agreement.

You think I wanted *this, Bryan?* I scrubbed a hand over my face. *You think I enjoy being away from my kids this much?*

That was only going to get worse during the hockey season. It always did; being away from them sucked when I was on the road, and now they were gone sometimes when I was at home, too.

And if I don't appease Bryan, then they might be gone all the time except like one weekend a month.

My blood ran cold.

Bryan wasn't one to bluff. If I didn't figure out some kind of in-home childcare solution, he would absolutely be in his attorney's office, making sure we had to drag our asses back to family court. The judge last time had already been salty with me over being gone so much throughout the year, but Bryan had assured her that we would make it work during the regular season, then resume a normal custody schedule during the off season.

If we got that same judge again... fucking hell.

And wasn't it just my luck that for all Bryan hated being at the mercy of the hockey schedule, he had a serious thing for hockey players. Now he was quite openly dating one of my teammates—something the tabloids and social media were having a *ball* with.

Fuck my life.

How the hell did he even still have a libido? Because mine had been dead and gone for months before I'd finally dropped the hammer on the divorce. I couldn't even jerk off these days, while *he* was sending my teammate to games and practices with a very smug smile on his stupid fucking face.

And now he wants our kids to be with him—with them—all the time? Over my dead body.

Of course he could've brought this up at any time during the off season. Any time during the past few goddamned months. But no, he'd waited until I was almost walking out the door to training camp to drop this bomb on me.

Probably because he knew I wouldn't be able to line someone up in time, so his petition for full custody would be a slam dunk.

Were you always this underhanded and conniving? What the hell?

The more pressing question, though, was what was I supposed to do? It had taken me until the twins were two to be comfortable leaving them with their grandparents overnight. They were six now, and I still didn't like the idea of anyone other than a relative or close friend watching them. Now I was supposed to... what? Hire someone, then leave them alone with the boys for hours and hours while I went to training camp? And for *days* at a time while I was on road trips?

I rubbed my eyes. Then I snatched my phone off the counter. I was on a private group chat with several friends from back home who I trusted not to leak screencaps and whatnot. Even if they didn't have a solution, they'd let me vent and bitch.

> I don't suppose any of you know someone who's vetted and trustworthy that I can fly out here on a moment's notice to be a live-in nanny or something, do you?

God, just reading that was depressing. How was this my life all of a sudden?

The responses started quickly.

> Mike: Are you serious, or is your autocorrect fucking with all of us?

LOL Serious unfortunately. TL;DR, ex is being an ass.

Don: What else is new? He's always been an ass.

Now you tell me.

Jake: You have always been a slow learner.

(middle finger emoji)

Don: So you need someone to watch the kids while you're on the road or something?

If I want to keep joint custody, yeah.

Jake: No shit? He's going to try for full custody over it? What a dick.

Mike: Ouch, that's brutal.

Tell me about it.

Jake: Actually, I might know someone. Got a minute to FaceTime?

Absolutely. Thanks, man.

Seconds later, the FaceTime request came through, and I accepted the call. "Hey, what've you got?"

Jake cut right to the chase: "You remember Cameron Wright, don't you?"

I blinked. That was a name I hadn't heard in a while. "Of course I do. Why?"

"Because he's in a bind right now, too, and you guys might be able to help each other out."

"I'm listening."

"Right, so he'll have to tell you the whole story, but the

short version is that he and his ex split, and the guy sabotaged his job, too. So he's out of a place to live, out of a job, and—man, he's *really* fucking desperate right now."

"Oh, shit. I'll, um... Yeah, I can reach out to him." I paused and flipped to my contacts. Cam was still there, of course, but there were no texts. No calls. Not since I'd upgraded my phone, and probably not since two or three phones before that. I was horrified and a bit embarrassed to realize just how long it had been since Cam and I had talked. "I, um... I don't know if I have his current number."

"He hasn't changed it since before he moved to Portland, but hold on." Jake furrowed his brow at his screen, probably perusing his own contacts. He read off the number he had for Cam, and it did indeed match the one I had.

"Okay, great. I'll give him a call. Thanks, man!"

"Any time."

We ended the call, and I gnawed my lip as I peered at Cam's contact. He and I had never had any kind of falling out; we'd just sort of drifted apart as life took us in opposite directions. I'd tried to reconnect a few times, especially when I was back on the West Coast for a visit, but we always missed each other. He hadn't been able to come to my wedding, though he'd sent a really nice gift and a thoughtful card. Otherwise, we hadn't had much contact.

Though we hadn't spoken to or seen each other in a few years, I'd heard about him through the grapevine. Last I knew, he was working as a personal trainer, and if memory served, they had to have all kinds of CPR certifications and things like that. He'd always been good with kids, too.

I tapped the corner of my phone on the counter. Would it be weird if I reached out to him? I didn't think it would. Yeah, we'd dated for most of our sophomore and junior years in high school, back before I'd figured out I was gay and before he'd figured out he was a boy. We'd lost our virginities to each other. We'd done a lot of our adolescent experimenting together. Both the sex and the relationship had been awkward and weird because we'd been young and stupid, though I wouldn't have called either of them bad. Just... young and stupid. Naïve, more than anything.

Fortunately, we'd also broken up without any major drama. As we'd started figuring out our identities, we'd both become seriously introspective, and we'd grown apart as boyfriend and girlfriend. Eventually, we'd realized we were better off as friends. Nothing nasty. Nothing we hadn't been able to come back from. We were just growing up and growing apart, and we'd stayed friends until our lives had gone in separate directions.

Now, when I desperately needed someone's help, it turned out he was in a similar situation. If I could get in touch with him, maybe we could help each other out.

Admittedly, I liked the idea of hiring him. In fact, I was relieved at the prospect of possibly bringing him to Pittsburgh to watch my kids, and not just because it would fix this crisis my ex had created. I'd always trusted Cam. I knew he was good people.

And what could I say? I missed him. The years I'd gone without even seeing him suddenly weighed on my shoulders, and I wondered how the hell I'd let that happen. Losing touch with people wasn't unusual for those of us on the pro hockey trajectory—it was all-consuming, and trying to break into the majors was a long, arduous process. I'd left more than a few friends behind just because I'd been too focused on hockey to maintain the friendships, and I regretted that.

I especially regretted leaving behind Cam Wright.

Cam Wright, who was now in a bind at the same time I

was desperate for someone to look after my kids so I didn't lose custody.

Well, hell.

Maybe my ex's bullshit ultimatum would be a blessing in disguise after all.

CHAPTER 2

CAM

"There's no way I'm going to find another job now." I pinched the bridge of my nose and sighed. "He's made sure my name is mud at every gym in Portland, and it's spread to Seattle, too."

My mom huffed with irritation. "You should be able to sue him for that."

I dropped my hand and turned exhausted eyes on her. "With what? I can't retain a lawyer." Well, not unless I found one willing to accept sexual favors, since that was about all I had left to offer anyone for anything. I didn't say that to my mom, though.

She pursed her lips. "Maybe you just need to find something else to tide you over. Until this all..." She waved a hand like something flying away.

I so wanted to tell her that wasn't going to happen. Gym rats could have incredibly long memories, and that stupid asshole—the one on whom I'd wasted eight years I was never getting back—had made sure I was fucked in that respect. No one in the fitness community was going to want to hire Cameron Wright any time soon. At this point, I wondered if anybody would. Fucking hell.

Sighing, I pushed myself up off the couch. "I'm going to go send out a few more job applications. Can't hurt, right?"

"Good luck, honey."

Yeah. I'd need it. I trudged upstairs to the guest room I'd moved into since that semi-sentient piece of maggot-riddled roadkill had upended my life. It looked depressingly like a hotel room—my mom loved pastels, and she was also a bit of a minimalist. There wasn't much on the furniture in here except a bedside lamp, my phone and charger, and my laptop, plus a few odds and ends from my toiletry kit.

Most of what I owned was wedged into my mom's storage unit. The rest was in one of the boxes stacked inside the closet or the two suitcases parked in front of it, plus some clothes I'd arranged in the drawers. It was my mom's house, but it didn't feel like home.

Maybe because my whole life was on its ass and everything felt jumbled and scattered and... ugh.

Okay. I was too miserable to deal with job applications right now. I'd doomscroll for a little while, maybe watch a few videos, and *then* send applications out into the ether to be summarily ignored.

I grabbed my phone off the nightstand and flopped onto the bed.

And then I froze.

On the screen, there was a text from someone I hadn't heard from in a long time.

I stared at his name. Trev Allen. Wow. We hadn't talked in... four, five years? Something like that. I was suddenly overcome with nostalgia, memories from junior high and high school flooding my mind. Hanging out at lunch. Our comical attempt at dating. Screaming myself hoarse at his hockey games.

The last few years had been a bit of a whirlwind, and it hit me now just how much I regretted losing touch with him. He'd always been such a great guy. Even our stupid high school breakup had been anticlimactic. We'd gone out one afternoon, and after the matinee, we'd had a sort of awkward conversation where we agreed we were better off as friends. Then we'd grabbed whatever we could afford off the McDonald's $1 Menu and sat in his car, talking until we both got in trouble for breaking curfew.

God, wouldn't my life be better now if all my breakups were like that?

I definitely regretted all the time that had slipped by since I'd seen him, that was for sure. And now he was reaching out, so maybe I should see why before I wandered off into another nostalgic daydream.

I tapped my screen and read his text.

> Hey, Jake told me you're in a bind. Long story short, I'm in one too, and we might be able to help each other.

I blinked at the message. There was a flicker of disappointment that he wasn't just reaching out because he'd missed me. He needed something from me. Damn.

But also... he wanted to help? And what in the world could he need *my* help with? Last I'd heard, he'd locked down like a three-and-a-half-million-dollar-per-year deal with his hockey team. Though some of our mutual friends had mentioned that his divorce had been messy. Maybe his ex had taken him to the cleaners?

Boy, could I relate. At least Dickhead and I hadn't been

married. Somehow I suspected he'd have found a way to screw me over even harder.

Well, I was desperate, and I didn't exactly have any other help on the horizon, so... why not? And Trev did say he could somehow help me, so yeah, why not?

With my heart in my throat, I typed out a message.

> yeah, things got messy with my ex. What's going on with you?

He didn't read it or respond right away. Not surprising, I guess; his text had come through almost half an hour ago. I must not have heard it.

I was about to swipe away and start doomscrolling like I'd planned, but then the three dots appeared. I held my breath, waiting for him to hit Send.

After a solid minute, he finally did.

> Short version – ex is threatening to go for full custody if I don't lock down fulltime live-in childcare for the hockey season. Which starts really soon.

I blinked. Childcare? That was not a career path I'd considered.

But... did he say full-time? And *live-in*? That meant a paycheck *and* a roof.

> Not gonna lie, my friend, there isn't much I won't do these days. You just need a nanny basically?

> Basically. Do you have a car? If not I can get you one.

My jaw fell open. He'd *buy* me a *car*? Or lease one or

whatever? I mean, okay, he was a millionaire and all, but goddamn.

> I have a car. Pretty sure it'll make it to you. You're still in Pittsburgh right?

> Yep. I think it's like a 5 day drive. I can fly out and drive with you if you'd rather not go alone. As long as it's not my custody week.

As much as a road trip with Trev sounded like a blast, we didn't actually know each other anymore. Agreeing to move in with him and work with him was a massive leap already—one I couldn't afford *not* to make—but being cooped up in a car together for three thousand miles could get sketchy.

> I can make the drive. Are you sure about this?

> Absolutely. Not gonna lie, I'm desperate.

Pause.

> That sounds kind of dickish. I'm desperate for someone to take care of my kids. It really will be great to see you again, too.

I had to chuckle. Good save, my friend.

But I understood. My entire life had been turned on its ass recently, and I was pretty single-mindedly focused on finding a solution. *Any* solution. I wasn't out to use anyone or take advantage of them, but I was ready to jump on the first viable fix that came my way.

So could I really begrudge him reaching out to me with that same kind of desperation? And hell, if I showed up and he was an asshole—if he treated me like he didn't give a shit about me and only cared about getting out of his bind—then I didn't have to stay. I could stick around long enough to save some money, then bug out.

I was hard-pressed to imagine him being like that, though. Yeah, he was a rich and famous athlete now, but he was still Trev. Some of the guys from high school were still in touch with him, and they'd never had anything negative to say about him (well, aside from Jake, who was still salty that Trev had signed with Pittsburgh instead of somewhere on the West Coast).

Trev was also offering me a promising path to getting back on my feet. A place to live, a paycheck, and a car? Hell, I'd have taken him up on it even if we *had* been bitterly estranged exes.

> Send me the details. I'll leave as soon as I can.

Thank you, Cam. You're a lifesaver.

I smiled to myself. He was a lifesaver, too.

And what could I say?

I was thrilled to be seeing my old friend again.

It was one thing to be aware that my childhood friend was now a famous athlete and a literal millionaire.

It was another thing entirely to pull into the cobblestone driveway of a huge-ass house and have my GPS tell me, *"You have arrived at your destination."*

"Holy shit," I murmured as I eased my dilapidated Honda to a stop in front of the fancy brick house. Everything from the enormous windows to the manicured landscaping was flawless and just... *big*. I couldn't imagine living here as a single guy.

Which meant this was probably the place he'd bought with his ex, intending to raise their kids here. Even then, it seemed way too big for four people.

But was I going to look this multimillion-dollar gift horse in the mouth? No, I was not.

As I was getting out of the car, the front door opened, and I very nearly tripped and fell on my ass.

Holy. Crap.

Trev had always been incredibly fit. Playing hockey had kept him in tiptop shape, and he'd been goodlooking even through those awkward junior high years. He'd looked amazing in high school and college.

The man standing in the doorway now? Oh my God. That blue henley stretched snugly across ripped abs and pecs, and his biceps and forearms were mouthwatering. When my gaze landed on his narrow hips and holy-shit-are-you-kidding-me thighs, I had to force myself to meet his eyes instead. He'd been so lanky as a kid, and while he was still leaner than a football player or a power lifter, he was—fucking hell, most of my personal training clients would've sawed off limbs to look like that.

He'd also lost a lot of that youthful softness in his face. His jaw and cheekbones were more prominent now. Back in high school, he'd bemoaned his lack of anything to shave, but now he had a respectable dusting of dark stubble that just made him even prettier.

That perfect smile, though—that hadn't changed a bit.

"Wow," he said as he stepped outside, arms outstretched. "I can't believe how long it's been!"

"Right?" Dazed, I stepped into his hug. "It's been *too*

long." Those words were even truer when he embraced me so tight I could barely breathe.

How did I go this many years without one of your hugs?

I almost got choked up, but I managed to hold my composure, and as I stepped back, I cleared my throat. Gesturing at him and grinning, I said, "Didn't you say you'd have a hockey smile by thirty? Looks like you still have all your teeth."

He laughed, which... oh God.

When did you get so hot? Who gave you the right?

"Actually," he said, tapping the left side of his jaw, "I'm missing two."

"You are?"

He nodded as a blush crept into his cheeks. "The one in front is capped. The molar—I'll get an implant there after I retire."

I whistled. "I thought your old coach told you not to stop sticks with your teeth."

"Hey now." He pushed his shoulders back and feigned offense. "I'll have you know the one in back was from stopping a puck."

Grimacing, I shuddered. "Um. Ouch?"

"Seriously." He turned his head a little and pointed at a faint silvery scar just above the edge of his stubble. "Had to get stitches, too. It fucking sucked."

"Yeah? How much of the game did you miss?"

"Period and a half."

I snorted. "That sounds like you. Still bleeding and barely stitched together, but back out on the ice anyway."

Trev shrugged. "It isn't like I could feel it. It was still numb."

"Still. Dude." I chafed my arms. "So what about the one in front? Puck?"

"No, that was a stick. But!" He put up a finger. "I drew a four-minute double minor for it, and we were already in overtime in an elimination game for the conference final. So... it was worth it!"

"Wow. Cost you a tooth but won the conference championship? Nice."

"I couldn't complain." He scowled. "Well, except we got swept in the Cup finals, but hey, at least we got the conference rings."

"Could've been worse, right?"

"Definitely. But anyway, enough about my dental history." He gestured at the house. "Come on in. I'll show you around."

CHAPTER 3

TREV

EVER SINCE MY EX-HUSBAND HAD DROPPED HIS ultimatum, all I'd been able to think about was figuring out my childcare situation. When Cam had agreed to come and help me out, I'd been overwhelmed with gratitude, not to mention anxiety that Bryan would find some way to declare Cam unfit for the job.

Now Cam was here, and I could barely think.

Our mutual friends had mentioned him from time to time over the years. They'd talked about going out with him and his now-ex-boyfriend. They'd mentioned in passing that they'd all met up for a baseball or football game. There'd been holiday parties and birthday get-togethers, not to mention our class reunion, which I'd been unable to attend. There'd been photos and the odd video including Cam.

But somehow, now that I was in his presence, I was absolutely blown away.

When precisely had he had this incredible glow-up, and how had I not noticed?

One thing was for sure—I noticed it now.

He'd always been cute when we were teenagers, both before and after he'd transitioned. In college, same thing. I just wasn't ready for how breathtakingly well he wore thirty.

As I showed him around the house, I kept tripping over my own words and my own feet. Every time I glanced at him, I was startled all over again because my cute friend had grown up to be so fucking sexy.

He'd been working as a personal trainer, and he'd obviously practiced what he preached. The gangly kid from a decade ago was long gone, replaced by this man who wouldn't have been out of place in a row of marble statues. He reminded me a little of my team's skating coach—though he was only about five-foot-nine and fairly compact, he was *built*. Powerful shoulders. Defined arms. Flat abs.

The thin white fabric of Cam's T-shirt hinted at tattoos underneath, and my fingers itched with the need to trace those inked lines and curves. And while piercings had never really done much for me, I was intrigued by the telltale shape of barbells through each nipple.

Get a grip, Trevor. Jesus Christ.

Why was I getting so stupid over him? I mean, yes, he was way hotter than I'd anticipated. Mostly because I hadn't thought about whether I'd be attracted to him or not. I hadn't been attracted to anyone—hadn't *wanted* to be attracted to anyone—since before the divorce.

Was that what this was all about? My libido had suddenly awakened, and now I was hyperaware of how long it had been since I'd had sex? So I got utterly tongue-tied over my old friend?

Yeah, maybe.

But also...

I mean...

I was around ripped, hot men every day of my life. I saw them naked so often it didn't register.

Cam, though... My God, every inch of him registered, and the way my mind short-circuited whenever I looked at him—that went way beyond catching an eyeful in the locker room or checking out a teammate wearing a particularly nice suit.

Because it wasn't just his body. Yeah, he was hot as hell, but whenever he smiled, my train of thought completely derailed. Time had been incredibly kind to his physique and his gorgeous face, but there was so much more to it than that. So much that I hadn't even considered while I'd eagerly awaited his arrival.

He carried himself differently now. As a kid, he'd been a little shy, and he often moved or sat like someone who didn't want to be noticed. A complete wallflower except around his closest friends.

Adult Cam walked with his back straight. Shoulders square. The wallflower was a distant memory, replaced by someone who didn't hesitate to look the world in the eye.

Which... like everything else about him today... scrambled my damn brain. I barely recognized him, and yet I also couldn't see anyone *but* Cam. As if the whole time we'd been ugly duckling kids, it had been a foregone conclusion that Cam would grow into this confident, sexy man who was just so damn—

"Trev?"

I shook myself and met his gaze. Oh fuck. Had he been saying something? Had I?

He cocked his head, though there was humor in his eyes. "You zoned out. You still with me?"

"Yeah. Yeah. Just..." *Thinking things that would make this arrangement way too awkward.* I cleared my throat.

"Trying to remember if there was anything else I needed to tell you." I laughed nervously. "There's probably a lot. Like... about my kids, for one thing."

"That would be a good start, yeah." Some nervousness entered his expression. "I'm, uh... to be perfectly honest, I don't have a ton of experience with little kids. I took this job because I'm seriously desperate, and I'll absolutely follow your lead, but if you wanted someone with years of experience as a nanny..." He grimaced.

I waved my hand. "I didn't have shit in the way of experience before we adopted them. You're someone I can trust. We can figure out the rest."

That seemed to catch him off-guard. "You... haven't seen me in years, though."

"No. But I know you. And our friends know you." I paused. "Look, I'm desperate, too, but these are my kids. I wouldn't just grab some rando off the street and leave them alone with them. You've always been good people, and our friends who've still been in touch with you all this time would've told me if there was some reason to think you'd changed in a bad way."

"Oh." He blinked. "I'm, uh... I'm glad they put in a good word for me."

"They rave about you all the time. And Jake's the one who reached out and said maybe you and I could help each other." I hesitated, then decided to be a little more candid. "I'll help you, you help me, and I finally get to see you again. Kind of seems like a win all around, you know?"

His eyebrows rose, as did some color in his cheeks. "Oh. It's, um... It's great to finally see you again too." Dropping his gaze, he murmured, "It's been way too long."

I chewed the inside of my cheek. I wanted to ask *why* it

had been so long. Why every attempt I'd made to reach out to him had come up empty.

But now wasn't the time. He was here, and we'd have plenty of opportunity to catch up. It didn't all have to happen ten minutes after he'd walked in my front door.

"Anyway, uh..." I cleared my throat. "Let me show you your room, and then I can take you downstairs to the home gym."

That brought Cam back to life, and he looked at me with wide eyes. "You have a home gym?"

"I'm a professional athlete," I said, chuckling. "Comes with the territory."

"Ooh, sweet." He grinned, a little cautious mischief entering his expression. "So, do I get to teach your kids how to do burpees and squat with proper form?"

I snorted, pretending my head wasn't spinning as that trace of my old friend—the shy but devilish kid I'd grown up with—peeked through. "If you can get a pair of high-energy six-year-olds to sit still long enough, be my guest."

"Pfft. I've trained teenagers hopped up on pre-workout. Challenge accepted."

"Oh my God. *Anyway.*" I gestured down the hall. "Follow me."

He did, unaware of my heart doing wild things and my stomach doing somersaults. I really needed to get it together. He was going to be living here, after all. In my house. And I couldn't afford to have him leave because he caught me staring at him with nostalgic hearts in my eyes. Or getting a badly timed hard-on. Or both.

Dude. Seriously. Get a grip.

I held on to my dignity, at least enough that he hopefully didn't notice my brain spinning out, and took him up to the top floor. The boys' bedrooms were at one end of the hallway, the guest room was at the other, and mine was right in the middle. I took Cam to the guest room, pushed open the door, and flicked on the light. "It's all yours."

He stepped in, and his lips parted as he looked around. "Dude, this isn't a room—it's a *suite*."

I chuckled. "I mean, kind of?" Pressing my shoulder against the doorframe, I scanned the room, which... yeah, it was a suite. There was a small living room area, a full bathroom, and a bedroom. One kitchenette shy of a small apartment, really. "We set it up this way for my ex-mother-in-law. She..." I waved a hand and shook my head. "It was better to do it like this than not, let's put it that way."

Cam turned, eyebrows up. "Difficult to please?"

Rolling my eyes, I nodded. "I always thought mother-in-law stereotypes were exaggerated, but I have seen the light, let me tell you."

He grimaced. "That bad, huh?"

"Worse. But fortunately, she's not my problem anymore, and the bright side is..." I gestured at the room. "I'm not just sticking you in a tiny guest room. This way you can have some space to yourself, you know?"

He gave a slow nod as he looked around the room, and something in him seemed to deflate. No, that wasn't right—it relaxed. As if he were releasing a breath he'd been holding. Tension visibly melted out of his shoulders. "My own space," he murmured, more to himself than me. "That'll be —God, that'll be nice."

I cocked a brow but didn't ask. As curious as I was, I reminded myself again that he'd only just arrived. We still needed to catch up as friends, and he was also working for me now. The personal stuff could wait until I knew where we stood with each other.

"This is..." Cam shook his head and exhaled. Facing me again with wide eyes, he said, "You're sure this is all mine?"

"Well... yeah?" I gestured over my shoulder with my thumb. "Mine's up the hall across from the stairs. The boys' rooms are at the other end of the hall. We've all got plenty of room, and you're doing me a gigantic favor just by being here." I waved at his surroundings. "Giving you all this is the *least* I can do."

He looked around the room again, still obviously dazed. "Wow. This is... It's amazing. The room. The job." He met my gaze. "You're seriously saving my ass right now, and I'd have slept in a broom closet if it was all you had. This?" He motioned at the suite. "Is phenomenal."

"Well, like I said, you're saving my ass, too. I have no idea what I'd have done otherwise."

"Yeah. Same." Cam swallowed. Silence hung between us that I didn't know how to fill, and the moment threatened to get awkward. Then he shook himself. "You said you have a home gym?"

Grateful for the diversion, I said, "Yeah. Downstairs."

He grinned. "Show me the way."

CHAPTER 4

CAM

WALKING THROUGH THIS ENORMOUS HOUSE WITH TREV was nothing short of a miracle.

If I thought too hard about the odds of us making it here, I'd probably dissolve into tears. Or a damn panic attack. Something. Because what if his world hadn't gone sideways at the same time mine had? What if he'd decided that I'd blown him off too many times and he wasn't going to waste his time trying to reconnect again? What if he hadn't married his ex, and adopted their kids, and then gotten a divorce and found himself desperate for a nanny? What if he hadn't made it into the pros in the first place so he could meet the ex, afford the house, and—

The odds were probably some ridiculous number with a ton of zeroes to one. Somewhere on par with a meteor landing in precisely the right spot to smite my controlling, cheating, dickweasel of an ex-boyfriend. While I would've been seriously thrilled if that had happened, this was even better, and it... God, there were so many ways it could have *not* happened, and I was going to drive myself insane imagining them.

As we took the stairs down to the ground floor, I subtly pushed out a breath. Regardless of the odds, we were here. I had a job and a place to live. My best friend from high school was back in my life despite all the reasons he could've just pretended I didn't exist anymore. I had a bedroom—a damned *suite*—that was bigger than any apartment I could've afforded back home, and I *didn't have to pay rent.* Not a *penny* of rent.

And part of the deal included full access to his house (minus his bedroom and home office), which *also* turned out to include...

"Oh my God." My jaw actually went slack as I looked around Trev's basement home gym. "Dude. There are home gyms, and there are..." I flailed a hand.

He laughed. "Eh. Sometimes I don't like going to the training center, and I want to work out alone."

"Right, but..." I blinked a few times. "I trained some pro athletes back home, and none of them had a setup *this* nice."

"You should see our captain's house," he mused. "He's got a half-sheet of artificial ice in his basement."

I whistled. Okay, so Trev may not have had his own rink, but his setup was phenomenal. An elliptical, treadmill, recumbent bike, and stair machine, all from the best manufacturer on the planet. Top-of-the-line resistance equipment. A rack of dumbbells and another of barbell plates that would've made the owner of my last gym weep with envy.

None of it had that pristine, unused look either. It was all in great condition, but was obviously used regularly. I'd worked with a couple of wealthy clients back home who had home gyms that were utterly spotless—not a scratch or scuff on anything. It was for show more than anything—something to impress their rich friends or to be featured in home magazines or whatever.

Trev obviously made judicious use of everything in here, but he kept it clean and in excellent condition.

"So... I can use this stuff?" I looked at him. "You don't mind?"

"Absolutely. Have at it." He paused. "And yes, the boys are allowed in here, but only if they're strictly supervised. They know what equipment they can use"—he gestured at some mats and smaller dumbbells—"but they're kids, you know? They'll try to push limits."

I nodded. "Oh, I get that. One of the gyms I worked at didn't enforce their policies about kids, and they'd get into and on everything." I rolled my eyes. "I'm genuinely shocked the place didn't get sued into oblivion."

Trev grimaced, shifting uncomfortably. "Yeah. I can imagine. Some of my teammates bring their kids to the training center's gym, but they watch them like hawks, you know?"

"As they should. Do your kids like coming in here?"

He quirked his lips, then wobbled his hand in the air. "Sometimes? They're still too small to use a lot of the equipment, and they get bored if I'm in here for a long time. I don't like to keep them in here if they're getting restless because I don't want them to associate boredom and restlessness with the gym, you know?"

"Oh, yeah, that makes sense." I scanned the room. "I did work with some of the youth fitness groups, so maybe I can modify some things for them. Just so they can have fun with it."

Trev's smile made my knees weak. Oh my God, I'd missed this man. Unaware of my rush of butterflies, he said, "I'd be thrilled to have you work with them in here." He paused, smile fading a little as he gazed around the room again. "I've played hockey with a lot of guys who don't have a healthy relationship with exercise *or* food, and they've passed that on to their kids." Meeting my gaze, he added, "I don't want to do that to my boys."

"I don't blame you. I worked with a lot of clients who were the same way. Their own relationships with food and exercise, and what they did with their kids." I gestured at all the mats and kid-sized equipment. "I can make it fun for them. But kids don't need to be lifting weights yet. I'm sure they get plenty of exercise when they're playing."

He laughed and nodded. "Yeah. If I had that much energy, I could play an entire sixty-minute game without slowing down." He motioned toward the weights. "They just like to come in here and imitate me, you know? Dad's lifting, so they want to."

I smiled. "A lot of kids are like that. And it's a good opportunity to teach them correct form. Learning that young and internalizing it will cut down on injuries, not to mention bad habits they'll have to unlearn later."

"Exactly. I just don't want to put pressure on them."

"You don't have to worry about that with me."

Ugh. God. I'd missed this man's smile so, so much.

"Anyway," he said. "The gym is off-limits for the kids unless someone is in here with them." He gestured toward the door. "Come on—let me show you the yard."

His yard was, much like the house, huge. A tall white privacy fence encircled a long, narrow, and gently rolling lawn, and it was immediately obvious the kids spent a ton of time out here. Though the front yard was pristinely land-scaped, the backyard had a few areas of dug-up ground with dirty toy trucks and bulldozers scattered around them. The grass was mowed, but had definitely taken a beating from feet, bicycles, and whatever else kids could do to a surface.

Looked like heaven for a couple of high-energy kids.

The one thing that gave me pause, though, was the very large swimming pool off to the side. There was a waist-high fence around it with a padlocked gate, but still... kids and pools. I'd spent exactly one summer as a lifeguard, and though I'd been very fortunate not to see or experience much, I'd heard some horrific stories. The training alone was the stuff of nightmares; my instructor had even opened by saying, "Welcome to 1,001 horrible ways for kids to die," and she hadn't been entirely kidding.

Trev either remembered me talking about that or he saw the dawning horror in my eyes. "The boys know the pool is absolutely off-limits unless an adult explicitly tells them they can get in."

I arched an eyebrow. He and I were living proof that kids could hear all the reasons something was dangerous, then immediately forget when the dangerous thing sounded exciting. Bike jumps, stunts involving trees, extraordinarily stupid things on skateboards—we did it all. If anyone in our area had had a pool, well...

"Trust me," he said, his expression completely serious. "We didn't even put water in it until they'd taken swimming lessons, and Bryan and I have both explained to them how dangerous it is." He grimaced. "I think we even went a little overboard, because Zach was actually afraid of the water until a year or two ago, and Zane still doesn't venture *too* far away from the shallow end. They absolutely *love* swimming now, and it's a struggle to get them *out* of the pool when it's time to quit, but they do have a healthy respect for the water."

I considered that, then shrugged. "I mean, I don't want kids to be afraid of the water, but there are worse things than being cautious, I guess?"

"That's kind of where we landed. We still swim with

them a lot, and we want them to be strong swimmers. And like I said, they enjoy it now." He gestured at the pool. "It helps that they're still absolutely joined at the hip, so it's incredibly unlikely one of them would end up in the pool completely alone. If one of them fell in, the other knows to throw in some pool noodles and then come get help." He paused. "We've also taught them how to tread water, stay afloat, get to the edge..." He waved his hand and exhaled. "Honestly, with as much as we've done to make sure the kids don't drown, even as much as they love it now, I seriously considered just ripping the damn thing out or filling it with concrete. It stressed me out more than I enjoyed it for a long time."

"I believe that." I chafed my arms. "It would stress me out too. Why *did* you get a house with a pool if it was so stressful?"

He suddenly looked exhausted, and he shook his head. "Because Bryan and I were idiots."

I raised my eyebrows.

Trev gestured at the pool, the house, and the yard. "We were just so damn excited that we could build a big house to raise our kids in. I'd just locked down my contract with the Rebels, and we suddenly had more money than we knew what to do with. The idea of a huge house with our family..." He rolled his eyes. "Then we moved in, and suddenly it's like—shit, we've got toddlers and a pool. We've got this huge yard... that wasn't fenced at the time and backed right up to the woods. We've got stairs, stairs, and more stairs." Trev shuddered and looked at me again. "When we got divorced, I seriously considered selling it just so I could downsize to something a bit saner."

"Why didn't you?" I paused. "Why *don't* you?"

"Eh, the kids were getting older. Stairs aren't as much of an issue. The yard is fenced off now. The pool has a gate and the boys are stronger swimmers. Plus, they like it here. They were already confused about why Bryan was moving out and they were bouncing back and forth between the houses. Selling it just seemed like..."

"Too much?"

"On top of everything else, yeah. Or maybe that's a copout. I don't know." He looked in my eyes with a startlingly vulnerable expression. "I really try to be a good dad, but sometimes I wonder if I'm as bad at that as I was at being a husband."

The candor caught me off-guard. "You... don't think you were good at being a husband?"

"I mean..." He held up his left hand and pointed at the bare third finger.

I wanted to insist that a relationship ending didn't mean someone was a bad partner. It often meant they *had* a bad partner. Or it just didn't work out. Or any number of things.

But I didn't actually know why Trev's marriage ended, so I didn't want to offer up some platitude that hit him in a tender spot.

Fortunately, he didn't give me a chance to say something awkward, and he nodded toward the house. "Let's go back in. I'll show you the kitchen, and then we can bring your stuff in from your car."

Grateful for the subject change, I followed him inside.

On the way through the house earlier, I'd noticed a number of framed photos on the wall, but I hadn't actually stopped to take them in. As we went back down the hall toward the kitchen and living room, I slowed and stopped, gazing at the various pictures.

Trev halted as well, watching me take in everything on the wall.

They were photos of him and his kids, from back when they were tiny infants until some more recent shots of them in soccer uniforms and school clothes. The last week had been such a damn whirlwind, I hadn't even seen pictures of the kids I'd be tasked with watching, so I'd had no idea what they'd look like. They both had near-black hair and big brown eyes, and they had a more Mediterranean complexion than Trev, who was fair-skinned.

"So these are your boys," I said.

The smile that broke out on Trev's face almost made my balance waver. "Yep, that's them." He pointed at them each in turn. "Zane and Zach."

I squinted. "How do you tell them apart?"

He chuckled. "It's a lot easier in person. Zach is the extrovert. Zane is very much... not."

I peered at some of the photos, and now that he mentioned it, I could see the difference. One of the twins was usually making faces or some silly gestures, while the other seemed content to just smile for the camera. I picked out one with them dressed for soccer—one in a regular jersey, one a goalie. The goalie held the ball under his arm and smiled. The other had struck a funny pose with a giant, toothy grin.

"So, Zane?" I pointed at the goalie.

"You've got it." Trev laughed with obvious fondness. "It's funny, if they were playing hockey, Zane wouldn't be the one I'd peg for a goalie."

"Didn't you say hockey goalies are a little nuts?"

He snorted. "A little. But in soccer, Zane is *really* good at it. He tracks the ball so well, and it's hard for anybody to get anything past him. They're both a bit smaller than some of the other kids, but they're fast as hell. Plus Zach is fearless, so he'll just mow through the other players and score."

"Wow." I hooked my thumbs in my pockets and studied my old friend. "I'm surprised you don't have them playing hockey."

The smile faded a bit. "They know how to skate—I wanted them to learn as early as possible—but my ex-mother-in-law convinced Bryan that hockey was too dangerous."

I inclined my head. "She knows you play professionally, right?"

"Yep. And she hated that her son was with a pro hockey player." Trev made an irritated sound. "Doesn't help that she and Bryan had the conversation about the kids playing hockey while I was recovering from a pretty bad concussion."

"Oh my God. Seriously? Did she leverage your injury to scare him out of it or something?"

"That, and she took advantage of me being out of it to strong arm him into pulling them out of the program they were about to start." Trev's lip curled with disgust. "At that age, they weren't even going to be doing anything dangerous. But she got to him, I was too fucked up to say anything, and then by the time I could make an argument, there were too many other things to fight about." He sighed. "They haven't missed their window to try it or anything, but it's just such a bone of contention with my ex and his mother."

"Good Lord," I muttered.

"Right? So if the boys come to me and say they want to try it, I'll sign them up. But I don't want to push them and get them into the middle of an argument between their dad and me."

He sounded utterly defeated and heartbroken, but could I blame him?

"Well." I cleared my throat. "Does this mean I'll be taking them to soccer practice and games?"

His smile returned, and he chuckled. "Practices are Tuesday and Thursday, and games are Saturday." He clapped my shoulder and grinned mischievously. "Have fun."

I just flipped him off, which had him cackling. He knew how much I'd always hated soccer.

"Anyway," I said. "They're seriously cute. And you said they're, what, six now?"

"Yeah. They'll be seven in December." He laughed, gazing at a photo of the boys as toddlers. "Time really flies, let me tell you."

God, he was just so adorable when he was talking about his kids. I'd never given any thought to Trev as a dad, but it was obvious now that he was meant to be one.

"Well, speaking of your kids..." I loosely folded my arms. "We still haven't talked much about the job."

"Oh. Yeah. We haven't, have we?"

"To be fair, the last week has been a bit chaotic."

"It has. Come on, let's sit in the living room. You want a beer or something?"

As we headed in that direction, I said, "A beer would probably put me to sleep right now. Could I bug you for some water?"

"Of course."

He got us a couple of glasses of ice water from his ridiculously huge kitchen. Then we settled onto the couches in the equally ridiculous living room.

Trev sipped his water. "So, it won't be like keeping up

with a pair of newborns or toddlers." He grimaced. "They're well past that stage, thank God."

I laughed. "Ran you ragged, huh?"

He groaned. "I should've known I was in for it when another teammate with twins told me the first year would be like nonstop playoffs. No sleep and no breaks, except with no end in sight."

"Wow. And it's not as bad now?"

"Nah. Once they started sleeping through the night and we could let them play unsupervised, it started getting a lot easier." He had a fond smile firmly on his lips. "I mean, don't get me wrong—they've been a blast from day one. I love them. But that first couple of years..." He huffed a laugh. "I'm glad we ended up with twins because otherwise, we'd be one and done."

I chuckled. "I believe that. And now I get to jump in when they're older. Cool."

"Lucky you," he said with a laugh. "As for the job, there isn't much to it, honestly." He paused for another sip of water. "The only time it really becomes full-time is when I'm on the road. Otherwise, I'll still be here a lot. Even when I'm gone, they're at school during the week, so between drop-off and pickup, you do you. Plus they're at my ex's place every other week."

"Oh. So it's not like 24/7."

"Nope. And they don't need you to be constantly inter-acting with them when they're home. Make them food or help them make it. Take them to playdates or parks or whatever. Take them to soccer." He shrugged. "Some of their friends' parents turn themselves inside out trying to constantly provide stimulation and interaction, but Bryan and I both prefer to let the boys entertain themselves as much as possible. Either on their own or with their friends. As long as there's an adult nearby, and someone checks on them now and then..." A half-shrug this time. "They don't need someone looking over their shoulder every second of every day."

"Thank God for that. I think that would've driven me insane as a kid."

"Right?" He smirked. "Though I might start hovering a bit more when they get into middle school and high school. Because I'm pretty sure that's when the real problems start."

"You mean like kids sneaking off to smoke weed under the bleachers or cutting class to make out in the woods?"

Trev laughed, which made my heart flutter with nostalgia at our past as wannabe juvenile delinquents, but it also made my spine tingle. He'd always been attractive, but I still couldn't get over how *hot* he was now. The grown-up pro athlete version of Trev was seriously sexy.

And I was startled to realize that the dad version of him was attractive in its own way, too. The way he smiled when he talked about his kids or looked at their photos. Just... him as a dad. I couldn't explain it, but it did something to me that made it hard to think or speak around him.

Or maybe I was still overwhelmed by everything. Being here. Being out from under the disastrous fallout of my breakup. Being in the same place as Trev for the first time in too long. That was all a lot to take in, so I could probably forgive my brain for tripping over the most ridiculous things.

Fortunately unaware of one of those brain trips, Trev said, "Let me get something out of the kitchen. Be right back." Then he got up, and I absolutely did not take advantage of that moment to check out his ass in those jeans. He'd always had a nice ass thanks to hockey, but *goddamn*.

I took a long drink of water to cool me down, and about the time I'd reclaimed my dignity, Trev returned.

He sat on the couch and handed me a thick binder. "This is basically everything you need to know about the boys. We put it together for when we were traveling and left them with their grandparents for a couple of weeks at a time, and we've just kept it updated as time goes on."

"Handy," I said as I picked it up. On the front, someone had written *Zane & Zach Allen*. I opened the cover to the first page. On that was what must have been recent school photos of the boys, and below that, a list of the basics: birth dates, contact information for their dads and grandparents as well as pediatrician and dentist. There were even half a dozen numbers that looked to be associated with Trev's hockey team, probably to make absolutely sure someone could reach him in an emergency.

"It felt a little over the top even to me," Trev admitted. "But my mom said it was really handy when they needed to take Zach to urgent care after he took a fall on the playground, and also when Zane got stung by a bee. So... I guess it's better to be overprepared than under."

"Yeah, no, I get that." I thumbed through the pages, which had dividers labeled as *medical/vaccine history, school and teachers, playdate friend contact info,* and *activity info*. It was definitely thorough, and while some part of me did want to tease him for being as meticulous as he'd always been, I kept that to myself. After all, this was all information I might need. Just knowing I'd have it all at my fingertips settled some anxiety I hadn't even noticed yet. What if one of the boys got hurt? What if I needed to contact Trev while he was on the ice?

Yeah, this was on-brand for the Trev I'd always known, but I suspected I'd be relying on it, at least for a while.

"Wow, it even has foods they like?" I flipped to that divider. "That'll be useful."

"Zach is pretty easy," Trev said, "but Zane has some serious aversion to food textures. Like, just having them on the table for someone else can make him gag. We're working on it, but it's a process, you know?"

I nodded. "Sure, I get that. Are they allergic to anything?"

"They both get some mild seasonal allergies, but no foods or anything like that."

"Good to know." I met his gaze. "And since they're in school—do I need to help with homework?"

He grimaced apologetically. "If I'm on the road, then..."

"Trev." I smiled. "It's fine. You're giving me a place to live and a paycheck. I'm not going to bitch if I need to help the kids with their schoolwork."

That settled him a little, and he nodded. "Okay. Well. They do get a lot. It's still fairly easy at this stage. They're just about to start first grade, so it isn't exactly calculus or physics yet."

I snorted. "Thank God for that. Because I don't know if you remember, but Algebra is my archnemesis."

He laughed, unaware of what that did to my body temperature. "I remember."

"Uh-huh. And do you also remember how the gods favor no one, and you were eating crow after it turned out your archnemesis was Geometry?"

He rubbed his eye with his middle finger, and I snickered.

"*Anyway.*" He lowered his hand. "That's about all there is to it. And... thank you. I know it's a ton of upheaval to get here, but you're a lifesaver."

I made a dismissive wave. "Dude, *you're* saving *my* ass.

I'd have tried to help you out either way, but your timing was perfect. I needed this job."

From the way he looked at me, I thought he might ask about how exactly my world had turned on its ass. Eventually, he probably would, but I was way too tired to hash it out right now.

Fortunately, he just smiled and picked up his water glass. "Guess it worked out for both of us, didn't it?"

"Yeah." I smiled back. "Guess it did."

CHAPTER 5

TREV

Cam was here. Yesterday, we'd moved his things into the guest suite. This morning, we'd made a grocery store run to stock the kitchen with things he liked.

Now came one of the parts I had not been looking forward to—introducing him to my ex-husband.

The ideal setting would be someplace neutral, like a coffee shop or a restaurant. Bryan and I could usually be trusted to be cordial in public, even when tensions were running hot.

But this was an unusual situation. Bryan hadn't been thrilled about my solution to his ultimatum, and I had a feeling this introduction could go off the rails without much provocation.

So, out in public wasn't going to work. In private, we had two options—the place he and I had shared, or the place he was currently sharing with my teammate. My teammate, who I had to play alongside at training camp in just a few days.

Though I rarely put my foot down about much, I made

an exception this time. Especially since he'd been the one to make the ultimatum, we were handling introductions on my terms... and on my turf.

Which was why, at around three in the afternoon, my ex-husband's gleaming black Mercedes-Maybach S pulled up in front of my house. I stepped outside, keeping my expression as neutral as possible, and waited.

He got out, and my stomach knotted the same way it always did when I saw him. It was a mix of resentment, regret, and hurt. From the moment I'd realized we were speeding down a one-way street to divorce, my emotions had been a clash of good and bad. I couldn't be in the same space as him and not get a twinge of *what the fuck did I ever see in you?* right alongside the pang of *what happened to us?*

I tamped them down, same as I always did, and watched him come around the car.

He, on the other hand, was wearing his emotions on his sleeve.

Or rather, his one emotion—irritation.

Halting an arm's length away, he glared at me. "Are you really serious about this? About hiring *him* to look after our kids?"

"Yes." I glared right back at him. "I trust him. And you didn't exactly give me a ton of time to find someone who—"

"You could've found someone besides him," Bryan hissed. "When I said to find someone to watch the kids, I didn't mean your old piece of ass."

I gritted my teeth. "That's ancient history. We were *kids*. And might I remind you that our boys spend half the time *living* with your *current* piece of ass, so..." I shrugged flippantly.

Bryan rolled his eyes.

"And I'm not dating Cam," I went on. "That was high school, for God's sake."

Another eyeroll, this one accompanied by a caustic laugh. "Yeah, but I'm sure you wouldn't mind a rematch, would you?"

For a second, panic flared in my chest. What the hell? Had I said something when we'd talked last night that gave away that I was suddenly reattracted to Cam?

Bryan must've seen the questions in my eyes, because he crossed his arms and scoffed. "Oh, please. The whole time we were married, all someone had to do was mention his name, and you'd either get all mopey or starry-eyed." He scoffed. "Don't tell me you wouldn't jump his bones again the second you had the chance."

I drew back, startled by his anger but also by how right he was. I didn't let it show, though, and coolly said, "Even if that were true, that isn't why he's here. He's here because you put me between a rock and a hard place, and I just got incredibly lucky that Cam was also in a bad spot." I showed my palms. "Go back to our old arrangement, and I won't have any reason to keep him around. Your call."

He held my gaze. I held his. My heart thumped against my ribs as my own dare hung in the silence between us. Fuck, what if he took me up on it? What was I supposed to tell Cam then? *So hey, my ex said he'd work with me after all. Here's some gas money to head back to Seattle.*

Shit. Should've kept my damn mouth shut.

"I'm only responding to your ultimatum," I said evenly. "And if you want to reject Cam and take me to court, you're going to have to explain to the judge why my high school ex is a problem, but your boyfriend isn't."

His jaw worked, and I was admittedly relieved. I had a feeling he knew I'd cornered him, and he really didn't have much choice. Unless he could come up with some massive dealbreaker of a reason to say Cam wasn't qualified or safe to watch our kids, he was just going to have to suck it up and live with it.

Finally, he pushed out a sharp breath. "Well, let's get this over with. I at least want to meet the guy before he's alone with the kids."

I was irritated, but I'd still call that a victory. So, without a word, I gestured for him to follow me inside.

Cam was in the living room, sitting on the couch and looking at something on his phone. When we walked in, he looked up, and his nerves were plain to see. I offered a smile that I hoped registered as, *Don't sweat it. We've got this.*

It didn't seem to help.

"Cam, this is my ex-husband, Bryan. Bryan, Cam."

Cam rose, and they regarded each other uneasily as they shook hands over the coffee table.

"I've heard a lot about you," Bryan said, his tone polite but taut.

"Have you?" Cam glanced at me and managed a nervous laugh. "All good things, I hope?"

Expression sour, Bryan muttered, "He's never said a bad word about you."

Cam stiffened, looking at me as if to ask how he was supposed to respond to that. I wasn't even sure, if I was honest, because I was struggling to keep my temper in check.

Really, Bryan? You want to have this conversation right in front of him?

Some arguments from the past scraped across my memories.

"You two dated in high school. Why do you care so much about him?"

"Yeah, we dated, but he was also my best friend."

"Right. 'Best friend.' Because that"—Bryan had gestured sharply at my face—*"is how people look when they talk about their best friend."*

In the present, keeping my voice and face as pleasant as I could—neutral, anyway—I gestured at the couch and recliners. "How about we all sit? Anyone need a drink?"

"Not one I can have before driving home," Bryan gritted out.

Cam just shook his head.

We took our seats. Cam was on one end of the couch. I was on the other, a whole cushion between us. Bryan sat stiffly in one of the recliners, looking like he wanted to be anywhere but here.

"I can relate," I didn't say out loud. *"So how about we just be civil and get this over with?"*

I cleared my throat, but my ex-husband spoke first.

"So, Cam, what were you doing before?" Bryan sounded bored. "Trev never mentioned you working as a nanny."

Cam fidgeted. "I'm a personal trainer."

"Yeah?" My ex's eyes flicked toward me. "Not exactly a childcare job, is it?"

"Bryan," I growled.

"What?" He put up his hands. "It's a reasonable question!"

"I've never done full-time childcare," Cam said. "But I worked with kids at the gym sometimes, and I've done plenty of babysitting since I was a teenager."

"That's not the same as—"

"They're not newborns," I said. "They don't need someone who has a Ph.D. in nannying." I paused. "And it wasn't like you or I had much experience when we brought them home."

Bryan scowled and rolled his eyes.

"Is it just me?" he'd asked, exhausted and threadbare on the third or fourth day at home with the twins. *"Or are we in way over our heads?"*

"I'm pretty sure we are." I'd scrubbed my hand over my face and sighed. *"But our parents figured it out. We will too."*

And we had. Little by little, sleepless night after sleepless night, we'd figured it out. Now, despite plenty of mistakes along the way, not to mention all the upheaval from our divorce, the boys were thriving.

Cam shifted with obvious discomfort, which made anger surge in my chest. It reminded me of that sleep-deprived, frustrated feeling like I was about to snap at the slightest provocation. I hated it, and I couldn't wait for this conversation to be *over*.

"Look," I said to Bryan, "Cam is and always has been responsible. Being a personal trainer is exactly the kind of career I'd expect for him because it requires someone to be conscientious, detail-oriented, and focused on an individual's specific needs." I inclined my head. "All the things you raved about with your last trainer?" I gestured at Cam.

Bryan pressed his lips into a thin line.

"And at the end of the day," I went on, "I *know* Cam. Have for most of my life. I can hire a nanny with a stack of references, but I won't know them. Not like I know Cam."

My ex huffed an ugly laugh. "Well, I should hope you don't know a new nanny like you know him."

The last remaining tether on my temper *almost* snapped. *Almost*. Especially as I watched the confusion, realization, and embarrassment flicker across Cam's face.

Heat rushed into my own face as I growled, "Are you done, Bryan? Can we do this like civil adults, or what?"

He glared right back at me. "I mean, how civil do you want me to be about you hiring your ex to watch our kids?"

"That was high school," I ground out. "Cam and I were friends a lot longer than we were a couple. And, again, it was *high school.*" I narrowed my eyes. "Or do we need to talk about the man you allegedly didn't start screwing until after we separated? Because if he's okay around the kids, then—"

"Tim's job isn't to watch the kids," Bryan threw back. "He's my partner. You brought Cam here specifically to watch our boys, so I think I'm well within my rights to—"

"You're well within your rights to ask him about his experience with kids. Not disrespect him and act like something from when we were *teenagers* is relevant here."

I hated how utterly uncomfortable Cam looked as I exchanged barbs with my ex-husband. I fucking hated everything about this conversation.

And I could tell from Bryan's eyes that this would absolutely escalate into the kind of screaming match that had been the soundtrack of our last year as a married couple.

Not today.

I put up my hands and schooled my tone. "Look. Do you have any questions for Cam that are relevant to his ability to do this job?"

Bryan's jaw worked. Then he slid his gaze toward Cam. "How's your driving record?"

Without a word, Cam picked up a manila folder he'd left on the end table, and he handed it over to Bryan.

Bryan opened it, and as he flipped through the pages, there was a mix of calm and irritation in his eyes. As if he were relieved by the contents, but also annoyed that he had less ammunition to reject Cam.

I'd been through the folder myself. In the interest of putting my sons' well-being ahead of my bias toward Cam, I'd scrutinized every page when he'd given it to me last night. It included a state and criminal background check, both of which were pristine. From his last job, he had a state-issued certification allowing him to work with children in the state of Oregon. His first aid training was up to date, and his CPR qualifications included AEDs. There was also a copy of his driving record, which had a couple of minor speeding tickets and an accident in which he wasn't found to be at fault. That was it.

From what I'd read about nanny qualifications, he wasn't missing a thing. He'd even taken some basic child development courses in college.

For a last-minute Hail Mary live-in nanny, we honestly couldn't have done any better than Cam.

Bryan perused the pages just like I had, and the silence stretched on awkwardly as he (I guessed) searched for something to pick apart. I wouldn't have been surprised if he gave Cam grief about the speeding tickets, just for lack of anything else.

Go ahead, Bryan. Then we can also talk about how much my insurance dropped after I took you and your lead foot off my policy.

And that was to say nothing about his boyfriend, who I knew for a fact had driven my children *and* had nearly run over a fan last season while peeling out of the training center parking lot.

Do it, Bryan. I dare you.

Cam shifted on the couch. "I, um... I have copies of my credit report, too. If you need that."

Bryan arched an eyebrow, silently asking if Cam was fucking with him. Which he might've been—ex-boyfriend notwithstanding, Cam wasn't usually one to suffer assholes.

"Some people want to see it." Cam shrugged, glancing at me with an innocent expression. "I'm an open book, so..." He spread his hands.

"I don't care about your credit." Bryan tossed the folder onto the coffee table with a quiet slap. "I'm not the one who has to worry about you paying rent. That's Trev's problem."

I fought back an eyeroll. Cam was unsuccessfully fighting back a smile. From the glint of mischief in his eyes, I wondered if he wanted to mention to Bryan that he wouldn't be *paying* rent.

Fortunately, he left well enough alone. Knowing Bryan, he'd yank on that thread and decide Cam was just a gold digger. He was here for rent-free access to my house and would only do the bare minimum to keep from getting fired.

A comment like that would be on-brand for Bryan, which made me wonder for the thousandth time this week what in the hell I'd ever seen in him.

I didn't let that thought linger.

Before I could speak up, Cam said to Bryan, "Listen, I know this a little weird for you. I get it. But Trev is getting me out of a really bad spot. And hopefully I can make things easier for both of you when hockey season starts." He paused. "Anything you want to know to make this all easier for you to stomach, just ask. I mean it—I'm an open book, especially because you guys are trusting me with your kids."

Bryan blinked, apparently caught off-guard. "Oh. Uh." He chewed his lip. After a moment, he asked, "Has Trev shown you the binder?"

Cam nodded. "Yesterday. And I read over most of it last night. In fact..." He turned to me. "I wanted to ask you—

there's a note in the section about Zane's food texture issues. Something about an ice cream place and asking them to put toppings on top." He furrowed his brow. "I didn't quite understand what that meant."

"Oh, right," I said. "There's a place out in Sewickley that mixes toppings into the ice cream. The boys love to go there, but Zane absolutely does not like anything mixed in. So just mention it to the person behind the counter. They're always cool about it."

"Oh! Okay. Okay, I thought it must be something like that, but—" He waved a hand. "Anyway, I just wanted to make sure I was reading it right."

I flashed a quick smile. I knew Cam was conscientious about things like that, but knowing he'd actually taken the time to read the binder and notice that kind of small detail was reassuring. It made me even more certain that I'd made the right call bringing him out here.

Apparently it had a similar effect on Bryan. Though he was still clearly not enjoying this, the hostility ebbed minutely.

"He's really not as picky as he sounds," Bryan said. "He likes to try new things, and he loves different flavors. Textures just really throw him off."

"Oh, I get that," Cam said. "My mom is like that, honestly."

"Is she?"

"Mmhmm. Growing up, I thought it was normal to always ask for tomatoes on your sandwich only to pick them off half the time."

Bryan's lips parted. "Really?"

"Oh, yeah. I finally asked her about it when I was a teenager. She said she loves the taste of tomatoes, and they really add to a sandwich, but if the texture is even slightly off..." He made a face and shook his head.

My ex-husband glanced at me. "That kind of sounds like Zane with lettuce."

"It does," I said with a nod.

Cam's gaze flicked back and forth between us. "So he likes it, always asks for it, but will pick it off if it's not exactly right?"

"If it's even a little bit wilty..." I gestured like I was throwing something over my shoulder.

Cam wrinkled his nose. "I mean, can you blame him? There is nothing worse than lettuce when it's all..." He shuddered.

"Oh God." Bryan made a face. "Now that you mention it..."

I almost gagged myself.

At least that got us onto a more cordial path. The rest of the conversation was—well, it wasn't chill and friendly, but it wasn't so full of swipes or barbs. By the end, Bryan accepted Cam's role as our children's nanny during my custody weeks. And though he obviously wasn't thrilled about it, he signed the letter my lawyer had written up that stated as much. Of course Bryan could still find other reasons to come after me for full custody, but I wasn't saying no to a paper trail.

"Well." Bryan faced Cam and extended his hand. "We'll probably be seeing a lot of each other."

"Looking forward to it," Cam said brightly.

They shook hands, and then I showed Bryan out.

Though he didn't say a word, I'd been married to him too long not to recognize his body language. The sharp foot-steps. The hard set of his shoulders. The way he resolutely did not look at me, even when I opened the door for him.

I stepped outside and closed the door behind me so we'd have some relative privacy. "Well?"

He faced me, all his irritation on full display. "What?"

My own irritation threatened to bubble up, but I kept myself calm. "You've met him. You've agreed to him watching the kids during my custody weeks. Are we good now?"

He huffed and broke eye contact. "It isn't like I have much choice, do I?"

"This whole situation *was* your choice," I reminded him.

"It wasn't a choice." Bryan snapped, and there was a hint of hurt at the edge of his voice. "I wasn't doing it for fun, okay?"

"Then why were—"

"Because I'm trying to move on with my life," he gritted out. "And it's impossible to do when I still spend half the goddamned year at the mercy of your schedule."

I straightened. "So, what? I'm being unreasonable because I—"

"It's not you being unreasonable." His tone shifted to one full of fatigue and even some defeat. "Joint custody is what it is. I can't move out of Pittsburgh as long as you're signed with the team."

"And I can't sign with another team because our custody agreement is contingent on my no-move clause. This isn't easy for either of us."

"No, it isn't. But when we're trading off custody once a week, I can get into that groove. When it's at the mercy of hockey, though? And practices, and team meetings, and every other goddamned thing that drags you out of the house?" He shook his head emphatically. "I can't do it, Trev. I just fucking can't. *You* signed with the Rebels. Not me. I want to be able to live my life without the team having me on the same short leash they have you on."

I gritted my teeth. "So you started dating another player?"

"That's different," he growled. "Tim comes and goes, just like you did. I can't do much about that. But that doesn't affect my custody of the boys." With a heavy sigh, he looked right at me. "This hasn't been fun for me, you know. Being divorced. It's—it hasn't been easy, and it hasn't been fun. I'm just trying to get my damn life into something more consistent and predictable."

I swallowed. I'd been so furious with him—not to mention freaked out—over his ultimatum, I admittedly hadn't given much thought to where he was coming from. Not beyond the certainty that he was trying to screw me out of joint custody. And even though I was tempted to point out that it was his choices and actions that had led to us splitting up, that wasn't even worth revisiting. It wasn't like we could go back, and it sure as shit wasn't like I wanted to.

As my thoughts caught up, though, I peered at him. "If this is just about getting your schedule into a groove—why the short notice?"

He tsked and rolled his eyes again. "Because hockey season is about to start? And I didn't want—"

"And you weren't willing to give me some time to make a solid long-term plan?" I flailed a hand. "I get it, okay? But you couldn't even cope with our current arrangement for a few extra weeks while I locked something down?" I gestured at the house behind me. "*And* you get pissed at me when I do the best I can in the very, very tight window you gave me? What do you *want* from me, Bryan?"

He held my gaze for several long, uncomfortable seconds.

Then he turned on his heel and headed for his car, throwing over his shoulder, "I'll see at the usual time to pick up the kids."

Before I could respond, he was in the car. The engine rumbled to life, and he pulled away, leaving me alone on the porch steps of the house we'd built together.

What the fuck did I ever see in you?

What happened to us?

CHAPTER 6

CAM

I could tell by Trev's gait that Bryan's departure hadn't gone well. They'd been out there a little longer than I'd expected, and now Trev was practically shuffling through the foyer and back toward the kitchen.

And like, was I even surprised? Though things had settled down enough for us to get through that uncomfortable conversation, the animosity between them had been impossible to ignore. The first couple of minutes after they'd gone outside, I'd just closed my eyes and taken a few deep breaths, relieved *that* was over.

Trev hadn't had a chance to decompress, and from the way he was moving—from the way he looked ready to face-plant on the nearest horizontal surface—I suspected he'd been far more stressed by the whole thing than I was.

I rose from the couch to join him in the kitchen. "Hey. Everything okay?"

"Yeah." He gave a heavy sigh as he trudged to the fridge. "I need a beer. You want one?"

"Uh. Sure. Yeah. I'll take one."

He pulled out two bottles, cracked them open, and

handed me one. In silence, we moved back to the couch where we'd sat earlier. He dropped onto the cushion, then he took a deep pull from his beer. With a heavy sigh, he let his head fall back against the couch and closed his eyes.

Ugh. Seeing him like that was heartbreaking. Some part of me struggled to fathom the two of them together. That there'd ever been a time when they were all about being in love and planning a future and starting a family. They'd married and adopted kids. They'd built a house. It was hard to picture that with the way they were now.

Except I knew all too well how a relationship could take a hard downward turn, leaving a smoldering crater where love and a future used to be.

I sipped my beer. "You okay?"

"Yeah." He wiped a hand over his face. With a heavy sigh, he pressed his beer bottle to his forehead. "I swear, he and I were happy once."

God, that was heartbreaking. The exhaustion radiating off him. The sadness and resignation in those words.

"It's hard when things go south." Ugh, that sounded so stupid and useless, but I didn't know what else to say. "You, um... Do you think he'll still let you hire me? Like, he won't find some way to weasel out of it?"

"Nah, he won't try to get out of it." Trev lowered the bottle and looked at me with exhausted eyes. "He's not happy, and he'll probably find reasons to bitch about you for a while, but he'll let it go." He stared at nothing for a moment. "Honestly, I think once he's had a few weeks of a normal every-other-week custody agreement during the regular season, he'll back off."

"You do?"

He gestured toward the front of the house with his beer. "He said something out there about how hard he's been struggling with having chaotic custody exchanges for half the year. Where both of our lives are dictated by the team's schedule, even though he shouldn't have to deal with that now that we're not married anymore." He brought the bottle up again. "Pretty sure he'll get over any issues he has with you after his first taste of the new schedule."

I thumbed the label on my own beer bottle. "Maybe? I mean, hopefully. But I don't think he likes me."

"Dude, I could've hired his own mother, and he'd have found reasons to complain," Trev grumbled. "He used to be really chill and easygoing, but ever since we separated, he's insisted on digging in his heels and pushing back on everything. Literally everything."

"Exes," I muttered. "What can you do?"

"Right." He took another drink. "By the way—that thing about the ice cream toppings..." He gave a little nod. "That probably got his attention and made him realize you actually give a shit."

"I figured it would."

He eyed me. "What do you mean?"

"I knew exactly what it meant. But he seemed like the kind of guy who'd try to quiz me and trip me up, so..."

Trev's eyebrow climbed. "Wait, so you didn't actually..."

"Pfft. Are you kidding? 'Ice cream toppings on top instead of mixed in.'" I rolled my eyes. "That is not rocket science, my dude." Grinning, I added, "But it does tell the uptight dad to knock off the suspicion that the nanny won't bother reading the manual."

Trev studied me for a moment, and I was worried he'd get mad that I'd done something admittedly manipulative.

I was about to apologize, but then he laughed and shook his head. "Well-played, my friend. Well-played."

Oh, thank God.

"You think it actually worked, then?" I grimaced. "And you don't mind me playing little head games to get your ex off my back?"

He scoffed and flailed his hand. "Are you kidding? The way he started coming at you sideways the minute you sat down, I wouldn't have complained if you'd torn into him. Your approach was even better, though. Play a little stupid, make it obvious you care enough about the boys to ask questions—" He raised his beer in a mock toast, then took a drink.

I laughed, more than a little relieved that I hadn't crossed a line. "Okay, so it worked. And there are few things in the world that everyone will agree on—one of them is that slimy, wilted lettuce is disgusting."

Trev chuckled. "You're not wrong." He sighed and played with the label on his beer bottle. "I'm sorry he was such an ass to you at first, though."

"Seems like he was mostly being an ass to you. Either directly or"—I gestured at myself—"by proxy."

He grunted. "Still. I didn't want you to be caught in the crossfire. If we could've swung this whole arrangement without you ever having to meet him, I would have."

"I had to, though," I said softly. "I understood that."

"I know. It just sucks." Trev's gaze turned distant. "Everything about it fucking sucks."

I watched him curiously, unsure if I should press. On the other hand, we were already on the subject, so we might as well go there.

I pulled my feet up under me and rested my beer on my knee. "What happened, anyway? Between the two of you?" I paused. "If, uh... If you don't mind me asking."

"Nah, it's fine." He took another swig of beer, then set the bottle on a coaster on the end table. Tilting his head back, he stared up at the ceiling. "I don't even know, honestly. Like, there isn't just one thing. I mean, I caught him cheating, so that was what ended it, but we were in trouble long before that ever happened. If he hadn't cheated, I think we still would've ended up divorced just because we were... I don't even know. It was a lot of little shit snowballing over time."

"So, death by a thousand cuts?"

"Something like that." His eyes fluttered shut as he sighed. "I guess it was just... like all the usual things that can put a strain on a marriage, but we didn't *fix* any of them. We'd argue about them, and we even went to counseling for a little while, but..." He shook his head and stared up at the ceiling again. "Nothing changed. Then one day, we could barely stand the sight of each other, and then I caught him cheating, and..." He waved his hand as if to say, *do the math.*

"That sucks," I said softly.

"Yeah. It's probably just as well we separated while the boys were still toddlers. It's not ideal, but we split before they were really engaged with the outside world. Like before they had solid memories of us as a family. I think it's easier for them to adapt." He pinched the bridge of his nose. "That's what I tell myself, anyway."

"There's probably some truth to it," I said. "I'm no expert on child development, but I think my parents' divorce would've been easier if it happened before I remembered them together."

He let his head loll toward me. "Yeah?"

"Well, yeah." I shrugged. "I remember them being good together. I remember them falling apart. And I remember the divorce. I think it would've been easier if the only thing I really remembered was them being divorced."

"Maybe?" Trev whispered. "I hope so, anyway. This

whole parenting thing has been nonstop trial and error, and I just hope the errors I've made haven't completely messed up my kids."

"I highly, highly doubt they have. You obviously love them and want what's best for them. Bryan obviously does too. I'm sure you've both made plenty of mistakes, but like, remember how often *our* parents fucked up?"

He managed a soft laugh. "Yeah. I do."

"Right, and we turned out okay. The people whose childhoods messed them up—they're the ones with parents who actually mistreated them, you know? Even at their worst, none of our parents did that. And I can't imagine you mistreating anyone except another hockey player who pisses you off."

Trev snorted. "Hey. That's not mistreatment. Fighting is part of hockey."

"Like that guy you sucker-punched during the playoffs?"

He barked a real laugh. "I didn't just punch him out of the blue."

I arched an eyebrow.

He rolled his eyes. "He slashed our goalie. *After* the whistle. And *then* like three seconds later, he shoved our captain, who was still getting up after a dirty check." Trev gestured with his beer. "If he didn't want to get punched in the face, he shouldn't have been acting like somebody who wanted to get his face punched."

"Uh-huh. Whatever you say."

He chuckled, and then he looked at me with a more serious expression. "You're right, though. About the rest of it. We're going to make mistakes with the boys." Sighing, he pressed back against the couch. "I just hope the ones we make and the ones we've made..."

"I really think you're fine."

"Eh. We'll see, I guess."

We would. But I suspected I'd still hold on to my opinion just as firmly after I'd seen him with his kids. Trev had always been the kind of person to fall all over himself and worry that someone was unhappy with him. It had actually been really cute, watching him with the boyfriend he'd had after me. The way he'd tied himself in knots, doing everything he could to keep that guy happy—it had been seriously adorable. The last month or so, when everyone but them had known a breakup was on the horizon, he'd been a mess. Not just crushed that his boyfriend was pulling away from him, but certain it was his fault somehow. That he hadn't done enough or been enough.

Which meant he must've been a wreck during the drain-circling period of his marriage.

My heart sank, both at that realization, and the guilt that I hadn't been in contact with him during that time. I had no idea if he'd have reached out to me, but at least I'd have been an option for him.

Out of the blue, Trev said, "You know what really sucks? I loved him. I still love him as my kids' other dad." He deflated. "But it's really, really hard to imagine ever being in love with him. Even though I can clearly remember the years when I was." He closed his eyes and gave a quiet, tired laugh. "God, that doesn't even make sense."

"No, it does."

He looked at me. "It does?"

"Are you kidding? I loved Daniel at one time. I mean, he love-bombed the fuck out of me and got me under his thumb, but there were still good times, you know? Sometimes I can even think back on those memories and enjoy them because it's like they happened with a completely different person."

Trev's eyes lost focus as he seemed to mull that over. "Yeah. Yeah, I get that, I think." He sighed and shook himself. "Just hard to believe things can change that much."

"I know what you mean."

Our eyes locked, and my heart thumped. Yeah. Things really could change a lot, couldn't they? The man who'd been my best friend through some of the most challenging years of my life—he was almost a stranger now. How we'd gone from being that close to not seeing each other for the better part of a decade was... I mean, I knew the sequence of events, but it was hard to wrap my mind around it all.

Apparently we were on the same page, too.

"Can I ask you about something?" Trev asked. "From the last few years? About..." He gestured at himself, then me.

My stomach tightened. *Here we go.* He was entitled to answers, though, and we were already prodding at some of his wounds, so why not?

Wordlessly, I nodded.

Trev hesitated, studying me uncertainly. "I tried to get back in touch a few times. Wanted to see you. But there was always..." He dropped his gaze and pressed his lips together, brow furrowed as if he were trying to find the right words.

I could read between the lines, though, and I sighed, rubbing the back of my neck. "I wanted to. I really did."

He looked at me through his lashes, the question unspoken but unmistakable. *So why didn't you?*

I stared down at my hands. "I'm probably a coward, or a pushover, or—I don't know. But my ex..." My shoulders slumped. "Every time I mentioned your name, Daniel lost his shit."

Trev's eyes widened. "What? Why? Was he jealous or something?"

I coughed a laugh. "Are you kidding? He was jealous of my *clients*. He was jealous that I still talk to our friends from high school. You?" I gestured at him. "Do you really think a controlling, insecure jackwagon of a boyfriend *wouldn't* be insanely jealous of the pro hockey player I lost my virginity to?"

Trev blinked, and he also blushed. I was probably blushing too; my cheeks were a little hot, and I had just casually made reference to the fact that we'd had sex a lifetime ago. Totally something I needed either of us thinking about right now when I was struggling not to openly drool over the seriously hot man he'd become.

Trev recovered before I did. "Being with someone like that sounds miserable."

"It really was. I should've left a long time ago, but..." I waved a hand. Because what could I do? It wasn't like I could go back and swipe left on him. I sure wished I could, though. It felt like I'd lost years of my own life because of him.

Years of my own life, and too many years with my best friend.

I made myself look in his eyes. "For the record, I wanted to come to your wedding. I really, really did. And he and I fought about it for like a month."

"What?" Trev stared at me with horror. "Jesus, Cam. I wanted you there, but I didn't want to cause problems with your boyfriend."

"I know. And it wasn't your fault. It was him being an asshole." My voice threatened to shake as I said, "He did a lot of shit while we were together, but I never forgave him for making me miss your wedding."

Trev sighed, and to my surprise, he slid closer on the couch and pulled me into a hug. "Not gonna lie—I thought you didn't want to be there. If I'd known you were with someone who was treating you that bad..."

I closed my eyes and wrapped my arms around him. "Nobody knew. I made sure they didn't."

He drew back and stared down at me, brow pinched. "But why? If you were so unhappy..."

I gave a heavy shrug. "That's how it works with people like that. In hindsight, I never should've given him the time of day. He had me so off-balance all the time, I was constantly scrambling to keep him happy. So I never really had a chance to stop and think, you know, this is kind of fucked up." Exhaling, I broke eye contact and shook my head. "And then one day, we'd been together for eight years, he'd mostly isolated me from my friends and family, and I barely even knew who I was anymore."

"Jesus Christ," Trev breathed. "That sounds awful."

"It was. It... Ugh. He criticized everything I did. *Everything*. Nothing was ever good enough, and I believed him. I was so wrapped up in trying to be better, I couldn't even see how bad it was." I paused. "There were some things I put my foot down about. He didn't like that."

Trev tilted his head. "Like what?"

"God, where do I start?" I rolled my eyes. "For one thing, he pushed me for a long, long time about getting bottom surgery."

Trev's lips parted. "Seriously?"

"Yep. And like, I don't even think it was a transphobic thing. If I'd been cis, it would've been something else. I think me choosing not to get more surgery was just an easy target for him."

"Jesus Christ," Trev growled. "I'm just glad he didn't actually push you into getting something you didn't want."

"He almost succeeded a few times," I admitted. "He'd always come at me about it when I was in a really low spot. Like right after my dad died, or after I had to stop working out for a while because of a car accident. My body was—I mean, I wasn't in as good a shape, you know?"

"I get that. It takes a ton of work, and one injury can set you back months."

"Right? So I gained some weight and lost some muscle tone, and even though I knew it was just part of the process and it wasn't forever, I didn't feel great about it."

"I can relate." Trev scowled. "And he used that time to pressure you about surgery?"

"Well yeah." I laughed bitterly. "What better time to make me consider making massive changes to my body than when I'm seriously unhappy about my body?"

Trev rolled his eyes, a low growl emerging from his throat. "For fuck's sake."

"Seriously. Fortunately, the guys—especially Don— were always happy to give me a reality check."

There was genuine relief in Trev's expression and the way his shoulders relaxed. "I'm glad they were there. I wish I could've been, but—"

"Daniel wouldn't have let you near me. He barely put up with me talking to the other guys. You?" I shook my head. "He'd have lost his shit. Hell, he was pissed that I sent you a wedding gift."

Trev's expression shifted from relieved to pained. "I just can't believe someone treated you that bad for so long. And pressuring you to get surgery? Fuck, dude. That's just..." He balled his fists at his sides. "Ugh. *Fuck* that guy."

"You're telling me." I ran a hand through my hair and

rolled my shoulders, which had started tightening up. They always did that when my thoughts turned to Daniel. "Anyway, like I said, I don't think he actually cared if I had bottom surgery or not. It was just an easy target to criticize and pressure me. If I'd gone through with it, he'd have found something else before I was even out of the OR."

Trev actually shuddered. "I can't even imagine. But I'm glad he didn't actually get you to go through with it if it wasn't something you wanted."

"It wasn't. Never has been."

"Good." He paused. "Err, I mean, not that you don't want the surgery. I..." He waved his hand. "That's your choice, of course. I meant 'good' like I'm glad you stuck to what you really wanted. Not what *he* wanted."

I smiled. "I know what you meant. And I agree." I gestured at my left arm. "The only lasting mark I have from him is this tattoo, and I plan to get it removed or covered up as soon as I can afford it."

Trev craned his neck a little, peering at the intricately detailed shark covering most of my upper arm. "Damn. It's a cool tattoo."

"It is." I ran my fingers over it. "I love the work she did, and it cost a fucking fortune. But..." I shook my head. "Every time I see it, I can hear Daniel badgering me to get matching tattoos." I tsked and rolled my eyes again. "I still can't believe I let him talk me into it."

Trev made a face. "Well, at least it can be removed and redone. Any idea what you'll get instead?"

"I don't know yet. I kind of don't want to make a decision until I actually get it removed. Like, let the skin be bare for a while so I know for sure that my next tattoo is because I want it, not because I'm eager to replace the shark."

"That's... That's a really smart way to approach it."

"Smarter than getting the tattoo in the first place," I said dryly.

"Eh, live and learn." He shifted around and pulled one foot up under himself on the couch. "So what was the straw that finally broke the camel's back?" He paused. "Jake said the fucker worked you over and put you in the situation you were in when I reached out to you. What happened?"

I took a deep breath and slouched against the cushion. "He cheated on me. With one of my clients."

Trev's eyes widened. "No shit?"

"No shit." I laughed bitterly. "And they both acted like I was overreacting when I dumped Daniel and refused to continue working with the client." My humor, what little there was, died away, and I exhaled. "The thing is, Daniel worked at the same gym, and he and his fuckboy concocted a story about me stealing from the till." I pinched the bridge of my nose as the memory and its ensuing fallout pressed down on my shoulder. Letting my hand fall into my lap, I added, "Got me fired and blacklisted from pretty much the entire fitness community in Portland. A good chunk of it in Seattle, too."

"Holy shit," Trev whispered.

I met his gaze as fatigue worked its way into my voice. "I swear to God, those allegations are bullshit. I think they all knew it, too, because no one pressed charges. So if you're worried about me doing—"

"Cam." Trev shook his head emphatically. "I wouldn't be moving you into my house to take care of my kids if I was worried about that. I know you."

I swallowed. For all he'd known, I'd been avoiding him like the plague for the past several years because I didn't want him in my life, but somehow, that hadn't tarnished his view of me.

"I know you," he said again. "I'm not worried. And I won't lie—getting to see you again was part of what made me reach out."

"It... It was?"

He nodded. "Once I knew you were in a bind, I'd have done anything I could to help. And I was in a bind myself, so there's that. But the chance to reconnect? That was on the list too."

Warmth rushed through me, and I smiled. "That was definitely a perk for me too. Not that I was in any position to turn anything down, but..."

Trev's tired but genuine smile chased away all the bitterness about my ex. Yeah, the last several years had sucked. Yeah, it had taken way too long to get out from under Daniel's thumb.

But I was getting back on my feet now.

And on top of that, I was with my best friend again.

For the first time in a long time, I could believe that everything would be okay.

CHAPTER 7

TREV

WHAT A DAY.

Lying in bed that night, staring up at the ceiling, I was both wide awake and utterly exhausted.

I'd introduced Bryan and Cam. That had gone about as well as could be expected. This evening, my ex and I had texted back and forth to coordinate, and we'd agreed I could start my custody week two days early. That would give the boys a chance to spend time with Cam before I had to be gone for the long hours of training camp. When the preseason kicked off, Bryan would take two extra days. In theory, this would ease everyone into Cam taking care of the boys while I was gone.

So, I'd go pick up the twins tomorrow. They'd meet Cam.

And hopefully, they'd get along with Cam.

I sighed into the stillness and rubbed my eyes. I wasn't worried about the boys getting along with Cam. I really wasn't. They were chill as could be and got along with just about anyone, including at least one teacher who'd made *my* teeth grind.

I couldn't imagine any scenario in which they clashed with Cam. I think I was just so worried about this solution—this Hail Mary without a backup plan—falling apart that I couldn't take anything for granted.

That worry was also front and center in my mind now that some of the other issues were out of the way. Cam had agreed to take the job. He'd come to Pittsburgh. Bryan had (if grudgingly) accepted Cam's role. The biggest logistical hurdles were out of the way.

In the whirlwind of getting Cam here from Seattle, I hadn't had much time to think about the two of us. I'd worried—and I still worried—how he'd get along with the twins. I'd been afraid Bryan would find some reason to veto the whole thing, leaving me up Shit Creek with no other solution on the horizon. And I'd been scared that too much time had passed. That Cam and I would be strangers, and maybe one or both of us had changed so much that we wouldn't get along anymore.

But I hadn't stopped to think about how much I'd missed my friend. Outside of hockey, almost every good memory I had of my youth involved Cam. And he'd been there for a lot of the hockey memories, too. There was no young Trev without Cam, and it was getting harder and harder to imagine adult Trev without him.

I'd desperately given him the benefit of the doubt all these years. Explaining to myself that there had to be some reason why he'd cut off contact. Why he hadn't come to my wedding. Why the North American continent hadn't been the largest distance between us.

In the back of my mind, though I hadn't admitted it to myself, I'd been expecting the explanation to be exactly what I'd gaslit myself out of believing: that he didn't want me in his life anymore. That he'd moved on from me.

So when it turned out there really was an explanation, and he really did still want me in his life...

When it turned out he'd missed me as much as I'd missed him...

I didn't know how to process that.

I also didn't know how to process the way my brain skidded to a halt every time I met Cam's gaze. Every time he laughed at something. Every time... fuck, every time he *breathed*. I still couldn't decide if this attraction just felt really strong because my dormant libido had very suddenly awakened, or if it really was that intense.

Because it sure felt that intense.

I closed my eyes and squirmed beneath the covers. I did not need to be rubbing one out to my friend. Especially not my friend who was now my kids' nanny. That would just be... weird. In fact, imagining making eye contact with him across the breakfast table, knowing I'd jerked off thinking about him...

Well, that took care of my hard-on.

I laughed into the silence at the absurdity of this whole situation. Being attracted to Cam wasn't a surprise. It really wasn't. I just hadn't banked on *how* attracted I'd be. On how absolutely jaw-droppingly sexy he'd be when he arrived at my door.

I've heard of having a glow-up, but holy shit.

He wasn't here for us to hook up, though. He was here so we could help each other out of some really ugly binds.

Which... now that I thought about it...

I mean, I hated his ex for how he'd treated Cam. Turned out I also hated him for being the reason I'd lost so much time with my best friend.

On the other hand, both of our exes being trash fires at

the same time had been the catalyst for landing us back in each other's lives. So maybe in the end, it wasn't so bad. We'd helped each other out, and we weren't strangers anymore. We were friends again.

As long as I don't find a way to screw this up.

Like, say, letting this attraction make me do or say something stupid and drive him right back out the door.

Sighing, I rubbed my eyes. I really hoped I didn't screw this up. I hoped this whole arrangement worked out, and not just because I wanted to hold on to joint custody of my kids. And if it *didn't* work out, I hoped Cam stayed in Pittsburgh or at least stayed in contact.

I didn't think I could handle missing him again.

Pulling into a parking space beneath this condo always gave me mixed feelings. The prospect of seeing Bryan, even for a few minutes, had me tense and irritated. Seeing my boys, though? That had me ready to jump out of the car and excitedly sprint up the stairs.

I shut off the engine and got out. There was a yellow sports car in the open garage, and I suppressed a curse. Great. Bryan's boyfriend was home. Just what I needed.

I headed up the stairs, trying not to grind my teeth. It bugged me, knowing this was my teammate's condo—that Bryan and I had come here together for social gatherings in our past life. Bryan *swore* he and Chats had never so much as flirted until after we'd separated, but I was dubious. Especially with as often as Chats liked to rub it in my face that he was with my ex-husband.

Naturally, that was exactly who came to the door when

I knocked. Shirtless, of course, because this man was allergic to covering up his abs unless a dress code required it.

He met me with a shit-eating grin. "Hey. Kids should be ready to go."

"Good. Thanks."

He gestured for me to come in, and I did, gritting my teeth the whole way.

Chats—Tim Chatsworth—was *exactly* Bryan's type. He was taller than me, and he had the hockey physique that was Bryan's catnip—powerful thighs, an ass that didn't quit, and six-pack abs. I liked to think hockey had been kind to me and that I wore the results well, but Chats was the player who had all the fans— men and women alike— openly drooling over him. He was probably hot as hell anyway, and the sport had chiseled him into something utterly stunning.

He was also an insufferable asshole, so apparently "opposites attract" wasn't a thing between him and my ex-husband.

I kept that catty thought to myself and joined the happy couple in the kitchen to catch up on everything before I left with the boys.

Chats leaned against the counter and grinned at me. He probably wanted me to roll my eyes or work my jaw— somehow let on that his smugness got to me.

I didn't give him the satisfaction, and instead turned a neutral look on my ex. "Do they have soccer this week? Or does that start next week?"

"They have practice on Thursday." Bryan narrowed his eyes a little. "I assume your *nanny* can handle that."

"That's his job," I said dismissively. "And the coaches have his email now, so he'll get notifications about schedule changes and moved games, too."

From the sour look on Bryan's face, he wasn't pleased by that, but I didn't care enough to read into why. Instead, I moved the conversation to catching up about school, though I was mostly kept in the loop there thanks to the teacher's emails. The year had just started, so there wasn't much going on yet that might be causing any issues for either of the twins. Right now they were still in that period of adapting to being in first grade instead of kindergarten, and they were thriving; a lot of their friends from last year were in their class, and they saw the rest at recess, soccer, and after school.

"So the boys are meeting Cam today," Bryan said flatly. "Is that right?"

I nodded. "Yes. He's at the house right now, so I'll talk to them about it in the car, and introduce them when we get home."

His lips thinned, and he exchanged unreadable looks with Chats. Facing me again, he asked, "And what happens if they don't get along? Or the boys aren't comfortable with him?"

I had a cold prickle of suspicion that he'd planted seeds of doubt in their heads. That he'd made sure they wouldn't get along with Cam and wouldn't be comfortable with him.

At the same time, though... no. That wasn't who he was. He might not have liked me or Cam, but he drew a very hard line at weaponizing the kids, at least in ways that caused them stress or anxiety. He'd happily weaponize them in ways that caused *me* stress and anxiety, like his custody ultimatum, but it was always well out of the twins' sight.

Keeping my voice even, I said, "If there's an issue, we'll address it. But you've met him." I inclined my head. "Is there any reason you can think of why he *wouldn't* get along with the boys?"

Bryan worked his jaw and shifted his weight as he crossed his arms over his chest. That was body language I recognized—when he couldn't refute an argument and was seriously annoyed by it.

Yeah, that's what I thought, I didn't say out loud.

Instead, I went with, "I don't think it'll be a problem. If it is, we'll figure it out."

He shrugged. "All right." I recognized that, too—he was sort of agreeing with me, sort of giving me enough rope to hang myself. Either way, he wasn't completely admitting he was wrong.

Fuck. No wonder our marriage had been so exhausting.

Finally, we were all on the same page, Bryan and Chats said goodbye to the kids, and we headed outside. Once the boys were buckled in, I got into the driver seat and pulled away from the condo.

As I headed out to the main road, I said, "So you guys know hockey season is starting, right?"

"Yeah," Zane said. "Dad told us."

"Okay, well, did he tell you we're going to do things a little differently this year?"

There was silence for a moment. Then Zach cautiously said, "We'll be staying with the new nanny while you're gone?"

Ah, so Bryan had filled them in. I tried to trust that he hadn't dripped any poison in their ears; that for all we could fight like cats and dogs, he really did draw the line at parental alienation. His boyfriend... well. One could hope.

"Yes," I said. "His name is Cam. He and I have been friends for a long, long time, and he's going to be living with us now."

"Oh," Zane said.

Zach made a quiet grunt of acknowledgment. Neither seemed particularly bothered by the whole thing. My teammates had babysat them a few times, and they'd stayed with family members before, so they were accustomed to people other than Bryan or me watching them. They weren't prone to separation anxiety like some kids their age. Hell, the first day we'd taken them to preschool, we'd been ready for them to cry and not want us to leave. Instead, they'd taken one look at the other kids and all the toys, and immediately forgotten we existed.

Still, I worried, because that was the kind of dad I was.

"Is that okay?" I asked. "Do you guys feel okay being with someone else while I'm gone?"

"Yeah," they both said.

"Okay. But you know you can text me or call me any time. I leave my phone with one of the trainers when I'm on the ice in case there's an emergency, so you can always reach me."

"We know," Zach said in that *God, Dad, we get it* voice kids did so well.

"I'm just making sure. And Dad is always around, too, if you need something."

"We know."

"Cam is there for you too," I assured them. "He's there just like a babysitter, except he lives with us. Does that make sense?"

"Yes." They sounded borderline annoyed now. *Come on, Dad, we're not stupid.* They weren't stupid, but I always erred on the side of overkill when it came to making sure they felt safe. Hopefully if a situation arose where they needed an adult, they could fall back on this conversation (and others) and know that they could rely on Bryan, Cam, or me. They could probably even rely on Chats, but if I was out of town, so was he, so... he didn't need to be part of the conversation.

Out of the blue, Zach asked, "Is Cam your boyfriend?"

"What?" I laughed, which came out a little high. "No! No, he's a friend."

"Oh. When are you getting a boyfriend?"

"I..." I glanced in the rearview, where two curious faces gazed back. Facing the road again, I said, "I mean, I just haven't—I haven't met anyone yet."

"But you've met Cam," Zane insisted. "He lives with us now like Tim does."

I pretended not to notice the flare of jealousy in my chest. I was not jealous of anyone living with or dating Bryan—Chats could *have* him—but yeah, there was still a part of me that bristled at their relationship. Maybe because Chats kept throwing it in my face. Or maybe because I still wasn't convinced the relationship had commenced *after* our separation.

Whatever. None of that was anything the kids needed to know about.

"We're just friends," I told the boys. "Cam lives with us because it makes it easier for him to do his job. But we're not boyfriends."

God, I wish we were.

Wait, what?

Dude. Stop it.

"Do you think Dad's going to marry Tim?" Zach's question didn't offer any hints one way or the other if he had any hopes about Bryan and Chats being in it for the long haul.

"Um." I tapped my thumbs on the wheel. "I really don't know. That's probably something to ask them."

"They won't say." Zane sounded affronted.

I hesitated, then cautiously asked, "Do you *want* them to get married?" I wasn't fishing for gossip or dirt; I genuinely wanted to know where they landed with this, and if there were any red flags I should know about.

"I don't know," Zane said. "I guess?"

"Tim's nice," Zach supplied.

"That's good," I said with a nod. It was, too. Both of my boys were like me in the sense that they tended to wear their emotions on their sleeves. If there was something going on with Chats—if they were uncomfortable with him, or if he'd said or done something they didn't like, or even if he was just too strict in his stepdad role—there would be tells. Their body language, their tone, their answers; even if they weren't telling me outright what the issue was, they would absolutely send up signals that something was wrong.

Chats had been in their lives since shortly after Bryan and I separated, and there hadn't been any negative signals from the boys. Nothing to indicate that Chats was a problem or that Bryan had told them to keep a secret from me. I subtly checked in like this every now and then, just to ease my own worries, but... so far, so good.

Maybe their dad and I had divorced bitterly, and maybe his new boyfriend and I couldn't get along, but as near as I could tell, they were both being good to the boys. That was enough for me.

After a while, Zach asked, "Is Cam nice?"

I smiled and glanced at them in the rearview. "I wouldn't have hired him to take care of you two if he wasn't."

They were apparently happy with that answer, because they didn't press for more about Cam.

So far, this was going well. They were unbothered by

this new person coming into their lives. They didn't seem nervous about meeting him.

And all the way home, I prayed this was a sign that I'd made the right decision.

Though the boys weren't fazed at all by the prospect of meeting Cam the nanny, I was nervous as I brought them into the house. Bryan's doubts needled at me; I didn't even know if he'd just been trying to make me second-guess myself or if he really was worried about Zach and Zane not getting along with Cam.

Whatever the case, it turned out none of us had anything to worry about.

As soon as I introduced them in the living room, the boys were alternating between grilling him about everything and excitedly wanting to show him their rooms and playroom.

I trailed behind as they led him upstairs and showed him everything. They dragged him to their closet full of board games and action figures. Showed him their soccer jerseys and gear as they chattered about the upcoming season. Brought him back downstairs to see the video game console.

"They can play that for an hour a day," I said. "No more."

Zane huffed and shot his brother a glare. "I told you we should've showed him when Dad wasn't here."

"Dad was going to tell him anyway," Zach retorted. "He told him *all* the rules."

Zane just rolled his eyes and grumbled something under his breath.

Cam glanced at me, eyebrows up and lips pressed together as if he were hiding his amusement. Oh, yeah, I hadn't mentioned to him that the biggest challenge around kids was trying not to laugh, especially when we were supposed to be disciplining them or something.

I mean, how the fuck was I supposed to keep a straight face when I was saying things like, "we don't tell Grandma her meatballs taste like boogers"? Or "it's not nice to pretend your plushies are farting on your brother"? When people said parenting wasn't for the weak, that wasn't what I'd envisioned.

During my moment of distraction, Zane looked at Cam and asked, "How do you know our dad?"

"We went to school together." Cam smiled fondly. "We met in..." He furrowed his brow and looked at me. "Was it fourth grade? Fifth?"

I rolled my eyes. "*Third*, Cam."

"Was it? I thought—oh. Oh, yeah, you were in Mrs. Vincent's class too, weren't you?"

"Unfortunately."

"Hey! That's how you met me!"

"Not that you remember." I chuckled and said to the boys, "We knew each other in elementary school, but then we got to be good friends in junior high."

"You didn't like Mrs. Vincent?" Zane asked, apparently clocking my "unfortunately" comment.

I wrinkled my nose. "She was mean."

"She was." Cam turned to the boys. "I missed *so* many recesses because of her."

Both boys recoiled in horror.

I snorted. "That was because you were always breaking the rules." Puffing out my chest, I added, "*I* never missed a recess in her class."

Cam rolled his eyes, and I suspected he was struggling *hard* not to flip me off.

"But you still didn't like her?" Zach asked.

"She was still mean," I said. "She was just... way meaner to the kids who didn't behave."

Zach looked at Cam, eyes wide with interest. "What kind of stuff did you do?"

"Nothing *you two* should try on *your* teachers," I warned, eying Cam.

"What?" He spread his hands, grinning like a jackass. "Do you really think I'd be a bad influence on your kids?"

"What's a bad influence?" Zach asked.

"Oh my God," I muttered. "Hey, why don't we all get in the pool? It's going to start getting cold soon, and you'll be at school, so you won't have as much time to swim."

That distraction worked like a charm. Both boys immediately took off up the stairs, probably to get changed.

"Well played," Cam said.

I rolled my eyes and elbowed him. "You're such a brat."

"Don't act like you didn't know."

"For fuck's sake."

He snickered, then gestured outside. "So are we swimming too?"

The thought of seeing him in shorts and nothing else sobered me right up, and I gulped. "Uh... Do you want to?"

"Are you kidding me? I haven't been swimming in ages, and your pool is gorgeous!"

I laughed, thankful he couldn't actually hear my heart going wild. "All right, all right." I gestured at the stairs. "Go get your swim trunks on."

When I came downstairs in my own swim trunks, the boys were waiting by the fence around the pool. Zane carried a couple of pool noodles, and Zach had a handful of weighted rings that could be retrieved off the bottom.

As I padded across the sun-warmed flagstones, I gestured at the rings. "Remember, you only use those when someone's watching. Tell me or Cam before you start tossing them in, okay?"

Zach groaned and nodded. "I *know*, Dad."

They both did, but I was never going to stop being extra careful where the pool was concerned.

I unlocked the gate, and the boys were in the water in two seconds flat. Zach had left the rings on the side, and they splashed and played in the shallow end while I sat on the edge with my feet in the cool water. As much anxiety as it gave me, having a pool with young kids, I loved watching them have fun in it. Now that the twins had gotten past a lot of their anxiety over being in the water, they couldn't get enough of swimming.

In fact, with the colder months on the horizon, I needed to look into some facilities around Pittsburgh with indoor pools. The one we'd signed them up for last year had closed, but there had to be more that were—

The sliding glass door opened and closed behind me, and I twisted around.

And... wow.

I did a double take as Cam stepped out onto the back deck.

Holy shit, you're hot.

His ripped physique was on full display except for what was covered by a pair of blue and gray swim trunks. He had on dark sunglasses, too, though he left those on the table before jumping into the pool.

He'd taken out his nipple piercings, which I appreciated. I didn't mind my kids seeing body modifications—their other dad had tattoos, after all, as did Chats and most of my teammates. But I really wasn't ready for a call from my ex-husband about, *"Tell me why our sons said you told them they could get their nipples pierced if I said it was okay?"*

Though Bryan was probably wise to it by now, especially after *"Dad said if it's okay with you, we can get tattoos."*

Kids, man. What can you do?

"Cam!" Zane called out. "Do you want to dive for rings?"

"Rings?" Cam looked around, then zeroed in on the stack of weighted rings. "Sure!" He swam over and grabbed them. "Who wants to go first?"

And just like that, they were playing a game—tossing rings into the water (the shallow end, of course) and retrieving them off the bottom.

As I watched, I couldn't help smiling. Whatever worries I might've had about Cam and the boys getting along—they were gone. I wasn't naïve enough to think this would all be sunshine and roses. Getting along with him when they were all having fun was one thing. Listening to him when he told them it was time to do homework or chores—that was where things could get dicey.

This was a good start, though. A really good start.

And... okay, when was I going to stop getting butterflies every time Cam did something? Because this was getting a little ridiculous. Laughing at something? Butterflies. Coming upstairs from the gym, sweaty and shirtless? Butterflies. Just... *breathing?* Fuuucking butterflies.

And now here he was, making my kids laugh while they all took turns swimming to the bottom to retrieve the weighted rings. He didn't try to coax them into deeper water. He didn't give Zach grief when he struggled to get one of the rings. He didn't criticize Zane's form when he got tired and reverted to dog paddling. In fact, he helped Zane to the edge of the pool, and he kept both of them distracted with a long-winded story from our youth. The boys laughed their heads off at the story. I recognized it for what it was— giving Zane a chance to rest a little so he could swim more comfortably and safely.

Sure enough, after Cam's story, they returned to their game, and Zane was back to swimming the way he'd learned in his lessons.

After a while, the boys got bored with chasing rings, and they were content to splash around on their pool noodles. While they did that, Cam hoisted himself onto the edge beside me. I was glad I had the responsibility of keeping an eye on the kids right then; it kept me from shamelessly ogling my gorgeous and half-naked friend's perfect, wet body.

Watching them with a smile, he leaned back on his hands. "Can you imagine if we'd had a pool like this when we were kids?"

I made a face. "We'd have spent half the time cleaning pine needles out of it, and the rest of the time, it would've been too cold."

He tsked. "But that one or two days every summer where it was hot? Man, they wouldn't have been able to drag us out."

"I know, right? We'd probably *still* be in it."

We both laughed and kept watching the boys playing in the water.

I loved this. Enjoying a relaxed summer afternoon with my sons, and also chilling with the friend I'd been missing so much for so long. As furious as I'd been with Bryan for his ultimatum, I could almost kiss him for it now because it was the reason I had Cam here.

In between games, the boys swam over to us.

"What's for lunch?" Zach asked.

I pretended to give it some thought. "I was thinking I could grill some burgers. Sound good?"

Both boys lit up. "Yeah!"

I chuckled. "Figured I wouldn't have to twist your arms. Maybe another half our or so, I'll start cooking?"

"Okay!"

They started to push off from the side, but then Zane pointed at Cam's chest. In an intensely concerned voice, he asked, "What happened?"

Cam glanced down. My stomach flipped as I realized my son had been indicating the silvery crescent-shaped scars on each of Cam's pecs. Panic knotted my guts as I scrambled for an explanation that would make sense to a six-year-old while not making a trans guy feel uncomfortable.

Cam, however, responded without missing a beat. "Oh, I had surgery a few years ago. But it's all healed now."

"Did it hurt?" Zane asked with all the innocence of a child.

"When it was healing, yeah." Cam shrugged. "But afterward, I felt a lot better."

"Oh. So like my dad's foot."

Cam tilted his head, flicking his eyes toward me before asking, "What happened to your dad's foot?"

"It was hurting him," Zane explained. "He went to the doctor and they fixed it. He had crutches for a while, but now he's better."

"Oh." Cam smiled. "Yeah, it's kind of like that. It hurts for a little while, but then it doesn't anymore."

"Oh. Okay." And with that, Zane and his brother were focused on something else—this time, using their pool noodles to stage swordfights in the water.

"They're really not bothered by much, are they?" Cam asked.

"No, they're not. They're curious about things, but I've found as long as we take them seriously and give them an answer, they're like—okay, curiosity satisfied, moving on."

"You don't say." Then Cam turned an uneasy look on me. "That's, um... That's okay, right? That they saw my scars? And asked about them?"

"Yeah, of course." I shrugged. "I just hope it didn't make you uncomfortable. Him asking about it, I mean."

"Nah. Kids are just curious." He studied me. "When did you have ankle surgery?"

"Ankle—*oh*. Not me. Bryan. He ruptured his Achilles tendon—must've been two years ago, I think?"

Cam grimaced. "Ouch. One of my coworkers did that. She was in so much pain for *ages*."

"Bryan was, too. It was awful. Like, I've had some pretty painful injuries from hockey, but I'll pass on that one."

"Good call. And I think I'll pass on some of those hockey injuries." He chafed his arms. "I made the mistake of watching a compilation of worst hockey injuries last year, and... ugh. No, thanks."

I laughed and elbowed him, pretending not to notice the frisson as bare skin brushed bare skin. "You didn't have to watch all of those, you know."

"I know. But it's kind of like a trainwreck. It's hard to look away."

"You're not wrong. I just don't watch the compilations

because there's always a chance I'm *in* them." I shuddered. "I'd just as soon not watch some of my greatest hits, thank you."

"Well," he said dryly, "you could try not getting fucked up as often?"

Rolling my eyes, I elbowed him again. "Shut up."

He just cackled.

God, it was good to have my best friend back.

CHAPTER 8

CAM

IF I HADN'T ALREADY HAD LITTLE HEARTS IN MY EYES starting the day I'd arrived in Pittsburgh, I'd have absolutely had them now. Yeah, yeah, yeah, Trev was hot, and he was cute, and I was a sucker for his smile, and—I mean, what about him *didn't* make me stupid?

But I was *not* prepared for what it felt like to watch this man with his kids.

Most dads obviously loved their kids and would move heaven and earth for them. There were some dads, though, who were also utterly in love with *being* dads, and their entire world was a thousand times brighter whenever their kids were around.

Trev fell very firmly into that second category, and it was the cutest thing ever. Watching him watch them—the way he smiled, the way their antics made him laugh—this was a man who absolutely adored his children, and it made me all fluttery inside.

He didn't let them walk all over him, either. When the boys fought over a pool toy, Trev told them both to sit in the poolside chairs for two minutes and cool down. Afterward, he had them apologize to each other, and warned that if they fought over the toy again, that would be the end of pool time for today.

He wasn't mean or loud about it, just very matter-of-fact and firm. They apparently took his warning to heart, too, and there wasn't any more arguing.

The boys seemed pretty well-behaved anyway, and they got along better than I had with my siblings. Maybe because they were twins? I didn't know. They had all the energy I would expect from a couple of six-year-olds, especially six-year-olds who were playing in a pool, but they seemed pretty easygoing too.

And they were still young enough to be absolutely delighted when Trev got into the water and joined them for a few games. They'd been enthusiastic when I'd played with them, but their dad? That was the highlight of their day, I thought.

At one point, we even put them on our shoulders and let them whap at each other with pool noodles, both of us laughing hysterically as they gleefully battled it out.

After that, we left them to play on their own, and we reclaimed our spots on the edge of the pool. As Trev hoisted himself up beside me, and I was so mesmerized by water running down his flawless body that I almost didn't hear him speak.

"I should get lunch going." He stood and reached for a towel, oblivious to me ogling his massive thighs or the way his shorts clung to his narrow hips. "Burgers still sound good to everyone?"

"Yeah!" the boys cried.

Trev smiled, looking so utterly adorable, then turned his attention to me. "What about you?"

Me? What about...

Lunch, Cam. He's asking about lunch.

I cleared my throat. "Yeah. Yeah, burgers sound great. Can I help with anything?"

"Nah, I got it." He gestured at the boys, who were now busily whacking each other with the pool noodles again. "Just keep an eye on them."

I gave him a playful salute, and he gave me a little wink that made me grateful for the water keeping me cool right then.

Pull yourself together, Cam. The fuck.

Though both boys loved swimming, Zach got out when Trev fired up the grill. He stayed glued to his dad's side, and Trev patiently explained to him everything he was doing. He even let his son turn some of the burger patties while he watched him like a hawk.

I got back in the pool to keep Zane entertained, and also to cool myself off and, like, not sit there and ogle Trev. Someone needed to keep an eye on Zane, and I wasn't doing that if I was perving on his dad.

So, I kept him busy and myself distracted, and I managed to not make an ass of myself while Trev and Zach finished making lunch.

We ate outside on the deck, and after lunch, we moved inside. While the boys went upstairs to play, Trev and I—still in our swim trunks—cleaned the handful of dishes.

As I put a couple of plates in the dishwasher, I said, "Zach seemed fascinated by you grilling."

A fond smile crossed Trev's lips. "Yeah. He really wants to learn to cook. He's been watching cooking videos with me and Bryan since he was little, and he's always interested in whatever we're doing in the kitchen." He paused, then added, "I can't wait until he's older so he can take on more. I know he's itching to try some things, but he's just not quite old enough yet, you know?"

"Like actually doing the grilling himself, and using a knife?" I asked. "And probably anything involving measuring?"

"Actually, they're both pretty good with measuring. They haven't learned much math in school, but they know how to match a fraction on a recipe to one on a measuring cup."

"Oh. Damn. Fractions will be a breeze for them then, won't they?"

"One can hope." Trev made a face. "Because they were almost the death of me."

"Yeah, I remember."

"Yeah, yeah, I'm sure you do."

I chuckled. "So they're both learning it—does that mean Zane likes cooking too?"

"He prefers baking. I think he enjoys the precision of it. Zach is fine with the precise stuff, but he really likes the chaos of cooking, where you can just throw stuff together and experiment. Zane is a bit more methodical." Trev paused. "He's surprisingly good at things like cake decorating, too. He's been asking us for months to sign him up for this one class in Sewickley, but it's for eight and over."

"Aww, bummer."

"Yeah, but I talked to the instructor, and she said she could let him in when he's seven as long as there's an adult with him. So he's signed up for one in December after their birthday."

I straightened. "Is one of my nanny duties taking your kid to a cake-decorating class? Because I will a hundred percent do that for free."

Trev laughed. "Really?"

"Are you kidding? I'm a personal trainer who was surrounded by rigid health fanatics for the past few years. Hell yeah, show me to the sugar class."

He snorted. "You know you're there to supervise, right? Not actually, like, eat the frosting and stuff?"

I shrugged. "And? Doesn't mean we can't lick the beaters when no one's looking."

"Oh my God." Trev rolled his eyes, but he was smiling. "You're a dork, you know that?"

"Are you only now just figuring this out?"

"No, no, I've known since third grade—*third* grade, Cam, not fourth or fifth—that you're a dork."

"Oh, Jesus. You're not going to let that go, are you?"

"That you forgot that entire year? No. No, I will not let that go."

"We barely even knew each other!" I crossed my arms. "And now that I'm remembering a bit more, I seem to recall you stole my crayons and never gave them back."

"I don't remember that."

I arched an eyebrow. "Got a little selective amnesia going on, do we?"

"I don't know what you're talking about."

"Yeah, Mrs. Vincent might've bought that, but I didn't then and I don't now."

He eyed me. "Do you have any evidence to back up your accusations?"

"Besides a lack of crayons?"

Inclining his head, he asked, "Are you saying you'd still have them now if I hadn't taken them back then?"

"So you admit to taking them?"

He huffed sharply. "Fuck you."

"That's not a no!"

He just rolled his eyes. *"Anyway.* It's still nice out." He nodded toward the sliding glass door. "Want to sit outside with a couple of beers?"

"Sounds perfect."

While I took our beers out to the deck, Trev went upstairs to check on the boys and let them know where we'd be.

He returned a couple of minutes later, and we sat at the wrought iron table where we'd had lunch earlier.

It was amazing how much quieter the yard was when it was just the two of us. There were birds chirping as a gentle breeze rustled some leaves and made water slosh lazily against the sides of the pool, and the afternoon felt still and calm.

We didn't talk much. We mostly just relaxed and drank our beer, and I basked in his company as much as I did the late summer warmth. I hadn't realized how much I'd missed him, and I vowed—same as I had at least a thousand times since I'd arrived in Pittsburgh—to never lose touch with him again.

I hadn't been prepared for how profoundly right it was to have him back in my world. For just how wrong it had been that we'd gone so many years without breathing the same air. Never again. No way in hell.

I also hadn't been at all ready for this version of Trev. Even seeing him on TV hadn't prepared me for the grown-up professional athlete, chiseled to perfection by his job.

I definitely hadn't been ready for the dad whose kids absolutely melted his heart. For as much as I knew what hockey could do to a man's body, why had no one warned me about how spectacularly attractive fatherhood could make someone?

I'd crushed on him a lifetime ago, both when we'd dated and—secretly—after we'd broken up.

That crush had *nothing* on what he was doing to me now.

CHAPTER 9

TREV

THE BOYS WERE MERCIFULLY EASY AT BEDTIME. I'd joked with Bryan that that was the gods balancing things out after the first two years, during which I was pretty sure he and I got about six minutes of sleep between us. Now, they might put up a little bit of a fuss if they were in the middle of something, but once they started their routines—baths, pajamas, brushing their teeth—they didn't really fight it.

By eight thirty, they were both out cold, leaving Cam and me with the rest of the evening to chill. We settled in the living room, this time with water instead of beers.

"So." He pulled his feet up under him on the couch and faced me. "You ready for training camp?"

"Hell yeah." I grinned. "I'm always excited for the season to get started. Though..." I grimaced. "I think camp kicks my ass a little harder each year."

Cam arched an eyebrow. "Could that just be that you're getting older?"

I glanced over my shoulder to make sure neither of the boys had snuck in, then flipped Cam off.

He snickered. "Hey, am I wrong?"

"You're three months older than me."

"Mmhmm, and I feel it at the gym sometimes, believe me."

"Says the guy who's making everyone *else* sore and miserable."

"Hey." Cam put up his hands. "People *pay* me to do that. I'm not there to judge their masochism."

"You're just there to indulge your own sadism."

He rocked his head from side to side in a gesture that was neither an admission nor a denial.

I laughed and rolled my eyes. "Eh, you're just like the trainers my team hires. My strength trainer is—ugh, she is *mean*."

"That bad, huh?"

"She's the reason some gyms have escalators. It's not because people are lazy—it's because no one can walk up or down stairs after doing leg day with her."

Cam barked a laugh. "Ah, she's *that* type!" He grinned. "A woman after my own heart."

"Yeah, I bet." I hoped the rush of warmth I got from his laugh and his grin didn't actually turn my face red. God, he was so cute. And hot. And just... so perfectly Cam.

Do you have any idea how much I missed you?

Or how much I want you now that you're—

Noo, no. Not going down that train of thought. Calm the fuck down, Trevor.

I cleared my throat. "If you decide to look into any personal training gigs, I can get you in touch with the team staff. They're always booked solid and turning away clients, so I'm sure they could refer people to you."

At that, Cam offered a soft smile that made my head spin. "Thanks. I'll keep that in mind. I, um..." He stared down at his hands for a moment, then shrugged as he returned his gaze to me. "I think taking a break from training might be good for me. Not forever—just enough to take a breather."

I tilted my head. "I thought you liked it."

"I did. I *do*." He sighed. "But my last gym got really toxic, especially after my ex started playing games. The way they all turned on me after he made those accusations?" Cam wrinkled his nose and shook his head. "It left a really bad taste in my mouth."

"I bet. But do you want to get back into it?"

"Eventually, yeah. I love training people. I just... need to stay away for a little while and shake off everything that happened in Portland."

"Makes sense to me."

"I'll keep that in mind, though—about getting in touch with the team's staff." He smiled. "Thanks."

"Don't mention it." I glanced at my phone and sighed. "It's getting late. And I have to see the evil strength trainer in question tomorrow morning, so I better get some sleep."

Cam chuckled. "Good idea."

We took our water glasses into the kitchen, then headed upstairs. I peeked in on the boys; they were both sound asleep.

In the hallway in front of my bedroom door, Cam and I both paused, and when I turned to him...

Oh, God.

Why do I want to kiss you so bad?

Yeah, right. As if I didn't know.

Somehow, I held on to my dignity, and I just cleared my throat and gestured at my bedroom door. "I'll, um, see you in the morning."

"Right." He smiled with an edge of shyness and uncertainty that I couldn't quite parse. "See you in the morning."

We both retreated to our bedrooms, and as soon as I was behind a closed door, I closed my eyes and exhaled.

I'm going to go insane while he lives here, aren't I?

Probably. But there weren't a whole lot of alternatives, and quite frankly, I wasn't interested in any. I liked having him here, even if his presence was plucking at the fraying threads of my sanity.

Was I always like this when I was attracted to someone?

Or was this just what happened when I hadn't wanted *anyone* in way too long?

That was quite possibly it. My sex drive had been so dead and gone since long before my divorce, I hadn't even *wanted* it to come back. I hadn't cared if I ever got horny or got off ever again.

Tonight... I was horny. And oh my God, I needed to get off.

I reminded myself again that it would be painfully awkward to face Cam across the breakfast table the morning after I'd jerked off to him. That was what had kept my hand off my dick every night since he'd arrived. Tonight, I wasn't so sure I could resist.

Then again, would it really make a difference? Because he was screwing with my concentration, and that wasn't going to get any better as long as he was living here. Seeing him in his swim trunks. Watching his powerful body in the water. Just... being around him. Yeah, it really didn't matter if I took care of this hard-on now; I wanted him, I was hard for him, and it was going to be just as embarrassing to make eye contact with him whether I got off or not.

So... fuck it.

I was paranoid about making any noise even though my

bed frame was remarkably quiet, so I stepped into the shower. By the time I was under the rushing water, I was rock hard and desperate for friction, so I got right to it. I had to bite back a groan as I closed my fingers around my dick. My toes curled into the hard floor, and the heat beneath my skin was almost enough to make the water hitting my back feel cool.

I squeezed my eyes shut and pumped myself furiously, imagining I was with Cam. Naked with him. Against him. Inside him. I imagined tasting his mouth. Sliding my hands all over his gorgeous body. His hands sliding all over me. God, I wanted to feel him. I wanted to hear him when he came. I wanted to turn him on and get him off any way he asked me to. Any way that made him hot.

When we'd dated, we'd wanted each other the way horny teenagers do—have hormones, want sex. This? This was completely different. I didn't want sex. I wanted sex *with Cam.* I wanted to be tangled up with him, buried inside him, absolutely coming unraveled with him. I wanted to feel the ripple of tension run through him just before he came, and I wanted to feel every tremor and every whimper while he rode his climax as long as I could make it last. However he wanted me to wring that pleasure out of him— fucking him, fingering him, going down on him—I'd do it all, and just thinking about doing any one of those things had me gasping for breath as my orgasm closed in.

In the second before I went over the edge, I had just enough presence of mind to clamp down on the cry that tried to escape my lips. The shower swallowed the shuddering groan as I unloaded all over my hand and the wall, thrusting into my own fist the way I wished I could be thrusting into Cam, until my knees nearly dropped out from under me.

Hand still around my cock, my other arm still pressed against the wall, I stood there for a long time, trembling and panting. Water continued beating on my back. My heart continued slamming against my ribs. Those sexy fantasies continued flashing through my mind.

Fuck, if any one of them came true now—if I got the chance to lay a single finger on him—I wasn't sure I'd survive it.

Though... dying by orgasm while Cam had his hands on me? I mean, I could think of *far* worse ways to go.

I laughed at my own thought, then pushed myself off the wall and turned to face the water. I shakily rinsed off and got out of the shower. After I'd dried myself and brushed my teeth, I climbed into bed, and goddamn—my legs were still shaking. My whole body was still vibrating.

Eyes closed, I replayed that ridiculously hot session in the shower. I was kind of surprised I didn't get hard again, though the night was still young. For now, I just basked in the solo afterglow, both relieved my libido had returned and half out of my mind because I wanted someone I couldn't have. Someone who was in bed right down the hall. Someone who lived in my house.

"Fuck my life," I whispered, rubbing my eyes with an unsteady hand.

Living with someone who I wanted so bad I couldn't think straight was seriously frustrating. And distracting. And...

Still a million times better than living with someone who resented me and despised me too much to even think about touching me.

No, I couldn't have Cam. And even if he wanted me, it was probably a bad idea because he worked for me, and because I needed him in very real, non-sexual ways.

But he was back in my life. He was saving my ass. I could fantasize about him in secret the same way I'd fantasized about other men I couldn't have. Being this close to him without being able to touch him would be frustrating, but it beat the hell out of not having him back in my world.

I could live with this.

I might need to stock up on lube and I'd probably wear out my elbow.

But I could live with it.

CHAPTER 10

CAM

WHEN TREV TOLD ME THAT TRAINING CAMP WOULD BE held at the team's practice facility, I'd envisioned something like where he'd played and practiced with his youth teams. A bleak, dark, concrete building with ancient vending machines and a sketchy concessions stand. A crooked bulletin board covered in flyers for skating and hockey classes, people looking for babysitters, and someone selling a lawnmower. Glass so marred by pucks that it was almost impossible to see through. The combined smells of over-cooked hot dogs, aged mildew, and piles of hockey gear marinating in adolescent sweat.

It had an ambiance that was somewhere between a crumbling bowling alley and a parking garage. Our friends had even had a betting pool to predict if and when there would come a day when all the overhead mercury vapor lights were working (no one had ever collected).

On some level, I knew professional players wouldn't have to make do with a shithole like that. An organization paying people that much money to play hockey could afford to give them a nice facility.

But I hadn't anticipated it being *this* nice.

For one thing, the place was *huge*.

Like, there were two whole rinks inside, plus a store selling team merch, a place to get sticks cut and skates sharpened, and—according to some signs—two workout facilities. There were three giant trophy cases out front, jammed full of enormous cups and plaques, plus the case that held the team's three Cups.

Everything was clean and new, the scents of coffee and rubber hanging in the air but not the stench of sweat or mildew.

I whistled. Wow. Swanky.

There was a concessions place that appeared to sell sandwiches, pizza, salads, and myriad other things.

The facility also had a coffee shop.

A coffee shop. At a hockey rink. Seriously. My Seattle heart was in heaven. They had the usual array of pastries and other snacks, plus machines to make every imaginable variety of coffee. And it smelled a lot more pleasant than the other place had. Definitely a plus.

Off to the side, tall windows overlooked a gleaming rink beneath bright LED lights. There were banners from the Rebels' past Cup victories, as well as a couple of retired jerseys and a scoreboard that probably didn't have a single burned-out lightbulb.

Rumbling across the ice was a Zamboni that looked like it had just been delivered fresh from the factory—pristine ads on the outside and machinery that seemed to be working, rather than just sputtering along while alarming tendrils of smoke curled up from the undercarriage.

Beneath the windows a long counter on which people were setting up laptops. Reporters, probably; some had jackets with logos from what I assumed were local sports networks, and at least two were wrangling large cameras onto their shoulders.

This was definitely a different world from all those practices and games I'd gone to when we were younger.

Zach snapped me out of my thoughts. "We have to get one of the papers before we go in." He pointed sharply at the front desk. "So we know where Dad's playing."

"So we know—wait, what?"

Zach sighed in that exasperated *"how can adults be so stupid?"* way that kids were so good at. "There's *two* rinks. We need to know which one he's on."

"Oh. Okay. Right." I continued up to the front desk. It was too high for the boys to see over, but I quickly zeroed in on what Zach had been talking about—a printout of everyone who'd be participating in training camp, split into three teams and listed in numerical order. I skimmed over it. "Okay, so it looks like your dad is on the gold team, which will be in Rink A." I looked around. "How do we get to Rink A?"

"We have to go up the stairs." Zane gestured at a staircase beside the front desk. Beside it was a sign: *To Rinks.*

Well, all right, then.

I glanced at the concessions counter. "Do you guys want any snacks or drinks before we go in?"

Their eyes lit up, and I had to wonder if I'd just inadvertently given in to something their dads didn't allow. Trev hadn't said anything about it, though, so we trooped over to the counter.

I ordered a gigantic bougie coffee that Trev's ancient practice facility *never* would've served. The boys each got a hot chocolate and a bag of fruit snacks. I also bought a couple of bottles of water; we were going to be here a while, so it couldn't hurt.

Snacks and drinks in hand, we headed for the stairs.

"You guys should see what your dad had to practice in when he was younger," I said as we started up.

"Was it small?" Zane asked.

I almost laughed at the innocent question. Small? Compared to this place? God yes. "It was tiny. But it was also really dark and run down." I paused. "Like if someone turned this place into a big haunted house."

"They should do that!" Zach said. "We could trick-or-treat and they could do a haunted house on the ice!"

"That would be great!" I said. "And they've got plenty of goalie masks, so it'll work."

Zane turned to me, brow furrowed. "Why would there be goalie masks in a haunted house?"

"You know, from—" I stopped myself. "Right. Right, you guys probably haven't seen those movies."

"We've seen *all* the hockey movies," Zach declared.

Zane frowned. "None of them used hockey masks in a haunted house."

Crap. I didn't need to be the reason Trev's kids suddenly started asking to watch *Friday the 13th*. "It was... one of those movies that almost no one has seen."

"So it was bad," Zane said.

Eh, I'd enjoyed them, but it was as good a reason as any to derail the conversation before I told them too much about some horror movies. "Pretty bad, yeah."

"No, thanks," Zach said.

"Yeah," Zane agreed. "Nobody wants to watch bad movies."

I just chuckled. Maybe someday I'd tell them just how much their dad loved stupid movies, and that included movies that were so terrible they were hilarious. In fact, that was something for them to figure out when they were in their *"oh my God parents are so embarrassing"* phases.

We found a place to sit in the bleachers, and we settled in to wait for camp to start. Trev had strongly recommended bringing seat cushions, and I was glad he did—the bleachers were hard plastic, and even with the cushion, my ass was feeling it after about fifteen minutes. The boys were still up and wandering around right now—all the kids were—but I suspected they'd appreciate the cushions too once they took their seats.

At about 8:15, they did exactly that, parking on either side of me and gazing out at the ice. A moment later, players started to trickle out of the locker room. A *lot* of players. The long list should've tipped me off—and Trev had said something about prospects, professional tryouts, and minor league players joining them—but wow, there were a *lot*. And this was only two of the three "teams" they'd all been broken into for training camp. The third wouldn't be out until later.

Above the ice, several offices had a balcony that overlooked everything, and a number of people in suits and Rebels jackets gazed down. If I'd understood some of Trev's comments from last night correctly, those were the general manager and other front office staff. The GM and the coaches (who were on the ice) would whittle down the long list of players to the opening night roster of twenty.

Better them than me, because that sounded like one *hell* of a task.

Beside me, Zane pointed sharply at the glass. "There's Dad!"

I followed where he was indicating, and sure enough, that was definitely Trev. He was just stepping onto the ice, and he glided a few feet as he fussed with his glove. Something about that look of concentration—even when he was just messing with his glove—gave me a fluttery feeling I didn't want to think too much about. This wasn't easygoing Trev hanging out at home. This was Trev at work, doing the thing he loved.

I'd always loved watching him on the ice. Not just in the heat of a game, but also when he was still relaxed and warming up. There was something amazing about seeing him in his happy place. In his natural element. The way he made everything he did look effortless, from the high-speed maneuvering to lazily skating backward while he chatted with a teammate.

From the time we were kids, he'd always had an air of contentment about him when he had on his gear. As if everything else in his world just fell away, and nothing existed except hockey.

I was glad to see that after his tumultuous divorce and all its fallout, he still seemed to find that calm and contentment out there.

And what could I say? Trev's practice facility wasn't the only thing that had been massively upgraded over the years.

I'd thought he looked hot at home. Grownup pro-hockey-player Trev on his skates with all his gear on? In the physique that professional hockey had blessed him with? *Whoa.*

"There's Dad," Zach said.

"I know," Zane snapped, and pointed sharply at Trev. "I just said—"

"No. *Dad.*" Zach pointed in another direction.

I craned my neck, and...

Aww, fuck me. Their *other* dad. The one who'd put Trev in a position to need me in the first place, and who didn't do a whole lot to hide how much he didn't like me.

As he came closer, Bryan smiled at the boys, but the expression faltered when he caught sight of me. The unspoken *Oh, you're here* came through loud and clear.

Um, yeah, dude? Because the boys want to watch Trev and you're the one who said he had to hire a babysitter. Where'd you think *I'd be?*

In fact, why was he here? He wasn't due to get the boys back until—

Ooh. Right. He was here because he was banging one of Trev's teammates.

Not an awkward state of affairs. Not at all.

As Bryan settled on the bench beside Zane, Zach came around and sat on his dad's other side. I didn't mind. I was the nanny. I would never begrudge either of them wanting to sit near one of their dads. Not even if Dad B *was* a complete douchewaffle in dire need of a visit from the Decent Personality Fairy.

My own catty thought amused me, and I pressed my lips together to suppress a laugh.

As the crowd on the ice thickened, Trev broke away, skating toward where we were sitting. When he held up a couple of pucks, the boys jumped to their feet and hurried down to the glass.

God, if there was one thing more beautiful than grownup Trev in hockey mode, it was Trev in Dad mode. The way his face lit up as he tossed pucks over to his sons was the sweetest thing ever.

Zach and Zane triumphantly held up their pucks, and Trev just smiled and smiled, fist-bumping them through the scuffed-up glass.

He was just about to skate away when another player came up and skidded to halt beside him. Trev turned, and the instant they made eye contact...

Holy shit. His expression went so dark so fast, it was like half the rink's lights had blinked out.

My heart jumped into my throat. What the fuck?

Oblivious to Trev's reaction, the other player tapped a stick—no, two sticks—against the glass. I hadn't realized until that moment that he was carrying two.

Both boys bounced excitedly, and they squealed with delight as the guy carefully put the sticks over the ice. Bryan rose and helped them catch the handles so they didn't get hit in the face or something. Then he and the other player exchanged smiles, the player tapped the glass with the back of his glove before he and Trev headed back toward their teammates, who were now gathering in front of a whiteboard.

As soon as the guy's back was turned, I understood.

Across his shoulders: *Chatsworth*.

So that was Chats. Trev's teammate and Bryan's boyfriend.

And now he was trying to one-up Trev with the twins?

My dude, that is low.

The boys sat down again, each clutching a puck and a stick. Bryan was smiling like the dickbag he was, somehow managing to combine fatherly warmth with ex-husbandly smugness.

I could not roll my eyes hard enough.

I did at least turn away when I rolled them, though. Bryan was just conniving and petty enough to decide I was copping an attitude—*uh-huh, guilty*—and use that to convince a judge I wasn't fit to take care of his sons.

Ugh. And Trev had been *married* to that piece of work? Fucking *why*, man?

Okay, I was one to talk, given the years I'd pissed away partnered with Daniel. At least we'd never had kids together. Yikes. We'd talked about adopting but had never pulled the trigger, and thank Christ for that. Daniel probably would've found ways to be a worse co-parent than Bryan.

Bullet dodged.

Maybe I should've been grateful Trev hadn't dodged that bullet. After all, even with all the hassles Bryan brought and kept in his world, I couldn't imagine he'd trade his twins for anything.

And if Trev and Bryan hadn't adopted the boys...

If they hadn't had a messy divorce...

If Bryan hadn't given Trev a bullshit ultimatum...

I'd still be living with my mom, unemployed and without Trev back in my life.

I guess every cloud—even a shitty-ex-husband-shaped one—really did have a silver lining.

CHAPTER 11

TREV

If I made it through training camp—never mind the hockey season—without dropping gloves with Chats, it would be a genuine miracle. Like the kind where a god actually came down, stood between us, and said, *"Whoa, hey, let's chill, guys."*

I hadn't liked Chats when he'd played for one of our rivals. I hadn't liked him when he'd signed with Pittsburgh. I hadn't liked him when he'd started flaunting his relationship with my ex-husband, especially when that had involved showing off bites, scratches, and bruises in the locker room.

But I was going to straight up rip out his still-beating heart through his ear canal if he got between me and my kids again.

Fortunately, either by sheer dumb luck or because Coach could see the writing on the wall, we were assigned to different teams for now. I was on the gold team, Chats was on the white team. One of the assistant head coaches directed the white team to the other rink, and Chats clomped out through the Zamboni gate with the others.

I fought the urge to look toward the bleachers and see if the boys followed Chats. I didn't want to think about whether that would make me jealous, or if it *should* make me jealous, or if I should feel anything at all.

I reminded myself they'd probably be following Bryan, not Chats, and that was okay. And even if they were following Chats, that was okay, too. It stung, sure, but their dads were going to date post-divorce. It was a *good* thing if they got along with our respective partners.

I just needed to ignore this jealous bone and not even think about wishing my kids would play favorites. No matter what happened, I was their dad. Period.

And if I wanted to stay employed and not get my ass traded out of Pittsburgh, I needed to focus on what was happening here on the ice, not in the bleachers.

I hated myself for letting him get to me. I also hated that shit like this could go beyond Chats, Bryan, and me, and that it could even go beyond the Pittsburgh Rebels. Whether I liked it or not (and I didn't) anything one of us did could affect other queer players. Though there'd been straight guys who'd had similar issues—one getting together with another's ex-wife or ex-girlfriend and dragging the drama into the locker room—we were held to a different standard. Only a handful of players in the League were queer, and if one of us fucked up, it immediately reflected on all of us, not to mention future players like us.

Simon Chowning teared up during an interview about his best friend being traded? Proof that queers were too emotional.

Brad Lange took an embellishment penalty after getting checked and acting like a wounded soccer player? Obviously the queer guys are weak and melodramatic.

Trev Allen divorced his husband? Gays aren't actually committed to their marriages.

Didn't matter that I could easily name a dozen straight players who'd shed tears during interviews, embellished injuries, or been divorced. Straight guys were responsible for their own actions, but anything one of us did was an indictment against all of us.

And if my ex-husband's boyfriend and I clashed where anyone who mattered could see it—our GM, a reporter, a fan with a camera—there'd be hell to pay for *all* of us going forward. I'd be strongly encouraged to waive my no-move clause so they could punt me out of Pittsburgh, and incoming players who were openly queer would be scrutinized through a filter of "are they going to cause us the same problems that Trev Allen did?"

Fuck. Fuck, fuck, *fuck.*

No matter how much of an asshole Chats was, no matter how much he and Bryan rubbed their relationship in my face, I had to just grit my teeth and smile through it. I had to act the same way I did when someone asked me an intrusive or obnoxious question during an interview—smile, be professional, and hope no one noticed me screaming internally.

God, I hated this so damn much.

It was the reality of my situation, though, so I did the only thing I could do—I shoved Chats and Bryan out of my mind and focused on hockey.

For the first hour-long session of camp, the coaches were running us through some intense offensive drills. This served to get us veterans back in the groove, of course. Mostly, though, it gave the prospects a chance to both learn from us and the coaches, and to shine. *No one* worked as hard as a prospect or a farm team player who wanted to make the cut during training camp.

And about ten minutes in, one of those youngsters was starting to seriously shine. Dave Bell was twenty, and after killing it in major juniors, he'd played all last year on our farm team. Though his stats had been excellent, he'd only been called up three times, and he'd never actually dressed for a game.

Today, it was impossible not to notice him or his determination. He played every drill like it was going to make or break a Cup final. He was on the smaller end—not quite five-foot-eight —but he had speed and agility to burn. He had grit, too; on his second run through the drill, he slammed Spaulding, one of our huge defensemen, into the boards hard enough to make the crowd gasp. During another drill, he sent a puck into the back of the net as if our two-time MVP goalie wasn't even there.

"Holy shit," my right winger, Houghtaling, said while we caught our breath between drills. "Where did this kid come from?"

I shook my head. "No idea." I tracked Bells as he zigzagged between a pair of defensemen, protecting the puck all the way. To Hoes, I said, "We do need a left winger on our line."

Hoes grunted. He and I had been linemates ever since he'd signed in Pittsburgh, and we'd cycled through several left wingers in that time. Our most recent linemate had signed with Vegas during the off season.

Now we had a spicy young winger who clearly wanted a place on the roster so bad he could taste it. Was the second line ambitious for a rookie? Absolutely. But stranger things had happened.

When we'd finished that cycle of drills and were sent to

the bench to hydrate, I skated up to Coach. "Hey, have you got anything in mind for Bells?" I found the kid in the crowd and gestured at him. "Number fourteen?"

Coach glanced at Bells, then peered at me from under the bill of his black Rebels baseball cap. "Why? You sniffing around for a winger?"

I shrugged innocently. "I mean, Hoes and I *do* need one."

"And you think a rookie belongs on the second line?"

"That's your call, not mine." I watched the kid jawing with some of the other prospects, unaware of us discussing his future with the Rebels. "He's really fucking good." Facing Coach again, I said, "Just thinking it wouldn't hurt to run him through some drills on our line. If it doesn't work, it doesn't work, but if he gels with us..." I trailed off into another shrug.

Coach pursed his lips, watching the rookie in question. Then he gave a sharp nod and met my eyes. "Worst-case, he'll learn a hell of a lot from you and Hoes." He clapped my shoulder. "You're good with the kids."

I laughed. "Uh, I thought I *was* still one of the kids."

He rolled his eyes. "Go get a drink, Trev."

Chuckling, I skated over to the bench to do exactly that. It was still kind of weird to be one of the veterans now. I was barely thirty, for fuck's sake! But hey, there were worse things than being one of the players who was good with the young guys.

Without thinking about it, I let my gaze drift toward the bleachers, and—

My boys were still there.

Zach gestured animatedly while Cam nodded along. Zane had Chats' stick leaning against his shoulder, and he was turning his puck over and over between his hands as he watched all of us on the ice. Apparently realizing I was looking his way, he straightened and waved.

My heart fluttered, and I waved back. Zach joined in. So did Cam.

Bryan was nowhere in sight, having no doubt gone to the other sheet to watch his boyfriend.

I wasn't proud of my internal fist pump or my silent *"Ha ha, fuck you, Bryan!"* Hey, I was as petty and vindictive as the next person, and after all our recent bullshit, yeah, I was going to bask in a little petty smugness over this minor victory.

Coach was getting ready to brief us on our next drill, so I pulled my focus back to practice.

But I *might've* kept on grinning for a while.

It didn't matter how much we stayed conditioned through the off-season—training camp kicked *everyone's* asses. And tomorrow morning, we'd be back out there to do it again.

With a groan that might've been a little melodramatic, I hauled my ass out of the car as my garage door rumbled shut behind me. At least I had a Land Rover, which sat up pretty high; if I'd had to climb out of a low sports car right about now, I'd have just sprawled on the cool concrete and stayed there.

Okay, I was being dramatic. I wasn't *that* sore. Not like I'd injured anything. Just... that feeling like I'd done a hard-core workout after a week or so of slacking off, even though I hadn't been slacking off. It was a good kind of tired and sore, but still... tired and sore.

And tomorrow, I'd have to do it all over again.

For now, though, I was home, and I could spend some

time with my boys during the relative quiet before the season started.

They were in the living room, sitting on the floor and playing a video game.

"Hey guys." I draped my hoodie over the back of a kitchen chair. "What're you playing?"

They excitedly chatted over the top of each other to explain the game to me. It was some kind of fantasy adventure game, which was their usual jam. Bryan had forbidden first-person shooters, and I'd agreed, but that had turned out to be a non-issue anyway because the kids just weren't interested in them. If it didn't have swords, dragons, and magic spells, they didn't want it.

Worked for me.

"Do you want to play with us?" Zane asked. "We can start a new game for you and show you how!" The excitement in his voice and in his brother's face melted my heart.

I smiled. "Definitely. Let me just check in with Cam first and then I'll join you, okay?"

"Okay!" they both said.

I looked around. "Where is he, anyway?"

"Downstairs. Zach, you can't use that spell with that sorcerer! He'll take your—no, use your dagger!"

I left them to it. They could argue while they played, but it didn't usually get too heated, and Bryan and I liked to let them sort things out. If it got out of hand, we'd step in, but it rarely did.

Keeping an ear tuned to the living room in case World War Twins broke out, I went downstairs. If Cam was down here, he was either working out or doing laundry, and since the gym door was open and the laundry room light was off, I could do the math.

I stepped through the gym's door and...

Oh.

Fuck.

Me.

He had his back to me, and he was doing a set of lat pulldowns. His shirt was off, giving me the most spectacular view of his powerful back. Cam wasn't a big guy—never had been—but I hadn't been prepared for how mouthwateringly cut and sculpted he'd become. I swear to God, my knees went a little weak as I watched his muscles work with his slow, controlled reps. And the sweat gleaming on his flushed skin... and darkening the ends of his hair... and rolling down the back of his neck... and...

I pulled my gaze away and gulped in a breath as I tried to compose myself.

The weights clinked into place, and I turned just as Cam did.

"Oh, hey." He got up and faced me fully, grinning as he absently ran a towel over his powerful arms. "You coming to work out after practice?"

I scoffed. "Not after training camp, no." I gestured over my shoulder. "I'm lucky I made it down the stairs, and the jury's still out on me making it back up."

"Oh, come on." He playfully swatted me with his towel. "You're a professional athlete. You can't be that worn out."

I arched a brow and inclined my head. "Have you ever done training camp? At this level?"

"No, but you have, so you should be used to it."

Groaning, I rolled my eyes. "There's no getting used to training camp."

"Drama queen," he muttered.

I flipped him off, and the way he laughed did more to screw with my blood pressure than that sweat on his skin had a moment ago.

What is wrong *with me? Jesus Christ.*

I cleared my throat. "Anyway. I, uh... I just wanted to check in with you. See how things went this morning."

"This mor—oh, at training camp?" He shrugged and rubbed the towel over his neck and shoulders, oblivious to what that was doing to my stupid brain. "It was a lot of fun. The boys know hockey better than I ever will, that's for sure."

I chuckled. "Yeah, they've really picked up a lot. They'll probably never play, but I could see them growing up to be analysts or commentators or something."

Cam pursed his lips. "I could see that. Zach would be a great commentator. Being an analyst sounds like it would bore him but fascinate Zane."

I couldn't help smiling. "You've figured them out."

"They're not hard to read. And their personalities make it really easy to tell them apart."

"I know, right? We admittedly struggled a little bit when they were babies, but as they got older and started interacting with the world, it was stupid easy."

"I can see that." Cam paused, and he started wiping down the machine he'd been using. "And this morning—it wasn't bad. Especially once Bryan went over to the other side."

I grimaced. "Yeah, I bet that was a bit awkward before he left."

"A bit." He glanced at me. "I thought you were going to tear his boyfriend's head off. Over that thing with the sticks, you know?"

Indulging in a frustrated groan, I nodded. "I considered it, believe me."

"I don't blame you. That was such a dick move."

I didn't know why I was so relieved that Cam was on

my side about this, but there it was. "Yeah. He likes to pull shit like that."

"And you haven't strangled him with his own innards yet, why?"

"I mean, there's the whole 'going to prison' thing. I'm told the League frowns on that, and I'm pretty sure Bryan would have a slam-dunk case for sole custody."

"Ooh. Yeah, you make a valid point." Cam glanced at me and winked. "So you just have to make sure you don't get caught."

The laugh that poured out of me felt amazing after my thoughts had turned to Bryan and his assclown boyfriend. "Yes. Exactly. I just need to not get caught."

"Well, if you need an alibi, you were here working out with me." He met me with puppy dog eyes that took me back to our high school days. "I swear, Your Honor, he was here the *whole* time."

I snorted. "You're a dork."

He shrugged as if to say, *Uh, yeah? No shit?*

I chuckled, but it faded as some of my earlier thoughts crept in.

Of course Cam immediately noticed. Tilting his head, he asked, "What's wrong?"

Sighing, I rubbed the back of my neck. "I'm... I guess I'm worried this crap with Chats and Bryan will bite all of us in the ass."

"How so?"

I explained my concerns about this affecting other queer players in—or coming into—the League. When I'd finished, Cam's expression didn't suggest that I was off-base in my thinking.

"Shit," he murmured, leaning his hip against the stair machine. "That's a lot of pressure."

"It is. And I don't think Chats cares, so it's on me, and..." I huffed out an exhausted breath.

He wrinkled his nose. "Is it too much to hope he ends up on the injured list for a while? Maybe a puck to the balls or something?"

I burst out laughing, which was a relief. "Stranger things have happened."

"Hey, I don't usually wish injuries on people, but I can make an exception." Cam gave me an innocent look and half-shrugged. "Especially since it would mean him and Bryan spending lots and lots of quality time together."

I snorted. "It's probably bad karma to hope, but..." I held up my crossed fingers.

He made the same gesture.

Chuckling, I motioned toward the stairs. "Anyway, I just wanted to touch base with you. The boys want to teach me their game, so I better get back to it."

"Oh, cool. I'm about done here, so after I grab a shower, I'll come watch."

Can I join you in the—

Trevor. Dude. For Christ's sake.

I cleared my throat. "Sounds good. Then we can figure out dinner. Maybe take the boys out since I don't feel like cooking tonight."

"Your call." He smiled. "I can cook too, you know."

The thought of him cooking dinner for my kids made me all stupidly warm and fuzzy inside. Of course he was going to cook for them. It was part of his job, especially once I started going out on the road.

But I was a colossal dumbass when it came to this man, and I apparently wasn't going to stop being one any time soon.

"We'll figure something out. I'll see you upstairs."

CHAPTER 12

CAM

I felt a little weird wearing a suit to a hockey game.

I mean, weren't people supposed to wear like jerseys and team hoodies and stuff? It was a sporting event, not a business meeting.

But since I was here as a family member of a player—or, well, an employee *supervising* the family members of a player—I was asked to adhere to the League dress code. Which was fine. I liked wearing suits and I thought I looked damn good in them. Plus, was I really going to argue with a dress code that required Trev to wear suits? Because that tailored medium-gray three-piece he'd worn out the door this afternoon was just... oh my God. I envied the fabric on his body as much as I envied the person who'd been tasked with measuring and fitting him. Goddamn.

So yeah, the League's dress code was a *thousand* percent fine by me.

It was just kind of surreal to be walking into a stadium dressed like this. Then again, it was also surreal to be going in through one of the Authorized Personnel entrances. Everything about this was definitely a new experience.

The boys didn't have to wear anything specific, and they both wore custom jerseys with their jeans. It had their dad's number, forty-seven, and instead of *Allen* across the shoulders, it read *Daddy*. Several of the other players' kids were wearing similar jerseys, including two infants who couldn't be more than four or five months old. They were all seriously adorable, especially Trev's boys, though I may have been *slightly* biased.

A woman in a maroon pantsuit came up to me. "Hi, you must be Trev's new nanny." She held out her hand. "Err, um, is that what you like to be called?"

I laughed as I accepted the handshake. "It's accurate, so... meh. My name is Cam, though."

"Cam. I'll remember that. I'm Kristina. My husband is Trev's linemate, Jackson." She paused. "Well, the guys all call him Hoes."

I blinked. "Hoes? Really?"

She rolled her eyes. "Our last name is Houghtaling."

"Ah, got it."

"Anyway, I just wanted to say hi." Kristina smiled at Zach and Zane. "He has the sweetest boys, doesn't he?"

"He really does. The apple doesn't fall far from the tree, you know?"

"You're not kidding. Trev is amazing. You know he even let us stay in his house for a little while when we first came to Pittsburgh?"

"Really? I mean, that does sound like him."

"It does, doesn't it? The team was happy to put us up in a hotel, but Trev and Bryan insisted on having us at their place until we moved into our apartment. It was only like two weeks, but it was so nice during that transition."

"I bet. I don't know how you all deal with uprooting every time a team makes a trade."

She quirked her lips. "Well, the paycheck helps."

"Okay, yeah, good point."

She chuckled. "Anyway. I just wanted to introduce myself. Are you sitting up in the partners' box?"

"Oh. Uh." I fought the urge to glance at Bryan, who'd walked in a few minutes ago. "I... Trev got us seats in the owners' box, so I think that's where we're sitting."

"Okay, no problem. But if you want to join us, consider yourself invited." She lowered her voice. "You're not a spouse or partner, but you're in charge of a player's kids. As far as we're all concerned"—she gestured at the others in the room—"you count."

I smiled. "Good to know. Thanks! Maybe at the next game?"

"Sounds good. Enjoy the game!"

She went to chat with some of the ladies she knew, and I subtly released a breath. I appreciated the invite, but I still wasn't sure if I should accept it. At this game, I had the excuse that Trev had already bought tickets in the other box. At future games... well, I wasn't sure.

Mostly because of who *else* would be there.

And it wasn't all in my head, either.

"If one of the spouses invites you up to the partners' box," Trev had told me this morning, *"you're more than welcome to go. But I'm about ninety-nine percent sure Bryan will be there, too. It's your call."*

The fact that he didn't say *"Fuck him—go sit wherever you want"* told me that maybe I wasn't imagining the potential for discomfort.

And more than anything, I didn't want to cause problems for Trev. Things were already messy and complicated with his co-parent dating his teammate. Since neither Bryan nor Chats seemed to be in any hurry to be adults and coexist with Trev, I didn't want to push my luck.

Jenni, who was apparently married to Martin, the team captain, came up to me right then, her infant on her hip. With her free hand, she took me by the elbow. "Come on. All the kids like to watch warmups from the Zamboni gate."

"Oh. Uh." I looked around, ready to call Zach and Zane, but they were already joining the small herd of children heading down the hall. Of course they knew the routine. Everyone here knew the routine except me and the babies. Hell, one of them even looked at me like, *Duh, it's warmups —are you new or something?*

At the Zamboni gate, the wives and girlfriends crowded against the glass, holding up the children who were too little to see over. Someone had wheeled over a small block, and the bigger kids—including the twins—stood on that, hands and faces pressed to the glass.

There was no one on the ice yet, but that didn't last long. Not two minutes after the boys got situated, a train horn sounded. Players started pouring out beside one of the benches; the away team, judging by the booing from fans and the kids.

Then the announcer's voice boomed: "Now taking the ice for warmups, please welcome your Pittsburgh Rebels!"

The crowd, thin as it was this early in the evening, went nuts, and the kids all started shouting and banging on the glass. Players in black and gold came out from beside their bench, and I could tell whenever a kid's dad emerged because of the delighted squeals and "Mommy, there's Daddy!"

After nine or ten players, it was Zach and Zane jumping

up and down and shouting to both Bryan and me, "There's Dad! There's Dad!"

Oh yeah. There he was. Fuuuck.

Was there ever going to come a time when the sight of grownup Trev didn't turn me into a quivering mess? Because if there was, it wasn't going happening tonight.

Seeing him in a game jersey was nothing new, but this was a game jersey at *this* level. At the very top of the sport he loved. With a logo on his chest from a team he'd watched as a kid, back when he hadn't known if he'd ever get into the League or what team he'd eventually land on.

Trev had made it. He was the hockey player he'd always dreamed of being.

Pride swelled in my chest, but I was also—I mean, who the fuck was I kidding? Trev was hot and I reacted accordingly. At some point, I'd have to get used to being around him at peak sexiness, especially since I lived with him.

But for now, hell—why not drool?

Not *openly*, though, if only because there were cameras around. And Bryan. I didn't need jealousy drama with Trev's ex-husband.

Throughout warmups, the kids all waved at their dads, and the various players came over to say hi. That was super cute. Some of the guys' faces were full of intense concentration while they skated and shot pucks, but the second they saw their babies, they turned into complete goo. They came right up to the gate and waved at their kids or did fist bumps through the glass. Some even pushed pucks through the hole that the photographers used, which had the littlest ones squealing with delight.

Martin was one of those "face of hockey" players—he was on the covers of magazines, the thumbnails for videos, and even a video game cover. Always with a fierce expression, full of intense concentration and competitive fire. But when he skated over and met his infant daughter's eyes through the glass, he went all gooey-eyed. He smiled and cooed to her even though she couldn't hear him, and when she waved her arms at him and giggled, he *melted*.

And then... Trev showed up at the gate.

And I was the one who melted. He high-fived his boys through the glass, and he smiled at them like they made his whole night. They banged on the glass and bounced with excitement as if this was the first time they'd ever seen him play.

He glanced up, and his gaze landed on me.

Was it my imagination, or did he freeze for a beat? His eyes widened and his lips parted.

What? Had he not expected me to be here? Was I supposed to—

He flashed me a smile and a sharp nod before shifting his attention back to his boys. He held up a finger—as much as one could in a hockey glove—and I thought he mouthed *"be right back."* Then he skated away, but he came back a moment later and handed a puck to the wife closest to the lens hole. When she took it, he tapped the glass in front of Zach, and she gave the puck to Zach.

Zane didn't protest at all. They both knew that whoever didn't get a puck at one game would get it at the next one.

Then they each fist-bumped their dad through the glass, and he skated back out to join his team. He didn't give me another look, and I was admittedly grateful for that. I was still jittery after that double take. What did it mean? Why had he looked at me like that?

And when had it started getting so hot in here? Would anyone mind if I went out and sprawled on the ice for a minute or two? Because goddamn.

"Take a picture," Bryan gritted out, "it'll last longer."

I turned to him. "What?"

He rolled his eyes. "Dude, you're not subtle." He gestured at the ice. At the players.

At his ex-husband, who I'd been staring at for I had no idea how long.

I gulped and shook myself. "I'm sorry, I have no idea what you're—"

"Oh, fuck off," he muttered, and stalked away. As he started chatting with some of the wives, acting like nothing had happened, I stood there like a dork, completely taken aback by his reaction.

On the other hand, he'd brought my temperature back down, so there was that.

I rolled my eyes, mentally gave him the finger, and shifted my attention back to the kids I was here to watch.

Jenni appeared beside me. "Warmups are almost over, so we're all heading up to the suite. Do you want to come sit with us?" She smiled. "It's usually reserved just for spouses, partners, and kids, but since you're here with Trev's kids, you're welcome to join us. There's plenty of room. "

"Oh. Uh. Kristine already invited me, but... " I glanced around, and my gaze snagged on Bryan. Any uncertainty I'd had about my decision was *gone*—no way in hell was I watching the game in the same space as him. Clearing my throat, I faced Jenni again. "I think... I think it might be less awkward if..."

Her eyes flicked toward Bryan, and she nodded as if she fully understood. Maybe she'd watched our exchange, or maybe she'd just picked up that everything in the orbit of the Bryan-and-Trev divorce was messy AF.

"Well," she said, "the offer is always open. And we don't

let drama kick up, so if you have any problems with anyone"
—she glanced pointedly at Bryan—"you just come to me."

"I will. Thanks." I smiled. "Maybe another night, I'll
come to the suite?"

"Of course. The offer is always open."

"Thanks."

She lowered her voice to a conspiratorial whisper. "I
won't lie, this is some uncharted territory for us. I wasn't
crazy about someone's ex still being in our suite, especially
after they had such a contentious divorce." She sighed. "But
he's dating a player *and* he's really close to one of the other
wives, and she invited him in, so..." Jenni waved her hand.

"Eww, that sounds... uncomfortable."

"It was. But we've got your back, okay? Especially since
you're here for them"—she nodded to Zach and Zane—"not
to stir up trouble."

"Thanks. I appreciate that."

I did. I really did.

But holy shit, was I grateful we wouldn't be sitting in
that box tonight.

CHAPTER 13

TREV

As we all clomped up the chute to the locker room after warmups, I was dazed. All thoughts of hockey had escaped my head, and I just... I needed a minute. To breathe? To pull myself together? Something. I was lucky I hadn't eaten shit on the ice; I'd been skating since I was a toddler, but tonight I'd suddenly been an unbalanced train wreck. How I hadn't lost an edge and fallen on my face would forever be a mystery. Muscle memory, probably.

I joined my teammates in the locker room, and I dropped onto the bench by my stall. Normally I'd strip off my jersey, have a drink, and do a little stretching, but this time...

This time I just sat there. I stared at the logo in the middle of the floor, and I let my mind race the way it had been trying to since I'd gone to say hi to the twins.

My whole world always lit up the moment I saw my boys through the glass. I loved it. I *lived* for it. Tonight had been no exception.

I just hadn't expected the way I'd feel the moment I saw Cam standing behind them.

He looked spectacular in that navy blue suit, and the instant I'd laid eyes on him, my whole world had lurched to a stop. For a second, I'd gone back to a time and place I hadn't thought about in ages.

It was only the caustic look from my ex-husband that had jarred me back into the present, at least enough to finish my routine. I'd given the boys a puck, then gone back and fumbled my way through the rest of warmups.

Now that I was sitting down and had almost twenty minutes before we returned to the ice, I let my mind go where it had been trying to go.

I'd never in my life—before or since—been as confused as I'd been about midway through my senior year in high school.

Cam and I had broken up at the end of the previous school year, but we'd stayed friends. Since we were both unattached when the winter formal dance came around, we'd decided to go together.

That had taken a ton of pressure off. I didn't have to awkwardly try (and fail) to connect with another girl. I didn't have to nut up and face the crushes I had on some male classmates, which I was trying desperately to ignore because, dude, what? I was straight. Right? *Maybe* bi? No, *straight*.

Except... none of the girls ever turned my head.

Just a couple of boys on my hockey team. And one in my history class.

But I obviously wasn't gay because why the fuck would I still get all loopy and stupid whenever I saw my ex?

In the crystal-clear lens of adult hindsight, it could not have been more obvious what was happening. At the time, though, awash with hormones, confusion, teenage angst, and denial over my sexuality, I hadn't had a clue. Was I just regretting our breakup? Trying too hard to ignore how much I wanted one of the guys?

Now, it was plain to see that my growing attraction to Cam coincided with the slow but dramatic evolution of his clothes and hairstyle. Looking back now, even during his most feminine periods, I couldn't think of him as anything but a boy. At the time, I'd had no idea he was quietly coming to grips with his gender identity. He'd had no idea that every time he cut his hair shorter or made his clothes more androgynous, a few more of my brain cells went rogue. When he'd asked my opinion of the chest binder he'd started experimenting with, I'd struggled to formulate an answer. Of course I'd supported anything that made Cam happy and I always would, but I'd been so fucking confused about why I couldn't stop staring at him the first time he wore one under his clothes at school.

Because he *feels good in it and I love seeing him this happy. Duh.*

Okay, yeah, but that shouldn't fuck with my ability to concentrate around him. Should it?

On the night of winter formal, I'd had some naively optimistic thoughts of us rekindling our relationship. The chemistry was obviously still there. We were still close even after we'd broken up. A boy could dream, right?

The morning of the dance, I'd received a text.

> Will you be mad if I don't wear a dress?

> Mad? Naw, of course not. Wear what you want.

> Unless it's that Joker costume you wore on Halloween. THAT IS A BRIDGE TOO FAR, MY FRIEND.

LOL Well fuck. There goes that plan.

LMAO Uh-huh. Nah it's cool. See you at 7?

(saluting emoji)

I hadn't thought much of it after that. Dresses had become less and less a part of Cam's wardrobe over the past year, so I honestly wasn't even surprised.

But I *was* surprised when Cam stepped out onto that familiar front porch.

I'd been halfway up the steps, and I just...

I mean, fuck. *"Not wearing a dress"* was one thing. My dumbass teenage brain just hadn't made it to the part where "not wearing a dress" to a formal event meant wearing a tux.

A black tux that had no business fitting that well.

He'd also cut his hair even shorter than before, adopting a very masculine look that was shaved almost to the skin on the sides with the top just long enough to style.

If I hadn't known any better, I'd have thought this was Cam's brother. But Liam had left for college last summer, and Cam didn't have any other siblings at home.

This was...

Holy shit.

The corsage tumbled out of my hand, its plastic container popping open and sending baby's breath and whatever else fluttering all over the steps.

"Oh! Fuck!" I doubled back to pick them up.

Once I'd recovered most of the flowers and some of my dignity, I joined Cam on the porch.

"Uh. Sorry." I gestured with the container, which now held a corsage that definitely wasn't worth wearing. "I guess... we can just skip this?"

Cam's laugh had lit up my whole world. "Yeah. We can

skip it. It, um... doesn't really go with the..." He'd gestured down at himself.

"I mean, if you'd given me some warning, I could've gotten a boutonniere."

"I did say I wasn't wearing a dress."

"Yeah, but there's not wearing a dress, and there's..." I gestured at Cam. "*Not wearing a dress.*"

He'd looked down at the tux, then back up at me, eyes full of nerves and worry. "So... does that mean... I mean, is this okay?"

"It's..." I gulped. "Uh... Yeah. Fuck, yeah. It's..." I shook myself and raked my eyes up and down Cam's body and rasped, "You look incredible."

And then he'd smiled, and my knees actually went weak. Attraction to Cam was nothing new, but *this?* Oh my God. It was like one of those movies where someone got a makeover and came out looking like a completely different person who was a zillion times hotter than before, except Cam had been hot to start with.

He cleared his throat, and some shyness crept into his expression. "Do you think anybody will be weirded out?"

I'd instantly been overcome with a sense of protectiveness that usually only reared its head when an opposing player threw a dirty hit on a teammate. The urge to drop gloves and make someone regret his life's choices.

"If they have a problem with the way you look," I growled, "they can take it up with me."

Turned out, no one who mattered had been bothered. Some of the mean girls looked down their noses. Some of the immature dudebros had asked when I'd gotten a boyfriend. But all of our friends agreed with me that Cam looked amazing, and we'd had a great time.

We didn't stay for the whole dance, though. A few slow

dances had turned into a few long looks I recognized from our recent past, and we'd been out of there by eleven. By the time I dropped Cam off long after our two o'clock curfews, we were well and truly back together. I'd been on top of the world, and—

"Hey. Trev." Hoes smacked my shoulder, jostling me back into the present. "You coming?"

"I—"

Oh. Fuck. The team was heading out to the ice.

Because it was time to play hockey. Professionally. Well, first we had to do our intros, since it was our home opener. But *then* we'd have to play hockey.

And my brain was someplace else. Jesus Christ.

As I waited for my turn to be introduced, I kept thinking back to the past. Our reconciliation hadn't lasted long after that dance. It hadn't ended badly, just abruptly, with Cam insisting "it's not you, it's me."

A month after that, he'd come out as trans. And if realizing he was a boy had made so many things make sense for me, I could only imagine how it had been for him.

Not long before we graduated, I came out as gay. Several of our friends had joked that now we could get back together for real, but we'd agreed to keep things the way they were. We were both still trying to process so much about ourselves, and we were also heading off to college, and it just... wasn't a good time. We were kids who didn't even know who we were; definitely not relationship material.

Looking back, it was so obvious that Cam had been coming into his own as a trans man at the same time I'd been figuring out I was gay. Being the naïve kids we were, we hadn't understood that, and we hadn't been able to be what the other needed at that time. Not as a couple, anyway. As friends, absolutely.

But we'd both been so confused about who we were, we just couldn't process that alongside a relationship. Cam wanted to find his footing in his new identity. He struggled with his body image, with believing he was attractive, with being sexual in a body that didn't match who he was. He just didn't have the bandwidth to be involved with anyone beyond friendship.

As for me, I was just a confused train wreck about my sexuality. I was afraid I'd be ostracized as an athlete if I came out. I was afraid that maybe I wasn't really *gay* because—in my eighteen-year-old brain—the only person I'd ever been with or *wanted* to be with was *technically* a girl.

Yeah. I know. I wasn't proud of it, and just thinking about that now made me cringe. I was glad I'd never said any of it out loud, especially to Cam. There'd been a lot of things I hadn't understood back then, and I was seriously thankful I'd kept them to myself. As an adult, I understood that Cam had always been a boy, and that my attraction to him made perfect sense now that I understood my sexuality.

And now, here we were. Older. Wiser. Living in the same space.

And one look at Cam in a suit tonight left me just as gobsmacked and stupid as I'd been that moment I'd seen him in a tux all those years ago.

For the same reason, too—because he was absolutely the most stunning human being I'd ever met. When we'd both been sixteen, he'd been everything in my sixteen-year-old eyes. When we'd been eighteen, and we'd both started really figuring ourselves out, I'd been confused about everything except how undeniably attractive Cam still was.

And now that we were thirty...

Christ. Sixteen- and eighteen-year-old me hadn't had a

clue just how jaw-dropping this man would be after we both grew up.

He'd come to Pittsburgh so we could help each other resolve our crises. I just hadn't bargained for him igniting another:

How the hell was I supposed to play hockey with this beautiful man nearby?

CHAPTER 14

CAM

I APPRECIATED THAT JENNI AND KRISTINA WANTED TO include me in the spouse's suite even though I wasn't a player's partner, but I really didn't want to chance any friction with Bryan. And by the time the twins and I had settled into the owners' box, I'd made the decision to stay here for every game rather than joining the wives. The tension between Bryan and me wasn't exactly subtle, and I didn't want to cause problems.

So... I'd stay out of their suite tonight and going forward. No point in making everyone in there uncomfortable.

That, and butting heads with him seemed like it was just asking for him to drag Trev to court and fight for full custody. I was *not* going to be the reason Trev lost his kids. With that in mind, staying away from him as much as possible seemed more than prudent.

What could I say? Working at a high-end gym with a ton of drama between divorcing high-society members had taught me a lot about conflict avoidance.

And anyway, it turned out, the owners' box was swanky as hell. Cushy leather seats. Free drinks of the alcoholic and non-alcoholic varieties. Tons of food. A handful of devoted staff members.

The view wasn't half bad either. We were sandwiched between the upper and lower bowls—a better view than the nosebleed section, but not quite as good as if we were down by the glass.

The boys were thrilled by it all. They were even happier when they found out one of the staff members would get them some snacks from the concessions downstairs—pizza for Zane, a hot dog for Zach, and sodas for both of them.

"They didn't do that for you last season?" I asked.

Zane shrugged. "Dad always took us to get snacks last season."

"Oh. We can do that at the next game if—"

"No way!" Zach grinned. "This is cool!"

I chuckled and let it go. I could talk to Trev about it later. Make sure he and Bryan were okay with this rather than expecting the boys to go through the concessions line like everyone else. Not that they seemed to have any issues with waiting their turn, in line or otherwise; I'd been to a handful of stores and restaurants with them, and they were always patient when they had to wait. They'd also been polite when they'd placed their orders with the staff member, and they thanked her profusely when she arrived.

I was probably overthinking things. Having someone run out of the luxury suite to pick up their game food was probably just a cool novelty for a couple of six-year-olds.

For an inexperienced nanny who really, really needed this fucking job, it was something to sweat bullets over.

Yep. Definitely overthinking.

I rolled my shoulders and tried to shake off the nerves. This wasn't my first outing with the boys, but it was the first where I was truly on my own. I couldn't reach out to Trev if I had a question. I could theoretically reach out to Bryan, and I certainly would if there was an emergency, but if I went to him over something stupid, I'd never hear the end of it. Or I'd never have to worry about watching the boys at a hockey game again, since I'd be on my way back to Seattle.

Breathe, Cameron. They're fine. You're fine. Bryan's not here to try to catch you doing something wrong.

Which... now that I thought about it, I was kind of surprised he hadn't come up here to be with the boys. He preferred to stay in the spouse's suite instead.

Because he wanted a break from being a dad? Because he wanted to hang out with the partners he knew? Because he wanted to give me a chance to fuck up so he could convince Trev to fire me?

I didn't know. I probably didn't *want* to know. At the end of the day, he was in another suite, I was in here with the boys, and I wasn't looking that glorious gift horse in the mouth.

While the boys ate their snacks, the pregame montage kicked on. The sellout crowd went nuts, roaring their enthusiasm as the clock ticked down to puck drop. After the montage, there was a brief segment by the sports commentators, which I couldn't hear very well.

Normally, the players would return to the ice, and then there'd be the national anthems, followed by puck drop. Opening night, however, began with player introductions. They were introduced in numerical order, each skating out onto the ice to the cheers of the crowd as their photo came up on the Jumbotron.

"From Seattle, Washington," the announcer's voice boomed, "number forty-seven—Trevor Allen!"

Zach and Zane cheered for their dad, and my balance

went a little wonky as his face appeared on the big screen. I was still not used to how attractive Trev had turned out to be. The thirty-year-old version of him decked out in his hockey gear, sweaty with finger-combed hair? It wasn't fair how smoking hot he was.

The announcer continued down the roster as each player skated out to the circle. When he was done, the players saluted the crowd, and then they moved to the bench or the blue line for the national anthem.

After the anthem, I asked, the boys, "So besides your dad, who's your favorite player?"

"Hoes," Zach said without hesitation. "He's Dad's linemate."

Zane nodded. "I like Hoes. But Petrovich is my favorite." He grinned. "I like goalies."

I chuckled. "I thought that was just soccer."

"No." He shook his head as he reached for his soda. "All goalies."

"Fair enough," I said.

I was a little surprised neither of them had mentioned Tim. They seemed to like him well enough. I left that subject alone, though.

Besides, the game was starting.

A couple of minutes in, someone broke off for a line change, and Zach pointed as he exclaimed, "Dad's coming out!"

I craned my neck, and sure enough, Trev had just gone over the boards. I shivered, and not from the coolness of the arena. Fuck, but I loved watching him in his element. Practice was fine and good. Playing at this level? When it actually counted and everyone was at full-speed? So hot.

He'd barely been out for a few seconds before he was engaged in a board battle behind Boston's goal. There was some fierce jostling and digging for the puck, and finally, Trev got it free. He sent it flying around the boards to where Bell was waiting, completely forgotten and unprotected by Boston.

The rookie immediately fired on goal. The sharp *ping* off the goalpost was audible even from up here, prompting an "oooh" from the crowd. So close!

Hoes caught the rebound and shot it... right into the netminder's glove.

The whistle blew, and everyone set up for an offensive zone faceoff. My heart was pounding from the short but intense play; I *loved* this.

Trev's shift ended. The fourth line came out, and they kept the action in the offensive zone. They didn't make much effort to score—Trev had told me once that the bottom six forwards were often tasked with tiring out the opposing players. They kept the players moving constantly, and never gave them any opportunities for line changes.

It worked, too. After a solid minute, the other team was utterly gassed. One got the puck and tried to pass it to another, but they were both so tired, it didn't work. The puck didn't go straight to the player it was intended to reach, and the recipient couldn't get to it in time. It sailed down the ice, and the refs blew the whistle.

The "goddammit" was palpable from the exhausted men on the ice. Since they'd iced the puck, none of them could go to the bench for a line change.

Pittsburgh's players, however, happily skated to the bench and let some fresh bodies come out.

Seconds after the faceoff, Pittsburgh's captain, Martin, scored the team's first goal of the season.

The crowd went wild, flying to our feet and screaming

as the guys exchanged high fives and the fatigued Boston players finally managed to leave the ice.

The action continued. Trev checked someone into the boards hard enough to make the glass flex, and the boys cheered. A moment later, he was on another player, trying to get the puck away when—

A whistle.

Play stopped, and even from this far away, I knew from Trev's body language that he'd been called. He shouted something at the ref and waved his arm. The ref shook his head and gestured toward the penalty box.

"Ooh," Zane said in the earnest voice of a six-year-old seeing someone getting in trouble. "Dad's getting a penalty."

"Stupid refs," Zach muttered.

I chuckled. "You don't even know what the penalty is for yet."

Zach shrugged dismissively. "Still stupid."

Trev apparently agreed, because he shouted all the way to the box while the ref skated out to announce the penalty.

Ignoring Trev's protests, the ref blandly said, "Pittsburgh number forty-seven. Two-minute minor. Slashing."

The crowd booed furiously.

On the big screen, there was a slow-motion replay. Trev skated up alongside the other player, and he used his stick to try to get the guy's stick off the puck. If I squinted hard enough, I guess I could see him graze the glove.

I rolled my eyes. Zach might've been incensed about any call against his dad, but I had to agree with him on this one. It *was* stupid.

The camera switched to Trev, who was not happy. He flailed his hand and shouted at the ref, and I hoped the boys weren't as adept at lip-reading as I was. Or if they were, they didn't quite understand what he meant by *"That's fucking bullshit and you know it. Jesus fucking Christ."*

I smothered a laugh and stole a glance at the twins. They were the sons of a hockey player—they'd be fluent in all the conjugations of the word "fuck" before they got to second grade. God knew their father had been an expert by the time I'd met him in third.

The Rebels' penalty kill took to the ice, but Boston's power play unit made mincemeat of them. Less than thirty seconds into the power play, they'd scored.

I watched Trev coming out of the box, and my stomach knotted. He usually took penalties gracefully (after he'd said his piece to the refs, anyway). Even when they were trash, he shrugged them off and moved on. But when the camera focused on his face as he crossed the ice, he looked pissed, but also... disappointed? In himself, maybe? He wouldn't make eye contact with his teammates. Not even as they smacked his back or arm and undoubtedly told him, *"Don't worry about it—we've got plenty of time to tilt the ice."*

It didn't get better, either. During a shift later in the period, he'd taken another penalty, this time for tripping. The twins had been furious over that, but Trev had been far more subdued this time. He'd hung his head on the way to the box, and he'd been staring down at his gloves instead of watching the replay.

Judging by the replay, it was a legit call. I remembered being livid when he'd taken a tripping penalty in high school, since the other guy had tripped over Trev's leg rather than Trev deliberately tripping him.

"Doesn't matter," he'd told me afterward. "Tripping is tripping, whether it's deliberate or not."

"But that's garbage! What's to stop someone from tripping over you or your stick on purpose?"

The response had been a wicked grin. "What makes you think we don't?"

Point taken.

At least no one scored on Trev's tripping penalty tonight, and in fact the Rebels had come incredibly close to a shorthanded goal. That had done wonders for the team's morale and momentum, and it wasn't long after the penalty that they scored. All's well that ends well, and all that.

But Trev still seemed distracted and off-balance tonight. His passes weren't as crisp as they usually were. His rookie linemate set him up for a *beautiful* opportunity to put a one-timer on goal, but Trev bobbled the puck. That had resulted in a breakaway that would've been costly had one of Pittsburgh's defensemen not stolen the puck back.

This wasn't like him. Especially not since he'd started playing at this level.

Come on, Trev. Where are you tonight?

I didn't know. I had a feeling *he* didn't know.

But a few minutes later, he was on his way to the penalty box.

Again.

CHAPTER 15

TREV

HOPEFULLY THIS GAME WASN'T AN OMEN FOR THE REST of the season. Not for me, anyway. The team did well for the most part.

Me, though? Christ. By the end of the night, I had the dubious honor of being number one in the League for penalty minutes this season. Of course that wouldn't last; this was the first night of games for the entire League, and there'd only been six games besides ours. Martin was number one in points, too, after two goals and an assist. Bells, my rookie linemate, was second overall for hits. By this time next week, we'd all probably be bumped down our respective lists. None of those stats or lists meant much of anything until at least a couple of weeks into the season.

But it was still weird to be number one for PIM. I rarely took penalties. Eight minutes in one game? I mean, okay, I hadn't deliberately tripped that one defenseman. Tripping was tripping, so it was a penalty regardless of intent, but it wasn't exactly a lack of discipline on my part.

The first slashing penalty had been bullshit, too. The second one, and the interference penalty? Yeah, those were on me. And they'd been stupid on my part. Just plain fucking stupid.

Stupid and *costly*. Two of Boston's four goals had been power play goals on *my* penalties. If their starting goalie hadn't been a sieve, we'd have been fucked. Fortunately, he'd let in five goals before being pulled halfway through the second period, and the backup goalie had let in two more. A 7-4 win on our home opener wasn't bad at all. 7-2 would've been even better.

God, I was not happy with how I'd played.

Since when did I let myself get *that* distracted over anything? The last time I'd played even close to this badly had been the day after I'd realized my husband was cheating on me. And today, it wasn't even anything bad—I'd just been wildly off-balance ever since I'd seen Cam in that suit, and my jaunt down Memory Lane had completely fucked my concentration.

Get a grip, Trev. Christ on a cracker.

The worst part? My boys had been watching. They weren't even like some of the other players' kids who'd get bored and stop paying attention. Zach and Zane were *riveted* to hockey games. So they'd watched every last minute of it tonight.

Fuck.

I'd had an embarrassingly terrible game a few seasons ago, but I hadn't worried about what the boys thought. They'd just turned three—they barely knew what was happening on the ice, and they were just excited about going to games and seeing their dad at the Zamboni gate or on the Jumbotron.

Now they were almost seven. They understood the game better than some kids their age who *played* hockey.

They'd know exactly how badly I'd played tonight, and they were never shy about telling me when I'd fucked up.

After practice one morning, Zane's voice had been full of disappointment as he'd informed me, "You were slow today."

"I know I was," I'd admitted, trying not to chuckle. "I'll be faster tomorrow."

"Good," he'd said with a sharp nod.

I hadn't told him I'd been deliberately taking it easy that morning. My knee had been bothering me since the previous night's game, and on the advice of my trainers—and my own instincts—I'd dialed things back a little. Better to just let my kids think I was slacking than tell them something hurt. Their disappointment wasn't fun, but it sucked a lot less than tipping my hand about even the slightest injury. Lesson learned the hard way.

So, as partners and kids started trickling into the locker room, I braced for my sons' inevitable admonishments. As I dressed, I catalogued potential explanations, looking for something that walked that fine line between saving face and showing them it was important to take responsibility for things. Something that didn't include *"well, I took one look at your nanny in a suit, mentally went back in time, and my concentration went all to shit."*

In other words... a complete fabrication. Because that was exactly what had happened, and I felt like an asshole for letting my team and my kids down, not to mention the fans. Like an absolute dumbass for letting something like that derail my focus. I felt like a failure.

I was just pulling on my T-shirt when Cam and the boys walked into the locker room. This time, his presence in that suit registered enough to send a shiver through me, but only for a second.

It was my kids who seized my attention.

As soon as they saw me, they ran across the room and almost bowled me over. I laughed as I tried to keep us all from tumbling onto the floor.

"You won!" Zach cried, hugging me tight. "That was awesome!"

Zane was practically vibrating with excitement. "It was so cool when you guys ran away with the puck during their power play! I thought you were going to score for sure!"

I couldn't help laughing again, and it was relief more than anything this time. Okay, they'd watched, and they'd seen all of tonight's fuckery, but they weren't fazed by it at all.

I guess it would take more than a bad game for me to fall from grace in the eyes of my sons. Definitely a relief.

"Hey, hey, it's the Allen twins!" Hoes called out.

They turned, and their faces lit up again. "Hoes!" Just like that, they were gone, trotting off to say hi to my various teammates. Of course the guys fawned all over them, talking about how much they'd grown and asking when they were going to start playing hockey like their dad.

I smiled as I watched. I'd never had any illusions that I was the only reason my boys loved coming into the locker room.

But their distraction meant I suddenly couldn't avoid my own. Especially now that I was—despite being in a crowded locker room—suddenly alone with Cam.

I turned to him, and thank God he was watching the kids and not looking at me. That way he didn't see my nervous swallow. Or the way my heart melted a little at the sight of that fond smile as he watched Zach and Zane interacting with the other guys.

I cleared my throat. "They really hate coming to games, don't they?"

He chuckled and turned those amazing hazel eyes on me. "Yeah. Definitely. They were just miserable the *whole* time."

I laughed, which helped me find some air. "Sounds about right. What about you? Did you have a good time?"

"I did! I always loved going to your games, but League games are something else."

"I know, right? It's definitely not the level I used to play when we were kids."

"God, no. I mean, even the Zambonis are shiny and new." Cam made a theatrically disgusted face. "What the hell is hockey without a Zamboni that's duct-taped together and has an ad for a company that doesn't even exist anymore?"

I barked a laugh. "Oh, yeah, I remember that thing. I bet the same dude is still driving it, too."

"Wasn't he like ninety back then?"

"Yeah, but my coach said he was like ninety back in the eighties, so who knows? He's probably immortal or something."

"Well, that's the dream, isn't it? Gain immortality and spend it driving a rickety Zamboni with a cigarette hanging out of your mouth."

I pursed my lips and half-shrugged. "I mean, he wasn't the guy who had to clean the locker room toilets, so..."

Cam made a face that was unreasonably cute. "Eww. That poor guy."

"Right?" I glanced over at the boys, who were listening intently as Hoes spoke. He was probably telling them some bullshit story again, and they were thoroughly entertained by it. Facing Cam again, I said, "I'm glad you had a good time. You don't have to come to every game if you don't want to, but..." I trailed off. I kind of hoped he *didn't* come to every game, if only so I could get my head out of my ass and remember how to play hockey.

He shrugged. "We'll see? The schedule looks pretty intense."

"You have no idea."

"Well, like I said—we'll see. I don't imagine you want the boys to always be out this late on school nights."

I shook my head. "Definitely not. But Friday and weekend games are fine. Just... don't feel like you have to bring them to all of those. Or come during Bryan's custody weeks."

His smile made the room sway. "I don't think you'll have to twist my arm to come to more of your games."

I returned the smile. I'd be fine. I'd be expecting him in a suit next time, so I'd be ready for it. I wouldn't get carried away thinking about the past or how hot he looked in the present. I'd be able to play hockey the way I was paid to do, without my head being someplace else.

I'd be *fine*.

Right?

CHAPTER 16

CAM

The Rebels' first three games were at home. I went to all of them—with the boys for the first two, by myself for the last one—and loved every minute.

The first game where I was on my own was admittedly kind of jarring. I was used to being responsible for the boys, and I was used to their company. Their comments about the game were funny and sometimes even observant in ways I wouldn't have expected from kids their age. They really knew the sport, and they'd taught me a thing or two.

Then it was just me, sitting alone in the owners' box with the staff, the owners, the general manager, and a couple of players who'd been healthy-scratched. I wondered a few times if I should've taken up Jenni or Kristina on the still-open offer to join the spouses and partners, but... no. Bryan was there with the kids, and I didn't want to create any tension. If one of the boys innocently interacted with me, Bryan could easily twist that into me pulling them away from him or some bullshit like that. Maybe I was paranoid, but he seemed just vindictive and conniving enough that I needed to be on guard about everything.

The kids were easy. The ex-husband was exhausting.

And then, right after that game, Trev and the team had gone straight to the airport. They'd be on the road for three games, which meant I had most of this week to myself. No Trev. No twins. Just this huge house that was suddenly devoid of all noise and activity that wasn't mine.

Not gonna lie—I wasn't sure what to do with myself. It was weird, being here without him. Without *them*. I hadn't seen Trev in almost a decade, but now I was losing my mind after he'd been gone less than twenty-four hours.

It reminded me of the way we'd been in school. Of that disappointment that would tug at me when the teacher took attendance and Trev's chair was empty. A whole day without him? Ugh. What the fuck.

Well, I was going to have periods of time where both he and the boys were gone, so now was as good a time as any to figure out how to handle it.

I could get in the car and go explore Pittsburgh. Trev and some of the Rebels spouses had told me about a few restaurants and shops I absolutely needed to try. They were especially emphatic about a few in the Strip District (whatever that was) and out in Cranberry (where some of the other players lived). Plus there were some parks that were great for walking while the weather was still nice. The various museums were supposed to be top notch.

But while I was a little stir crazy, I decided to save the exploring for when cabin fever set in. Right now, despite the restlessness, there was also something to be said for some quiet downtime with no one around and nothing pressing to do. I didn't quite know what to do with that, hence being twitchy about it, but I thought it might be a good idea to just... sit with it for a while. Just be by myself, enjoying the silent solitude and the lack of some urgent matter to attend to.

It was weird and not completely comfortable, probably because I wasn't used to it anymore. As I lounged on Trev's couch, chatting about nothing with the guys back home, I tried to think about how long it had been since I'd experienced the luxury of restless boredom. Not while I'd been with my mom before coming to Pittsburgh; I'd been panicking and flailing because my whole life had been upended and I didn't know what to do. The last year or so with Daniel had been its own shitshow, with me alternately walking on eggshells and fighting with the man I later discovered was porking one of my clients. In fact, even the years before that had been their own minefield as I vacillated between trying to keep him happy and scrambling to atone for whatever I'd done to piss him off.

Pressing my head back into the couch cushion, I stared up at the high ceiling and released a long breath. God, no wonder I couldn't relax into this. It was like I'd been in a constant state of fight-or-flight all this time, and now that the danger had passed, I didn't know how to reclaim my equilibrium. As the adrenaline drained away, I couldn't remember how to function.

Christ. I should've left Daniel ages ago.

Wasn't that the truth.

So, yeah. I needed to just sit with this and get used to being by myself without a dark cloud over my head or a fire that needed to be put out.

Of course, knowing that didn't make the twitchiness go away, and just because I wasn't going out didn't mean I had to sit here on the couch until I went insane. I could get up and move around. Maybe finish unpacking the handful of boxes that had arrived this week—things I'd left at my mom's house and she'd shipped after I'd confirmed I was staying with Trev for the foreseeable future. I could hit the gym downstairs. I could do... I don't know. Something.

I put my phone aside, pushed myself to my feet, and shuffled into the kitchen. There was a cabinet in there where I could keep snacks and munchies I liked, but when I opened it this time, something caught my eye.

It was a green-and-yellow box of Crayola crayons. Taped to it was a note, hand-written in blue crayon:

It was me. Sorry I stole your crayons in 3rd grade.
Trev

I couldn't decide if I wanted to laugh, swoon, or cry. It was such a funny and cute gesture, and it made me wish that much more that he was home right now. I didn't know what I'd do or say, only that I wished he was here.

But he's not, Cam, so pull yourself together and don't spend all this time pining.

I wouldn't. I really wouldn't. But... I did indulge in a moment to adore his cute little gesture with the crayons.

Just a moment, though. Then it was back to figuring out what to do with all this time to myself.

I left the crayons on the shelf, dug a protein bar out of a box, and closed the cabinet. Then I wandered the house.

When Trev had first given me a tour, I'd been aware of a lot of the photos on the wall, but hadn't looked closely at any besides the ones of his kids. Today, I paused by some of the framed photos I passed multiple times each day, and I actually looked at them. These were from Trev's hockey career, starting with his first couple of seasons in the minors and all the way through to the present. There were shots of young Trev holding up a trophy after his college team won or biting a medal after some international competition. An old framed photo showed an adorably young Trev grinning down at the Winnipeg jersey he'd pulled on over his shirt and tie at the draft.

Across the top of the wall, a row of eight-by-tens documented his professional career in his annual team portrait. First as a baby-faced rookie playing for Winnipeg's minor league affiliate, then after he was traded, playing for Pittsburgh's farm team. In his third season, he'd been on the starting roster for the Pittsburgh Rebels, and every portrait after that showed him growing up in that jersey. His features had sharpened. His haircut had gotten shorter and neater. His scruff had darkened to something I'd have killed to trail my fingertips over. He also seemed to evolve from a starstruck kid to a slightly overwhelmed early-twenty-something to a more confident man who knew he belonged there.

Maybe I was just feeling a little maudlin today, especially after the crayons, but I almost got choked up as I gazed at the portraits. I hated that I'd missed so much. Watching him on TV and reading about him in sports articles just wasn't the same. The absence of my best friend had weighed on me for a long time, and I resented Daniel for that more than I did a lot of his other bullshit. This visual of all the time Trev and I had lost—that was heartbreaking.

And what if I'd never caught Daniel cheating? What if we'd never split up? What we'd gotten married like we'd talked about, and I'd never found myself desperate for a solution to my living situation? What if Trev's ex hadn't given him an ultimatum at the same time my life had been in chaos?

I swallowed hard as I gazed at Trev's portraits. We'd lost

so damn much time, and it was only through dumb luck and asshole exes that we'd come crashing back into each other's lives.

That thought lingered for a second, and I chuckled to myself. We both apparently had terrible taste in men, but hey, they weren't completely useless if they'd made my path cross with Trev's again. Would it be petty to text Daniel and tell him that? Probably, yes, but it sure was tempting.

I laughed again in the silence of the hallway. No, I wouldn't actually do it, only because I didn't want to reestablish contact with him. A clean break was the best thing.

It was just super satisfying to imagine the look on his face.

I moved on from those portraits to the other images from Trev's career. The shot of baby-faced Trev celebrating a goal with Anson Harper, a legendary player who'd retired after Trev's first season with Pittsburgh. I could only imagine how much Trev's inner fanboy had lost his mind over being in the same locker room with that guy, never mind being on the same ice with him.

In fact... ah. The framed puck beside the photo made sense. White tape had been wrapped around it, and someone had written in black Sharpie, *Goal, Pit vs. Wash., Allen from Harper.* So that veteran had assisted on one of Trev's goals. God, I wished I could've been there to see him afterward. I could imagine him sitting at home afterward, clutching that puck like a gift handed to him by Santa Claus himself.

Beside that photo and puck was a larger image of Trev sporting a full playoff beard as he hoisted the Cup. The photographer had caught him mid-shout, and Trev was the very picture of joy and elation.

Beside that, there was a shot of Trev beside the cup, one baby in the crook of his arm, the other inside the Cup.

Wow. He'd been on top of the world that year. A new dad. Won the Cup. Still happily married. His dreams from the time when we were young had been to get married, have kids, and win a Cup as a pro hockey player. It was amazing to see him enjoying all three of those things at the same time.

I'd watched that win on TV. I'd celebrated as if I'd been there with him. My chest had been ready to explode from the sheer joy of watching him achieve one of his biggest dreams, and it had ached because I'd missed him so damn much.

I traced my fingertip along the edge of the picture frame. For years, I'd followed Trev's career from a distance, watching games and highlights whenever I could be sure Daniel wouldn't catch me.

It was weird to see them now while I was here. In Trev's house. Back in his life.

I was glad to see that while part of his world had fallen apart, not all of it had. His marriage had imploded, yes, but he still had his boys. He still had his career. Though the divorce had been hell and his ex-husband still insisted on being a pain in the dick, Trev hadn't lost everything.

And through it all, he was still the same sweet, amazing man he'd been when we were kids. More mature now, but still Trev. Still the friend I'd been missing all this time. Still the man I'd regretted drifting away from.

By a series of minor miracles, we were back in each other's worlds.

And like hell was I ever losing him again.

The restless boredom did not, in fact, kill me, though I wondered a few times if it might. An hour in the gym helped. Food helped. Watching Trev's game on TV helped.

But I was definitely not used to being alone without some panic to keep me occupied, and by the time I called it a night, I was both exhausted and wired. Tired from hours on end trying to chill, keyed up from all the thoughts that had been banging around in my skull all day.

And now that I was in bed, there was nothing to pull my focus.

Well... almost nothing.

Because spending a day alone, feeling untethered and occupying myself with photos of Trev and thoughts of him while I sat around in his house... had let me think about him. A lot.

Trev as a dad. Trev as a hockey player. Trev as the breath of fresh air he was after I'd wasted so much time with Daniel. Trev as the kid I'd experimented with who'd had the audacity to grow into a man who had no business being that goddamned gorgeous.

I closed my eyes and whispered some curses even though there was no one around to hear me. Alone in the darkness, all those thoughts of Trev coalesced into something that was both surprising and predictable—horniness that *needed* an outlet. I hadn't been interested in anything sexual in a long, long time—not since well before I'd stopped having sex with Daniel—but tonight...

Fuck. Tonight I was *almost* tempted to fire up a hookup app.

Almost, because that would've required effort and brain cells, and also, it would mean sleeping with someone who wouldn't be able to scratch this itch. He might be able to get me off, but he wouldn't be able to get Trev off my mind, and goddammit, I didn't just want an orgasm or sex right now—I wanted all that with *Trev*.

I wanted to run my fingertips over the planes and contours of his body, feeling for myself what time and hockey had done to his physique. I loved the sounds men made in bed—moaning, gasping, cursing—but right now, I only wanted to hear those coming from Trev.

God, I was stupid. Trev was my friend, and he was also my boss and my landlord. And like, the dude was a rich pro athlete. I'd seen the people hockey players dated. I was pretty sure every one of the Pittsburgh Rebels' wives and girlfriends were literal models, and though Bryan was a dick, he wasn't hard on the eyes. I'd have bet money that under his hoodies or suits was a body that wouldn't be out of place in an underwear ad.

I was fit and all, and I liked to think I was a good-looking guy, but I was also realistic. I was an unemployed personal trainer who'd had to drive his piece-of-shit car across the country to take a gig as a nanny in order to keep my head above water. Trev could do a *lot* better.

But that didn't mean I couldn't close my eyes and imagine the alternate universe where he wanted me. Especially since I'd visited that universe plenty of times over the past few years. I mean, it wasn't a big secret that when people were checked out of relationships, they fantasized about other people during sex with their partner.

The secret I would never admit out loud under torture was that, for the last three years of my relationship, it was fantasies of Trev that had carried me through sex with Daniel. Every time I came, it was to thoughts of Trev's tongue driving me wild or his dick pounding into me or his voice purring in my ear about how turned on he was.

"You're gonna regret this," Daniel had told me when I was leaving.

"Why?" I'd snarked back. *"Because I'll miss the sex?"* I'd scoffed and rolled my eyes, knowing I was hitting below the belt and not the least bit sorry about it. *"Please."*

He'd replied with a caustic laugh. *"You finished every time, so I must've been doing something right."*

I mean, yeah, he had me there. I'd always—*almost* always—come.

He'd just never know that it was less about his technique and more about the mind-blowing fantasies of my best friend.

And those fantasies had all happened before I'd been face to face with the man Trev had become. I'd seen him on TV and all, both playing and in interviews, but actually breathing the same air as him—actually seeing him in the flesh—was a million times better. I couldn't help but be turned on by the man he'd become in the years we'd been apart.

Okay, now I was *seriously* horny.

I put a little lube on my fingers and started teasing myself, closing my eyes as my brain went through its catalog of go-to Trev fantasies. Not just fucking me—though, oh my God, I wanted his dick in me—but with his face buried between my thighs. The thought of his mouth on me like my fingers were now—fucking hell, that had my toes curling already.

I usually moved between fantasies while I was getting off, but not this fast. Not one imaginary scenario after another, rapidly flitting between Trev fucking me over every imaginable surface to him going down on me until his jaw ached to me riding him until he came so hard he couldn't breathe. I wanted it all, and each turned me on more than the last. It was like getting all my fantasies remastered into high def. Or hell, remade with a far better and prettier actor. One who was light years out of my league, but inside my fantasy, wanted me more than anything else in the world.

Even his voice was sexier now. Deeper than when he was a teenager, and a little rough around the edges. What I wouldn't have given to have that voice growling in my ear, encouraging me to my climax while he chased his own.

"That's it, baby," I could imagine him purring. *"God, you feel amazing."*

I bit my lip and arched, my toes curling as those first sparks of a climax fired off. I usually let my orgasms build for a while, enjoying the ride until I was ready to let go, but I was too keyed up tonight. Too hot with need as my mind filled with images of present-day Trev driving both of us into oblivion. Too needy in ways I couldn't remember ever being.

So I let my fingers and that amazing mental porno send me into the stratosphere. I thought I heard myself cry out with abandon, but all I knew for sure was absolute bliss as the most intense orgasm I'd had in ages crashed through me.

I took my hand away before things got too sensitive, and I pushed out a ragged breath as the intensity started to ebb. I let my eyelids flutter shut, and I just lay there for a moment as those delicious aftershocks rolled through me. I couldn't remember the last time an orgasm—of my own making or otherwise—had left me dizzy and shaking like this.

There was no guilt this time, either. I wasn't deceiving anyone. Okay, I might've been lying to Trev by omission, but that was probably the best thing for my job and our friendship. There was no shame in not blurting out, *"So I totally jacked off thinking about you, and I had to peel myself off the ceiling afterward."*

The thought made me laugh drunkenly. Yeah, it was just as well I was keeping this to myself. But I wasn't lying to Daniel anymore because he wasn't here. His opinion, his pleasure—none of that mattered anymore. Only mine did.

And goddamn, the pleasure was incredible this time. My solo sessions would never be the same again now that I had updated Trev-shaped fantasies to play with. I didn't even feel the need to go looking for someone to hook up with or date. Who needed a stranger when thinking of Trev did more for me than most real-life guys did?

Hell, maybe it was just as well this was only fantasies. Maybe it was just as well I wasn't actually sleeping with Trev.

The sex would probably kill me.

CHAPTER 17

TREV

ROAD TRIPS WERE NEVER EASY. DIDN'T MATTER IF I was a kid riding drafty buses and staying in crap hotels or a full-fledged pro flying on charter jets and sleeping in high-end rooms—it took its toll. The jetlag. The early mornings. The late nights. As much as I loved traveling with my teams, and as much as I'd loved it since my youth days, it was still hard sometimes.

Being away from my boyfriend, then fiancé, then husband had been tough. About the time getting away from him had become a relief, I'd been grappling with constantly leaving my kids behind. Early on, they'd struggled with separation anxiety, which hadn't done good things to my head. The last couple of seasons, they missed me but didn't get scared that I wasn't coming home, so that was an improvement for everyone.

It still sucked sometimes, though. One of the hardest things had been after the divorce. I hadn't worried about Bryan talking shit about me to the boys—that was one line even he wouldn't cross—but I'd been startled to realize how much the lack of connection to him severed me from them.

He was reliable as the sun about getting them on FaceTime with me, which I appreciated. He kept me in the loop if there were any issues, like when Zane was down with a bad ear infection or when Zach sprained his ankle playing soccer.

But I hadn't realized how much I'd leaned on the sporadic updates throughout the day. The random photos of the boys. The texts about something silly one of them had said. The videos of milestones I hadn't been there to see. Even the messages about how this or that cartoon made him want to put an icepick through his own ear or how he couldn't take one more repetition of that obnoxious song.

The end of my constant communication with my husband had meant an end to all those little lifelines, which had been the beginning of me realizing—too late—just how much they'd kept me going. Without them, road trips became bleak and lonely, even while I was surrounded by my teammates. When Bryan had the twins, it was radio silence from the home front, and it was driving me insane.

When Cam had the boys, though?

> I have no idea where they found the markers or why they thought to color on each other's faces, but the picture is hilarious lol
>
> The boys wanted to show you their paintings from school today, so here's a pic!
>
> Your children have MASTERED the voice of Spud the Sparrow, so when you get home, we need to discuss my SUBSTANTIAL pay raise.

I chuckled at that last message as the bus took us back to our hotel after our morning skate. The twins were obsessed with this obnoxious cartoon featuring talking woodland creatures, and I wasn't at all surprised they'd taken to mimicking one of the characters. Or that Cam—who'd hated characters like that even back when we'd been the target audience of most cartoons—was annoyed by it.

> Could be worse. Trust me.

HOW??

> Look up Pirate Billy Bob on YouTube.

There was no response for a moment. I pressed my lips together, imagining the horror on his face when he saw those clips. Bryan had barely made it through the twins' Pirate Billy Bob phase, and it wouldn't surprise me if he started dry-heaving upon hearing the first few notes of its theme song. Hell, if things had been less tense, Cam and Bryan could've bonded over their hatred of children's programming. It was actually funny, imagining the two of them ranting about high-pitched sea shanties, overdone pirate voices, and nightmarishly creepy animation.

The thought made my humor fade a bit. Cam and Bryan having an exasperated conversation about Pirate Billy Bob was a fantasy. It made me think, for the millionth time—*what* happened *to us?*

Before I could go too far down that mental road, my phone pinged.

Jesus. Fucking. Christ.

What... What even IS this show? Your kids WATCHED it?

LOL They watch Forest Friends. Are you surprised?

Okay, Forest Friends is stupid and annoying, but this? WHAT THE ACTUAL FUCK?

Have you listened to any of the songs?

There's SONGS? I can't even get past the animation.

It's like someone tried to mimic South Park's style using some bottom-of-the-barrel AI, and it somehow came out looking both cheap AND like something in the uncanny valley.

You have to WORK at it to make something this bad.

You should really listen to the songs.

Absolutely the fuck not.

(chicken emoji)

(middle finger emoji)

(three chicken emojis)

(eyeroll emoji) (middle finger emoji)

Nothing came through for a minute or so, but about the time I was gathering my coffee cup and toque to get off the bus, there was another ping.

Oh fuck yooou

Goddammit. I'm going to have this stuck in my head all day.

I hate you.

That was followed by several rows of middle finger emojis, and I was laughing so hard I nearly dropped the phone and my coffee. I was probably going to pay for this, but that was okay. Totally worth it.

> I'd say I'm sorry but we both know I'm not. Getting off the bus and heading to a team meeting—TTYL

I'm Amazon Priming spider eggs right now. They'll all be hatching in your room when you get home.

I just laughed, pocketed my phone, and continued into the hotel. I followed some of my teammates into a small conference room for the team meeting, and I took a seat by Bells, Tremblay, and Hoes. We were early, so everyone was shooting the shit or playing on their phones while we waited for the coaches.

I was scrolling social media when some of the guys walked in, and I caught their in-progress conversation.

"—it's no fucking wonder you're playing better on the road." Spaulding smacked Chats on the back. "Maybe we should ban you from seeing him so you can pull your weight at home."

Chats met him with a big shit-eating grin. "Yeah, you wish. I'll get used to it."

Spaulding rolled his eyes as they walked past me. "Don't let Coach see it affecting your game, man."

"Nah, it's not." Chats gave my shoulder a shove. "Trev can vouch for me, though—that kind of cardio takes a *lot* out of a man!"

The response from our teammates was a mix of irritated

glares and—from the new guys—snickers. I just gritted my teeth and stared intently at my phone.

"What's he talking about?" Bells asked innocently. "Why can you vouch for him?"

I closed my eyes and pushed out a breath through my nose.

From Bells's other side, Hoes quietly said, "Chats is with Trev's ex-husband."

The rookie stiffened, and when I looked at him, he was staring at me in horror. "Oh. Shit. Man, I'm sorry. I didn't mean to—"

"It's fine," I said. He clearly wasn't convinced, so I added, "Chats just thinks it's a lot funnier than it is."

Elsewhere in the room, someone said to Chats, "Man, I don't get you. Is getting with someone's ex really that much a flex for gay dudes?"

I groaned, pressing my elbow into the armrest and rubbing my eyes with my thumb and forefinger.

Chats scoffed. "Nah, but when you see what someone else tosses out?" I could *hear* the smug grin on his face. "Trust me, this car doesn't have *nearly* as many miles on it as you think."

I was relieved that my teammates responded with muttered admonishments. The newer guys who'd laughed a minute ago were quiet now, having evidently read the room.

Whatever Chats said next, I couldn't make it out since he was a few rows back. Fine. I didn't want to know. From the tone of the hushed conversation, though, the rest of the guys weren't having it.

Well, thank God for that. I really couldn't have cared less that Chats and Bryan were together, but I had no patience for having it repeatedly thrown in my face. This wasn't the first time, and it wouldn't be the last. Though maybe now he'd stop doing it so much around our teammates, since they were clearly done with it.

Thanks for having my back, guys. Because otherwise I'm going to throw gloves with him.

Except there was that whole thing about our bullshit blowing back on other queer players. My life would've been so damn much easier if Chats cared about things like that and stopped acting like a twat. But no, I had to be the responsible adult who cared about other people like us. I had to be the one who quietly gritted my teeth through his crap so no one else got punished for "those gay dudes who can't keep their drama out of the locker room."

Ugh. I hated this.

Fortunately, our coaches came in a moment later, and the team meeting kicked off. I was only half tuned in. Embarrassment and anger bubbled beneath the surface. Even knowing my teammates were on my side didn't alleviate this humiliated feeling or the desire to curb stomp Chats.

It made me wonder what Bryan saw in him. He'd never been into guys who were mean-spirited and nasty. Then again, he hadn't been a vindictive asshole himself, so maybe they were birds of a feather now.

And this guy is around my kids all the time?

That thought made my stomach fold in on itself. I hoped—and I *believed*—that Bryan didn't put up with anyone talking shit about me in front of the kids. That was one of the few areas where we'd managed to remain civil. He even put his foot down with my ex-mother-in-law, who'd never been my biggest fan. She probably had all kinds of things to say about me now that I was her precious son's asshole ex.

I fought the urge to squirm in my seat as the assistant

head coach talked about... something. Whatever. I wasn't paying attention. I was too wound up about Chats and my kids and... just everything.

Fuck me. It was bad enough I was gone all the time. What if that was driving me away from my kids? What if their potential stepfather was adding his own little wedges to subtly widen the divide?

And it occurred to me that the whole reason Cam was living in my house right now and suffering through terrible cartoons was that Bryan had given me an ultimatum. That he'd threatened to try for full custody, pulling the boys even farther away from me.

What if that was the plan—to steadily chip away at my relationship with the twins until I was lucky to have a weekend a month with them?

And what if it worked?

I'd been distracted at our home opener because I was an idiot for Cam. In the games since, I'd had my head together, and I was already on track for a solid season. If I kept up my current points-per-game streak, and I didn't go down with any injuries, this could be a record year for me.

Tonight, though...

Tonight was not going to be a good game.

Ever since that bullshit from Chats during this morning's team meeting, I'd been wound tight and pissed off. I'd usually pass out right away during my pregame nap, but today I'd tossed and turned the whole time. As I'd gone through all my routines, gearing up and getting ready for warmups, I'd been distracted, and the distraction hadn't been nearly as pleasant as the home opener.

And then during warmups, Chats and I passed each other at one point and made eye contact. The grin that flashed across his face made me want to kick his skates right out from under him.

I hated this. I hated *him*. I didn't even know if his aim was to make me jealous that he had Bryan, or if he was just rubbing it in my face that he was getting laid while I—as far as anyone knew—wasn't.

Jealousy wasn't an issue. I still had some feelings about my divorce, but I didn't want Bryan back. Chats could have him.

The rest? I genuinely didn't care. So what if he was getting laid? I didn't even want—

That thought almost made me trip as I stepped off the ice and into the tunnel.

Up until recently, I *hadn't* wanted to get laid. My libido had been dead and gone, and if anything, I'd just wondered how the hell Bryan could be interested in sex or dating or anything at all. Hockey had barely interested me.

Oh, but my libido was awake now, and it had been ever since...

I shivered, goose bumps springing up under my gear as I clomped toward the locker room.

Ever since Cam had arrived.

Well... that was a pleasant, if mildly distracting and seriously frustrating, train of thought. Nothing was going to happen between us, and I was surprised I hadn't made an ass of myself living with him, but still. Beat the hell out of fixating on Chats and his bullshit.

And that kept me going right up until we were back on the bench. We were all standing for the national anthem, the stadium lights dimmed so people could focus on the flag and the singer. Bells and Hoes stood between me and Chats, all of their backs to me.

After the song had wound down, but just before the bright lights came back on, Chats turned around, and we once again made eye contact.

He smirked.

And he fucking *winked*.

And all those pleasant thoughts about Cam scattered.

If not for my mouthguard, I probably would've ground my teeth to dust as I dropped onto the bench. I needed to stop letting him get to me like this. He was a bag of dicks. He was an antagonistic piece of shit. Why was I letting him fuck with my mood, not to mention my hockey?

Hockey, Trevor. Focus on the hockey.

I tried my level best to do exactly that. Martin's line managed to pin Chicago into their own defensive zone, and one by one, they peeled away. Hoes, Bells, and I joined our top D-pair, and they too went for changes while the three of us kept the puck deep in the zone.

Bells managed a gorgeous shot on goal. Shit, this kid was going places; he only had a handful of points so far this season, but his instincts were on point and his shot was deadly. If not for the miraculous save by Chicago's goalie, Bells would've had the first goal of the game.

Fortunately, the goalie's rebound control wasn't that great, and Hoes managed to snag the puck away.

*Un*fortunately, one of Chicago's forwards knocked him off the puck, and suddenly all the action was heading to our end.

Spaulding, our veteran defenseman, wasn't able to get the puck away, but he did slow him down enough that one of the other forwards crossed into the zone first. The whistle blew—offside.

We seized the opportunity for a line change before the offensive zone faceoff, and—

"Don't worry, Trev." A smirking Chats smacked my arm as we passed each other. "You know I can always pick up wherever you leave off."

The impulse to roar with fury and snap my stick over my thigh (or his stupid head) almost got the best of me, but I just mentally cursed him out before taking my spot on the bench.

Son of a bitch. He's going to do it during games now? Really?

Yeah. Really. Because he was that kind of petty, immature jackass.

I wanted to say I got over it by the time I went out for my next shift. I wanted to say I shook it off and refocused on the game. I wanted to say I didn't let him fuck with my game.

I *wanted* to, but that would be a lie.

"Son of a bitch!" I shouted when my shot went miles wide. Before the words had even finished leaving my mouth, a Chicago player had the puck and passed it to another.

One who'd managed to get behind us *and* behind our D.

The crowd roared as he flew up the ice. Petrovich shifted left and right in the net, blocker and paddle ready as he anticipated where the shot might come in.

The player wound back, and Petrovich rose up to anticipate a top-shelf attempt... leaving his five-hole open for the dagger of a shot.

The red light came on. The goal song was barely audible over the ecstatic crowd.

I groaned and muttered a few curses as I watched the Chicago players skating by their bench for fist bumps.

One sloppy shot on my part, and now we were down by one.

Way to go, Trev. Way to fuck your whole team because your head's not in the game.

I dropped onto the bench and took a swig of water. My anger drained away in favor of just feeling like shit. I'd let my team down. Yeah, it was only one goal, and we were only halfway through the first period, but it was never fun to have to dig ourselves out of a hole. Knowing my stupidity had put us in that hole... ugh.

A hand landed on my padded shoulder, and I turned my head as Coach leaned down beside me. "You here tonight, Trev?"

My face burned, and I nodded. "Yeah, Coach. I'm good."

He studied me skeptically. Then he nodded, gave my shoulder a smack, and stood again to watch the action on the ice.

I needed to be here. I needed to get my head together.

Against my better judgment, I found Chats on the ice. He was fixated on a puck battle, jostling with an opposing defenseman while he waited for someone to get the puck free and pass it to him.

I gnawed furiously on my mouthguard. Why was I letting him under my skin? Why was I letting him fuck up my game?

Ugh. My kids are watching. The Pittsburgh Rebels fanbase is watching.

Ignore him and get it together. Fuck.

I told myself all that and more. Over and over and fucking over.

Can't say it really helped, though.

CHAPTER 18

CAM

Sitting on the couch in Pittsburgh Rebels pajamas, Zane furrowed his brow at the TV. "Dad's having a bad night."

Beside him, Zach scowled and nodded.

They weren't wrong—Trev was on another planet. He'd been playing so well after that bumpy first night, but now... Jesus. We weren't the only ones who noticed, either.

"I'm not sure what's going on with Trevor Allen tonight," a commentator said. "He hasn't had a single shot this game, and he seems to be going for a new personal record for turnovers. And if Petrovich hadn't been on his toes, there would've been an own goal against Pittsburgh for sure."

"I don't know, Joel," the other replied as the camera watched Trev and three other players battling for the puck against the wall. "But I tell you what, if I'm Coach Larson and my second line center is playing like this tonight, he's playing on the fourth line in the next game."

"Or he's spending some time on the bench," the first

said. "Because *this* isn't what anyone expects from Trevor Allen."

"Well, I hope Tim Chatsworth is ready for some second line minutes, because he's probably getting promoted soon."

"Then let's hope Allen gets his head together, because Chats on a good day still doesn't hold a candle to Allen on an off day."

The commentators continued remarking on whether Trev or Chats was worthy of that spot and how the team was in trouble if Chats was the best they could do to take Trev's place.

As they yammered on, Zane frowned. "I don't like it when they talk about Dad like that."

"I don't either," I admitted. "It isn't nice."

"They just don't like him because they can't play like him," Zach declared.

"Is that right?"

He nodded sharply, glaring hard at the screen. "Dad's boyfriend says that announcer guy was healthy-scratched more than he ever played."

"Oh really?" I asked. "What does that mean?"

"It means he was benched," Zane said in that *"oh my God, what did you* think *it means?"* tone that kids did *oh* so well.

"Oh," I said. "So he sat on the bench most games instead of playing hockey?"

"Duh," Zach said with total seriousness. "His team wanted to *win.*"

I snorted. These were *definitely* Trev's children.

But this was also definitely not Trev's night, and I was worried. When we'd exchanged texts this morning, he'd been himself. Later, though, his responses were brief and kind of... disengaged? Not like he was blowing me off, but like his heart wasn't in it.

Just like his heart wasn't in the game right now.

My stomach knotted with worry. As the camera followed Trev skating toward the bench with a defeated look on his face, that worry intensified.

Where are you tonight, Trevor?

I wasn't any less worried when the game was over. They'd gone into overtime, and ultimately lost in a shootout. None of Trev's mistakes had been terribly costly tonight, aside from some turnovers that had resulted in scoring chances, but he hadn't really helped much either.

When he FaceTimed with the boys after the game, he looked and sounded exhausted. Still obviously thrilled to see them, but like he was ready to collapse, too. And I didn't think it was just from the game.

While I supervised the twins brushing their teeth afterward, I texted him.

> Hey. Want to FaceTime again? With just me?

The reply came as I was tucking the boys in, and I read it after I'd stepped out into the hall.

> Yes please. In my hotel room now.

> Give me a minute.

I headed into my own bedroom, shut the door, lay back on my bed, and sent the FaceTime request.

One thing became apparent the instant he was on the screen—the smile he'd put on during his call with the boys had been doing a *lot* of heavy lifting. Now that he wasn't trying to pretend everything was okay, the fatigue really came through.

"Hey," I said. "I wanted to ask without the boys around—are you okay?"

Trev sighed and wiped a hand over his face, letting even more exhaustion come through. "Yeah. It was just a rough fucking night."

"So I noticed."

He grunted. "Bet Zach and Zane noticed too."

I acknowledged that with a subtle nod but added, "They're absolutely sure your next game will be better, though."

His smile was halfhearted at best. "Glad they still have faith in me."

"Of course they do." I paused. "What's going on, though? Just an off night, or...?"

Trev stared at something off-camera for a moment. Then he deflated a little more. "What's going on is that playing on the same team as my ex's new boyfriend fucking sucks." Trev sighed and scrubbed a hand over his face. "And the fact that he's a dick about it..." He trailed off, waving his hand. "I don't know what to do."

I winced. "That really sucks. Doesn't anyone do anything?"

He gestured dismissively. "My teammates got on his ass about it. I'm sure he'll cut back a little around other people, but any chance he gets, he smirks at me and just gives me these looks..." Trev rolled his eyes and growled something the phone didn't pick up. "I'm so sick of his bullshit."

"What about your coaches, though? I'm surprised they let that kind of crap slide."

Trev pursed his lips. "I think they know. They definitely know I'm... off my game. But I'm not sure I actually want to bring it up to them."

"Why not? Because of everything you said about it affecting other queer players?"

"That, and also because at the end of the day, if they want to separate us..." His shoulders slumped. "If they want to separate us, they'll have a much easier time unloading me than him."

I stared at him. "What? But... I mean, you're on the second line and your stats are way better. Why would they keep him?"

Trev exhaled as if this whole line of conversation exhausted him. "The short version is that I signed my extension while we were low on cap space. In theory, I could probably be pulling another million, maybe even a million and a half every year."

I whistled. "Damn."

"Eh." He shrugged as if $1.5 million wasn't that big of a deal. "Then Chats came onboard. The thing is, we'd just lost one of our most expensive players to free agency and the second most expensive had retired. Our GM had cap space burning a hole in his pocket, and that was when there were still some concerns that Martin wouldn't come back after his hip surgery." He blew out a breath and rolled his eyes. "So instead of chasing down some top-notch players or signing players he could use for trades, he signed Chats for *way* more than he's worth."

"Ooh, so it was like a perfect storm."

"Yep. An injured captain, a stupid GM, and a cocky

bottom six forward who was happy to relieve the team of valuable cap space."

"Your GM sounds like a dumbass."

"He was. Oh God, he was. Fortunately, they fired him last season." Trev rolled his eyes. "Shame they didn't drop the axe before he traded a future Hall-of-Fame goalie, let a generational talent defenseman walk during free agency, and signed Chats to a six-year deal."

"Holy shit," I breathed.

"Right?" Trev scratched the back of his head, then let his hand fall into his lap. "So if shit really hits the fan and they want to separate us, it's going to be a lot easier to offload the cheap top six forward with a year left on his contract than the overpriced bottom six with four years left."

"That sounds..." I made a face. "Would they really do that? I mean, can't they like fire him or something?"

"They can terminate his contract for cause, but I don't think they'd go that far with this. Not unless it gets really out of hand and starts disrupting the locker room."

I inclined my head. "It isn't doing that already?"

He made a noncommittal noise. "We're a couple of grown-ass adults. I doubt the club is interested in policing something like this. They're probably just quietly hoping we'll unfuck it ourselves without anyone having to intervene."

"Do you think that's doable?"

"Maybe? I'm just trying to stay away from him as much as I can. I really just need to learn to ignore him. This is... I don't know. It's just childish, being this fucked up over someone acting like an asshole."

I wanted to tell him that wasn't true at all. That he shouldn't have to just knuckle through one of his teammates being a jerk. It wasn't childish to be pissed off that a coworker was creating a hostile work environment.

I got it, though. Even if it was perfectly justified, it *felt* childish. Been there, done that, in the time between my breakup and when Daniel had gotten me fired.

I wished more than anything I could hug Trev right now. Being this far away when he was this out of sorts—that was frustrating.

Before I could say anything, Trev pressed back against the headboard and swallowed. "I think I'd be a lot less fucked up over this if I wasn't also struggling with being away from the kids."

Oh. *Oh.* Yeah. That would throw someone off the rails.

"I bet that's hard," I said, because I didn't know what else to say. "They're looking forward to you being home, though."

His smile wasn't even close to halfhearted. "They'll be at Bryan's when I get back."

My heart sank. "They will? Oh. Right. Yeah, they will."

Frowning, he nodded. "And they'll come back to my house just in time for me to go on another road trip."

"Jesus. Bryan won't let you adjust the custody agreement at all? Not even with this many road trips on top of each other?"

"Not without going back to court," he muttered. "And if we do that, I suspect he's going to try to angle for full custody."

"Do you think he'd get it?"

"Don't know." Trev looked right at me. "But I don't want to take the chance and find out."

"Oh. Yeah, I can understand that. At least it's only for half the year. Once the season's over, you'll be home."

"That's true. I just hope they can wait that long. Like they don't start thinking I'm—"

"They don't," I said gently. "Trust me."

His eyes begged me to mean that.

"They don't," I repeated. "They'll be thrilled when you get home. I promise."

At that, he grimaced. "It shouldn't be a novelty. Their dad being home. It's... I always felt guilty leaving them when I was on the road, but I feel even worse about it now. Not... Not because I have any issue with you. You're great with them and they adore you. But... I don't know. It's like these road trips where they're home with you—it feels like I'm even more of a failure. Or worse of a dad. Or... I don't know." His shoulders sagged and his voice wavered a little. "I used to leave them at home with their other dad. Now I take them away from Bryan *and* I leave them, and it's..." He trailed off again, sighing heavily.

"It makes you feel like you're not there enough," I whispered.

"I'm *not* there enough. And I mean it—it has nothing to do with you. You've been great for them, and you've been a lifesaver for me. But what kind of dad only gets his kids half the time, and then he's gone for half of *that* time?"

"A dad with a really demanding career and a cockweasel for an ex-husband, so you're doing the best you can to play a shitty hand?"

He managed a laugh at that. "Cockweasel, huh?"

I shrugged unrepentantly. "Am I wrong?"

"No. No, you're not wrong." His humor evaporated, and he stared at something off-camera with unfocused eyes. "Sometimes I feel like Bryan did this—the new custody arrangement, I mean—just to make the boys resent me."

"How do you mean?" I tilted my head. "Do you think he's trying to alienate them from you?"

"I mean... maybe?" Trev sighed. "But I worry he's hoping that eventually they won't want to come to my house anymore because I won't be there anyway. And then maybe I'll... I don't know, give up joint custody? Or the boys will ask him to let them stay with him more? I..." He rubbed the back of his neck. "Sometimes I think he would never be that vindictive. And then other times..."

I bit my tongue, because oh yeah, I could totally see Bryan being that vindictive.

"And then there's the part where his boyfriend is *such* an asshole." Trev pressed his head back against the padded headboard. "I don't *think* he says anything in front of the kids—from what I've seen, he's good with them. But then sometimes I worry he does and... I don't know. But when it's him and me? Or when we're around the team?" He rolled his eyes. "Like dude, okay, I get it—you got Bryan. I lost him." He waved a hand. "Whatever."

"Does he want you to fight him for Bryan or something?" I asked. "Like does he need you to be jealous?"

"I don't even know. Sometimes I think he's just trying to make me fuck up on the ice."

"Why would he do that? Doesn't it screw over his own team?"

"It does. But if I fall apart, they'll drop me to the bottom six and bump him to the second line."

I scowled. "That's a bit mercenary."

"No shit." Trev suddenly looked even more exhausted, his eyes losing focus as he quietly added, "Sometimes I think he's succeeding, too."

I schooled my expression so he didn't see my wince as

the commentators' remarks echoed in my mind. "Was he getting to you tonight?"

Trev laughed bitterly. "Was it that obvious?"

"I mean..." I half-shrugged. "I've watched you play enough to know when you're having a rough night."

"That's an understatement," he muttered. Then he shook himself and met my gaze. "I'll get it together. Tonight was a bad night, but I'll be okay."

"Okay. Well. If you're not, you know how to reach me."

"Thanks. I appreciate it. And thanks for talking to me tonight." He smiled weakly but genuinely. "I still feel like shit, but I feel better."

"So it's an upgrade from the shit you felt like earlier?"

That made him laugh. "Yes. Yes, a very nice upgrade. Thank you." Humor fading, he said, "I should let you go."

"Are you going to be able to sleep?"

He seemed to think about that. "Probably better than I would have if we hadn't talked."

"That's a start, right?"

The smile came back to life. "Yeah. It's a start. I'll take it."

"Works for me."

We ended the call a moment later. I lay back on my bed and stared up at the ceiling, my dark and silent phone resting in the middle of my chest. I hated seeing Trev this unhappy. And I hated that there was no escape from it. Even if Bryan and Tim split up, Trev would still be stuck with both of them in his life for the foreseeable future. Plus he'd still be dealing with the custody shitshow.

There'd been a time in my life when I'd have scoffed at the thought of sympathizing with a millionaire athlete. Especially recently when I'd had to move back in with my mom because I'd suddenly been without a job or a place to live.

Oh, you've got problems, Mr. Moneybags? Cry me a river, pal.

But tonight, the sweetest, most loving father I'd ever met was hurting because someone he'd tried to love was using their kids to make him miserable. He was stuck in an impossible situation with his ex, with his teammate, and with his boys. No amount of money could chase away that kind of pain.

Is it really too much to ask for Trev to catch a break?

CHAPTER 19

TREV

AFTER THE LAST GAME OF THAT THREE-GAME ROAD trip, our plane touched down in Pittsburgh at around four in the morning. I'd had just enough caffeine to keep me awake so I could drive home, and then I faceplanted in bed until my alarm went off. At least Coach had moved practice to noon instead of ten.

When I finally awoke, the house was painfully silent. For a moment, I thought maybe the kids were outside or otherwise playing quietly, but then I remembered they'd gone back to Bryan's yesterday. The day before? Hell, the days were all blurring together.

Damn. I hated these road trips that were during my custody week, and then got me home right before the boys went back to his place. I missed when we just went with the flow, and Bryan would let me take them if I was gone during my usual custody period. His hardass approach might've made things easier for him, but it meant I had to go long stretches without seeing the twins, and that was killing me.

Worse, I was worried the boys were resenting me. That

they thought I didn't *want* them here, or that I didn't care, or... something.

I closed my eyes and sighed. Well. This was a great train of thought to kick off the day.

I got up and shuffled in to take a shower. That helped a little, even though it gave my mind time to wander down some depressing tracks. By the time I was drying myself off, I'd resolved to text Bryan later and see if I could at least chat with the boys.

First things first... breakfast.

As I came downstairs, I didn't see Cam anywhere, but when I went to pour my coffee, I realized he was outside on the back deck.

And I was halfway across the deck before I realized he was wearing a pair of gym shorts and...

And that was it.

Though we were into October now, the summer heat was still hanging on, and apparently he intended to take full advantage while it lasted.

Oh my God. Nearly his entire incredible body was on full display. One look, and my brain went completely blank except for how much I wished I could trace my fingertips over every inch of him. Or my tongue. I wanted to—

I shook myself and looked away before I embarrassed myself.

Of course Cam picked that moment to twist around and look up at me. "Hey. How was the road trip?" He paused. "I mean... aside from your ex's dickcheese of a boyfriend."

I laughed dryly as I took a seat on one of the other deck chairs. "Aside from him and that one game, it was all right."

He smiled. "That's good."

I half-shrugged. "I got through it."

Cam studied me. "You okay?"

I nodded. "Yeah. Yeah. Just..." I wanted to say it was jetlag. And flying in stupidly late. And... something other than the truth. But this was Cam, and I could tell him the truth. As I gazed at my kids' scattered toys in the otherwise empty yard, and my shoulders sagged, and I wasn't sure I could hold back the truth if I wanted to. "Just sucks, being away from them and coming home just in time for them to go to Bryan's place."

He winced. "I figured that was still bothering you."

"Of course it is." I huffed a sharp, frustrated breath. "The only time I've seen my boys lately has been when Bryan brought them to a game, plus the *one* day I had with them before I hit the road." I fought back a surge of unwelcome emotions. "It fucking sucks."

"Yeah, it does. And it shouldn't be like that." He flailed a hand in the general direction of the road. "You guys live so close together—it's stupid that there can't be some flexibility."

"Right? And it's..." I pressed my lips together as I tried to gather my thoughts.

Cam tilted his head. "What?"

I thought about it a bit more, then sighed. "It's not just that I don't see them. It's who *does* see them. I'm gone all the time, *and* their dad's boyfriend hates me." I raked my hand through my hair and exhaled hard. "Their dad's not too crazy about me either. I'm just worried..." I chewed my lip, unsure how to finish.

Cam wasn't so hard up for words: "You're worried that'll rub off on the kids."

Wincing, I nodded. "Even if no one's talking trash, I mean..." I dropped my hand into my lap and held Cam's gaze. "The boys aren't stupid, you know? They can pick up on the tension. And the fact that I'm not around. Like... a lot."

He tilted his head. "Is that the core of the issue? Not that Bryan's camp is going to turn the boys on you, but you being gone?"

My throat tightened, and I avoided his eyes as I nodded again. "Especially now." My shoulders sagged. "What if they notice that when they come to my house for my custody weeks... I'm gone?" I looked at him through my lashes, and shame coiled around my heart as I whispered, "The way the hockey schedule is, they could go *weeks* between seeing me."

"That's not your fault, though," he said softly. "They know you have to go with the team."

"But what's it going to do to them when they keep coming over to my house and it's just you?" I winced. "I... I don't mean you're not—"

"I know what you mean." Cam's smile was gentle. "I get it. You're worried they're going to start feeling your absence more because you're gone when they're supposed to be with you."

I flinched and nodded.

He gave a quiet scoff. "Kind of have to wonder if that was Bryan's plan."

I stiffened. "You... picked up on that too?"

"Are you kidding?" Cam made a face and shook his head. "Who the fuck drops an ultimatum like that on their co-parent with almost no time to figure out a solution unless he *wants* you to fail?"

I sat back, startled to hear my own thoughts coming from his lips.

He tsked. "It's pretty fucking obvious, isn't it? I mean, if he wanted to actually work with you and figure out an arrangement that was best for the kids, he'd have given you some time. And he wouldn't have come up with an arrangement in the first place that meant your kids—your *six-year-old kids*—will have to be without one of their parents for long stretches at a time *just* because he wanted a more predictable schedule." Cam rolled his eyes and made a disgusted sound. "Nobody has kids because so they can have a predictable schedule."

I managed a halfhearted laugh. "Isn't that the truth."

"Right? And I mean, I could be biased because I don't like Bryan, I think he's a dickhole, and I hate how he treats you. But that's really how it looks to me."

I chewed my lip, not sure what to say. As much as I couldn't stand my ex-husband, I bent over backwards looking for ways to give him the benefit of the doubt when it came to his parenting. He *was* a good dad. But... maybe Cam was right. Bryan could be the world's greatest dad, but he was a shitty co-parent, and it was taking its toll.

"It sucks," I admitted. "Especially because there isn't much I can do. If this starts hurting my relationship with my sons..." I couldn't even finish the sentence because it hit me hard to imagine this whole shitshow—whether it was Bryan's deliberate sabotage or not—damaging the relationships I had with Zach and Zane.

Cam touched my arm. "Trev. I need you to listen to me, okay?" He sat up and faced me fully, his expression serious but not unkind.

With no idea where this was going, I nodded. "Okay?"

"When I first got here, you said you weren't sure if you were a good dad."

I swallowed, dropping my gaze. This was not something I wanted to think about on top of everything else. "Yeah. I did."

"Okay. Well. For what it's worth, your boys get super excited when I tell them you'll be FaceTiming with them soon."

I met his eyes. "They do?"

"Oh, yeah. Then when I say they can stay up and watch the game if they finish their homework, they sit down and do it without a single complaint." He motioned toward the door to the garage. "And whenever they hear your car after practice or a game, they go nuts that Dad's home."

My throat tightened, and I wasn't sure why.

"All those videos I send you?" he went on. "The pictures? Those are because the boys ask me to. Every single one."

I had to cough to get my breath moving. "They—really?"

"Yeah." Cam smiled. "They don't resent you for being gone. They miss you, and they wish you were home, but they know you're just doing your job."

I winced. "Doing my job, and not living with them even half the time. What kind of dad has their kids scrambling to make videos so he doesn't forget they're alive?"

Cam's lips parted. "What? No, it's *nothing* like that!"

I held his gaze, hoping like hell he'd elaborate, because I was dubious to say the least.

"Trev." He shook his head. "They *adore* you. No, I won't bullshit you and tell you they like it when you're gone. They miss you." He shrugged. "It is what it is. But they love talking with you. They..." He laughed softly. "My God, they get *so* excited when they watch you play hockey. Whether it's on TV or in person."

I swallowed hard. "Really?"

"Of course. Yeah, I'm sure they would love it if you and Bryan still lived together and you could be home 24/7, but that's because they love you, not because they think you're abandoning them."

I didn't know what to say to that. Or how to say it without falling apart, because his words had found their way to a tender spot I hadn't even known existed.

"No parent is perfect," he went on softly. "But the two people whose opinions matter the most think the world of you."

Fuck. He was going to make me cry. "Really?" I whispered.

"Really." He smiled and squeezed my arm. "Trust me."

I did trust him. It was hard to believe that the divorce and the distance hadn't tarnished my image in my kids' eyes, but Cam was not someone who'd blow smoke up my ass. If there was anyone on the planet I could trust to sit me down, look in the eye, and say, "Trevor, you need to unfuck things," it was him.

When he said my boys thought the world of me, I could take that to the bank.

Eyes stinging, I smiled. "Thanks. I... definitely needed to hear that."

"Any time. And I assume this means you want me to keep sending you all the pictures and videos they tell me to send?"

"Yes, please," I said. "Send them all."

"I will. I promise." He narrowed his eyes. "Including the ones of them imitating Spud the Sparrow, you motherfucker."

I barked a laugh, which felt *so* good. "Do it, and I'll steal your phone and change all your ringtones to Pirate Bob songs."

"Oh my God." He shook his head and rolled his eyes. "You're a dick."

"Eh. Don't act surprised."

"I'm not."

I chuckled, grateful for the levity that gave me a chance to pull myself together. The dam wasn't going to hold, but I wasn't going to collapse right here in front of my longtime friend.

Clearing my throat, I gestured over my shoulder. "I'm, uh... I need to go eat something. I've got practice at noon."

"Okay." Cam smiled that adorable smile that I'd missed so much. "You want me to throw something together?"

I didn't think I had the headspace to cook today, but I shook my head anyway. "Nah. I'll just grab something quick on my way. And it's your day off, so..."

He shrugged. "Day off or not, we're still basically roommates. If you want something, just say so."

Oh, I wanted something. But I didn't dare say it out loud.

And after our conversation, I was feeling a little too raw for that anyway. More than anything, I needed a moment to myself, so I quickly bowed out of the conversation to go upstairs.

Alone in my bedroom, I leaned against the door. Without Cam around to see or hear me, I couldn't hold back all those emotions that had been trying like hell to crash through, and I didn't try. I didn't even know why I was this emotional. I wasn't that kind of guy. Maybe I was just sleep-deprived. Maybe I just really, really missed my kids.

But I was pretty sure it was because what Cam had told me—it had shaken something loose in me.

"No parent is perfect, but the two people whose opinions matter the most think the world of you."

God. Cam. Way to hit me right in the feels.

For most of my life, I'd wanted nothing more than to be

the best hockey player I could be. For the past almost-seven years, all I'd wanted was to be the best dad possible to my two boys. More and more, I'd been terrified that for all I'd succeeded in becoming that hockey player, I was a failure as a father.

I couldn't make my marriage to their other dad work. I had to hire a nanny to fill in all the time I couldn't spend with them during my custody weeks. I saw them on Face-Time more than I saw them in person.

I was a fucking awful dad.

But maybe...

Maybe I'd been wrong.

They were excited to see me? They wanted Cam to send me videos of them? They missed me but didn't resent me?

God. Cam. I needed to hear that. I needed to hear it so damn bad. It hurt to hear it, but it also fixed a lot of cracks that had been driving me insane.

Leaning against my bedroom door, I wiped my eyes and tried to catch my breath, not that it did much good.

This wasn't the first time I'd cried since my divorce.

But it was the first time they'd been tears of pure, bone-deep relief.

CHAPTER 20

CAM

I was glad to put Trev's mind at ease. He deserved to know how much his kids loved him and how little Bryan and Tim were succeeding at undermining him (because if that wasn't what they were doing, I was the fucking Pope).

But there was something about the interaction that left me a little... uncomfortable.

Not the conversation itself. That had been fine.

The issue was when he'd been walking out to join me. My phone screen had picked up his reflection, and I'd taken that moment to shamelessly ogle him...

Which had given me the opportunity to realize he was looking at me strangely. And to notice how he quickly looked *away* before he sat down to talk with me.

It wasn't the first time that had happened since I'd moved in, and it was... weird.

It was especially weird when I thought about how sometimes he'd see me before or after a game, and he'd pause like he was... I don't know, surprised to see me? He knew I'd be there, though. Or like something about seeing me threw him off-balance? I couldn't figure it out, and though I wanted to give him the benefit of the doubt, I wasn't sure I liked it.

I was probably reading way too much into it because I was used to Daniel. I'd spent a lot of time seriously on edge around him because a sidelong glance could mean he was getting ready to tell me I'd pissed him off somehow. Or avoiding looking at me usually meant there was a fight brewing. About what, I wouldn't have a clue until he finally blew up at me. I'd just have to walk on eggshells and worry myself sick until he finally told me if I'd loaded the dishwasher wrong, hadn't been putting out enough, or had committed some cardinal sin I didn't even know would bother him.

That was probably it. I had no idea why Trev looked at me the way he did, or why he sometimes seemed startled to see me even though he knew I was there. I couldn't explain it.

But my twitchiness about it probably had a lot more to do with Daniel than with Trev. Which meant it wasn't fair to get annoyed with Trev or be suspicious.

Brushing off those thoughts as best I could, I threw on a pair of sweats and an old T-shirt, and came back downstairs to join him in the kitchen. He was topping off a travel mug with coffee, and when he met my gaze with a smile, there was a hint of telltale redness in his eyes. That honestly didn't surprise me since we'd been getting into some tough emotional territory earlier. A few times, he'd looked like he was ready to lose it right then and there; that he'd made it into the house was probably a small miracle. That was why I'd tossed in a joke to give him a chance to collect himself—I knew him well enough to pick up that he'd been fighting hard to keep his emotions from spilling over.

I didn't acknowledge any of that out loud. He'd be

embarrassed if he knew I'd caught on that he'd probably been crying earlier.

I hated that, but he was probably still raw, and any assurances that "dude, guys can cry—we all do" wouldn't help much.

So, I just pretended not to notice.

"You heading out?" I asked.

Nodding, he screwed the lid onto his mug. "Yeah, in a minute. And I'll be back in time for dinner if you want to eat together. We're reviewing film after practice, though, so I'll be at the training facility for a while."

"Cool. We'll figure something out. I hadn't thought that far ahead."

"Me neither." He sipped his coffee. "There's like five games on tonight if you want to watch one."

"Hell yeah. Who's playing?"

"Um..." Trev took out his phone and frowned as he scrolled something on the screen. "Let's see... Houston at San Jose, New York at Seattle, Vancouver at Montreal, Detroit at—ooh, Detroit's playing Atlanta. That's guaranteed to be a fun game."

"Oh yeah? They rivals or something?"

"They've knocked each other out of the playoffs every year for the past five years. Detroit's beaten them three times. Atlanta's swept them twice." He grimaced. "Things get *heated* when they meet up."

I whistled. "I bet. Sounds like fun!"

"Perfect." He put his phone in the island beside his coffee. "Maybe we can indulge in a pizza or something while we watch."

"Ooh, sign me up." I chuckled and gestured over my shoulder toward the basement stairs. "I'll just put in an extra half hour in the gym so I don't feel guilty about it."

Something flickered across his face, but before I could parse it, he cleared his throat and said, "I don't think you really need to feel guilty, do you?"

"No. And I encourage my clients not to because..." I waved a hand. "Toxic relationships with food and exercise and all that." With a quiet laugh, I added, "But I also know how quickly and easily I'll slide into eating less-than-healthy and being lazy at the gym, so..." I half-shrugged. "I just try to stay on top of it."

"Fair enough. I have to do that during the off season."

"You? Really?" It took all I had not to rake my eyes up and down his gorgeous body. Even in a hoodie and track pants, he was still lean and *smoking* hot.

He laughed softly. "We burn like two thousand calories per game, and that doesn't include practice and off-ice workouts. So it's really, really easy to get into the habit of 'eh, I can eat whatever the fuck I want because I'll be burning it off later.' I try to eat the way I'm supposed to, but not gonna lie: by the end of the season—especially the end of the playoffs—I'm definitely slacking."

"With all the traveling you do? I'm not surprised."

"Oh, it's not just traveling." He sipped his coffee again. "I just get lazy." He flashed me a grin that had no business making my spine tingle. "With a personal trainer living with me, maybe I'll stay on top of things."

"As we both order pizza tonight."

"Eh." He shrugged.

I chuckled. We'd be fine. I really did encourage my clients to cultivate healthy relationships with food and exercise, and it didn't do anyone any good to obsess over it. Treating food as a reward and exercise as a punishment was a recipe for disaster. But I was pretty sure we could find some balance between eating and working out during his off season.

I leaned against the island. "So, you said you're doing film review today? What do you guys even do for that? Just watch your old games or something?"

"We do that, but mostly, we're watching the team we'll be playing next. Which, in this case, is Salt Lake City." He grimaced. "They've got one of the best power plays in the League, and there's already rumors that their goalie will get the netminder MVP award."

"Whoa. So... tough team to play against."

"Very." Then he snickered. "One of my teammates— Hoes? He does voices while we're watching them sometimes."

"Yeah?"

Grinning, Trev nodded. "Drives our video coach nuts, but it's kind of hard for him to tell Hoes to knock it off when even he's laughing so hard he can't speak."

"So, even at this level, you're all still just a bunch of kids who goof off in class."

He quirked his lips, then shrugged. "Pretty much, yeah."

"No wonder you love it so much."

"Guilty."

We both laughed. After a moment, though, he sobered, and he met my gaze. "By the way—thanks. For what you said..." He tilted his head to indicate the deck outside. "I've been having a really tough time. About everything with the kids. So... I needed to hear that."

I smiled. "Any time. I think anyone would be a mess right now. Playing tug-of-war with your ex over your kids..." I wrinkled my nose. "That's going to fuck with anyone's head, you know?"

Letting his shoulders drop, he sighed. "Yeah. Because no matter what we do, they're stuck in the middle. I'm just glad they don't resent me as much as they probably should."

"Trev." I shook my head. "They don't, and they shouldn't. Yeah, they might have some complicated feelings about the divorce, especially as they get older, but I think they can see as well as anyone that you're doing the best you can."

"God, I hope so," he whispered.

I couldn't handle seeing him that upset, so I stepped closer and hugged him. As I pulled him in tight, I said, "Trust me. They love you. And no parent is perfect, you know?" I stroked his hair. "You're doing fine."

Trev sighed heavily and held me against him. "Thank you."

"Don't mention it." After a long moment, I loosened my embrace, and we pulled apart.

And whatever I was going to say next—because I'd had something on the tip if my tongue—fell away when I met those familiar, stunning brown eyes.

Holy shit, you're the most beautiful man I've ever seen.

When I recovered from my two-second mental record-scratch, I realized...

He'd locked eyes with me too. And he'd tensed as if he'd been startled. Or his own train of thought had derailed.

My heart was beating hard, and with my chest still touching his, I had to wonder if he could feel it. Or if his was doing the same.

Was he...

Were we...

His eyes flicked to my mouth, that subtle gesture flooding my brain with memories of our past life, and holy shit, I wanted one of us to work up the courage to lean in and—

An alarm on his phone screamed to life.

We jumped apart, both gasping. He snatched the phone off the kitchen island and swore under his breath as he silenced it.

"Damn it," he whispered. Then he met my gaze with apologetic eyes. "I, uh... I have to go."

"Right. Yeah." I cleared my throat. "Don't be late for practice."

"I won't." He laughed, and was I imagining how nervous he sounded? "Uh... dinner and watching a game when I get back?"

"Sure. Yeah. Sounds great."

He flashed me a quick smile. Then he left the kitchen.

I let out a breath, both frustrated and relieved that the moment had passed. Just as my heartrate was starting to tick down, though, I noticed Trev's travel mug on the island.

"Shit!" I grabbed it and jogged toward the door.

Just as I was getting to it, he was coming back in, and we nearly collided, which almost sent the coffee cup flying. Somehow, we both stayed on our feet, and I kept my grip on the mug.

"You uh..." I held it up. "You forgot something."

He laughed, and was he blushing? Oh fuck me, he was blushing. "Thanks," he said as he took it. "Now I won't pass out on the ice."

We both chuckled, and he left for real this time.

Alone in the hallway, I leaned against the wall and closed my eyes. God, I was so confused. One minute, I was weirded out by the way he looked at me when he didn't think I'd notice. The next, we were bantering like old times.

And the one after that, we were so close, looking at each other like we might—

No. That wasn't who we were. Not anymore. I was working for him and helping him out of a jam his ex had put him into. *He* was helping *me* out of a jam that *my* ex had put me into.

Everything else? That was high school. A pair of clueless teenage dumbasses marinating in too many hormones. We were adults now. Friends. Employer and employee, if I really wanted to keep the lines clear.

We both needed each other too much right now to indulge in the kind of recklessness.

Not even if Trev's eyes had told me he wanted it as much as I did.

Like almost every kid I knew growing up—well, aside from Trev, who'd been deeply ensconced in hockey by kindergarten—I played soccer in elementary school. Only two seasons, though. My parents had signed me up for the first season because every kid I knew was playing and I'd wanted to join. Then they'd put me in for the second because, "You're still learning—once you get the hang of it, it'll be a lot more fun!" and "You wanted to play—you can't possibly hate it that much."

They were wrong. I *had* hated it that much, and there'd been no third season. Soccer was awful and boring and stupid, and I wanted no part of it. As a teenager, when some self-righteous classmate had informed me I was going to Hell (I don't recall why, it could've been any number of things), I'd snarked that if she was right, that probably meant an eternity being forced to play soccer.

Years later, I still thought any hell for me would be soccer-oriented, but I'd revised my stance a little. Rather than playing the awful sport for all eternity, I would instead be condemned to stand on the sidelines and make small talk with parents while we watched *other* people play soccer.

I demand a raise.

Again? What now?

I replied with a photo of the soccer game.

LOL You still hate soccer, don't you?

(grimacing emoji)

LOLOLOL Hey it could be worse.

How?

They could be playing hockey. YOU would be the one airing out all their gear. (gagging emoji)

But I wouldn't have to watch soccer.

No but you'd have to deal with the smell of hockey gear.

Still not really seeing the downside if soccer is the alternative.

OMG stop being so dramatic. At least it's only like an hour. Football games are 3 business days long.

I swear to God if you get these children into football while I'm employed (knife emoji)

Worse than soccer?

(knife emoji)

LOL brb registering them for football.

You're a dick.

(halo emoji)

I chuckled as I lowered my phone and shifted my attention back to the field. Zach was on his way out with two other forwards. In the goal, Zane was laser-focused on the activity in front of him—poised and ready for action, but calm and collected.

"It's a good thing they play different positions," one of the moms, Sheryl, said to me. "I don't know how you'd tell them apart otherwise."

I laughed. "Well, the numbers on their jerseys..."

"Still. If you can't see the number..." She waved a hand.

She did have a point. Admittedly, I was grateful Zane wore the bright blue goalie jersey while Zach and the other players wore yellow. I was getting better at being able to tell the boys apart, but it was definitely easier when they were dressed for soccer.

And that was probably the one and *only* concession I would *ever* make in favor of this sport. Everything else about it could go straight to hell.

Another mom appeared beside me. "So which one is yours?"

"Oh. Uh." I scanned the field. "The goalie, and number—"

"Oh! You're here with the hockey player's twins!"

"Yeah." I didn't know why my face got hot. "I'm their nanny."

That seemed to slightly short-circuit her brain, though

she recovered quickly, and we made that excruciating small talk that soccer parents did. I wondered if it bothered her, the kids having a male nanny. I'd definitely encountered some people who were weird about it. Most didn't seem to care, though.

Maybe they didn't think anything of it. Or maybe they were just glad Bryan wasn't here.

The thought made me chuckle, but I kept it to myself.

After a period of time during which empires had probably risen and fallen, the ref blew the whistle. Both teams trotted toward their respective sides of the field, and a mom opened up a container of orange slices. The kids grabbed handfuls of oranges along with their water bottles, and they snacked while they listened to their coach giving them a pep talk.

"You looked good out there," she told them. "In the next half, let's work on not letting them take away the ball, okay?"

The next half?

The next—

Wait. It was halftime. Fucking hell—it was only *halftime*?

Jesus. I was going to be here until I was seventy, wasn't I?

The coach's pep talk wrapped up, and the players focused on eating, hydrating, and talking to each other. I checked in on the boys, making sure they had enough water and they both had some orange slices. They were far more interested in hanging out with their friends than talking to me, so I left them to it.

Still keeping an eye on them, I texted their dad again.

It's only halftime. I just sat through eternity, and now I have to sit through it AGAIN?

I heard they're thinking of making it like hockey. Three periods instead of two.

You won't be able to afford me if that happens.

(violin emoji)

(middle finger emoji)

As much as I hated soccer, I did enjoy this part—the snarky texts with Trev. It was something we'd started doing as soon as we'd gotten our first phones, and I hadn't realized how much I'd missed it until we'd picked it up again.

I knew I wouldn't be Zach and Zane's nanny forever. This job definitely had a shelf life. And that was fine.

But God help me, even after I found another job, I was never letting this friendship slip through my fingers again.

CHAPTER 21

TREV

I HAD A RARE DAY OFF FROM ALL THINGS HOCKEY, AND the boys were with Bryan, so I spent it being as lazy as humanly possible. I slept in. I spent a solid hour scrolling my phone in bed. I indulged in a late breakfast delivered from a nearby café. There wasn't a lot of downtime like this during the regular season, so I made sure to take full advantage. I wished I could've spent it with my kids, but I tried not to dwell on that. They'd be back soon.

Even while I had a lazy day, I did still like to keep up on my workouts, so I spent some time in my home gym. Nothing too strenuous, of course. A good run on the treadmill, some low-intensity weightlifting, and maybe another twenty minutes on the bike. Then I could figure out what to do with the evening.

I was maybe fifteen minutes into my twenty-minute run when the stairs creaked. I bit back a curse; Cam was coming in, wasn't he? And I doubted he was just here to ask me a question or something.

I was right—he was wearing shorts and sneakers and carrying a towel, which meant he was here to work out.

Oh God. Do you have any idea how distracting you are like this?

I didn't say a word, though. We exchanged smiles as he got on the elliptical beside the treadmill I was on, but neither of us spoke. As he got started, I stared straight ahead, focusing on the yard, the windows, a spiderweb in a tree—anything but the gorgeous man beside me.

I both loved and hated seeing him work out, especially when he wasn't wearing a shirt. I didn't want to stare at him and make things weird. At the same time, I didn't want to take my eyes off him. He was just so...

My God, Cameron. Do you have any idea how sexy you are?

Maybe he did, maybe he didn't, but I sure did. And it was killing my concentration.

At least I was almost done on the treadmill, and when the timer went off, I whispered a prayer of thanks as I shut off the machine. Then I moved to the lat pulldown.

Which... only made things worse.

Because I had arranged this gym without giving any thought to the possibility that my incredibly hot best friend would be using it with me, and the lat pulldown was facing the elliptical.

Which was currently occupied by Cam.

Shirtless Cam with his powerful back and shoulders on full display, not to mention his legs. And those gym shorts weren't doing a whole lot to make his ass look any less appealing.

As he moved, sweat rolled down his back, sliding along the grooves between his sculpted muscles. It traced the edges of some of his tattoos. Made others glow as if they were freshly inked.

And of course, I knew from experience that if he were

facing me, I'd see sweat gleaming on his chest, too, and the barbells in his nipples would catch the light, and—

I had to tear my gaze away from him. Jesus, I was going to embarrass myself one of these days, wasn't I? Drop a weight. Trip over my own feet. Something.

Fuck it. I couldn't concentrate, and I was going to lose my form and hurt myself.

Fine. I could cut my workout short, then make up for it later tonight or at the training center tomorrow. I needed to get out of here before I hurt myself or embarrassed us both.

I cleared my throat as I got up. "I'll, uh... I'm going to head upstairs."

"Already?" He turned to me. "Taking an easy day?"

"Yeah. Yeah, something like—it's my day off, you know?" I forced a laugh. "Might as well enjoy it."

He eyed me as if he saw right through to my internal freakout. Then he shrugged. "Okay."

I nodded sharply and headed for the door, eager to make my escape.

I didn't get far, though.

"Trev. Look at me."

There was a sharp edge to his voice that caught me off guard, and I turned to him. He stepped off the elliptical and faced me. His expression was closed off, but something in his eyes echoed that sharpness. He absently dried his hands on the towel he was holding, and he kept his gaze fixed right on me.

I inclined my head, silently asking what was going on.

His eyes narrowed a little. "I need to know something. And don't bullshit me."

I showed my palms. "Okay. Sure. What's on your mind?"

He studied me for a painfully long moment, then asked

in a flat voice, "Does it bother you that I work out without a shirt on?"

I stiffened. "What? Why would it—what makes you think it bothers me?"

"I don't know. You just seem..." He chewed his lip, and he held his towel against his chest, as if making a subtle attempt to cover up. "The way you look at me when I'm working out, or whenever I don't have a shirt on. You just don't seem comfortable whenever I'm..."

"Oh. Fuck." Shame, embarrassment, and horror swept through me. Shaking my head, I said, "No. No, it's—it doesn't bother me in the least."

Cam's brow knitted as he watched me, his eyes asking me, *So then what's the problem?*

I thought fast, but every possible attempt I could think of to sidestep the truth just made me certain he'd feel more uncomfortable and self-conscious. He knew damn well I'd been in locker rooms with naked men almost daily for years, so why should I be bothered by a shirtless guy on a treadmill?

Honesty was risky because I might embarrass myself and look like an idiot, and it might make things supremely awkward between us. Still, it was the only approach that didn't have the potential to hurt his feelings or make him think I saw anything wrong with him or his body.

So... fuck it.

I took a deep breath and pretended my heart wasn't slamming against my ribs. "I have no problem with you working out shirtless. Or doing *anything* shirtless. None at all." I swallowed hard. "It's just, whenever I see you like that, it completely scrambles my brain because—God, Cam." I had to fight the urge to look him up and down. "You're fucking *hot*."

Cam's lips parted. "Come again?"

Frustration and embarrassment vied for dominance in my chest, and I couldn't look him in the eye as I repeated, "You're fucking hot."

"I..." He shifted a little, the squeak of his sneakers giving away the subtle movement. "Are you serious?"

"Yes." I made myself look into his disbelieving eyes. "You've always been cute. You've always been attractive. But the way you are now..." I indulged in that impulse to look him up and down, and when I met his gaze again, I rasped, "I wasn't avoiding looking at you because you made me uncomfortable. It's because every time I look at you, I forget how to think."

He stared at me. "You... Are you saying you want me?"

I pushed out a breath, my heart pounding so hard he *had* to be able to hear it. "Yes. More than I've wanted anyone in..." I shook my head. "More than I think I've ever wanted anyone."

For long seconds, he was still and silent. Eyes wide. Lips parted.

When he finally broke the standoff, he didn't speak. He didn't make a sound.

He closed the distance between us, curved a hand behind my neck and—

Oh, God. Yes.

There wasn't a trace of tentativeness in his kiss. The shyness of the first kiss we'd shared as kids—his first kiss and mine—was a distant memory, replaced by this assertive confidence that made my knees shake. He wasn't forceful or aggressive, but holy shit, he knew what he wanted and he took it without question.

I fucking melted. Wrapping my arms around him, I couldn't help but whimper into his kiss. When he teased my lips, I opened them, welcoming his tongue into my mouth.

I'd never been kissed like this. Not once in my whole goddamned life. Never like I was exactly what this man craved. Never like he knew this was exactly what *I* craved, and he was going to give me all this and more.

Yes, please, baby. Fuck yes.

There was no hiding how turned on I was, either, and Cam clearly wasn't bothered by it. He pressed against me, grinding against my thickening hard-on, and my head spun even faster. Oh yeah, my libido had definitely returned with a vengeance, and I wanted Cam so bad it almost literally hurt. Now that I had his gorgeous body against me and his talented mouth working mine—fuck, I'd never been one to go off in my pants, but there was a first time for everything.

Cam drew back and stared up at me with wide eyes. He was panting. So was I. His hand was still firmly on the back of my neck, and I wanted his damn mouth again.

"Does that..." I paused to catch my breath. "Does that answer your question?"

"Uh-huh." He sounded as dazed as I felt. "Yeah. Yeah, it does." He swept his tongue across his swollen lips. "Now I feel like an asshole for thinking you were—"

I cut him off with a soft kiss. "No. I'm the one who made you self-conscious because I was too stupid to—"

And *he* cut *me* off with a kiss. Grinning, he said, "Why don't we just agree that on some level, we're both still the same dumbasses we were in high school?"

I laughed. "I can get onboard with that." I bit my lip. "I, uh... I really didn't mean to make you think I was—"

"It's fine." He laughed and shook his head. "I should've known you of all people..." He waved a hand. "Anyway.

We're good now." His eyes narrowed a little as he drew me back in. "Like, *really* good."

"You're not kidding," I murmured just before he claimed my mouth. God, I loved the way he kissed now. All the tentativeness from our younger years was a distant memory—he was assertive bordering on aggressive, and he seemed to know exactly what to do with his lips and tongue to make my knees weak.

Is this real? Am I really kissing you? Holy shit, this is real.

I'd been worried that his half-naked body would get me embarrassingly hard, but it definitely wasn't embarrassing now. Not when I pressed my erection against him and he responded with a low moan.

Oh, fuck yeah.

Then Cam drew back again, and when he looked down at himself, he made a face. "Ugh. I'm disgusting. If we're going to—I should... I need to get a shower."

I licked my lips. "Any chance you want some company?"

Cam's eyes widened. "If, um..." He swallowed, raking his eyes over me. When he met my gaze again, he said, "If we get in the shower together, we're going to end up in bed."

"Sounds to me like a feature, not a bug."

His eyebrows flicked up. "Yeah?"

"Uh-huh." I slid my hands up his back. "When I say I want you—I mean it. Completely."

Cam gulped. "So if I said that after we shower, I want you to dick me down until I can't move, you'd be game?"

All the air rushed out of my lungs as a shiver went through me. "Keep talking like that, and I'll fuck you over a bench right here in the gym."

He bit his lip, a gesture that had no business being that

sexy. His eyes were beautiful anyway, and now they were absolutely on fire with need. "That's... not much of a deterrent, you know."

"Fuck," I whispered. "No, it's really not, is it?"

"No. It isn't."

"So." I tipped my head toward the stairs. "Shower?"

His grin said it all.

I'd go to my grave wondering how we made it upstairs, out of our clothes, and into my shower. I was lucky I could walk, never mind navigate stairs, but somehow, we got here without one of us falling or something.

And now, every fantasy I ever had blinked out of existence because nothing—fucking *nothing*—stacked up to holding Cam's sculpted, naked body against mine. Hot water rushed over both of us, and we managed to soap up and rinse off, but we were mostly focused on kissing and touching. My cock was rock hard between us, and every time Cam moved, the friction almost drove me out of my damn mind.

"I don't even know where to start," he breathed. "I just... God, I want you."

Goose bumps sprang up all over my skin beneath the rushing water. "Me too. And this is—I mean, this is a pretty good start, right?"

"Yeah, but..." Cam licked his lips. "I just want to do everything, you know?" He slid his hand between us, down over my dick, and my moan almost drowned out his whisper of, "I've been fantasizing about you so much since I got here."

I rocked my hips, fucking against his palm because I was

desperate for friction. "Me... Me too. And I swear, I've got stamina, but I'm probably going to come way, way too soon."

The wicked grin that curled his lips almost made that prophecy come true right then and there. "Can you come more than once?"

I gulped. "I mean, after I've recharged a bit, yeah."

"Good." He nudged me back a step, and I hissed when my shoulder blades hit the cool wall.

And in my split second of distraction, Cam went to his knees.

Suddenly the wall was the only thing keeping me upright as his talented lips and tongue enveloped my dick.

"Holy shit," I ground out, staring own at him. I wanted to enjoy the view—drink in the sight of his naked body and wet hair and his lips around me cock, but I'd been teetering on the edge before his knees had touched the floor. "Oh my God. Cam, I'm..."

I couldn't help rocking my hips a little, and that moan—that thrum of his voice around the head of my dick—took me there in an instant. I managed to brace against the wall and shout "I'm coming!" a heartbeat before he definitely *knew* I was coming, and he kept pumping me as I unloaded in his tongue.

My knees almost shook out from under me. I had no idea what kind of nonsense tumbled out of my mouth as I came in Cam's, but holy shit, I was surprised I didn't pass out or something.

And at least the heat of the shower probably masked some of my blush. I had *never* gone off that fast. Not even our first time together, and that was saying something.

Slumping against the wall, I tried to catch my breath and not die of embarrassment, especially as Cam rose.

"That was hot as hell," he purred.

"What?" I laughed nervously. "Me going off in two seconds flat?"

"Turning you on so much that you came that fast," he said as he draped his arms around my neck. "I *love* doing that to you."

Then he had my mouth, the taste of my own cum on his tongue making my head spin even faster.

Christ. I'd come, but I was still so turned on I couldn't see straight.

I slid my hands down over his perfect ass and murmured, "I promise, I'll last longer the second time around."

"I figured." He grinned against my lips. "And I doubt this will be the last time I blow you, so..."

"Oh my God," I whispered, shivering between him and the wall. "Please tell me I'm not imagining this."

"Not unless we're sharing a hallucination."

"That would be a feat." I put my hands on his waist and turned him, nudging him against the wall. "But it wouldn't be a fair if only I got off, right?"

Cam bit his lip, arching off the wall. "Yeah? What do you have in mind?"

"Standing up is kind of awkward for oral," I said, sliding my hand down to his hip. "And it's a good way to break our necks if we try to fuck."

The laugh that burst out of him made me almost as dizzy as my orgasm had. Holy hell, this man was gorgeous. "Yeah, shower sex is... hazardous."

"Mmhmm. But you always liked when I used my fingers before." I raised my eyebrows.

He whimpered softly. "Uh-huh. I did."

"It's been a while, though. You might have to guide me a little."

"Just be gentle and slow."

I grinned. "Okay, *that* much I remember."

"Good." He guided my hand between his legs, which was all the green light I needed.

It had been a long, long time, and we'd both been clumsy and clueless back then, but with some trial and error, I'd learned to get him off. And it turned out, some things were just like riding a bike.

"Oh God..." He closed his eyes and pressed back against the wall, rolling his hips as I made light circles with my fingertips. "Fuck..."

"That good?"

Eyes still squeezed shut, he nodded. "Y-yeah. Oh my God..."

Maybe we should've waited until we were in bed, because I wasn't so sure I could hold myself up. The rush I got from turning him on like this made my knees weak and almost turned my spine to liquid.

I'd manage, though. Whatever it took to keep him moaning and trembling like that.

I pressed my other forearm against the wall for balance, and I found his mouth with mine. His kiss was less deliberate and calculated this time, but no less intense —it was messy and needy, breathless and hungry. He gripped my shoulder in one hand, my hair in the other, and every whimper and moan vibrated across my lips and made the whole room spin. I was barely even aware of the hot water anymore. Nothing existed except Cam getting hotter and hotter as I teased him and kissed him and held him and—

Fuck, I couldn't believe this was real. That he'd kissed me in the gym. That he'd dropped to his knees and blown me. That I was fingering him closer and closer to oblivion.

That I might... Oh my God, I might get to hear and feel and make him come right here, right now, in my shower.

I broke the kiss and touched my forehead to his. "You are so fucking hot," I slurred. "Jesus, Cam."

He clawed at my shoulders, trembling hard between me and the wall as he rutted against my fingers. "I want to come. And... I want you to fuck me. I'm..." He trailed off into a moan.

"I'll absolutely fuck you," I said hoarsely. "Any way you want it."

The strangled sound he made was too damn sexy for words. His fingernails dug into my shoulders, and he shuddered hard, arching off the wall as he whined, "Oh my God..."

I stared at him, utterly mesmerized as he started to fall apart in my arms. That I was the one doing this to him— blew my damn mind.

"Let me see you come," I pleaded. "Fuck yeah, baby, let me—"

He gasped, and then cried out, his voice echoing off the marble walls as he bucked between me and the wall, rubbing hard against my fingers and swearing and nearly falling to pieces.

If I hadn't already come myself, I'd have gone off from this alone. No fantasy, no porno, no prior experience— nothing held a candle to Cam unraveling into oblivion in my arms.

With a harsh, ragged breath, Cam slumped against the wall, panting and trembling, still holding my shoulders in a painful death grip. "Holy shit..."

"That is so hot," I murmured.

He grinned and kissed me lightly. "You're telling me. I was the one coming."

"I know. And I want you to be the one coming again."

Cam bit his lip. "Good thing neither of us has anywhere to be today, isn't it?"

"Uh-huh. Good thing." I reached back and turned off the water. Without the rush of the shower, my voice echoed in the suddenly silent bathroom. "How about we move this into the bedroom so I can fuck you?"

Cam closed his eyes and shivered as if the question alone had reignited his orgasm. When he opened them again, they were full of fire as he rasped, "Bedroom. Now."

CHAPTER 22

CAM

WE MADE IT AS FAR AS STARTING TO DRY OFF BEFORE we were all over each other again. Still dripping from the shower, we leaned against the cold bathroom counter and made out as if an orgasm apiece hadn't done a thing to calm us down. I usually needed some time to recover, same as he did—one of those things I'd had to get used to once I'd started taking T—but I was raring to go already. Still too sensitive for him to try getting me off again, at least for a little while, but this? Kissing and dragging our hands all over each other's bodies? Oh yeah, I could handle this.

We were still wet, though, and we finally separated long enough to towel off. I didn't mind, especially because it gave me an amazing view of his beautiful naked body. I couldn't help raking my eyes up and down him, marveling at the incredible things professional hockey had done to his physique. He had the six-pack abs my clients could've killed for—not the hard-edged look of someone who'd dehydrated themselves for a photo shoot, but the smooth contours between the toned muscles. His whole body was lean and toned and chiseled—every inch the professional athlete. There were also some bruises of varying ages, which was pretty normal for a hockey player.

He wasn't erect at the moment, but I'd been up close and personal enough with his hard-on both in the past and today to know exactly how much he was packing. While his body was extraordinary, absolutely fitness magazine material, his cock was completely average—fucking perfect as far as I was concerned.

I'd been fantasizing about getting drilled by him because I missed good sex, because I wanted Trev in particular... and because what could I say? Between his size and the powerful muscles in his legs and ass, I knew without a doubt it was going to be the fuck of my life.

Yes, please. Please, please, please.

He glanced at me, and then our eyes locked, and he grinned. His expression reflected the same lust and surprise that still heated my blood. I wanted him so bad I could barely see straight, and I still couldn't believe we were here. I couldn't believe that just a few minutes ago, I'd knelt at his feet, taken his cock between my lips, and swallowed his cum. Or that he'd fingered me into the stratosphere. Or that we were anything but finished fooling around.

He tossed his towel aside and stepped closer, wrapping me up in those strong arms as he kissed me. He had a couple of inches on me, but not so much that we had to strain to kiss while we were standing. We fit together almost perfectly, and I loved it.

And I loved that this man—Trevor Allen—was the one holding and kissing me. I'd misread him so badly in the gym, and I felt awful for that.

Drawing back, I looked into those beautiful brown eyes. "I'm sorry, by the way. For thinking... in the gym..."

He blinked as if he wasn't sure what I was talking about,

but he quickly caught up. "No, it's okay." He carded his fingers through my hair. "I'm sorry I made you think I didn't want to see you like that. Because holy shit, I definitely do."

I grinned and pulled him in closer. "I think we're on the same page now."

"Mmhmm, we definitely are." He slid his hands down my back and over my ass, and he murmured, "Oh my God..."

I concurred; I couldn't remember the last time someone had made me feel so sexy. Or the last time I'd wanted someone this much.

"We're on the same page," I whispered. "Maybe we should get on the same piece of furniture?"

He laughed softly. "Good idea. Then I won't have to concentrate so much about keeping my balance."

Ah, so we were *definitely* on the same page.

In the bedroom, he pulled back the covers, and I climbed into his enormous bed. Instead of going around to the other side, he came in after me, wrapping an arm around my midsection and pulling us close together. Heat rushed through me as his lips skated up my spine and his hardening dick pressed against my ass.

"I've been going nuts with you in the house," he murmured against the back of my neck. "From the day you got here, I've wanted..." He pulled his hips and my ass flush together, his cock thickening between my thighs. "Would you be offended if I told you I've jerked off thinking about you?"

I didn't even recognize the helpless sound that escaped my throat. "'Offended' isn't the word I'd use." I covered his hand with mine and squeezed my thighs together to give him some friction. "What did you think about when you were jerking off?"

"Everything," he rumbled. In between kissing the side of my neck, he went on, "I came so damn hard the other night. Just... thinking about... God, just thinking about *you*."

I closed my eyes and squirmed. "Yeah?"

"Mmhmm." The arm around my midsection tightened as his hot breath rushed past my neck. He kissed along my hairline, his cock still moving slowly but rhythmically between my thighs. "I'm not kidding when I say I came hard. Surprised I didn't black out."

Christ, I loved hearing all that arousal and need in his voice.

Some uncertainty crept in, though, and he asked, "That isn't weird, is it? That I was thinking about you and..."

"Not at all." I twisted around to find his mouth with mine. "Especially not after I've been doing the same thing."

His fingers twitched on my skin. "Oh yeah? And what have *you* been thinking about?"

"Mostly you fucking me." I rolled over to face him fully. "The details don't matter. I just really, really want..." I trailed my fingertips along the underside of his hard-on, drawing sighed profanity from his mouth.

"You really do want to get dicked down, don't you?"

"Like you wouldn't believe."

He laughed, but there was a hint of uneasiness in his expression.

I touched his face. "What?"

"I, uh..." He hesitated. "Listen, I don't want to hit the brakes or kill the mood or anything, but..." He looked at me shyly. "The last time we did anything like this, it was before you transitioned."

I nodded. "Yeah, it was. And it was back when we were young and stupid."

"That too. And I still remember what you liked back

then, but if anything's changed—anything you don't want me doing or touching, or that you like now that you didn't before—I'm all ears."

I smiled, running my fingers down the middle of his chest. "I need more time to recharge in between orgasms now. And there's some positions I don't like now, but that has more to do with my back than anything."

Trev's eyebrows flicked up. "You hurt your back?"

"Jacked it up a little a few years ago." I rolled my eyes. "Got lazy about my form while I was deadlifting, and I'm still paying for it."

He made a face. "Ouch. So certain positions..."

"I mean, I can do the usual. Nothing super acrobatic. But like, my back can get a little bitchy when I'm on top for a long time."

That brought a quiet laugh out of him, and he relaxed a bit. "Well, that probably won't be an issue."

"Oh yeah?"

He nodded. "Aside from when we were in the shower, I can usually last pretty long, you know? But for some reason, if someone's riding my dick..." He whistled and shook his head.

"Ooh," I said with a grin. "So if I want a really intense quickie, just climb on and ride it?"

The way he bit his lip and squirmed sent tingles up my spine.

"So, longer recharge and be careful of your back. Anything else?" He ran his thumb over my pierced nipple. "Do you like these touched?"

I shrugged. "There isn't much feeling, honestly. I got them because I like how they look."

"Good to know. And I like how they look, too." He slid his hand down my side, then around to my back, and when his lips met mine, I couldn't help the soft moan. Trev had been a good kisser when we were teenagers. As an adult? Oh, *God*. He was an *artful* kisser now.

He broke away again and looked in my eyes. "Okay, before we get too carried away again—do we need condoms?"

Oh. Huh. Yeah, that was probably something to figure out sooner than later.

"Up to you," I said. "I tested negative for everything on the planet after my ex cheated."

"Thank God for that," he muttered. "What a dick, though. And I did the same after Bryan cheated—all negative."

I smirked. "Does this mean we both have really bad taste in guys?"

"Probably." He bent to kiss beneath my jaw. "But I think we're making up for it now, right?"

"Mmm, yes. Definitely." I dragged my palm up his back. "And, um—we don't need condoms for, uh, other reasons, either. If you want to fuck me in the front."

He lifted his head, eyebrows up. "Yeah?"

"Mmhmm. There's nothing—you don't need to worry about it. Trust me."

"I trust you, but I meant—do you still like it like that?"

"Oh hell yeah." I grinned. "Front, back, mouth—I'll take it wherever you want to give it."

The way he bit his lip and shivered sent a surge of need through me. "God, now I don't even know what I want to do." He rubbed his hard-on against my thigh. "I really want to make you come again, though."

I squirmed under him. "Please do."

Those gorgeous eyes gleamed with hunger. He shifted

onto his side and trailed his fingertips down my belly. "I always loved doing this before."

I parted my thighs. "You were always damn good at it, too." He really had been. Even in our clumsy, clueless teenager days, he'd always had magic fingers, and that hadn't changed. Still a soft, gentle touch, just less tentative now. More sure than he'd been back then.

Jesus Christ, this was sexy. Lying here, kissing, teasing each other with our hands—I could do this all damned day. Or until we both came again. Or—whatever, I just loved it.

I couldn't help rocking my hips to egg him on. Some guys took that to mean they should work their fingers harder —ouch—but just like in the shower, Trev's touch stayed light.

He moved his fingers down a little, exploring carefully. When he found my entrance, he teased gently, as if making sure he wasn't crossing a line. I rocked my hips some more, moaning into his kiss, and he definitely got the message— two fingers slid inside.

"Oh my God," I whispered, arching my back as he worked his magic both inside and out.

"Like that?" He was grinning, but there was a hint of uncertainty in his voice. As if he really wasn't sure I was into this.

"Are you kidding?" I slurred. "That is so good."

He claimed my mouth again, and fuck me, I couldn't get enough of anything he did.

I didn't want to hog the fun, though, so I wrapped my fingers around his dick, and I was rewarded with a gasp and a mumbled, "Jesus fuck."

Then we were making out again. He fingered me as I stroked him, and before long, we were both breathing so hard, it was a miracle we could still kiss.

It had been way, way too long since I'd been with someone who was this enthralled with my responses. Someone who was clearly driven by what I liked and how I reacted.

Sex that's a two-way street—what a fucking concept.

I could have easily come again just like this, but that wasn't what I wanted this time. I wanted his dick. Right the hell now. I didn't care where or in what position—I just needed every inch of him buried in me. *Now.*

I broke the kiss to tell him exactly that, but he spoke first.

"Do you, um..." Trev licked his lips. "Do you still like it when someone goes down on you?"

Oh. Oh, now *that* was an intriguing thought.

I squeezed his hand between my thighs as I squirmed. "I love it."

"Yeah?" He laughed softly and blushed. "I swear I'm better at it than I was as a teenager."

I snorted. "Baby, we're *all* better at this than we were as teenagers. And yes, I fucking love it, so be my guest."

His grin made my toes curl. So did the way he kissed me until I was panting all over again.

"One request, though?" I asked as I tried to catch my breath.

He raised his eyebrows.

Grinning, I said, "I wasn't kidding when I said I wanted to be dicked down. And I really, really want it."

Trev licked his lips. "So go down on you, and then plow you like a driveway in Calgary?"

I snorted, and he chuckled.

"I wouldn't word it quite like that," I said, still laughing. "But yes. *Please.*"

The heat in his eyes had me squirming all over again.

"Hell yeah," he purred, and kissed me one more time.

And then...

Oh, hell. Trev pushed my thighs apart, and he went to town on me. His tongue—oh fuck, his tongue was perfect. Even better than his fingers had been—just enough pressure to light up every nerve ending, not so much that I got overly sensitive.

I was sometimes too tense to come like this, especially after I'd already gotten off once. I was too afraid the soft touches would turn hard enough to hurt, and it was impossible to relax enough to get off.

That... was not an issue this time.

For the first time in I didn't know how long, I was completely relaxed. Completely surrendered to my partner's ministrations, confident he could—just like he always had—read me well enough to know if it was too much, too little, or just right.

It was just right. Holy fuck, it was exactly right. Perfect circles that got faster but not harder. The odd hum or moan to let me know this turned him on as much as it did me. The way he held my hips firmly, but not painfully. Everything about his touch said that even after all these years, he was still intuitive enough to keep me sliding into delicious bliss, and he was determined to do exactly that.

I closed my eyes and let him lick and tease me until I was ready to lose my damn mind. And he kept going, gently drawing me toward that brink with all the eagerness of a needy, horny man and all the patience of someone whose biggest turn-on in the world was his partner's pleasure. I raked my hands through his wet hair, and he rewarded me with a muffled whimper.

As I stared down at him, he flicked his eyes up to meet mine, and that was nearly enough to send me into oblivion.

The fire in his eyes. The heat. The hunger. The desire in his touch. All from the most amazing man I'd ever known.

Oh my God, I can't believe you want me this much.

But I couldn't *not* believe it. Every sweep of his tongue or thrum of his voice chased away that disbelief, and if any remained, they turned to ash in the heat of his undeniable arousal.

I wanted him to make me come, but more than that, I wanted him to fuck me. And if he got me off a second time, I'd be way too sensitive.

"T-Trev..." Almost sobbing with pleasure and need, I pleaded, "Fuck me. Please. Until I can't—" I ran out of words, but from his low groan, he read me loud and clear.

Before I could even find my breath, he was over me in an instant, and we both gasped as he thrust inside. Trev moaned, letting his head fall beside mine. He withdrew slowly, then slammed in again, and I dug my nails into his back. His very average-sized dick was exactly perfect to fill me completely and turn my vision white. Every thrust had me calling out things I didn't even understand, and that was to say nothing of the helpless, choked sounds he made as he fucked me.

I pushed a hand between us, and he lifted up just enough to let me start teasing myself. As soon as I did, he groaned, and a shudder ran up his spine as he murmured, "Holy fuck, you're so *tight*."

He thrust himself home again, and all I could do was moan and babble, pleading for more and harder and faster and *more*, and Trev delivered. He used those strong thighs and that powerful ass to ride me so hard he knocked the breath out of me while I kept working myself closer and closer to the edge. I couldn't get enough. I was so damn turned on, so absolutely ready for his every thrust, and as good as I felt in that moment, I may as well have been coming already. The whole room spun. My whole body was electrified. I heard myself crying out his name and begging for more, but mostly I was just consumed with this white-hot pleasure of him moving inside me.

"Oh God," he whispered shakily. "God, I'm gonna come. I'm..." He trailed off into a moan and rode me even harder, and that was all I needed. My orgasm had been building for a while, but it still seemed to come out of nowhere. I cried out and arched and swore and absolutely lost myself as he rode me through wave after wave of pure bliss. I rocked my hips to drive him on, and then he thrust as deep as he could and cried out as he came too. He gave a few more sharp, erratic thrusts, as if he could get just a little deeper, and then he slumped over me, shaking and panting.

Closing my eyes, I wrapped my arms around him and pulled him down. He buried his face against my neck, and for a long, perfect moment, we just lay like that—Trev still inside me, the two of us tangled up in each other as we trembled and caught our breath.

I stroked his hair and smiled to myself.

Because this was perfect.

CHAPTER 23

TREV

On one hand, it was fucking surreal to be cuddled up naked in my bed with Cam, my whole body still vibrating from some amazing sex.

On the other, it made perfect sense. Like despite the wildly different paths our lives had taken, this had always been destined to happen.

Of course Cam was here. Of course my arm was around him. Of course his hot skin was against mine, his short, damp hair tickling my chin as he rested his head on my shoulder.

Of course I'd just had the best sex of my life with him.

I closed my eyes and ran my hand up and down his arm, just basking in everything. His warmth. The post-orgasmic bliss. Being here with him.

It was Cam who finally broke the silence. "I want to say this was totally unexpected. But it also feels like... it wasn't?" He shifted onto his side and met my gaze. "Does that make sense?"

"Probably not, but it makes sense to me."

He laughed and leaned in for a soft kiss. "Well, whatever. I liked it."

"Me too. After the divorce, my sex drive was completely gone. And like, I didn't even care that it was. I didn't *want* to want sex." I carded my fingers through his hair. "The day you showed up, though…"

His eyebrows rose. "Yeah? You've… for that long?"

Sure I was blushing, I nodded. "I meant what I said downstairs—you're fucking hot."

He laughed softly, and he was blushing too. "You're, um… You're not so bad yourself." He drew back a little and looked me up and down, and when he met my gaze again, he was grinning. "Time and hockey have both been kind."

I snorted. "Says the man who can't feel all the aches and pains from both."

"Eh." He gave a dismissive shrug. "I can enjoy the aesthetic without feeling the pain. Works for me."

"Asshole," I muttered, and pulled him closer. He was still grinning when our lips met, but his mouth quickly softened into a toe-curling kiss. Was it any wonder this man had driven me to distraction ever since he'd come to Pittsburgh? In fact…

I broke the kiss and met his gaze. "Remember the home opener? How I kind of forgot how to play hockey that night?"

Cam made a face as if to ask, *You're bringing that up now? Really?* "Um. Yeah?"

I ran my palm up his back. "That was because of you."

His eyebrows flew up. "It was?"

"Mmhmm." I chuckled, my cheeks warming at the memory. "I was good right up until I saw you at the Zamboni gate with the boys. Something about the way you looked in that suit…"

Cam blinked. "Seriously?"

"Yeah. I just... I don't know. One look at you, and my concentration was gone." I didn't dare explain exactly where my mind had gone. That would be a little *too* sappy and weird.

He stared at me, and then he laughed quietly. "Damn. I honestly had no idea. I wondered where your head was, but I didn't think..." He trailed off, eyes flicking toward my lips before meeting mine again. "I really didn't have a clue."

"Well, good." I smoothed his short hair. "Then nobody probably knew, so they just thought I was having a bad night."

He grinned wickedly. "Is it safe to assume you're not having a bad night tonight?"

I laughed and pulled him closer. "Absolutely *not* having a bad night tonight."

We sank into another kiss. For ages, we just kissed and held each other. I doubted there'd be much more for a while; I could absolutely go multiple rounds, but I needed to recharge for a bit first. Cam seemed to be fine with this too, just making out without trying to get each other turned on again. I loved it. I loved just kissing and touching without any goal in mind. How long had it been since I'd been in bed with someone who appreciated lazily touching instead of chasing orgasms?

Too long. Way, way too long.

My libido had flared back to life the moment I'd laid eyes on Cam, but I hadn't realized until now how much I'd been missing this. How much I loved being touched. Kissed. Held. If he told me he only wanted this going forward—just kissing and cuddling and not having sex—I didn't see myself complaining.

My God, how did I not know how bad I'd been needing affection?

That wasn't to say I didn't want sex with him again. Just thinking about moving inside him, tasting him, driving him wild—hell yeah, I wanted all that and more. But this? His hands all over me? Our bodies pressed together? His mouth moving decadently with mine? I couldn't get enough.

After a while, though, he drew back, an unspoken thought creasing his forehead.

Alarm zipped through me. "What? You okay?"

"Yeah. Yeah, I'm..." He swallowed. "Look, I don't want to kill the mood, but I think we should make sure we're on the same page."

I lifted myself up to put some space between us. "Okay. Sure. What about?"

"About, um... what we're doing, I guess? Like, is this just sex? Or...?"

I thought about it. "I... I don't know, honestly. I don't want to punt or anything but... what do *you* want it to be?"

"Well, I mean..." He shifted a little, but he kept a hand on my arm, so he wasn't pushing me away. "The thing is, I just got out of a long and awful relationship. And you're still finding your footing after your divorce. Plus I work for you." He ran a fingertip along the edge of my jaw. "I think we're way too close to ever be just casual fuck buddies without any connection, but we don't need to put a name on it yet, do we?"

His comment took me by surprise, and I had to chew on it for a moment. He was right, though; for as much time as we'd gone without seeing each other, we'd been incredibly close as teenagers. Which was probably why we'd been able to break up so amicably, now that I thought about it. Even after we'd been physically intimate for the better part of a year—a line that we shouldn't have been mature enough to cross and come back from—we'd still *fiercely* held on to our friendship.

That was probably because having him in my life had always meant more than being able to get naked with him. After we'd broken up, we'd both been figuring ourselves out in ways that were bedrock-shaking, and I couldn't imagine going through that without him and our strong bond.

And then I went almost a decade without you. Fuck.

He was here now, though, and that bond was as strong as it ever was. He was absolutely right—there was no getting intimate without getting *completely* intimate.

I moved my hand from his waist to his back. "I think you're right. We'd never be able to do the casual hookup thing. But... not putting a name on it?" I nodded. "That's a good idea. Because I have no idea what we're doing, or what I want us to be doing. Only that I don't want to stop."

His little smile made my spine tingle. "I don't want to stop either." The smile shifted to a wicked grin. "Especially not after you made me come that hard."

A laugh burst out of me, and I was grateful for the break in tension. "It isn't like you're that difficult to get off."

"Pfft. You'd be surprised."

I blinked. "Seriously?"

"Oh yeah. Without killing the mood by going into detail about my ex, let's just say the sex wasn't what kept me in that relationship."

"Wow. And you put up with that for... eight years?"

"Eight and a half years that I'm never getting back." He teased my nipple with his thumbnail, raising goose bumps all over me. "So, if you're game to help me make up for lost time..."

A soft moan slipped free, both from his touch and from

the prospect of more. "I am a *hundred* percent onboard with that."

"Good. Me too."

I kissed him, letting it linger for a moment. "Are you, um—going forward, are you still good with skipping condoms?"

Cam shrugged. "I don't see why not. As long as we're honest if we sleep with someone else and we use condoms after that."

A strange feeling flared in my chest. At first, I thought it was jealousy at the idea of Cam hooking up with someone else. Then I realized it was... maybe revulsion was too strong, but this impulse to say, *"I am absolutely not interested in fucking anyone else. Period."*

"I'm good with that," I said.

He smiled, but then sobered. "I, um... I assume we should keep this out of the boys' sight."

I considered it. "Yeah. Just... until we know what we're doing. If we think there's more happening than just—"

"I get it," he whispered. "We don't want to confuse them. Or get their hopes up. Or..." He waved his hand. "It's definitely better to keep it on the DL for now."

I felt guilty about that, and I wasn't sure why. Lying to my kids? Hiding Cam? I didn't know. But keeping this cat in the bag was definitely the smart move for the moment.

"In the meantime..." I searched his eyes and cautiously spoke. "Do you, um... Do you want to sleep in here tonight?"

The way his face lit up—oh God. My heart.

Eyes and voice full of hope, he asked, "Do you want me to?"

"I don't know if I can go another round," I said, "but... yeah, I do want you to sleep here." I swallowed. "With me."

Cam laughed, unaware of how fast that made my head spin. "If we go another round, I won't be able to walk tomorrow." He lifted his chin and stole a long, soft kiss. "But I would love to sleep here."

I couldn't even define what I felt in that moment. The rush, the ache in my chest, the almost uncontrollable urge to laugh with ridiculous giddiness. I wrapped my arms around him and pulled him in close, and his languid kiss would've had me on my knees if we'd been standing.

No, there was no casually hooking up with Cam. I had no idea what exactly I felt for him, or what kind of relationship was possible between the mature adult versions of us. But I knew to my core that sex with this man could never be detached or casual.

The condom issue was fully moot for me. I would absolutely tell Cam if I slept with someone else or wanted to, but that was about as likely as me telling him I'd decided to give up hockey and join a monastery. I didn't want anyone but him. If he slept with someone else... well, I wasn't so sure how I felt about that, but we were less than an hour into whatever this was. I didn't feel right demanding exclusivity yet. Especially not when he was still licking his wounds after a long overdue breakup.

But me?

As far as I was concerned, other men had ceased to exist the moment he'd kissed me tonight.

CHAPTER 24

CAM

I winced as I rolled over in bed. My hips did not feel like they were properly connected to my body anymore.

Worth it, though, I thought with a grin. *Totally worth it.*

Beside me, the man whose tongue had made my soul leave my body was still asleep, breathing slowly and softly. This was a new experience. I'd woken up with guys before, and I'd seen them sleeping before, but never Trev. I mean, unless you counted those times I'd fallen asleep against him during a movie or when he'd slept through part of a road trip with me and some of our friends.

Waking up to the morning light resting on his face in the bed we'd rumpled... definitely a new experience, and one I was going to savor.

God, he was such a good-looking man. His heavily stubbled jaw and cheekbones were sharply defined, and I could've stared at those full lips all day long. He'd been cute as a teenager, but as a grown man? Holy shit, he was chiseled and sexy and just... Honestly, it was a genuine miracle I'd kept my hands off him until last night.

Well, and I also hadn't realized the attraction was mutual. Now that I did? Game fucking on.

My petty, spiteful side allowed in an intrusive thought about sending Daniel a photo of me and Trev. Both of us naked in bed, his spectacular physique on full display, very obviously announcing that we'd slept together. And I'd accompany it with a screencap of one of his parting texts. The one that said, *You'll never do better than me.*

Sure about that, Daniel? Because this ripped hockey player with a magic tongue, a fantastic dick, and stamina for days is one hell *of an upgrade.*

I wouldn't actually send it. Of course I wouldn't.

But it sure was fun to fantasize about Daniel's ego imploding at the realization that I had, in fact, done better than him.

I chuckled to myself. It was hard to believe I'd ever been worried that man and I would split up. Turned out, losing him was the best thing that ever happened to me.

I turned and gazed at Trev.

Losing Daniel was the *second* best thing that ever happened to me.

It was still hard to believe we'd landed here again after all these years. At the same time, it made perfect sense. Of course we were here. Of course we'd found our way back to each other. Back to the intimacy that had been so easy even back when we'd been immature and inexperienced. When we'd still been figuring out who the hell we were.

As inexperienced teenagers, we'd been clumsy and clueless, but we'd just laughed off the awkward moments. We'd learned what we could (thank you, books and internet), and we'd experimented. Even as we'd stumbled into my gender dysphoria and his confusion about his sexuality, it had never been bad. Maybe not great, but always... kind. That was the word. Kind. Giving. Loving.

As experienced adults who knew who we were and what we liked... holy. *Fuck*.

Right then, his alarm went off. He jumped, then felt around for his phone. When he found it, he peered at the screen, shut off the alarm, and tossed it back on the nightstand. I thought he might go back to sleep—did he have multiple alarms set like I did?—but instead, he rolled toward me. When his sleepy eyes met mine, he smiled, unaware of how criminally adorable he was.

"Hey," he rasped. "Morning."

"Morning." I trailed my hand along his arm. "I'd kiss you, but..." I wrinkled my nose.

He laughed. "Yeah. There's mouthwash in the bathroom. I'll take a raincheck."

I grunted. "Perfect."

"Perfect?" He grinned, looking tired and even a little drunk. "Last night was perfect."

"Oh my God." I rolled my eyes. "Could you be any cornier?"

"Probably. But I'll need coffee first."

"You're such a dork."

"Mmhmm." He groaned softly as he scooted closer and gathered me in his arms. His stubble grazed my forehead just before he kissed the top of my head. As I cuddled against him, he murmured, "I didn't hear you complaining about me being a dork last night."

I laughed, closing my eyes and basking in his warmth. "Well, to be fair, your mouth was too busy to make dorky jokes, so..."

Trev chuckled. "True."

"Are you going to be able to move tonight?"

He scoffed, and as his fingertips drifted along my spine, he said, "We didn't go *that* hard."

I pulled back to peer up at him. "Oh really? So you were half-assing it?"

Trev rolled his eyes and drew me back in. "Shut up."

I laughed, and from the way his body was shaking, he was laughing too.

"To answer your question," he murmured, "yes, I'll be able to skate tonight." He paused. "Did you still want to come to the game? Even if the boys are with Bryan?"

"Obviously. I love going with them, but I also like to just be able to focus on the game, you know?"

"So you're not bored of hockey yet?"

I eyed him again. "I've been going to your games since we were like eight. If I'm not bored of it yet, it's not gonna happen."

That got an adorably sweet but tired smile out of him. "You didn't get bored back then?"

"Are you kidding? Especially once you guys started checking—I mean, what's not to love?"

"Ooh, so you just came to watch people knock me around." He rolled his eyes. "Gee, thanks."

"What? No! I came to watch you knock people around. Which... you did. Eventually."

He just laughed, kissed my forehead, and reeled me back in again. In his youth hockey days, he'd been a little afraid of hitting, and he'd been slammed into the boards many, many times. Then two things had happened at once—he'd had a growth spurt, and he'd started hitting back. By the end of that season, he wasn't getting knocked around anymore. Not as much, anyway.

And now? Well, now there was nothing timid about him on the ice.

I couldn't wait to watch him play tonight just like I couldn't wait to watch him any night.

I trailed a fingertip up his back, making him shiver. "How much energy do you think you'll have after the game?"

Trev gasped, squirming in my arms, and his thickening hard-on brushed against my hip. "Oh, I think I can find some energy tonight."

"Yeah?" I pressed against him. "What about this morning?"

He groaned softly. "I have to leave soon for the morning skate." He loosened his embrace, and I had a second to be mildly disappointed before he added, "Plenty of time for a quickie, though."

He was not wrong.

I'd always loved watching Trev play hockey. I'd always thought he was sexy on the ice.

When I was watching him from the owners' box with a head full of dirty thoughts and memories? Ooh, God. Two amazing weeks into this, that novelty hadn't even begun to wear off.

In the days since we'd started fooling around, we'd been at it every chance we could get. He'd been gone on a road trip the last few nights, and he'd flown in late last night, so we hadn't done much for a few days. Well, aside from this afternoon; he'd *almost* been late getting out the door because—I mean, what can I say? He had the audacity to come down the stairs in a bespoke brown suit, and I didn't think I was out of line thinking he should rail me over the back of the couch before he left. The fact that he spent almost twenty minutes licking me until I came before he finally manhandled me around and fucked me? Well, that had been his choice.

I smothered a laugh at my own stupid thought. I'd been in this ridiculous, giddy headspace since the first night I'd wound up in his bed, and I loved it. I loved the way just seeing him move made my whole body light up with memories of his hands or his mouth on me, or of his cock moving inside me.

It didn't help when the guys came out for warmups. There was a particular stretch hockey players often did that was both obscene and hilarious. They'd kneel on the ice with their knees as wide as possible, then lean down onto their hands and... Listen, I wasn't the only one who thought it looked like they were trying to fuck the ice. I'd teased Trev about it plenty of times when we were younger.

Tonight, watching those narrow hips move like that while I remembered having my legs wrapped around them before he'd left for the airport a few days ago? Oh, fuck. Was it hot in here?

Squirming in my seat, I fought back a smile just so a stray camera didn't catch me looking as loopy as I felt.

Did I ever feel this way with Daniel? Because if I did, I don't remember.

Eh, who the fuck cared? I felt it with Trev, and I couldn't get enough.

At least I didn't have the boys with me right now. It was again Bryan's custody week, so they were down in the spouses' box, and that was fine. I still felt weird as hell whenever I started getting this stupid over their dad while they were sitting right here. And I did feel a bit guilty about keeping our relationship—whatever it was—out of their sight. I understood why we were doing it, and I didn't want to confuse them or upset them or get their hopes up about something, but I did feel guilty. Did it make sense? Maybe. Maybe not. Or maybe I was just worried about how things would go if and when we finally did tell them.

That was a bridge I'd have to cross eventually, but I was just thankful it wouldn't be tonight.

The game kicked off, and it was intense right from the get go. After a hard fight to get out of the defensive zone, Trev and his linemates went to the bench while another line came out. Now they were headed back out after the fourth line had ground the other players to dust in the offensive zone. Toronto's guys had been out for about two and a half minutes apiece according to the reader board, and it showed. They were slowing down. Their passes were weaker and less precise.

Exactly the right time for Pittsburgh's well-rested second line to attack.

And attack, they did. Bells stole the puck away from an exhausted defenseman, and he passed it to Trev, who then sent it flying to Houghtaling. Hoes fired it on goal, and—

Everyone roared to their feet as the goal light came on. Hoes, Trev, and their teammates celebrated as the exhausted Toronto players trudged back to their own bench.

The camera zeroed in on Trev as he and his teammates slapped Hoes on the back and shoulders, and that huge smile did nothing to calm me down. Trev was sexy no matter what. Exuberant, triumphant Trev? Be still, my heart.

Of course, now Toronto had fresh bodies on the ice, and they didn't waste any time after the faceoff. One of their centers was a lot smaller than anyone else on the ice, and he whipped in between players like they weren't even there. He was fucking fast, protecting the puck all the way. A defenseman managed to knock him into the boards and off the puck, but he couldn't get out of the defensive zone. The next thing I knew, Toronto was doing exactly what Pittsburgh had done: exhausting the opposition in their own end, and once the fatigue started to show, they started peeling off to bring in fresh players. Pittsburgh couldn't get off the ice, and Toronto's upper hand was getting stronger and stronger with every pass and with every rested player who hit the ice.

So it wasn't much of a surprise when they scored. Now the game was tied, 1-1, and Trev's line headed for their bench.

The camera landed on Trev.

Sweaty, flushed, disheveled, exhausted Trev.

Fucking hell.

I again squirmed in my seat. *Would* he have anything left after the game? He'd said he would, but after his morning skate, this afternoon's quickie, and tonight's intense game, maybe he wouldn't? Or I could do all the work. Blow him. Get on top and ride him. I just... wanted him. Bad.

When I shifted in my seat for the umpteenth time, my thigh rubbed up against the small plastic bottle in my pocket, and that didn't help me calm down at all.

Maybe I was being stupidly optimistic, but on the way out to the first game after we'd started sleeping together, I'd slipped the tiny bottle of lube into my pocket, and I'd kept it with me at every game since. I hadn't needed it yet—so far, we'd always made it home, and Trev's mouth had always made the need for lube a moot point—but I was seriously keyed up tonight. Screwing around this afternoon had only made me hungrier for him, and from the longing look he'd given me on the way out the door, that feeling was mutual. I hadn't needed my "just in case" lube yet, but I'd be riding home from the arena with him, and if Trev was as wound up as I was...

Yeah. I might need it.

We'd probably make it home before that became an issue—always did—but hey, no harm in being prepared in case he wanted to spontaneously rail me, right?

I bit my lip and squirmed. Would it be wrong to make a reservation at the hotel across the street from the arena?

Maybe not wrong, but probably not necessary. We had our beds back at the house. Hell, the shower again. The bathroom counter. The living room. The kitchen island. The garage door. Wherever, I was game.

Assuming Trev wasn't gassed from the game, of course. That happened sometimes.

Eh. I was optimistic, though.

But God help me if this game went into overtime.

CHAPTER 25

TREV

TONIGHT'S GAME WAS A TOUGH ONE. A GRIND FROM start to finish. Toronto was always hard to beat, and they were stingy as fuck about goals against; they made us work for every goal we ever scored on them. Hoes scored in the first period, and they'd promptly answered. After that, nobody was scoring despite both goalies getting hammered with shots. We *finally* slipped another puck past their netminder just before the end of the second period. With ten minutes left in the third, we had a 2-1 lead and Toronto had started to flag a bit. We'd foolishly thought we had the game in the bag, which gave Toronto a chance to tap one in during the last minute of regulation.

Overtime was five minutes of seeing how much our fans' hearts could handle. Rush after rush, shot after shot, multiple near misses on both sides.

No goals.

The shootout had everyone on pins and needles. My teammates and I sat on the edge of the bench, barely breathing as we watched players on either side take their shots.

Toronto's third shooter put one in. Lucky me, I was Pittsburgh's third shooter. I could either score and keep the shootout going, or miss and we'd lose the game. No pressure or anything.

Seeing the puck slam into the twine was such a relief, it was almost orgasmic.

Four shooters later, Hoes scored, and the fans nearly blew the roof off the arena. I was as elated as my teammates, but also relieved the game was finally over. We had our two points, and now I could strip off my gear, shower, get dressed, find Cam, and get back to the house. Maybe I was just flying high from the game, maybe I was just deluding myself into thinking he'd be interested, but I was quietly hoping Cam still had some energy left tonight. Now that I finally wanted sex again, I couldn't get enough. Especially when it was sex with him—so, so damn *good*. Even a game going to a shootout couldn't drain me—not after we'd only managed a quickie this afternoon after I'd been gone for a few days. We had the last three nights to make up for, damn it.

Though Cam wasn't here with the kids tonight, he still had a pass to come downstairs after the game. He didn't come into the locker room, though. I said hello to my boys, chatted with them about the game, and then hugged them goodbye before they left with Bryan. After that, when I went to leave myslf, I wasn't at all surprised to see Cam waiting outside the locker room, but—oh hell. The instant I met his gaze, I almost stumbled. I doubted anyone else could see what I did, but I sure saw it—the hunger in those stunning hazel eyes.

I gulped. Cam suppressed a grin.

Neither of us said a word. I supposed we didn't have to.

And we didn't dare anyway because there were still some cameras and potentially hot mics nearby.

So I kept my mouth shut until we got in the car, and so did Cam. Once we were alone, he let go of a groan. "Oh my fucking God. You guys just *had* to go to a shootout tonight, didn't you?"

I turned to him, arching an eyebrow. "I thought you liked shootouts."

"Yeah, they're fun—but not when they go to a million shooters, and definitely not when I'm losing my fucking mind because you're down there on the bench instead of rearranging my insides!"

I burst out laughing even as heat flashed through me. "Were you—were you getting horny up there?"

"Just a bit, yeah," he said without an ounce of repentance.

Fuck, I was glad we'd waited to have this conversation until we were in the car; I didn't need anyone seeing me getting hard. "I, uh... I didn't realize hockey turned you on that much."

"It isn't hockey. It's—I can't really explain it. Something about watching you play after we've fucked is just..." The seat creaked as he shifted around.

"Oh." I swallowed. "Really?"

"Uh-huh. Plus you've been gone the past few nights, so..." He turned to me and raked his eyes up and down my body. "Any chance you have anything left tonight?"

Oh my God. He was going to be the death of me.

"Pretty—" I cleared my throat and tried again. "Pretty sure I've got some left."

"Good. Maybe don't worry too much about the speed limit on the way home?"

"I never do." I started the engine. "Seat belt?"

"Right." He pulled his on. "As if I'd ever *not* wear one when *you're* driving."

"Shut up."

He snickered, and I chuckled even as I rolled my eyes.

"Too bad your car is so flashy," he teased. "We could go park somewhere."

I laughed, suddenly breathless. "Goddamn. I knew I should've bought something more subtle."

"Please. You always said you were going to get a fancy car if you ever got to this level."

Some warmth rose in my face, and I shrugged. "Okay, but I didn't think that would get in the way of getting laid."

Cam snorted. "You're so classy and romantic, Trev. Never change. But maybe step on it?"

I laughed. As I started out of the parking space, I glanced at him and grinned. "Or I could drive extra slow and—"

"Fuck you," he muttered. "Come on. I'm horny. Let's go."

I laughed. "But you're so fun to tease."

"I'm even more fun to fuck."

Pursing my lips, I rocked my head back and forth. "You make a valid point."

"Uh-huh. That's what I thought."

We exchanged looks, and the hunger smoldering in his eyes had me unbearably hard. I'd just *had* to buy a place out by the practice facility instead of close to the arena, hadn't I? Fucking hell.

On the other hand, the drive back would give me more time to tease him into oblivion. I could live with that.

Outside the garage where players parked, there was a section of sidewalk where fans often gathered before and after games, hoping for autographs. Sometimes I stopped.

Sometimes I didn't. They were mostly nice, and it was fun to see them light up.

Tonight, I needed to get us home. Like now. Ideally before one or both of us burst into flames from pure horniness.

On the other hand...

I grinned to myself and pulled into the lane where my teammates and I usually stopped.

Beside me, Cam stiffened. "What are you doing?"

I flashed him a grin. "Making you wait, just because it's fun to make you squirm."

Then I turned to the fans and rolled down the window.

"Oh, you asshole..." Cam muttered just loud enough for me to hear.

I snickered, but quickly shifted my attention to the fans standing beside the car. I thought for a second this might've been a bad idea—the flirting with Cam had left me in a somewhat... visible state of needing him. But I was in an SUV that sat up pretty high, and it was dark out, so nobody could see much. And hell, it actually gave me a sec to calm down so I could drive comfortably.

Cam didn't say a word as I signed photos, pucks, and a jersey for gathered fans. He kept his expression schooled, too—smiling at people when they peered across to see who was riding with me. I was probably going to get asked about this later—about who my "mystery man" was—but the fans were polite and so was Cam. He may not have been media-trained, but he knew how not to offend people or tip them off that there was any tension inside the vehicle.

Especially since it wasn't bad tension. It wasn't like we were fighting; I still wondered sometimes if fans had picked up on that whenever I'd stopped with Bryan beside me. He *was* media-trained, and he was very good at putting on a happy husband face, but sometimes you could just *feel* it.

Tonight, there was nothing negative, just me relentlessly teasing the helplessly horny man sitting beside me. Teasing myself, too, but that would just make everything hotter once we finally tore off these clothes. As I made my way down the line, I wondered more than once if I should've just waved at the fans and kept driving. We all did that sometimes—the fans appreciated when we stopped, but we were hardly required to—and I'd have been miles down the interstate by now. Almost home. Almost fucking Cam.

Yeah, definitely a good thing the fans couldn't see much beyond the top of my steering wheel, because I was far from calming down. So much for driving comfortably. By the time I made it to the end of the line of fans, I was shocked I wasn't out of breath.

Finally, though, I was done. I waved at the fans, rolled up the window, pulled away from the curb, and managed to avoid squealing the tires in my hurry.

Now that we were safely away from the fans, Cam dropped the façade and growled, "You are *such* a dick."

I laughed, squirming myself because oh, yeah, I was way too horny for this. "You know it'll be worth it when I make you come."

The groan he bit back was seriously sexy.

As we got on the freeway, I had to adjust myself, and his quiet cackle said he'd absolutely noticed.

"You brought this on yourself, you know."

I shot him a look. "I could take the long way home."

"You could. But you won't."

He wasn't wrong. And I wasn't giving two shits about

the speed limit, because... God, I wanted him. Having him this keyed up beside me was equal parts fun and frustrating.

Are we there yet?

I reached across the console and slid a hand over his thigh. Fucking hell, I loved the way he whimpered when I did that. Especially when I moved higher, letting my finger slip along his crotch.

"Fuck, Trev..." he breathed. "I want you so bad."

"Likewise," I said, wondering when my voice had gone hoarse. "Shame we don't have any lube, or I'd pull over and fuck you across the backseat."

He whimpered softly. "You think I'm leaving the house around you without lube?"

I glanced at him, eyebrows up.

He dug in his pocket, and I'll be damned if he didn't hold up a small bottle. At first glance, I'd have thought it was hand sanitizer, but the logo caught the light and my breath hitched.

"Holy fuck..."

"So, about fucking me across the backseat?"

I shifted around, which didn't make the hard-on any more comfortable. There were a few parking lots and backroads around here that I could get to in short order, but...

But I was driving a Land Rover. Not exactly inconspicuous like the battered old sedan we'd lost our virginities in. If someone saw us, and if they recognized my car...

Fuck. Not a good idea.

And we still had at least twenty minutes before we got home.

Time to improvise.

I licked my lips. Still keeping my gaze firmly on the road, I said, "Undo your pants. And belt."

He stiffened for a second, but before I could say anything, his belt buckle jingled. I bit my lip. Jesus Christ.

Then he lifted himself off the seat a little and rucked his trousers down. Not far, but definitely far enough.

"Lube?" I rasped, offering my free hand.

The cool liquid touched my fingertips, and I breathed a string of curses. Should we chance it and just pull over right here on the freeway? Because that was tempting. So, so tempting.

But... no. Partly because it was in public, and partly because I wanted to be peeling Cam off the ceiling by the time we got home.

I reached across again and slid my hand between his thighs. He rutted against my fingers, spreading his legs wider. A harsh breath escaped his lips as I started teasing him with my slick fingertips, and the seat creaked as he arched and squirmed.

I was definitely out of breath now, and it was a struggle to keep my gaze fixed on the road as I wound him up. I drew slow, light circles that had his breath hitching and his hips pushing against my hand, and I wondered more than once if I was going to come in my damn pants before we got home.

"God, Trev..." He pressed back against the seat. "Fuck..."

"Oh, we'll get there." I circled a little faster with my fingers, and I reveled in his helpless moan as he arched off the seat. "I want to make you come first."

He made a choked sound. Then he grabbed my wrist, but he didn't pull my arm away. His grip was painfully tight, and he kept my hand firmly in place as I was teasing him, as if he were telling me *"don't you dare fucking stop."*

The sounds he made were unreal. Fuuuck. My only regret in that moment was that I couldn't look at him. A stolen glance here and there, yes, but I had to focus on the road. I couldn't stare at him and drink in the sight of him unraveling from my ministrations.

As I followed a ramp off the freeway, I asked, "Is that good?" I sounded like I was pleading. Probably because I was. "Tell me, baby. Tell me if you like it."

The response was a soft whimper. His grip tightened on my wrist, and he ground out, "You're gonna make me come."

"Yeah?" I panted. "That what you want?"

"Uh-huh. God." He rubbed harder against my fingers. "Goddammit, as soon as we get home, I need your dick."

All the air rushed out of me in a ragged exhalation. "You want to get fucked?"

"Hard," he gritted out through clenched teeth. "God, I want..." He trailed off into a breathy moan. "Trev..."

Fuck it. I didn't want to be a danger on the road, and I also didn't want to miss this. So... I pulled over.

We were into one of the winding dark roads leading toward Sewickley, and there was no one else around. With my hazards lighting up the night all around us, I turned to him. He had his head pressed back against the seat, his back arching and his lips parted as he pushed out a ragged breath. He was a wreck, and I was doing this to him, and I could not possibly get any more turned on.

"Come for me," I begged. "God, baby, I want to watch you come." I was almost there myself, and I wasn't even touching my dick; just thinking about him climaxing had me this close to exploding.

"Trev..." He squeezed his eyes shut and arched off the seat. "Oh, fuck..."

I moved my fingers just a *little* faster, and I was rewarded with a throaty cry as he almost levitated off the seat. I was mesmerized, loving the sight and the sound and the feel of Cam coming right there in my passenger seat. He kept coming, kept crying out and shaking and gasping, until he finally tugged at my wrist. I got the message—back off before he got too sensitive.

I did, and he exhaled and sagged against the seat, still panting and trembling all over.

"Oh my God," he slurred.

I grinned, and holy shit, in that moment, I wanted nothing more than to climb across the console and rail him until I was a shaking mess too.

Not out here, though. It would be just our luck that a cop would pull up and see my bare ass bouncing in the glow of their high beams, and nobody needed *those* resulting headlines.

Cam let his head loll toward me, and even in the low light, the fire in his eyes was unmistakable. "We should get home. Because you need to get off, and I need to get fucked."

He didn't have to tell me twice.

"Get those pants and shoes off," I rasped. "Because we're not going to make it into the house."

I didn't have to tell *him* twice.

It was maybe fifteen minutes from there before we pulled in my driveway, but it felt like days. Especially as Cam squirmed his way out of everything below the waist.

As the garage door opened, I growled, "Tilt your seat back."

The seat's mechanism clicked and clanked, and I was easing into the garage as Cam was easing back.

"Do we need more lube?" I asked as I put the car in Park.

"No. Just get over here."

I shut off the engine and pressed the button to close the door. Then I unbuckled my seat belt and climbed over the console. As I settled between his parted thighs, I couldn't help a soft moan. Almost there. Fuck.

"God, Trev," he murmured. "Fuck me?" The trembling plea in his voice almost did me in.

"Absolutely," I growled. His body heat radiated through our suits, and I wanted to strip it all away so there was nothing between us, but there wasn't time for that. I needed to be inside him more than I needed to be naked, and I was struggling enough with my belt and zipper. With Cam's help, I managed to get my pants open and pushed down enough to free my dick and—

"Fuuuck…" I moaned as I buried myself in him. Tight. Hot. Slick. So damn perfect. I let my head fall beside his as I pulled out and thrust in again. This wasn't the best position in the world—screwing in a car always meant a little contorting and adapting—but I didn't care because I was moving in him. I had him. His thighs around my waist. His arms around my neck. My mouth on his. My cock buried in him.

It was *perfect*.

"You feel so good," I whispered. "Jesus… *Cam*…"

He moaned, rolling his hips to drive me on, and I thought he got even tighter. I squeezed my eyes shut and buried my face against his neck, absolutely lost in how incredible he felt.

Then he shifted a little, and he must've been resting his foot on the dash or something, because he found some *amazing* leverage. Every thrust I took made the world spin faster. I had no idea what I was saying, or if it was even words, only that I couldn't shut up as I kept fucking into him and he kept driving me on. I was distantly aware that my libido had been dead and gone very, very recently, but it was alive and well and on fire with need for this gorgeous, insatiable man.

"Oh my God," Cam whined. "You feel so..." He trailed off into a whimper that had no right to be that sexy, and I couldn't hold back anymore. I roared as I thrust for all I was worth, trying to get as deep as he could take me as my orgasm crashed through me. The release took my breath away, and for long, perfect seconds, all I could do was come.

With a heavy sigh, I relaxed, slumping over him. Cam wrapped his arms around me, and I let my head fall gently on his shoulder. Neither of us spoke as he stroked my hair and I caught my breath.

Little by little, the smoke cleared. My head stopped spinning. Reality came back into focus, and I lifted myself up to meet his beautiful eyes.

My words came out slurred as I asked, "Do you always carry around a bottle of lube?"

Cam's grin was equal parts wicked and adorable. "When I'm going to be around a smoking hot hockey player who enjoys fucking me..." He half-shrugged. "Kind of seems like a good idea to be prepared."

I snorted and let my forehead rest on his collarbone again. His suit jacket muffled my voice slightly as I murmured, "Feel free to be prepared like that in the future."

He carded his fingers through my hair, sending goose bumps prickling down my spine. "I'll keep that in mind." Beat. "And the lube in my pocket."

"Good idea."

CHAPTER 26

CAM

Unsurprisingly, Trev and I fell effortlessly into the perfect rhythm of a couple in their honeymoon phase. In bed whenever we had a chance. Texting and FaceTiming whenever we could.

The sex was off the charts. I'd never experienced a man who couldn't get enough of me, and it was addictive. Just the way he'd look at me whenever one of us walked into a room would make my toes curl. Being desired was familiar. Being *craved*? Being the reason a man lost his train of thought or—as had happened at practice a couple of times—nearly lost an edge? That was very, very new, and I loved it. He wasn't kidding about being hot for me when he saw me working out, either; I'd lost count of how many times we'd ended up going at it right there in his home gym.

And that was to say nothing about talking. Lying in bed. Driving back from a game. FaceTiming until all hours of the night. Sitting on the couch long after the boys had gone to sleep. My mom had once mused that she wondered if we'd ever run out of things to talk about, but if the last few weeks were any indication, that wasn't happening any time soon.

My life looked nothing like it had a year ago or even three months ago. I was in a new city, working a new job, and absolutely loving every second I spent with the man I'd been away from for too many years. Kind of felt like the universe was doing me a solid after running me through the wringer with Daniel.

I'd take it.

The boys turned seven the first week of December, and as luck would have it, the Rebels were in town. Trev felt guilty that he had a game on their birthday, but the twins were thrilled, especially when the Jumbotron read, *Happy Birthday, Zach & Zane Allen!* and the whole crowd applauded.

Their dad scoring a goal that night was the icing on the cake, and they were bouncing with excitement when we met up with him after the game. I was pretty sure their giant smiles and tackle hugs reassured him that they weren't even a little bit upset that he'd had to work that night.

The Saturday after their birthday, Trev hosted a party for them. Apparently Bryan had wanted to throw one, too, and he'd conceded that the house was a better venue. Trev said he was welcome to come as long as they kept their issues out of the kids' sight, and he tactfully requested that Tim not attend.

But then the boys had asked if Tim was coming, and Trev hadn't had the heart to say, *"No, your dad's boyfriend is a giant bag of dicks, and if he comes in my house, I'll drown him in the pool."*

So... there we all were—Bryan, Tim, Trev, and me—in a sea of children and parents, trying to keep everyone entertained, happy, and fed.

It wasn't as bad as I expected. For one thing, the weather was unseasonably nice, so we could let all the kids outside to play. For another, as much as Tim could be an asshole to Trev, he was great with kids. That was apparently enough for him and Trev to pretend they liked each other while they showed all the kids how to hit pucks into a net in the backyard. Or maybe he was just media-trained enough to know that if a video surfaced of him being a jerk to Trev at a children's birthday party, it wouldn't go over well with the team.

Whatever the case, I was relieved. I had fully expected today to be a struggle of trying not to throat punch Tim or Bryan. There was still that temptation just because it was kind of my default state with both of them, but it was tempered today. They were behaving. Trev was happy.

What I severely *under*estimated, though, was how stupid I'd be around Trev.

Like, I already knew that watching him with kids turned me into a swooning dork.

And I knew that he was so damn hot that my brain shorted out whenever I saw him.

And—the most recent development—I knew exactly how hard this man could make me come.

But still, somehow, I was not prepared for those three to come together into a perfect storm of distraction.

The boys had been at Bryan's until the party, which meant Trev and I had had the house to ourselves this morning, and we'd taken full advantage. Now I couldn't look at him without remembering how hard he rocked my world every time we were alone.

And I also couldn't look at him without going a little wobbly because he was just so damn cute. When a girl tripped on the deck and skinned her knee, he'd been gentle and kind, helping her to her feet. He'd sat her down on a deck chair, where he'd carefully cleaned the wound, put a colorful Band-Aid on it, and then showed her a scar on his own knee.

"I got that falling off a bike," he told her. "Had to have six stitches."

She'd sniffled as she'd looked at the silvery scar, then peered up at him with wide, tear-filled eyes. "Did it hurt?"

"Uh-huh. It hurt a lot." He gestured at the Band-Aid on her knee. "And they didn't give me one of those." He tsked and rolled his eyes. "Just one of the plain ones."

That got a giggle out of her, and a moment later, she was off and playing in the yard with the other kids.

I stood next to him on the deck as we watched her and everyone else romping around on the lawn. "Falling off a bike, huh?"

He muffled a laugh. "That's the official story."

"Mmhmm. And how much is it worth for me to not tell her the truth?"

Trev shot me a look and narrowed his eyes.

I shrugged with mock innocence.

He huffed, shook his head, and muttered just loud enough for me to hear, "You're an asshole."

"And that's not a bid for my silence, so..." I started to walk toward the deck stairs, but he grabbed my elbow, hauling me back as I cackled.

"Tell her," he warned, "and I'll tell all the kids where you got that scar on your finger."

"Which finger?" I held up the middle one, keeping it tucked against me so no one else saw. "This one?"

He snorted. "No. The other one."

"Go ahead." I shrugged. "Do you really think I'd be embarrassed if you told a bunch of first graders that a shark bit me?"

"No, but you might be if I filled in the part where the

shark was two feet long, dead as a doornail, and you stuck your finger in its mouth to see if its teeth were sharp."

I huffed. "Still a better story than—"

"Shut up." His cheeks turned a satisfying shade of crimson, and I didn't even try to hide my snickering.

And that just added another dimension to all the reasons Trev was a walking, talking distraction today. All those memories from our youth—I didn't get nostalgic about many things, but it was hard not to when I thought about growing up with him and our friends. Even the time we'd been walking on a beach and found a dogfish that had washed up with the tide. Yes, I'd stuck my finger in its mouth, and yes, I had a hell of a scar from it. The part he'd left out was that he and Don had each promised to pay me five bucks if I did (hey, that was a lot of money back then). So it was really their fault.

To this day, his parents believed the story that he'd "fallen off his bike" when he'd cut up his knee. He'd sworn the rest of us to secrecy because his parents would've had his head if they'd found out he'd crashed said bike into a parked car while riding with no hands (something his mom had warned him about a million times).

Just like they still believed to this day that every time our group of friends went to the theater, we were absolutely *not* bribing people to buy us tickets to R-rated movies. And Trev and I had never once bought tickets to movies we never saw so we'd have an alibi for the two or three hours we spent parked somewhere. Though that last one almost blew up in our faces once when his parents saw a film that we'd claimed to see, and they'd tried to strike up a conversation about it. I still didn't know how we'd managed to bullshit our way out of that one.

Those memories were all swirling in my head today

alongside everything that existed in the present. It wasn't that I wanted the kid version of him now that I was an adult. It was just that all that nostalgia and all the years of friendship and our clumsy attempts at love—we had a ton of history together, and all that history combined with everything we had now made it impossible to keep my feelings for him casual. We were the sum total of everything we'd ever been, everything we'd ever done, and everything we were doing now, and nothing in the world had ever felt more right or more perfect.

I'd told him I wasn't ready to jump into an official serious relationship because I'd recently had a messy breakup, but honestly, it didn't feel like anything I needed to get over. Not anymore. That whole shitshow of a relationship—all eight years of it—and its disaster of an end felt like a flicker of bullshit in the lifelong timeline of Trev and me.

As I watched Trev, all I could think was... Daniel who?

I wanted today to last forever, and I couldn't wait to get him alone tonight, and oh my God, I was so stupid for him.

I was a grown-ass adult. I could handle keeping my hands to myself.

But I'd have been lying if I said my brain didn't go completely blank every time I heard Trev's voice or caught a glimpse of him. One minute, he was being adorable with one of the kids, carefully and patiently showing them how to hit a puck. The next, the sun would hit him just right and he'd be somewhere between *so fucking cute* and Greek God.

Then he'd glance at me, and our eyes would lock for a second, and he'd give me a little wink or a lopsided grin, and by some miracle, I wouldn't drop my damn drink. One smile would send me back to our childhood. The next would send me back to this morning.

And it was perfect. All of it. I couldn't wait to get him alone, but I also adored watching him like this.

It was startling, and yet it made perfect sense. As if I couldn't believe the depths of my feelings for him, but at the same time—I mean, no shit, I had tons and tons of feelings for him. We hadn't wanted to put a name on this thing or go too fast, but it wasn't like we'd just met. It wasn't like this was the first time we'd been close. We weren't starting from scratch—we were picking up where, I realized now, it had been a mistake to leave off.

Or maybe we'd needed the time apart. We'd both needed time to mature. Time to figure out who we were and what we wanted out of life.

It just seemed inevitable that we'd eventually find our way back to each other, and now that we had...

I sighed as I watched him helping a tiny boy maneuver a puck with a hockey stick.

Why is it that every time I look at you, I'm surprised by how much I love you?

The relative quiet after the party was amazing.

All the guests were gone. Everything had been cleaned up (and credit where it was due—Tim and Bryan had stayed until that task was done). The boys were in their rec room upstairs, playing some new video games they'd received as gifts. Nothing to do now but wind down.

After Trev put the leftover birthday cake in the fridge, he exhaled. "Well. That was fun." He looked at me. "Did you enjoy yourself?"

"I did. Kind of glad to have some quiet now, though."

He pushed out a breath. "Me too. I love having a house full of kids, but I also love when they go home."

I laughed. "Seriously. It was fun, but the quiet afterward is nice too."

He grunted softly. Then he glanced up at the ceiling before looking at me. "While they're upstairs playing their games..." He gestured for me to follow him. "Can you give me a hand with something in the basement?"

"Sure. Yeah."

I didn't think anything of it until we walked into the laundry room and he said, "Shut the door?"

Shut the door? Uh. Okay.

I did, and I watched, puzzled, as he pulled some dry towels out of a laundry backset and tossed them into the dryer. Then he started it up, the machine rumbling loudly to life in the small room.

Before I could ask questions, Trev pulled me in by my hips and kissed me.

Oh. *Ooh.*

Okay, *now* I knew what he was thinking.

I wrapped my arms around him and returned his hot, hungry kiss. He was already hard, too, so we were definitely on the same page.

"We have to be quiet," he whispered between kisses, the sound barely carrying over the dryer. "Completely quiet."

"Uh-huh. Got it."

He groaned softly and went for my neck. "I was going to wait until we went to bed, but God, I want you," he purred. "Right fucking now."

My answer was a whimper that hopefully translated to, "*Yes, please.*"

It must have, because in the next moment, we were unzipping flies and rucking down pants.

"We don't have any lube," I panted. "We'll... just go slow at first?"

Trev paused as if I'd caught him by surprise.

He seemed to catch up quick, though, because he hoisted me up onto the edge of the dryer, pushed my thighs apart, and—

"Oh, fuck," I breathed shakily, carding my fingers through his hair. "Trev..." I let my head fall back against the cabinet and tried like hell not to make a sound. That wasn't easy. Not with the things this man could do with his tongue.

How the fuck was I supposed to stay quiet? Especially when I managed to open my eyes and look down at him.

Oh my God, that was a sexy view. His strong hands gripping my thighs. His face buried between my legs as he went to town on me. The heat in his eyes when he glanced up.

And just like the first time and every time, his tongue was absolute magic. He always seemed to know exactly how much pressure to apply—where that fine line was between *that feels so good* and *ow!*

If he kept that magic up, he was going to make me come. And if he made me come, "quiet" wasn't going to be a thing.

"Fuck me," I demanded through my teeth. "Please?"

He gave one last mind-blowing circle with his tongue, then pushed himself up. As I wrapped my legs around his waist, he asked, "Think lube will be a problem now?"

"Shut up and fuck me."

I hadn't even finished the sentence before he was inside me. Trev shuddered and swore, and then he thrust again. He buried his face against my neck, and he fucked into me like a man possessed. I dug my nails into his shoulders and my teeth into my lip, fighting back a cry that desperately wanted to escape. He just... Christ, he felt so fucking good.

"We can take our time when we go to bed," he murmured against my skin. "And we will." He thrust again, using my neck to muffle his groan. "But I just... needed you. Right now."

"M-me too." I ran my fingers through his hair. "God, Trev..."

He made a low, throaty sound, then gasped. "Fuck, I'm gonna—I'm gonna come." His shaky voice barely carrying over the whump-whump-whump of the dryer. "Fuck, Cam, I'm—"

"Come, baby," I whispered. "Don't hold back."

Oh, he didn't. He thrust a few more times, hard and deep, and then a choked moan escaped his throat as he shuddered. I rocked my hips as much as I could in this position to drive him on until he relaxed with a heavy sigh. Then he thrust all the way in, making the dryer's feet scrape on the concrete as he somehow—God, somehow—didn't make a sound. The dryer's noise and vibration had nothing on the way he trembled with the force of his orgasm and what looked like a ton of effort to stay quiet.

Abruptly, he exhaled, then relaxed, sagging against me.

I just held him while he caught his breath.

"Holy shit," he breathed into my shoulder.

"Uh-huh." I held him tight, still panting and shaking myself.

"Fuck, that was fast." He laughed, sounding a little drunk. "You're going to make me a minuteman after all, you know that?"

"And?" I grinned, running my fingers through his hair. "Quickies are fun."

"Uh-huh. They are." He kissed me and let it linger for a long moment. When he looked in my eyes, his were full of fire. "You still need to come, though."

Before I could gather my thoughts, he'd pulled out and slipped two fingers into me.

Closing my eyes, I bit my lip and gripped his shoulders. "Jesus, Trev..."

He said something, but I was too turned on to process it. Then his mouth was on mine, and I just held on while he kissed me and drove me into the stratosphere with his hand. The way his fingers worked inside while the heel of his hand pressed just right—fucking hell, this man was magic.

I broke the kiss with a gasp and pressed my head back against the cabinet. "Trev... fuck..." I thought he growled some encouragement or... I don't know. Something. All I knew for sure was that he was so, so damn good at this, and I was so close, right there, so close to that edge and—

Trev's kiss silenced the cry I didn't even know I was releasing, and he kept me quiet as he kept me coming, and he didn't let up until I shakily grabbed his wrist.

"Holy shit," I breathed when I could form words again.

He had the cockiest grin on his swollen lips. "You were supposed to stay quiet." He sounded *thoroughly* pleased with himself.

"I did." I braced a hand on the edge of the dryer just to keep from trembling apart. "I knew you'd shut me up."

He snorted. "Yeah, well." The grin turned to a wicked look. "Later tonight?" He brushed his lips across mine. "I'm going to be peeling you off the ceiling all over again."

I shivered, because this man had absolutely earned the right to have this much bravado about his sexual prowess. "Going to take you up on that."

Desire gleamed in his eyes, and I was tempted to suggest we say to hell with it, go up to one of our bedrooms, and get on with that second round. But we weren't alone in the house, so... no. Later.

Trev helped me down to the floor, and once I was steady on my feet, he reached past me to shut off the dryer. Instantly, the house was still and silent. No voices or movement filtered down from the upper floor, so the boys were probably still in their playroom. They probably hadn't even noticed or cared that we were gone.

We stepped into the gym, grabbed a couple of towels, and cleaned ourselves up. When we'd finished fixing ourselves up, we were both still a tiny bit flushed; if anything, we looked like we'd just moved something heavy.

I did feel a little guilty as I followed Trev back upstairs. Was it weird, sneaking off for a quickie while the boys were awake?

But he glanced over his shoulder, grinned, and winked at me. If he thought it was okay, then... I mean...

On the first floor, I went into the kitchen, desperate for some water. He continued upstairs, probably to check on the boys. A minute later, he came back down and joined me.

"They didn't notice we were gone?" I asked, still not quite sure how I felt about this.

"Pfft." Trev pulled a glass down from the cabinet. "They've got brand-new games. About the only thing that'll pull their heads up from those screens is the sound of the ice cream truck."

Okay, he had a point. The kids weren't addicted to their screens, and they'd put them down if they were asked, but they did have brand-new games. Those were going to keep them engrossed for a while until the novelty wore off.

"So it isn't weird, then?" I asked. "Ducking out while they're awake and..."

Trev chuckled. "Nah. I thought it was, but from what

I've gathered on parenting boards, everyone sneaks out for a quickie sometimes."

"Yeah?"

"Mmhmm. Where do you think I learned the trick of turning on the dryer?"

"Oh." I snorted. "And here I thought that was just supposed to enhance the experience."

"I mean, two birds, one stone..." He shrugged.

I laughed and rolled my eyes, and it was startlingly difficult not to step in close and put a hand on his waist or steal a kiss.

I sipped my water instead, grateful for the cold. "For the record," I whispered. "I've never dated—or, well, done whatever this is with someone who has kids. So I'm not quite sure where all the lines are."

Trev nodded. "I know. And it's my first time dating as a single dad." He let his gaze drift toward the stairs, and he sighed, letting his shoulders drop. "One minute, I feel like it's no big deal. The next, I'm afraid I'll completely screw up their childhood if I do something wrong."

"Is that dating as a single dad, or just parenting in general?"

He pursed his lips, then laughed as he shifted his focus back to me. "Definitely parenting in general." He grimaced as he brought his glass up to his lips. "I love my kids and I love being a dad, but I won't tell you for a second that it's easy."

"No, I figured that out." I paused. "Especially because there's so much... *soccer*."

Trev choked on his water, very nearly spitting it on me.

I cackled. "You deserved that!"

"What? For fucking you?"

"No! For making me go to soccer!" I paused, then shrugged. "Fucking me gets you a lot of leeway."

He rolled his eyes, put his glass aside, and wrapped an arm around my waist. "You're a brat."

For a split second, I was afraid we shouldn't do this out in the open, but... the boys were very firmly ensconced upstairs, and neither was particularly stealthy coming down the stairs. So it was perfectly safe to let Trev wrap me up in his arms. It was safe to let him claim a long, lazy kiss.

Or two.

CHAPTER 27

TREV

I'd kept my word last night and made sure Cam's world was thoroughly rocked. Keeping him quiet hadn't been easy, but I was always game for a challenge, and getting him to unravel like that without crying out was... incredibly rewarding.

The only downside was that my neck and hips were a little bitchy when I stepped out on the ice for our morning skate. Eh, some stretching would help. I'd be fine.

My jaw was sore, too, but I didn't really need that for hockey. Well, aside from chirping at other players and chewing the hell out of my mouthguard, anyway, but whatever.

All in all? Zero complaints. Ten out of ten, would make him shake like that again. And soon, we'd have the house to ourselves again so I could make him scream. As much as I hated when my boys went to Bryan's, this new arrangement was a hell of a lot better than spending my non-custodial weeks being miserable and lonely.

Goose bumps sprang up under my gear and base layer, and I bit back a grin as I leaned down to pull on my socks.

Even Chats couldn't get under my skin today, and boy, did he try. He was determined to get me to admit that I was jealous of him and Bryan.

Not today, Satan.

"You're lucky, Trev," Chats said with that shit-eating grin as he taped his stick.

I had to bite back a laugh because I suspected I knew where this was going. "Oh yeah?" I eyed him, hoping he took my expression as one of boredom. "Why's that?"

Smirking, he tore off the tape and put the roll aside. "Almost sent a picture to the family group chat this morning instead of just to Bryan." He barked an obnoxious laugh. "Good thing I caught myself, isn't it?"

I just rolled my eyes. I hated that he had any business at all on our family group chat. I hated... Well, I hated him, but that wasn't news. Keeping that boredom on full display, I leaned down to lace up my skates. "I mean, you do you, I guess? I wouldn't have seen it."

"Dude, you're on the family group chat," he snarked.

I laughed and shot him a grin. "Well, yeah, but you didn't know? I muted you ages ago."

The stunned expression made me chuckle. He had that look of a grade school bully who'd just had his cleverest insult turned back on him—completely confused, offended, and embarrassed.

Perfect.

"Wait, we can mute teammates?" Bells asked. "Well, shit. I wish someone had told me that."

"Of course we can." Hoes glanced up from taping his sock. "I've muted Tremblay and Arnolds for—"

"Oh, fuck you, Hoes," Tremblay said from across the room. "I blocked you two seasons ago because you wouldn't stop sending me pictures of your—"

"Wait, what?" Spaulding chimed in. "What the fuck, Hoes? I've been asking for pictures of your dog for ages, and you're spamming Tremblay with them? You dick."

As the banter went on and got increasingly ridiculous, I just laughed. Good thing there weren't any cameras or hot mics in the room right now. Though I kind of wished a camera could catch Chats looking like someone had flipped his birthday cake on the floor.

Sorry, dude. I'm not taking your bait, and nobody else is playing your games either.

I really shouldn't have been feeding the animosity between us, but it was just so satisfying when I could turn some of his obnoxious bullshit back on him. He'd made it clear that he desperately wanted me to be jealous and pissed about him and Bryan. My apathy was his kryptonite.

What could I say? His crap didn't bother me nearly as much now that I was spending every available minute driving Cam wild. If we weren't having sex, we were bantering as effortlessly as we had when we were kids, or curled up in front of a movie, or talking about whatever until we couldn't keep our eyes open.

Chats just wasn't going to get to me now that I was this happily distracted by the hot, funny, amazing man waiting for me at home. He could try, and I knew he would, but it wasn't happening. Not anymore.

I picked up my stick and gloves and headed to the ice to join my teammates for our morning skate. We'd practice this morning and then play tonight. And later on, I'd be in bed with the hottest man I'd ever touched.

Time to focus on that instead of the jackass my ex-husband was with for some reason.

This game was *wild*, and the hometown crowd was loving it.

Minneapolis pulled their starting goalie in the first period after he let in five goals on seven shots. The backup was a brick wall, but we still had a 5-1 lead. All we had to do was hold on to it.

On the bench, Hoes clapped my shoulder. "You think you've got another one in you?"

I glanced up at the timer and shrugged. "Still thirty-five minutes left to play. I think I can get another in." I grinned at him. "You gonna set me up?"

"Are you kidding? When was the last time you were actually on hatty watch?"

I laughed, admittedly a little giddy. I hadn't had a hat trick in three seasons, and I'd only been on hatty watch twice in the last two. Tonight, I'd been so damn close to a *natural* hat trick; two goals in the first ten minutes of the game, and I'd almost picked up a third in the dying minute of the first period. That ping of the puck hitting the crossbar would haunt my dreams.

So no natural hatty tonight, but still plenty of time for a hat trick.

"What do you say, rookie?" Hoes leaned past me and looked at Bells. "Think we can get Trev his hat trick?"

"Fuck yeah." The rookie fist-bumped both of us. "Let's do this!"

Of course my linemates would still absolutely take a shot if they saw one, but especially when we had a comfortable lead, it wasn't unusual to try to set someone up to complete a hat trick.

I was getting another puck in tonight, damn it. I was practically salivating at the thought of hats raining down on the ice. It had been too damn long, and I was too damn close with a ton of hockey left to play.

The comfortable lead didn't stay that way for long, though. Minneapolis got a breakaway that tilted the ice hard in their direction, and suddenly all the action was in our defensive zone. Our third line and the D-pair completely fell apart at the worst possible time, and in seconds, the score was 5-2. A minute and a half later, 5-3.

"Get out there," Coach barked to the top line, his irritation coming through loud and clear. I got it—sometimes a strong lead like that was dangerous because while the other team got motivated, we got lazy and took our foot off the gas. Now we were only up by two instead of four, and a two-goal lead could vanish *fast*.

The top line finally got things moving in our favor. The zone entry took a few tries because Minneapolis's defense were on their toes. Then we were offside, and our guys tried again, but it was still a struggle.

Finally, though, a beautiful stretch pass from Spaulding to Tremblay got us onside in the offensive zone.

Tremblay fired on net, and the goalie froze the puck. A whistle let our exhausted top line and D pair come off the ice while my guys and I went over the boards with the second pair. Showtime.

I narrowly lost the faceoff. Their center sent the puck screaming toward one of his wingers, who was already on his way to the neutral zone.

The winger caught it, but Hoes flattened him with an open ice hit and whipped the puck along the boards. It flew around the end of the ice behind the goal, right onto Bells's stick.

"Trev!" he called out.

I was ready when he passed to me, and the puck landed right on my tape. I'd planned to go for a one-timer, but there was suddenly a dense screen between me and the goal.

Instead, I whipped the puck to Hoes, and before anyone in that screen could shift left to get in his way, he one-timed it *right* into the back of the net.

As we crushed him in celebratory hugs, he shouted above the cheering crowd, "Next shift, Trev! Next shift!"

"We've got a bigger lead now." I smacked his helmet. "That's the important thing!"

"Okay, then." He shrugged as we headed toward the bench for fist bumps, calling over his shoulder, "No hat trick for you!"

"Damn it, Hoes!"

He laughed as we skated down the line for fist bumps.

Coach kept my line out since our shift had been fairly short, though he did swap out the D pair. We set up at center ice, and this time I won the faceoff. I passed to Spaulding, who got us into the offensive zone, and then we started cycling the puck, passing around and around as we steadily closed in on the goal.

Hoes got the puck, but instead of sending it to Bells like he'd been doing in the cycle, he passed it back to Spaulding. That threw Minneapolis off for a half a second, which was when Spaulding passed it to me.

I wound back for a one-timer and—

The ping off the iron almost drew a curse out of me... until the puck bounced off the goalie's shoulder and right into the net.

The fans went wild, and I'd barely pumped my fist before the first hats started landing on the ice. My linemates and defensemen celebrated with me, and then we were off to the bench again, the ice littered with hats as more came down and the scoreboard showed 7-3.

This was hockey. Things could turn around in a hurry

and we could still lose, especially since we still had a whole other period to play. But this was a damn good place to be.

And I had my hat trick. My first in too long.

My first with Cam in the building.

The thought made me shiver as I took a seat between Bells and Hoes on the bench. While the ice crew started collecting the hundreds of hats, I grinned to myself. I was sure everyone thought it was because I'd scored my fifth career hat trick. And to some extent, it was.

But it was also because there was a gorgeous man up in the owners' box who'd no doubt help me celebrate later tonight.

I stole a glance at Chats, who was staring out at the ice, chewing aggressively on his mouthguard. To anyone watching, he was just focusing. Concentrating. Readying himself for his next shift.

But I knew.

He was fuming. He was still pissed he hadn't made it under my skin earlier, and I had no doubt he was mad that my hat trick would overshadow his game-winning goal.

Sucks to suck, asshole.

I grinned to myself for the rest of the period.

CHAPTER 28

CAM

WHILE ZACH SPENT THE AFTERNOON AT A FRIEND'S house, I drove Zane to the art center in Sewickley. The day the boys had turned seven, Zane had eagerly reminded Trev that he was now old enough for the cake-decorating class, and could he please sign him up ASAP?

Trev hadn't forgotten. In fact, he'd signed him up months ago, and he'd emailed the instructor a week before the twins' birthday to double-check he'd secured spots for Zane and me. Though I was there to supervise Zane, I had to register as a student myself for head count purposes. I had no idea if Trev had had to pay for me or not, and he'd hand-waved any concerns I had about it.

So... fine by me. Free cake decorating class? Twist my arm. Though I did make sure we both had a reasonably healthy breakfast beforehand—light on sugar, heavy on protein and everything else. If we were going to be main-lining sugar all afternoon, I needed to make sure we balanced it out with breakfast and dinner (not to mention the lunch and snacks I'd packed).

I was kind of amused at the thought of Daniel seeing me

now, going to a class where I, along with the child under my care, would undoubtedly be sugared up by the end. He'd been *militant* about "clean eating," to the point of shaming his clients for indulging in things like wedding cake or a birthday dessert. Like, dude, if someone was leading a mostly healthy lifestyle, they weren't going to derail that by having a goddamned tiramisu on their birthday or some cookies on Christmas.

Small wonder my client retention rate had beaten his by a mile. Not that that had done a damn thing to keep me employed, but that was another story. People deserved to enjoy their lives, and sometimes that meant eating things that weren't approved by the man who preached fire and brimstone about "food is fuel, not fun" to clients who just wanted to be healthier.

Ugh. What had I ever *seen* in him?

Well, he was history now, and today I was going to have a good time—and a shitload of sugar—with Zane while he learned how to decorate cakes.

He was the mellower of the twins, but he was practically bouncing in the backseat on the way to the class. We'd spent a solid hour last night looking at pictures of decorated cakes, with him gushing about all the techniques he wanted to learn. It kind of blew my mind, this first grader who was still getting the hang of writing full sentences and capitalizing words but was like a miniature pastry chef when it came to this.

"Do you think they'll let us use fondant?" he chattered. "It looks hard, but I want to try it!"

I glanced at him in the rearview and smiled. "Maybe? I think it's just frosting and icing this time."

"Ooh, maybe we can use royal icing!"

Jesus. I hadn't even known what royal icing was until

he'd shown me a series of YouTube videos about it, and I knew for a fact that if someone had asked seven-year-old me what fondant was, I wouldn't have had a clue. This kid was going to be a pastry chef someday for sure, either professionally or as a hobby.

I realized as I continued into Sewickley that Zane reminded me a lot of young Trev. In third grade, while we'd still been trying to get our heads around fractions and multiplication, Trev could rattle off hockey stats like a pro commentator. He'd struggled with reading aloud in class, but ask him about the playoff race or the trade deadline, and he could talk forever about who was likely to snag a wild card spot and who should be traded. I hadn't known nearly enough to say how accurate any of his commentary was, but it sure sounded like he knew what he was talking about.

Zach was that way with soccer and video games. Zane? Baking. Anything that had to do with baking, he was passionate and knowledgeable beyond his years. Clearly nurture over nature in this department, since the twins weren't Trev's biological sons, but it was seriously cute to see his personality rubbing off on them. Not surprising either, given how enthusiastically he encouraged them to explore and talk about their passions.

And this man had ever worried for a second that he wasn't a good dad?

Dude, no. Just no.

I pulled into the parking lot behind the art center's building, and I practically had to sprint to keep up with Zane on the way inside. We followed some signs to the kitchen, and—wow. This place was impressive. The kitchen classroom was huge, with a large table at the center for instruction and demonstration.

The teacher was a plump woman in her fifties with a

bright pink mohawk and a nose ring. As soon as we walked in, she met us with a bright smile. "You must be Zane?"

He nodded shyly.

"Well, welcome to cake decorating. My name is Marci." She looked at me. "And you're his chaperone?"

"Yes." I extended my hand. "I'm Cam."

We shook hands, and she said—staying very pleasant but still serious—"I usually ask parents and chaperones to be as hands off as possible. The whole point is for the kids to learn, and they learn much better by doing." She shifted her attention to Zane. "If you get frustrated or you're not sure about something, you can always ask me or Cam, okay? This is a class, so no one's expecting you to get everything right the first time. Got it?"

Zane nodded again, and a little smile broke through.

"And besides," she went on in a stage whisper, "making a mistake in cake decorating just means more cake and frosting. So…" She shrugged.

That got a laugh out of Zane, and I decided I absolutely adored Marci. Zane could be a little bit of a perfectionist—the type who got frustrated if he didn't master something his first time out—so I appreciated her reassurance. I didn't know if Trev had given her a heads up about it, or if she'd just worked with enough kids to know how frustrated they could get when learning a new skill, but either way, fine by me.

Zane and I took a couple of chairs around the large table in the middle of the classroom. Along the side of the kitchen, there were several trays of cupcakes on the counter, but no sheet or round cakes in sight.

Zane furrowed his brow. "Wait, this is for cupcakes?" He sounded disappointed.

Panic fluttered behind my ribs. "Um…" Shit. What if

that wasn't what he wanted? He'd been looking forward to this for ages. What would—

"Cupcakes are easier to work with in the beginning," Marci said cheerfully. "The things you learn today will work on bigger cakes, too, but we like to start people small."

Zane still didn't look convinced.

I thought fast. "It's like the tutorial levels on a video game. You want to learn those before you reach a boss level, right?"

Chewing his lip, he nodded. "I guess, yeah."

"Right. So think of these like that."

He seemed to consider that. Then he turned those puppy dog eyes on me. "After the class, can we try it on a real cake?"

"Uh." I swallowed. "Well, we were going to watch your dad's game tonight, but maybe tomorrow? If you want to?"

That brought him back to life, and he smiled. "Okay!"

Phew. Crisis averted.

While we were still waiting for people to settle in, Zane started chatting with an older girl sitting next to him, and I texted Trev.

> Did you know this was a cupcake class?

Oh. Shit. I might've? Is Zane mad?

> He was a little disappointed, but I convinced him it's like a video game tutorial.

Good thinking. And it worked?

> Yep. But now he wants to do a boss-level cake at home.

Pretty sure we can make that happen.

I stared at his message, then glanced at Zane. Then I started typing.

> I told him he and I would do it, but maybe that's something for you and him?

Uh, you've taken the class, not me.

> I can supervise. (wink emoji)

Oh. Yeah. Because you count as adult supervision.

> I do today, don't I?

Yes, you do, and I seriously appreciate you doing this with him. And defusing the situation when I fucked up and put him in a cupcake class.

> We'll settle up when you're back in town (wink emoji)

Damn right we will.

> Ok class is starting. Text later.

The class was pretty basic. Marci started by showing everyone the basic process of making a few varieties of frosting, which was fairly straightforward but had a lot of steps. Fortunately, there was a handout with the recipe and detailed instructions, so neither of us would have to memorize any of it.

"Once you have this," she told us, "you can add different flavors and colors. That way you don't have to mix up a batch every time you want to change something."

Well, damn. There was me learning something in this class. Not that I'd given it a ton of thought before, but it hadn't occurred to me you could just make a big ass bowl of frosting, and then modify smaller portions of it.

Duh, Cam.

For starters, Marci just had the kids use a plain off-white frosting and do very basic lines and dots on a piece of waxed paper. Using the piping bag was a challenge for Zane, mostly because his hands were smaller than everyone else's. Fortunately, Marci found one that was thinner and easier for him to manage, and after a few practice stripes, he was handling it pretty well.

He did get a little aggravated, though, when his rosettes didn't come out the way he wanted them to. After four tries, Zane's still didn't look like Marci's examples.

He glared at his failed attempts. "It's hard!"

"It's okay!" I touched his shoulder. "Remember what she said? Mistakes just mean more cake and frosting!"

He looked up at me, a mix of confusion and frustration in his eyes.

I tipped my head toward the waxed paper and whispered, "If they're not pretty... just eat them."

He blinked. Then he grinned, unaware of how relieved I was that I'd made the right move. He swept one of the rosettes onto his finger and stuck it in his mouth. I took one too, and we shared a conspiratorial chuckle.

"You're just learning, too," I reminded him. "You don't have to be good at something on the first try. Most people aren't."

He sighed, peering at the remaining rosettes.

"You know I used to watch your dad play hockey as a kid, right?"

Zane looked at me. "Yeah?"

"Do you think he was as good then as he is now?"

Zane's eyes widened, as if he'd never imagined his dad being less than incredible at hockey. "He wasn't?"

"Of course not." I shrugged. "I mean, he was good, but if he'd tried to play for the Rebels back then..." I grimaced and shook my head. "It's a tough sport, and it took him a long time and a lot of work to get where he is now. And I guarantee you when he first started skating, he fell down a *lot* more than he stayed up."

Zane shifted his gaze to the frosting blobs.

I squeezed his shoulder. "It just takes practice. That's all." I paused. "Sort of like the games you've been playing. You didn't beat them all on the first try, did you?"

He sighed. "No."

"Exactly. So just keep at it. You'll get there."

He eyed the frosting, then nodded and held up the bag. "Can you put a little more in it?"

"Of course." I spooned some more frosting into the bag, then handed it back to him.

He was hesitant at first, as if he were afraid to make a mistake.

I touched his shoulder. "Go ahead and make a mess. The more you do it, the easier it'll be. I promise."

Zane peered up at me uncertainly. Then he looked down at the waxed paper in front of him, shrugged, and... made a mess. One squeeze of the bag, and the frosting overshot the place he'd been aiming for and landed on the rosette next to it. I had a split second to panic, thinking he was about to have a meltdown, but the giggle stopped me. He adjusted his grasp on the bag and tried again, this time with a bit less force. A few more blobs happened, but then...

Then one of the rosettes came out looking like a rosette. Still messy and not quite what Marci had effortlessly done, but it was enough of a proof of concept that it seemed to sharpen Zane's focus. He shifted around, steadying himself on his elbow, and carefully squeezed out another novice rosette. The next few were significantly better, and one was actually damn close to what his instructor had showed us. I had to wonder if he'd just been putting so much pressure on himself, expecting it to be as easy as Marci made it look, that he'd psyched himself out.

I could relate.

When Marci had the students apply what they'd learned to some cupcakes, Zane moved in with the focus and precision of an assassin. Carefully, he pointed the tip at the cake, gave a little squeeze and a turn, and...

"Look!" He sat up and pointed at the rosette. "I got it!"

"You did! Want me to get a picture?"

"Yeah!" He carefully held it up next to his gap-toothed grin, and I snapped a photo on my phone.

Of course, I sent it to Trev.

> This kid's a fast learner.

By the time Trev responded, Zane was already eating the perfectly rosette-ified cupcake.

> Wow! Tell him I said great job!

I did, and that prompted a big grin with crumbs gathered at the corners of Zane's mouth.

This kid was something else, just like his brother.

Just like their dad.

God, no wonder I'm so stupid for Trev.

I focused, though, and continued helping Zane practice the various techniques he was learning. The class broke for lunch in the middle, and we both happily ate the sandwiches I'd packed. I'd worried briefly that Zane might not be hungry, but like me, he seemed to love the switch from something blindingly sweet. The turkey and cheese sandwiches were a nice balance to the steady stream of sugar we'd both been eating since the class started.

As we reconvened after lunch, Marci chirped, "Now I'm going to show you how to make a *filled* cupcake." She held up a melon baller. "Step one... scoop out the middle."

I worried that Zane might balk at that part, since he wanted to be decorating larger cakes instead of cupcakes, but he was actually quite into it. Like me, he probably hadn't given a ton of thought to how the filling got into a cupcake. He seemed fascinated, and when Marci turned the kids loose to fill a couple of cupcakes, he was excited as he tried to decide between the different fillings.

He ultimately settled on raspberry for one and chocolate cream for the other. The first cupcake broke apart when he used the melon baller, but he didn't get discouraged or upset this time. He just went a little slower on the second one, and the center came out without much fuss. Using the bag to add the filling went smoothly enough; he'd had enough practice with it so far that he seemed to understand just how much would come out when he squeezed it.

The rest of the class went smoothly. Zane had a few frustrating moments, but talking him down was even easier now that he'd seen himself get the hang of things after a few tries. He was still determined to have perfect results, but he was giving himself grace while he learned the various movements.

In the end, he had half a dozen elaborately decorated cupcakes placed carefully in a cardboard carrier, which he asked me to show his dad. The congratulatory *"those look awesome—save one for me, okay?"* text from Trev lit up Zane's whole world.

I'd worried that a four-hour class might be too much for a seven-year-old. I'd been prepared to bail early if I thought he'd had enough, or we could step out for a few minutes if he needed a breather. It wasn't like this was an SAT prep class or something; if he missed a segment, someone would probably fill us in.

By the time we left the art center, though, Zane probably would've happily sat through another four hours. Marci raved about how much she enjoyed having him in her class, and two of the moms mentioned that he was amazingly focused and well-behaved.

"I'll pass the word along to his dad," I said on the way out.

Zane was all smiles, carrying his carton of finished cupcakes down to the car, and he chattered excitedly about all the ideas he wanted to try on a bigger cake.

"The cupcakes *are* fun, though," he admitted as I pulled out of the parking lot. "Do you think we can make some?"

"Sure, yeah, we can make some. Not today, but maybe this week?"

"Okay." He was quiet for a moment, and then, as I was sitting at a red light, he said out of the blue, "I wish Dad could've come."

I glanced at him in the rearview. He was gazing out the window, a touch of sadness in his expression. "Yeah?"

"Yeah. I know he's gotta go with his team. But sometimes I wish he didn't have to miss stuff."

I winced. "That has to be tough. I know he misses you guys a lot while he's away." I flicked my gaze to the mirror before refocusing on the road. "He says the highlight of his day is FaceTiming with you and Zach."

"He does?"

"Of course. And he knows it's tough on you and your brother." I paused. "Marci said she has more classes like this during the year. Maybe we can see if your dad wants to do one with you after hockey is over."

Zane looked up, meeting my gaze in the mirror. "Yeah?"

"Sure. Would you like to do that?"

His smile warmed my heart. "That would be fun!"

I nodded, fixing my gaze on the road as the light turned green. "I'll talk to him about it."

Hopefully I hadn't just put my foot in my mouth and committed Trev to something he wouldn't enjoy. Though I really struggled to imagine him objecting to doing something that one of his boys enjoyed. Especially something they wanted to do with him.

Besides, he made me go to soccer, so he could *live* with cake-decorating.

I picked up Zach from his friend's house, took the boys home, and fed them dinner. After hearing his brother talk about the class, Zach was suddenly interested in it himself, so I made a mental note to mention it to Trev later.

Then we packed their schoolbags into the car and I drove them over to Bryan's condo. At least Tim was on the road with Trev. He was probably driving Trev nuts, but he could handle him better than I could handle two-on-one. God, I hated that guy.

Bryan let us in, and the boys hugged me goodbye before wandering into their bedrooms. Alone in the kitchen, Bryan and I managed a cordial conversation, which was a lot easier without Tim lurking nearby. I brought him up to speed on homework; Zach was struggling a little with the latest math unit, and Zane was having a hard time with the reading module.

"Reading?" Bryan eyed me. "This kid basically taught himself to read. What's he struggling with?"

"Honestly? I think he's bored with the story. He comprehends the sentences and words just fine, but he'd rather eat glass than read it. I had him read something else that was about the same level, and he blew through it like it was nothing."

Bryan chewed his lip. "That doesn't bode well for reading textbooks later."

"Probably not."

"Great. Well, I'll talk to Trev about it. We'll figure something out."

I nodded. "Maybe we can each take him to the library. Let him pick out some books that interest him. He'll have to slog through stuff he doesn't enjoy later, but we might as well encourage him to read what he *does* enjoy."

"True." After we'd touched base on a few more things, Bryan walked with me to the front door. As I put my shoes back on, he asked, "So how is it, working for Trev?"

I shrugged. "It's been great. The kids are a lot of fun, and he got me out of a really bad spot."

"Yeah, seems like a pretty sweet deal for you, isn't it?" There was an odd edge to his tone that hadn't been there earlier, and it brought me up short.

I met his gaze. "I mean, yeah?" I shrugged again. "It's a great deal."

He grinned knowingly and nodded. "Well, I honestly wasn't too surprised when I met you. When I told him he had to get full-time childcare if he wanted to hold on to joint custody, I kind of figured he'd hire someone he could bang, too."

I jumped like he'd slapped me. "I—excuse me?"

Bryan laughed in that condescending, *oh, you sweet summer child* way. "Ah, so you don't know him that well after all, do you?"

Irritation tightened my chest alongside confusion, and the confusion made the irritation worse. I'd been with Daniel long enough to know this game—he was trying to keep me off-balance. Gaslight me into thinking I was the idiot for not knowing the "truth" that he was making up. I hated that it succeeded in keeping me off-balance; not because I thought he might be right, but because I couldn't figure out what his angle was. What was he trying to do? Shame me into admitting I was sleeping with Trev? Weaponize that relationship against his ex-husband? Just fuck with my head?

Keeping my voice calm and devoid of that irritation, I said, "I haven't seen him in almost a decade. You were married to him." I half-shrugged. "You probably do know him better than me at this point."

The concession landed exactly the way I'd hoped—now Bryan was the one off-balance, staring at me and shifting his weight.

"So what made you think he was going to hire a nanny he could bang?" I asked as conversationally as I could. "Because it's news to me."

Bryan narrowed his eyes slightly, as if *he* were trying to figure out *my* angle. Then he schooled his expression. "I mean, we all know what Trev's number-one priority is."

"The twins."

Bryan huffed a laugh. "You would think. But... no. That man's life is and always has been hockey."

Anger surged through me, but I tamped it down. I wasn't going to take his bait.

"Hockey is his passion," I said evenly. "But he still—"

"Hockey is his *life*," Bryan cut in. "And now that he's hired you, he's got all his bases covered." He started ticking points off on his fingers. "Someone to watch the kids. The house is taken care of. He keeps joint custody so he doesn't have to pay me child support. And he doesn't have to put any time or effort into meeting a new partner or hooking up." He made a sweeping gesture at me and smiled coldly. "All-in-one, leaving him able to focus on hockey. What's not to love?" Before I could reply, he gave a dry laugh. "I don't blame you, honestly. He's hot as hell, and I'd bang a hot rich guy who was paying me to live in a million-dollar house."

"Ah. Well." I gestured around the condo. "That explains a lot, then."

The fury that crossed Bryan's face was deliciously satisfying. "Excuse me? I moved in with him because we're dating. Not because—"

"Mmhmm. And I moved in with Trev because I'm working for him. But if you can make crass, obnoxious assumptions about our arrangement, then..." I shrugged as flippantly as I could. "Fair's fair, amigo."

He stared at me, face full of equal parts shock and anger.

Then he rolled his eyes and muttered, "Go fuck yourself," before closing the door in my face.

I chuckled on the way down to the car. As I drove out of the parking lot, though, my amusement and satisfaction ebbed. I was still angry and irritated, sure, but another feeling started to worm its way in, and I couldn't get comfortable.

I knew Bryan was wrong about me. I hadn't taken this gig so I could jump into bed with Trev.

But... what if he was right about Trev?

I told myself over and over that Trev had stopped reaching out to me because I hadn't answered him. He wasn't the type to go where he wasn't wanted, and when I didn't respond, he took that to mean I didn't want to be in contact with him. He didn't reach out this time because he expected a readily available piece of ass—it was because one of our mutual friends had told him I was in a bind, and Trev had a solution to both of our situations. He hadn't made a single move or even flirted with me. Hell, I'd been the one to kiss him after I'd cornered him into admitting he was attracted to me.

None of that added up to a man who'd opportunistically hired a nanny/boytoy combo.

So why had Bryan's words still made it under my skin? He'd just been fishing for dirt and trying to stir things up. I knew that. And yet...

What if some of it—any of it—was true?

What if I was just a convenient sure thing for Trev?

Of course that didn't sound like the man I'd known a *lot* longer than Bryan had. Of course it didn't sound like my best friend. Of course it didn't sound like the man who'd looked at me like there was nothing he wanted more than to taste me.

But my whole world had been yanked out from under me just a few months ago. My foundation felt shaky.

What if...

What would I do if Bryan was right?

CHAPTER 29

TREV

ON THE BUS BACK TO THE HOTEL AFTER OUR MORNING skate, I scrolled through the photos I'd gotten from Cam since I'd left for this road trip. The cake decorating class with Zane. Zach playing basketball with some neighborhood friends. Both boys holding up their trophies after their soccer team's season-end banquet.

I smiled as I looked at each photo for the millionth time. And as I read the messages Cam had sent with them.

> Zane already wants to sign up for the advanced class. He loves it!

> I think Zach wants to go out for basketball. He's getting really good!

> I think it's bullshit that I don't get a trophy for coming with them to all those evil soccer games. (skull emoji)

That last one made me laugh, which soothed the ache deep in my chest. These long road trips had always been a bear, but they'd been especially hard since Bryan and I had adopted the twins. Now that I only had them every other week? Now that some of those weeks were swallowed up by these trips? It fucking hurt. I loved my career, but being away from Zach and Zane was a lot harder than I'd anticipated, and that had only gotten worse since the divorce.

Since the divorce, and since Bryan had decided to make everyone's lives more complicated by getting with someone who was not only my teammate, but also the most insufferable bag of dicks I'd ever shared a locker room with. Who knew it could actually be *more* miserable to be divorced from him than it had been to live with his cheating and all his other bullshit? Or that he'd find the most antagonistic and inescapable man to be his new boyfriend?

And what if things got ugly with Chats and the team decided to separate us?

I closed my eyes and pressed my head back against the seat. I had to do everything I could to get along with that asshole. Don't take his bait. Don't engage. Don't even look at him. If it wasn't about hockey, I didn't need to interact with him, and I wouldn't. Not if our bullshit could get me sent to another team in a city where my kids didn't live. I was missing enough of their lives without letting my ex's douchecanoe boyfriend make things worse. If things escalated enough, even my no-move clause wouldn't keep me here. Not forever.

The bus came to a stop and the doors squeaked open. I looked up and realized we were back at the hotel, so I gathered my phone, coffee, and headphones and followed my teammates off the bus.

I was kind of in the mood to go to my room and wallow in this funk. Look at texts. Look at photos. Hate my life.

But I was saved from that by an announcement that we'd be reviewing film in twenty minutes. Just enough time to go upstairs, change out of my suit and into a pair of sweats, and come down to the conference room.

I sat between Hoes and Bells. Reviewing film wasn't my favorite thing in the world, but it was a welcome distraction today, so I didn't complain.

We'd be playing Anaheim tomorrow, so our video coach, Gavin, cued up some clips of that team in action. First it was special teams.

"Their power play is first in the League by a *mile*," Gavin said, "so let's stay out of the box tomorrow, all right?"

"Anyone gets a major or a double minor against this team," Coach warned from the front row, "you're bag skating for a week."

That prompted grunts and nods. He might've been kidding, but maybe not. Any penalty was dangerous against this team, but Anaheim was deadly. Against New York last week, they'd scored twice on a double minor, putting them one ahead in a game they ultimately won 5-4. A five-minute major had proven disastrous for Seattle—during that extended man advantage against the second worst penalty kill in the League, they'd scored *four times* in what ended up being a 5-1 victory.

So... yeah. Staying out of the box tomorrow would be a really, really good idea.

I leaned over to Hoes. "Fingers crossed the refs don't fuck us."

"Right?" He rolled his eyes. "If we take another penalty for someone tripping over nothing, I swear to God..."

I scowled and nodded. Three nights ago, Tremblay had taken a tripping penalty after someone had pretty much tripped over his own damn feet. We'd managed to kill that penalty, at least. The same couldn't be said for the one Bells took in Boston. We'd ended up down a goal because they

got a power play after the refs called Bells for interference...
after the other player crashed into *him*.

Such bullshit.

Gavin moved on from special teams to one of
Anaheim's other deadly weapons: odd man rushes. "This
includes," he groused, "one-on-zero rushes." He looked
pointedly at a section of chairs. I couldn't see who he was
glaring at, but I suspected it was the second and third defensive
pairs, who'd let a few too many people squeak behind
them recently. Nothing made the D pairs look worse than a
single player leaving them in the dust and attacking the goal
unchallenged. The goalies did the best they could in those
situations, but they didn't appreciate being left completely
on their own.

And apparently Anaheim really, *really* liked doing that.
On the screen, one of their forwards broke away, whipped
past a startled defenseman, and started sprinting up the ice
with three people on his heels and nobody in front of him
but the goalie.

In a cartoonishly high-pitched voice, Hoes narrated,
"After him! He's getting away!"

Snickers rippled through the room.

As the player on the screen whipped left, then right,
trying to fake out the goalie, Hoes shrieked, "Oh God!
What do we do? What do we do?" The player fired the
puck into the net, and Hoes's melodramatic howl of despair
had us all doubling over with laughter.

"Hoes," Gavin warned, but the grin in his voice kind of
killed the sternness.

"Sorry, Coach," Hoes said. The devilish glint in his eyes
said he was anything but.

He wasn't done, either. During a video of a board battle,
he muttered, "Goddammit, Carl, you're stepping on my—I

just polished my skate, you dick! Look at it! Look, you've scuffed—"

"*Hoes.*"

"Wait! Wait! That's *my* puck! Where are you going? Come back here at once!"

Gavin just facepalmed, and he didn't succeed in hiding his own amusement.

As the player onscreen passed the puck, Hoes said, "Here—you think *you* can do better? You take it. Maybe you can—oh, hey, you got a goal."

All around him, our teammates were vibrating with laughter. How Hoes managed to keep a straight face when he did this, I'd never know.

We wrapped up not long after that, and I doubted anyone was more relieved than Gavin. Film review was a necessary part of the process, but it could be seriously boring, especially for a bunch of hockey players who weren't wired to sit still.

It ended eventually, though, and the coaches dismissed us. We had the rest of the day to chill now, since our game wasn't until tomorrow afternoon. Some of the guys were heading out to play golf. Others were chilling in their rooms or going out in search of food. I had dinner plans with Hoes and Bells, but not for a couple of hours yet.

I thought I heard some of my teammates making noise about going to a go-cart track, but that might've been just to antagonize Coach. Though he hadn't banned us from going to places like that, he hated it when we did. Apparently a couple of his teammates during his playing days had gone to a less than reputable track, and though I wasn't exactly sure what happened, three of them had ended up missing that night's game. So... he preferred if we didn't tempt fate.

Go-carts did sound kind of fun, though, and as long as it was a reputable place, then we could—

"—don't you, Trev?"

The sound of my name turned me around a half-second before I registered that it was Chats. "What?"

He smirked. "I was just saying, if Bryan keeps working me as hard as he does, I might end up on LTIR. You know what that's like, don't you?"

There was a time very recently when that would've set my teeth on edge and made me see red. This time, I just chuckled, rolled my eyes, and turned back around to keep walking. His taunts about being with my ex-husband weren't nearly as effective anymore. Not when I'd be Face-Timing naked with Cam later tonight. The thought made me shiver and—

"Hey, don't be jealous," Chats called after me. "Not my fault you downgraded from him to the hired help."

That stopped me in my tracks a split second before I could tell myself not to take the bait. Several of our teammates halted too. Some were glaring at Chats. Others were watching me like they thought I might drop gloves with him right here in this hallway.

His shit-eating grin got bigger. "What's wrong, Trev? Did I hit a nerve? Is that—"

"Chats." Spaulding put a hand on Chats' chest and tried to herd him away. "Don't. That's not—"

"No, no," I said through my teeth. "Let him talk. The fuck did you say, Chats?"

The jackass kept grinning as he nudged Spaulding's hand away. "What's wrong? Had to screw the nanny since the janitor turned you down or something?"

"Dude, that's not cool," Hoes said.

I didn't know if he meant outing me as being with Cam,

or acting like anyone who qualified as "the help" was beneath him. Either way, I appreciated it.

"What?" Chats shrugged, grinning like the jackass he was. "I'm not wrong. Am I, Trev?" He inclined his head. "You know I'm right about—"

"I know my personal life is none of your fucking business," I snapped. "And it's not for you to share with the rest of the team, whether it's true or not."

"But it *is* true. We all know it is."

Some of the guys rolled their eyes.

"Chats." Hoes stepped in between us. "Fucking stop, man. It's bad enough you rub it in his face at every opportunity that you're with his ex. This?" He grimaced and shook his head. "Come on. This isn't cool." He must've seen what I did—Chats smirking and getting ready to say something else—because he added, "Or do you just get off on having another man's sloppy seconds?"

That—along with the snicker that went through the group—knocked the grin right off Chats' smug fucking face.

He swore under his breath and stalked away. Some of the guys followed, chirping at his back because why the hell not?

I just exhaled and rolled my stiff shoulders. I'd never liked the idea of anyone being someone's sloppy seconds—it was gross to talk about people like that—and I didn't think Hoes was okay with it either. That wasn't his style. But he'd known exactly what would get under Chats' skin and bring him down a few necessary pegs. Maybe the end justified the means this time.

Either way, I wasn't going to bitch about anything that sent Chats storming out of the room and out of my face. Fuck, he was exhausting.

Hoes watched him go, then shook his head and turned to me. "You okay, man?"

"Yeah, I'm good. Thanks for stepping in."

"Don't mention it." He made a disgusted sound. "Chats needs to shut the fuck up."

"No kidding," Bells said. "What's his deal, anyway?"

I was exhausted just imagining trying to answer that question.

Hoes didn't have that problem, though. "He's been desperate for Trev to be all pissed off or jealous because he's with his ex. It got old a *long* time ago."

"Yeah, it did," I muttered. I glanced around, making sure only my two linemates were within earshot before I admitted, "I fucking hate that asshole."

"You and me both," Hoes grumbled. He tilted his head. "That thing he said about your kids' nanny—is that true?"

The heat in my face was probably a dead giveaway, so there wasn't any point in lying. And why should I? I wasn't embarrassed to be with Cam. I just hated the way Chats had outed us.

"Yeah," I said. "We've, um... We've been dating for a little while."

Hoes nodded sharply and grinned. "That explains a lot."

I cocked a brow. "Oh really?"

"Yeah, it does," Bells chimed in. "You've just seemed more... I don't know... Settled, lately?" He looked at Hoes as if to ask if that was the right word.

"Close enough," Hoes said. "Just... Chats hasn't been getting under your skin as much. I figured you must've either decided he wasn't worth the blood pressure spike, or you'd moved on from your ex."

I laughed nervously as some more warmth bloomed in my face. "I, uh... I didn't think anyone had noticed."

Bells shrugged. "Eh, I didn't really put the pieces together until Hoes did."

"I had my suspicions," Hoes said with a smug grin.

"Did you?" I narrowed my eyes. "Why?"

He scoffed and gave me a shove. "Oh for fuck's sake, dude. You're not exactly subtle."

I straightened. "I'm... I'm not?"

"No." He shook his head and gestured for us to start walking. As we fell into step with him, he said, "I can tell the minute he walks into the locker room. I thought it was just because he was bringing in your kids, but then I realized it happens even when he's by himself." He smacked my arm with the back of his hand. "Like I said—you're not subtle."

I looked at the rookie for confirmation, and he nodded.

"Great," I muttered. "Why can't the two of you be this observant on the damn ice?"

That prompted protests from both of them, and they talked over each other as they defended their innocence. I just laughed as we continued toward the elevators.

I was still pissed about the exchange with Chats, but I felt better. And I was grateful for my teammates who'd stepped in. They didn't put up with his shit, whether it was harassing me or being an elitist asshole who thought people were beneath him.

I played with a lot of good guys, and I was glad they had my back.

Unfortunately, the road trip only went downhill from there.

Maybe it was demoralizing loss followed by the late flight followed by the early morning. Maybe my coffee hadn't made it into my system yet as I joined my team for yet another morning skate.

Or maybe I was just tired of my asshole teammate.

Whatever the case...

"For fuck's sake." I whirled on Chats after he "accidentally" slashed me during a drill. "What is your fucking problem?"

"What?" He laughed, putting up his gloved hands. "What are you talking about, man?" He nodded sharply. "Come on. We gotta finish the—"

"Fuck the drill," I snapped. "We're finishing *this* right here, right now."

His eyes widened. Then they narrowed as a sly, triumphant grin came to life. "Yeah? So what? You wanna drop gloves or something?"

"You'd like that, wouldn't you?" I growled.

I was distantly aware of a whistle blowing. Of one of our coaches yelled something. But I kept my glare fixed on Chats and his smug fucking face.

"I don't need to fight with you," he said with a smirk. "I already won. And I get to put my dick in it every time I'm—"

"Yo, hey!" Tremblay grabbed Chats' shoulder and tugged him back. "Come on, dude. Give it a fucking rest."

"What?" Chats laughed. "I'm not the one who's butthurt and can't move on!" To me, he said, "If it didn't bug you, you wouldn't get all pissy every time you see me with him. Must be tough, knowing I'm getting that—"

"Shut the fuck up!" I snarled as Hoes put a hand on my chest, not quite holding me back but ready to if the need arose. I scoffed and shook my head. "Christ, Chats." I gripped my stick so hard, I was amazed it didn't break even through my gloves. "I don't *care* that you're with him. You can fucking have him. The only reason I still have to put up with you two is because we're teammates and I have kids with him. Otherwise, I would be more than happy to never lay eyes on either of you again."

He barked a sarcastic laugh. "Just admit it, Trev—you hate seeing us because you hate being reminded that he's not putting his—"

My hold on my temper snapped, and I threw my stick as I lunged for him.

Hoes was ready, though, and he held me back, shouting, "Whoa! Whoa! Trev—easy, man. Easy!"

Petrovich joined in, taking my arm as I shook off my glove.

Spaulding and Arnolds held on to Chats, who was shouting at me to come on, come on, bring it, though his voice was muted through the cotton in my ears.

A whistle blew. It had blown several times, I realized now, but I'd been so single-mindedly focused on Chats that it hadn't registered.

"Enough!" Coach bellowed. "Both of you!" He skated in between us and shot us each a venomous look. "What the fuck is going on?"

Chats opened his mouth to respond, but Martin scowled and said, "Chats is antagonizing Trev. *Again.*"

Coach exhaled a cloud of exasperated breath into the air, and then he pointed sharply toward the locker room. "Chats. Trev. Go shower and change, and then we're going to talk." He paused. "And if I hear that you so much as *looked* at each other between now and then, there will be hell to pay, and bag skating will only be the beginning. Am I clear?"

"Yeah, Coach." I picked up my gloves and stick and started my skate of shame. I fully expected Chats to be on my heels, running off his mouth anyway because he just couldn't help himself. There were voices behind me, though. Angry ones.

Yep, running off his mouth. Just not at me. Whether it was at Coach or our teammates, I didn't know, but I was grateful for a head start so I could calm down.

I tore off my gear and stomped into the shower. As the water ran over my head and neck, I closed my eyes and tried to will myself to chill. I was pissed, but I still had a game tonight—assuming Coach didn't healthy scratch me—and I'd already caused enough headache for my team today.

I hated this. I hated that we were grown men, but my ex-husband's boyfriend had dragged me down to his level and gotten me to snap, so now we were both going to get reamed out by Coach like a couple of kids. And what the hell? I'd been flying so high yesterday. So unbothered by that asshole's bullshit.

I hated myself for letting Chats get to me. I hated that I'd lost my cool, and we'd clashed during practice. Fortunately, it hadn't been open to the public since it was a morning skate at the host team's arena, but there were reporters here. There were *cameras*.

By now, our scuffle was probably all over the internet. If Chats hadn't texted Bryan about it, Bryan had probably heard by now through social media. I was terrified to even look at my phone when I got back to the locker room.

It's going to get back to the boys.

Fuck. I let my face fall into my hands and groaned. Our GM no doubt knew about it, and my kids would know about it, and *fuck my life.*

The more I thought about it... the less I was bothered by

the things Chats had said. I didn't give two shits that he was with Bryan. If they made each other happy, then more power to them. It meant two less assholes in the dating pool to make *other* people miserable.

I had my kids. I had Cam. I had my career. I didn't need or want Bryan, and I didn't care what Chats thought.

I just didn't like the constant juvenile shit that went above and beyond chirping. I didn't like how this could fuck with my relationship with my kids, or how it could hurt my career or reflect on other queer hockey players.

I *especially* didn't like getting called in to face Coach alongside Chats. But ten minutes after my shower, there I was, sitting there like a kid waiting to find out how much detention he'd be serving.

At home, Coach would've taken us into his office, but there was a small office used by away team GMs and coaching staff, and he set us up in there.

In the silent office, he glared at both of us. "The most pressing question I have right now is, can the two of you idiots play on the same team? Or do I need to have Eric start shopping one of you around for a trade?"

Oh fuck. We did not need the general manager getting involved.

"I don't have a problem playing on the same team as him," I said evenly.

"I don't either," Chats said, sounding perfectly media-trained and professional.

Coach's eyes flicked back and forth between us. "So... why are we having this conversation? What exactly is going on here?"

Neither of us answered.

Coach huffed an impatient breath. "Is this about him taking up with your ex-husband?"

I winced. Then I looked pointedly at Chats. *He* could answer this one.

"It's just chirping, Coach," he said with a shrug. "I didn't think he'd take it that seriously."

I pressed my lips together so hard I was surprised my teeth didn't break through them.

Coach eyed Chats. Then me. Then Chats again. With a heavy sigh, he said, "Can I trust you two to put a lid on this particular brand of *chirping* going forward?"

"Yeah, Coach," we both said. What else could we do? At least this way, Coach was giving Chats some rope. If I didn't let myself react to any of his taunting going forward, he'd hang himself. Problem solved. I could do that.

And that was probably what Coach was angling for— some way for his grown-ass adult players to iron their shit out without him needing to seriously intervene.

Fine by me as long as the bullshit actually stopped.

Coach dismissed us, but I didn't get far.

"Trev."

I stopped just shy of the door. So did Chats.

"You can go, Chats." Coach gestured at me. "Close the door and sit back down."

My heart jumped into my throat. I didn't dare look at Chats, and I did as I was told.

When we were alone again, Coach sighed and folded his hands on the desk. "Look, I'm not stupid. I can see what's going on here." He shook his head. "You're not the problem."

Swallowing hard, I nodded. There was a "but" coming. I could hear it from a mile away.

Coach pushed out a long breath. "I'm going to have to get Eric involved at this point. I can't let it escalate beyond where it already has. And son, if the decision was mine, you wouldn't be the one getting traded." He grimaced. "But I can't promise Eric will agree. With as volatile as this is getting—with as volatile as it has the potential to get—Eric might ask you to waive your no-move clause."

My stomach somersaulted. I'd known that was a possibility, but hearing someone actually say it turned my blood to ice. "And if I say no?"

He shrugged tightly. "Don't count on getting re-signed."

My heart sank, and I wanted to argue, but... I really couldn't. Trading me would keep me playing. If I wasn't re-signed, and especially if the other GMs knew *why* I wasn't re-signed, they'd probably assume I was the problem child. I was the gay player who couldn't keep his personal life out of the locker room and couldn't resolve my issues with a teammate. I wouldn't be a very enticing unrestricted free agent with that much baggage.

Fucking hell.

"I understand," I whispered. "And I know it's not the club's problem, but if I get traded out of Pittsburgh..." My throat tightened, and I muffled a cough. "The custody agreement I have for my kids..."

Coach winced. "I understand. I do."

He didn't have to say it, though. The club was—and had to be—every general manager's top priority. It wasn't at all unusual for fathers to be traded to the opposite coast from their spouses and kids. Some families didn't even bother to move with their player because there was no guarantee he'd be there long enough to be worth the effort. They'd spend the regular season doing the long-distance thing, and then he'd go home for the off-season. Well, most of the time; the pandemic had kept families separated on opposite sides of the US-Canada border. I had literal nightmares about being traded somewhere and having something like that happen again.

Even without another pandemic or crisis, the fact was that if I was traded... my kids weren't coming with me. The judge had made that very clear. Our custody agreement had a clause that if I was traded or signed with another team, we'd switch to an amended version. It would reflect the new living situation, and during the off-season, we'd have our normal joint custody, plus some extended periods for me. For the regular and postseason, though, I'd be, at *best*, a one-weekend-a-month dad.

My team's front office was aware of this, but they could still ask me to waive my no-move clause to resolve the shit between Chats and me. And if I didn't, they could just... not re-sign me.

It didn't matter that Chats was the instigator. The two of us together made for a toxic locker room, and Eric was going to unfuck that in the most inexpensive and advantageous way he could.

Which most likely meant that if Chats and I didn't fix our shit, my days in Pittsburgh were numbered.

After we'd returned to the hotel and I was alone in my room, my mood started to dim even more. My thoughts had been stuck on the exchange with Chats, as well as the one with our coach.

I liked to think my teammates backing me against Chats would work in my favor if Coach or Eric needed to get rid of one of us, but I wasn't optimistic. Eric wouldn't look past the numbers unless things *really* got out of hand and Chats proved himself to be a cancer in the locker room. One who caused issued with *multiple* teammates or staff members. To my knowledge, Chats only fucked with me, so if the club got rid of one of us, the problem would be solved without costing the team more money than necessary.

Which meant I really didn't have much of a choice except to ignore him as much as possible and to not take his bait.

But it also made me realize how tenuous my situation was, and not just with Chats. If I didn't toe the line on the team, I'd be sent someplace else where I wouldn't be able to see my kids often. And if I fucked up on the home front, I'd lose what little time I had with them.

Chats had somehow picked up that I was, at the very least, hooking up with Cam. So had Hoes and Bells. Which meant we weren't being as discreet as we probably should've been, at least while we were finding our footing together.

And... what if we *didn't* find our footing together? What if we realized that even as mature adults, we couldn't make it work any more than we had as teenagers?

I wiped my hand over my face. If I fucked up in my handling of Chats, I could end up anywhere else in the League, far away from my kids. If I fucked up with *Cam*, I could lose him as my boyfriend, my friend, and the man who took care of my kids. I could lose custody of Zach and Zane.

I swore under my breath and rubbed my eyes with the heels of my hands. I'd been so caught up in how good it felt to be with Cam—not to mention how relieved I was to have my childcare situation squared away—that I hadn't stepped back to look at the big picture.

I could lose my kids over this.

Not completely, of course. I'd still be one of their dads,

and I'd still see them. But if things got worse with Chats or they imploded with Cam, and I couldn't find another live-in nanny to take care of my kids when I wasn't home, I'd have my custody reduced to one or two weekends a month. And those weekends could easily fall during road trips or when I had back-to-back games. How flexible would Bryan be about that? Would I have to take him back to court for it?

Would the boys resent me because the only times I saw them were still dominated by hockey?

I didn't even give a shit that Bryan would undoubtedly ream me for child support. I didn't care about the money—I cared about having a relationship with my sons.

I cared about not failing as their father, and now I was worried sick that I was going to do exactly that.

I *couldn't* lose what little time I had with the twins already. And that meant I couldn't lose Cam as their nanny. Not until I could line someone else up to take his place.

But then he'd be out of a job. And I'd probably lose my friend, not to mention the man I was quickly starting to feel things for that I thought I'd forgotten how to feel.

How the hell do I do this without ruining my relationships with three of the most important people in my life?

CHAPTER 30

CAM

I HADN'T BEEN ABLE TO RELAX SINCE THE conversation with Bryan a few nights ago. I'd managed to put on a chill and happy face when I'd FaceTimed with Trev, though I'd begged off from any spicy chatting. Even the platonic conversations took more work than they should have; as soon as the screen had gone dark each time, I'd been back to wringing my hands and worrying myself sick.

I was being irrational. Bryan was just trying to get under my skin, and apparently he'd found a way to do exactly that. It didn't mean he was right about anything.

But something about that interaction had jarred another set of uncomfortable feelings that I couldn't shake off. It was as if he'd knocked me out of the clouds and back down to earth, and while he'd been full of shit, he'd jostled me enough to make me see some of the ugly things I'd been carefully ignoring. I'd been so caught up in how amazing it felt to be with Trev again, and how much I loved this new thing between us—even if it didn't have a name yet—that I hadn't let myself think about any of the potential drawbacks.

I still wasn't letting myself get to them yet. I kept circling back to everything Bryan had said, and I knew myself: I was focusing on those so I didn't have to stare down everything I'd been trying to ignore.

But none of that was helping me sleep. Or think. Or just relax once in a goddamned while.

So I finally did what any grown-ass man with an ounce of sense would do in this situation: I called my mom.

"Things are going good with him," I said. "But there's a part of me... I don't know. I can't decide if I'm just being paranoid after Daniel, or if there really is a reason why this is all going to blow up in my face. And I'm kind of afraid to find out."

"That's reasonable," Mom said. "Nobody enjoys looking things like that in the eye."

I grunted in agreement. "You're not wrong. But... I don't know. Am I just looking for a reason to pull the plug on this? Because I don't want to pull the plug on it."

"Is there any reason why you'd want to?"

"Not really. I'm just as crazy about him as I was in high school." I paused. "I'm tired of his ex-husband, though, that's for sure."

Mom huffed a laugh. "He's an ex-husband. I doubt you're the only one who's tired of him."

"You're not wrong," I grumbled. "But now he's figured out I'm dating Trev, and he's just... *ugh*. He's insufferable."

"Oh Lord. He's giving you grief for that? Hasn't Trev put a stop to that?"

I sighed. "He doesn't know about it. Not... not yet."

"Why not?"

"He's on the road, and it just started. I'm... I don't even know if I *should* tell him. Things are already so strained between them, and they still have to co-parent, and..." I groaned. "It's just so damn *messy*." Rubbing the back of my neck, I admitted, "And the ex—he's said some shit that's got me thinking things I really don't want to think about."

"Oh really?"

I took a deep breath and told her about the conversation with Bryan. About how it had been needling at me for days, and how I didn't want to believe Trev was using me, but after Daniel, I was afraid to trust anyone. Even the man who'd been my best friend since we were kids.

"I don't even know what to think anymore," I said. "I know Trev, but I've got so damn many trust issues now, and I..." I pushed out a breath. "Am I losing my mind?"

"No, you're not," Mom said. "And I think if you told Trev everything you just told me, he'd understand why you're confused and worried."

Something about her tone gave me pause, though. As if there was an unspoken "but."

I sat back and stared up at the ceiling. "What am I missing? Because it sounds like I'm missing something?"

"Well, I mean, I'm concerned that..." Mom trailed off.

I sat up a bit, my stomach knotting. "Concerned that... what?"

She didn't answer immediately. Then she took a deep breath. "Listen. I adore Trev and I always have. You know that."

"Right," I said, not sure where this is going.

"But... you're working for him. And you live with him. If... Honey, if things go off the rails with him, you're going to be back to where you were with Daniel. Except you'll be twenty-five hundred miles away from me and the rest of your support network."

That knot turned into a cold ball of lead. I chewed my

lip as I watched myself tugging at a loose thread on the hem of my shirt. "I don't think he'd... I mean, he's not like Daniel, you know? It's *Trev*."

"There was a time when you didn't think that was Daniel, either."

"No, but he showed his true colors a long time ago. Trev has always been good people."

"He has. But you're putting an awful lot of eggs into this basket. Even if Trev doesn't turn out to be like Daniel—and I don't think he ever would—you two could still break up. Things *could* get messy. And then what? You'll either be stuck living with him and working with him, or you'll be out of a job *and* a home." She paused. "What if you want to quit the job? Or get your own place? How will that affect your relationship with him?"

I swallowed. I wanted to insist Trev would be fine with any of that. But Bryan had left me full of stupid doubts, and Daniel had left me full of trust issues, and now I didn't know what to believe.

"I don't... I don't know. I really don't."

"You might want to think about it, Cam," Mom said gently. "I think Trev is the last man in the world who'd take advantage of you or toss you out, but I don't want to take anything for granted. Not after what Daniel put you through." She sighed. "And the wealth difference between you two—that's not always a good thing either."

"What do you mean?"

"Money is power," she said. "It can be controlling, even if the person with the money isn't trying to use it that way."

"I don't think Trev would, though."

"I'm sure he wouldn't. But think about it—if you decided right this second that you wanted to break up with him, would you stop and reconsider how that would affect your job and your housing situation?"

"I..." Something cold trickled down my spine. "I mean, yeah? But that doesn't mean he's—"

"I don't think he'd lord it over you," she said softly, "but it exists. It means you're not nearly as free to leave the relationship as he is. That kind of imbalance—that can cause problems."

I pressed my lips together. A million protests flew to the tip of my tongue about how Trev would never do that, but she was right. If Trev wanted out, it wouldn't affect his job, his house, or anything financial. He'd have to hire a new nanny if I bailed, but his stability would be unchanged.

My stability?

My stability leaned *hard* on how much Trev liked me and wanted to keep me around, either as his nanny, his boyfriend, or both. If he decided I didn't need to fill those roles, I'd be out on my ass.

Fuck. That wasn't good.

"I don't know what to do," I admitted. "I adore him. And I love this job. I *need* this job. I... What do I do?"

"I don't know, honey. But think about it. And maybe sit down and have a frank conversation with Trev about it. It won't be comfortable and it won't be fun, but you two need to be on the same page. Especially if you're going to continue with any part of this arrangement—living with him, working for him, or dating him."

I swallowed so hard, it was probably audible on her end. "Okay. I'll, um... I'll give it some thought."

"And you'll talk to him?"

"I'll talk to him." I didn't know how to bring it up, or when, or—or anything. But Mom was right. This wasn't something to let fester.

We ended the call not long after that, and I stayed where I was, staring at the ceiling as I turned my silent phone between my hands.

What the fuck was I supposed to do now? Yeah, I needed to think about it and discuss it with Trev, but... *how?* Where did my fear and insecurities end and Trev's true colors begin? How did I bring any of this up without scaring him off? He already had to deal with Bryan's bullshit, not to mention's Tim's, and he couldn't get away from them. Why would he want to sign up for more bullshit with me?

Ugh. Fuck my life. I'd been squicked out by Bryan's remarks about sleeping with Trev. And unsettled by his comments about hockey being Trev's biggest priority over everything else, including his kids and definitely including me.

But even as they'd bothered me, I struggled to imagine it was true. Suggesting that Trev would use someone just because they were convenient and useful—it didn't *fit.*

The things my mom said, though—those worried me. A lot. And now that she'd pointed them out, they were exactly what had been lurking beneath the surface. I hadn't wanted to think about them, as if ignoring them might make them less real, but now that she'd dragged them out into the light, there was no avoiding them.

I just didn't know where to go from here.

I adored Trev. I wanted him. I felt things for him I never had for anyone else, including Daniel.

But my mom was right. If things didn't work out between us, I'd be out of a home *and* a job.

There was also a non-zero chance I'd lose my friend again. That was even more unthinkable than us breaking up. I hadn't realized how much I'd been missing Trev until he'd come crashing back into my life, and the thought of returning to that—of having that void in my world that I couldn't ignore—was heartbreaking.

How did I navigate all of this so I didn't lose the man I'd always loved?

CHAPTER 31

TREV

I WAS A MESS FOR THE REST OF THAT ROAD TRIP. EVERY time I saw Chats or heard his voice, I was overcome with frustration and a million other emotions. I wanted to drop gloves with him. I wanted to beg him to just be happy with Bryan and leave me the hell alone. I wanted to backhand him into next week for disrespecting Cam.

But mostly, he was just a reminder of how raw I'd felt ever since our last run-in. Of all the thoughts that had been swarming in my head like a black cloud of mosquitoes. I had to play nice with Chats if I wanted to stay in Pittsburgh... but what about Cam? How was I supposed to navigate things with Cam without upending my relationship with my kids *and* my relationship with him? What the fuck was I supposed to *do*?

I tried to keep all that beneath the surface in the locker room, and I tried like hell to hide it when I FaceTimed with Cam. I didn't know how successful I was being. My teammates seemed to keep Chats at bay with silent looks. We hadn't struck any sparks off each other in the past couple of days, which was great.

My interactions with Cam, though... those worried me.

Because I didn't think I was being all that slick about hiding this emotional turmoil from him, but he still didn't seem to notice. He didn't seem to want to chat much, and he wasn't interested in fooling around on-camera. He barely wanted to FaceTime at all. After our game in Montreal, I'd thought we were going to chat when I got back to the hotel. Instead, I was met with a text.

> I'm sorry, I'm just wiped out. I'm going to call it an early night. Talk tomorrow?

We'd texted the next day, and we'd FaceTimed, but only briefly because I'd had to catch a flight. Two nights later, after a demoralizing loss in Toronto, we'd chatted, but again, not for long. He'd smiled and laughed several times, but his eyes had given him away—his heart wasn't in it. It was like he was on another planet, or just didn't want to talk to me, but I'd been too much of a coward to ask why. I told myself it was better to do this in person than over text or FaceTime. Was I being a coward? Probably.

I was worried. Distracted, too, and my game reflected it. I'd gone three games in a row without a point, and last night —the final game of the road trip—I hadn't even notched a shot on goal. Coach hadn't talked to me yet, but I could see it in his sidelong glances that I needed to get my shit together ASAP unless I wanted another one-way conversation.

At least we were finally home today. I had no idea if that would improve things with Cam, but it got me back on familiar turf and away from Chats. I'd take it.

My flight came in super late last night, and Cam had already been asleep in his own room, so I'd left him to it. This morning, he'd been out when I got up, and he'd come back twenty minutes later with some grocery bags. I'd helped him put things away, but the conversation stayed superficial and... not cold, but not warm either.

Something was wrong. I could feel it all the way to my damn core. But I also had a mountain of uncomfortable things I needed to bring up, and I was afraid to start that conversation. It was going to be a self-fulfilling prophecy, wasn't it? When I told him I was afraid of messing things up with him... I'd mess things up with him. When I told him I was afraid to lose him as my kids' nanny... I'd lose him as my kids' nanny. When I told him I was afraid of losing him entirely...

God, I couldn't even think about that.

Yeah, I was probably a coward, but I wasn't used to having quite this much on the line. At least when I'd confronted Bryan about cheating, I'd had my anger to rocket me past my fear of everything that would happen once we got that all out in the open. Divorce was terrifying, especially with kids involved, but I'd been too pissed off and hurt to let the fear get a word in edgewise.

This time, there was no anger. Not between me and Cam, anyway. Hurt, yes, but not because Cam had done anything wrong. It just hurt to think I might lose this amazing thing between us.

Except... maybe I already had lost it. The lack of eye contact and conversation from the man who'd barely spoken to me the last few days? The way he hadn't been at all interested in sexting or even just casually texting?

Fucking hell. How had it gone so wrong, so fast? And what was on *his* mind? What had gone wrong on *his* end?

I couldn't handle this standoff anymore.

The long silences between me and Bryan had been a relief more often than not. At least when we weren't talking, we weren't fighting. The moment I'd realized that had been the moment I'd known divorce was on the horizon.

It didn't feel anything like that with Cam. Whenever he left a room or avoided interacting with me, I was hit with this impulse to drop to my knees and beg or cry or... *something*. I wasn't actually going to do anything that melodramatic, and I'd been thinking about cooling things off between us anyway, but that was how those moments left me feeling.

Finally, after I came back from practice the second day I was back in town, I decided enough was enough. Cam was in the gym downstairs, and while I didn't like to interrupt his workouts, I couldn't handle this tension for another minute.

He was on the treadmill, and he glanced at me when I came in, but focused out the window. I took a deep breath and came closer. "Hey. Can we talk?"

He winced.

"Cam. Talk to me. Please."

He wouldn't even look at me.

I tried again, struggling not to sound as desperate as I felt. "Did I do something wrong?"

He flinched. Then he paused the program on the treadmill. After the belt had slowed to a stop, he rested his hands on the siderails and sighed. Still not looking at me, he said, "No. No, you didn't do..." He raked a hand through his sweaty hair. "I don't think anyone did anything wrong."

I studied him, completely confused. Shit. What was going on? I stayed quiet, letting him gather his thoughts and figure out what to say. I definitely had no idea what to say.

Finally, he exhaled hard and rolled his shoulders, and after a moment, he met my gaze. The amount of pain in his eyes almost sent me back a step.

"I'm sorry," he whispered. "I don't... This has nothing to do with any feelings I have for you. It's..."

I swallowed. "Is this about us? Dating? Or, uh, whatever we're doing?"

Avoiding my gaze again, he nodded.

Though I knew the answer, I asked anyway: "Do you want to end it?"

The flinch made me want to wrap my arms around him, but I couldn't. Not this time. Because I knew what was coming.

"I don't *want* to," he whispered. "But I..." He cleared his throat and finally looked at me again. "I need to, Trev. I'm sorry."

There should've been some relief that he was dropping this hammer. He was saving me the heartache of trying to spell out why *I* needed to call it off. But all I could feel in that moment was panic that the most amazing man I'd ever known was slipping away. Again.

"But why?" I pleaded softly. "Cam, we can—"

"I need this job. I need this place to live." He swallowed hard and shook his head. "If things fall apart between us—if we break up and it gets ugly—then I don't just lose you. I lose *everything*. Same as when everything went to shit with Daniel."

I blinked. "I would... I would never do that to you."

"I know. But what if we *do* break up?" He struggled to hold my gaze, and his voice wavered. "How do you really see that playing out? I keep living here and watching your kids, even while things get super uncomfortable and we both start seeing other people?" He grimaced and shook his head. "And that's the *best-case scenario*. What if things aren't amicable and we can't stand to be around each other? This"—he gestured to encompass the house—"is all yours. I have nothing. I have nowhere to go except back to Seattle to start all over. *Again.*"

Jesus. While I'd been wringing my hands over all the reasons why this could blow up in my face, it hadn't occurred to me how badly it could blow up in his.

"I'm sorry, Trev," he whispered. "I don't want to do this. But I'd rather we end things now while we can go back to being friends so I can keep working for you and living here. I'm scared that if we keep doing this, things might turn ugly, and..." He trailed off, shaking his head.

What could I even say? No, I'd never toss him out on his ass, not even if things went to hell between us. But what right did I have to expect him to have faith in that? We weren't married. There was nothing legally obligating me to make sure he was on his feet. At best, I was pretty sure I had to give him a minimum of thirty days before kicking him out, but that was about it. He'd be out of a job, out of a home, and in a city where he didn't know anyone but me.

Would I have wanted to stay in a relationship in his position?

No, I would not.

So what right did have to expect him to want to stay in one?

I exhaled. "Okay. Okay, I get that. But I don't want to lose you. And not just as a boyfriend or as someone taking care of my kids. I already lost so damn many years with you, and I don't want to go back to that."

"I'm not leaving," he insisted. "As long as you want me here, I'm here. I don't want to lose you either. I just... I can't let the lines blur." He winced as he added, "I can't risk losing all my stability—*again*—if things don't work out between us as a couple."

"I get that. I do. I promise. And... I don't want that for

you either. I want you to be safe and have stability." It took some serious effort to swallow. "If that means we have to give this up, then... Then that's what we have to do."

There was still pain in his eyes, but his posture relaxed a little. "Thank you," he whispered. "I'm sorry. I wish we could do..." He trailed off again, rubbing the back of his neck with an unsteady hand. "I really don't want to do this. Just so you know."

"I know," I said. "I'm sorry I put you in this position."

"It took two."

"Still. I'm sorry."

"So am I."

Uncomfortable silence hung between us, and I had no idea how to fill it. What else was there to say? What would make the situation better instead of worse?

Cam flicked his eyes toward the door. "I'll, um—"

"I'll get out of here," I said evenly. "I'm sorry I interrupted your workout."

That seemed to catch him by surprise and leave him slightly off-balance. He avoided my gaze and picked up his towel. "I... I've already cooled down a bit, so I'm just going to grab a shower and..." He swallowed, and he didn't finish the thought.

Then he quickly toweled off the treadmill, grabbed his water bottle, and disappeared out of the gym.

Leaning against the wall, I listened to his footsteps fading up the stairs. There was movement above me, then nothing, so he must've continued up to the next floor.

With a heavy sigh, I wiped a hand over my face.

Okay. Okay, it was done. We'd had the hard conversation and we were back on the same page. Everything was the way it needed to be. Everything was good.

So when would I start feeling better?

CHAPTER 32

CAM

THIS WAS HELL.

I'd thought the aftermath with Daniel had been awful, but this post-relationship coexistence with Trev was torture. I didn't get angry whenever I saw him the way I had with Daniel. I *hurt*. I physically *ached* for him, and not just for his touch. After all those years without my friend, I'd had a taste of life with Trev again—of my world being on its axis because Trev was back in it—and now... this.

When we'd talked things through, I'd insisted I wasn't going anywhere. I'd just wanted the lines to be clearer. I'd meant every word of that.

But now that we were actually living what we'd agreed to, I wasn't so sure I could keep doing this after all. I needed this job and I needed the room in Trev's house. Plus he needed someone looking after his kids, at least until the hockey season was over.

But every time I saw him or heard his voice, or every time one of the boys mentioned him, I died a little inside. I hated myself for not being able to have faith in him that he wouldn't screw me over if things went to shit. I hated everything about this situation, especially how inescapable it felt.

I hadn't spent another night in the place I'd shared with Daniel after I'd busted him cheating, but we'd still had to cross paths. I'd had to move out and give him back my key. We'd still worked together for that brief period before he got me fired. Just that level of interaction—being in the same eleven-thousand square foot gym without seeing or speaking to each other—had been fucking miserable.

And somehow, that didn't hold a candle to living in the same house as Trev.

Nothing had blown up between us. No one had done anything wrong. We—or, well, I—had come to the painful conclusion that being more than friends was a bad idea.

Since then, it was hard to coexist with him at all. I missed him as much as I wanted to be far, far away from him. Sleeping alone was excruciating. I didn't even care if we had sex; I just missed having him in bed with me. The nights when he was on the road were a relief because at least we would've been separated anyway. When he was sleeping across the hall, I tossed and turned all goddamned night.

And from the sound of it, he did too. His bed was pretty quiet, but it did make some noise, and the muffled creaks and groans that filtered through the walls as he tossed and turned made me feel even guiltier. Trev was such a sound sleeper most of the time, but lately, not so much. Then in the mornings, he'd be bleary-eyed and clinging to his coffee cup as he avoided looking at me. I had to imagine that every time he left for practice or a game or the airport, he was breathing the same sigh of relief I was.

We didn't FaceTime when he was on the road anymore unless it was so he could talk to the kids. After he'd chatted with them, I'd get him up to speed on anything about what was going on in their world, and then we'd end the call. No more long conversations when we both should've been sleeping. No more sexting after we'd hung up. Just... silence.

It didn't even feel like we were friends anymore. There was no hostility or animosity, but everything else had evaporated. The banter. The nostalgic conversations about our past life. Just the *friendship* that had been missing for so damn long.

Three weeks after I'd said we couldn't do this anymore, I couldn't *take* it anymore. I hurt for him more than I'd ever hurt for Daniel. I missed him. I wanted to get away from him. I loved him. I was pissed at him for no rational reason besides *"you exist and I can't have you."* I was relieved every time he left the house. I was terrified he was going to fire me and send me away.

It was exhausting, and it fucking hurt. I had to do something, damn it, and every mental flowchart landed on the same solution: get out.

Go back to Seattle? Find another job here in Pittsburgh? Start over someplace else? I didn't know. Just... get out of this house and this miserable situation.

Sometimes I thought I could hold out until the hockey season was over. Trev could focus on hockey between now and then, and once the off season started, he'd have months to find someone to take my place. That way I wouldn't be throwing him off his game or leaving him in a lurch.

I didn't want to hurt him any more than I already had, but this wasn't getting any better for either of us.

It didn't help that Trev wasn't great at hiding how much this was hurting him. He had always been the type to wear his feelings on his sleeve, and he wasn't taking this well. I could see it in the set of his shoulders and the way he avoided looking at me whenever he could help it. It came out in his voice, which was flatter than I'd ever heard it; not like he was gray-walling me or blowing me off, but like he just didn't have the heart to put any emotion into his words.

And it showed in his hockey game too.

I was no expert at the sport, but there were nights when Trev seemed to understand the game even less than I did. When he'd get the puck on his stick and suddenly not seem to know what he should do with it. Or when a teammate would send him a pass because he was wide open, and the puck would just go sailing past him; that happened sometimes anyway, but it was conspicuously frequent now. The commentators noticed. His coach evidently noticed, because Trev had been knocked to the third line for the last couple of games. Even the boys noticed.

"I don't think Dad likes hockey anymore," Zane said one night as we watched a game on TV.

"You don't?" I asked.

He shook his head. "He's playing like my friend Hayden did right before he quit soccer."

I almost whistled. The lack of enthusiasm was definitely coming through if a seven-year-old could pick up on it.

And I didn't imagine any of this was going to get any easier for Trev as long as he had to keep coming home to me. It wasn't getting any easier for me either.

Maybe waiting for the end of the season was a bad idea. Maybe I needed to rip off this bandage sooner than later. Or be proactive and find some people in the area who might be able to take my place, so once he hired them, I could exit stage left. Or... something. I needed to do something to break this tension before one or both of us lost our minds, or before it started doing serious damage to his career.

One way or another, something had to give, and soon.

I couldn't keep hurting Trev or myself like this.

CHAPTER 33

TREV

"Oh. I wasn't expecting—" Bryan stared at me through the condo's open door. Then he recovered, put on a smile, and greeted the boys, who were standing behind me. After they'd gone to put their stuff down in their rooms, he turned to me, and his momentary confusion had returned. "I... thought Cam would be bringing the kids by."

"He's busy," I said flatly. "And they are my kids, you know."

He pursed his lips. "Yeah, but you had—there was practice, so—"

"Well, it's me today."

Bryan studied me. "Did you two... you and Cam..."

I winced. "We're, um... We're working on some things."

That was a half-truth. Yeah, we'd broken up. I hadn't been able to give Cam an argument for why we *shouldn't*— not without compromising his sense of safety—but for the last few days, I'd been tying myself in knots trying to come up with a solution. Now I was almost certain I'd found one, but I had no idea if Cam would go for it. I had no idea if there was any saving us. All I could do was try. I'd just wanted to wait until the boys were out of the house so they didn't overhear anything. Now they were with Bryan, so...

"I need to get going," I told him.

"No about updates about the boys?" Bryan demanded. "There's absolutely nothing?"

I paused. Truth be told, I didn't know if there was. I'd been too distracted and too much of a mess to be the parent my sons needed. And things had been too weird with Cam for me to check in with him to see if I needed to pass something on to Bryan. God, I was just winning all over the place, wasn't I?

I made a mental note to make up for it when the boys were back at my place, because they sure as shit deserved better than that. Cam did too, and hopefully I'd have the chance to smooth things over with him.

And Bryan...

Well, I wasn't usually one to be petty, but he could figure it the fuck out this week. God knew he'd left Cam to do the same a few times. Hopefully I could be forgiven for being petty this one time. I was exhausted. From Chats. From Bryan. From this canyon between me and Cam. I needed to have a conversation with Cam and unfuck our situation, and I—

"What is going on with you?" Bryan snapped. "Look, whatever drama is happening between you and your boyfriend, it shouldn't be interfering with how we parent our—"

"But it's okay for *your* boyfriend's bullshit to drive wedges in all over the place?" I threw back with sudden fury, making both of us jump.

And now that I'd said it—fuck it. I wasn't taking it back.

"Did he tell you he outed me and Cam to the team?" I demanded.

Bryan's eyebrows jumped. "He—what?" Then he scoffed. "Everyone already knew you two were—"

"No, they didn't. They suspected, but nobody confirmed anything until *your boyfriend* decided to trot it out. And not only that, but he managed to insult the hell out of Cam in the process." I glared hard at my ex. "What's it like, huh? Being with a man who thinks someone like Cam is *beneath* him? Just because he's a nanny?" I made a disgusted sound. "I knew you loved the high life, but I didn't think you were into the hardcore elitist types."

His lips parted, which made me think I'd revealed something about Chats that he either hadn't noticed or hadn't wanted to acknowledge.

And while I was on that tirade, another piece clicked into place.

"You know, when I got together with Cam, Chats' bullshit stopped bothering me. I stopped caring." I narrowed my eyes. "And then lo and behold, you and Chats are suddenly convinced Cam and I are fucking."

"Which you were," he snapped, though his anger was waning in favor of embarrassment.

"Yeah. I was." I shrugged. "And I won't apologize for that. But doesn't it tell you something when the reason you figured us out was that your boyfriend's bullshit wasn't getting under my skin anymore?"

Bryan blinked. "What?"

"Oh, come on." I scoffed, letting the sarcasm drip. "Chats was relentless about rubbing it in my face that he was with you. And yes, it bothered me. It was fucking annoying, and it—look, we're done, but it still hurt, okay? He can have you, but yeah, it sucked, being reminded every goddamned day that he was screwing you."

Some color drained from Bryan's face.

"Do you know how hard that is?" I demanded. "Trying to do my job while someone is constantly there and constantly reminding me that he's fucking my ex-husband?"

"That's..." He swallowed. "Yeah. That's... really unprofessional."

"Unprofessional?" I scoffed. "How about fucking heartless? Cruel? Just goddamned obnoxious?" I threw up a hand. "I'm not one to question your taste in men, but why the hell are you with someone like that? Is that the example you want to set for our kids?"

Bryan opened his mouth, probably ready to let fly with something defensive, but he hesitated. He closed his mouth. Shifted his weight. Maybe my last question had gone too far, but I didn't take it back. It was something we both had to consider when we picked post-divorce partners.

Gentler now, I said, "I'm not telling you how to live your life. Date whoever you want. As long as they treat you and the kids well..." I gestured dismissively. "I don't care." Holding his gaze, I let some of the hurt and worry take over for the anger in my tone. "Is someone like him really treating you and the kids well? Really? Because he's good with kids, but if he's that much of an insufferable asshole to—"

"I get it," Bryan snapped, and he folded his arms. "Look, he really is a good guy. To me and the kids." He showed his palms. "I... I didn't know he was—"

"Bullshit you didn't," I hissed. "Maybe you didn't know what he was saying in the locker room. I can accept that. But you can't honestly say you didn't know he's been trying to antagonize me ever since the two of you got together. Or that you haven't been helping."

His jaw tightened.

I went on, "I don't care if your new partner likes me. I

genuinely don't. And me and you—we don't have to be friendly. As long as we can co-parent, I don't give a fuck." I stabbed a finger at him. "But don't fucking pretend you had a problem with your boyfriend making things worse between us, or that watching him act like that won't have a negative impact on our kids."

To my surprise, he actually looked chastened. He avoided my gaze and gnawed his lip.

"He let it get far enough to jeopardize both his career and mine," I said. "I don't know if he told you, but we're *both* on thin ice over it."

Bryan tensed. "You won't... You won't lose your careers," he insisted, sounding more like he was trying to convince himself. "One of you might get traded, but—"

"You don't think people will find out why? You don't think it'll get around that we had to be separated because of locker room drama? The League still has a hair up its ass about queer players. You don't think people will perceive it as two queer guys fighting over a man, and that won't translate into guys like us having no place in a locker room?" I set my jaw. "And I'd ask if it's crossed your mind that if I get traded because of this bullshit with Chats, then I'll be even farther from our boys. But hey, you'd have primary custody and I'd almost never see them, so that would work out great for you, wouldn't it?"

To my surprise, that seemed to hit a nerve, because he lost even more color. He avoided my gaze, his eyes unfocused as he apparently reeled from what I'd said.

"I..." He swallowed, shaking his head slowly. "I don't—I want you see the boys. I don't want to take them away from you."

"Could've fooled me," I growled.

I fully expected him to lash out, but his shoulders

sagged a bit further. Knowing him as well as I did, I had to wonder if he hadn't been *consciously* trying to separate me from our sons, but was realizing now that was exactly what he'd been doing.

Now that I had his attention, I went on, softening my tone a little. "I don't care if you're with Chats, okay? I don't. I really, really fucking don't. But whether I like it or not, I *have* to co-parent with you, and I *have* to coexist with him." I threw up my hands. "Something has to give here, okay? And it can't be me this time."

Again, I fully expected him to snap at me. I expected him to give me shit for putting this on him. Even when a ball needed to be firmly in his court, he never took it gracefully.

This time, though...

He chewed his lip as he met my gaze. "We, um... Yeah. We do have to co-parent. And you and Tim..." He glanced down the hall as he trailed off.

"I don't know what else I can do." My voice wavered a little. "I'm trying to be everything I'm supposed to be right now. A teammate. A dad. A co-parent. I..." I flailed a hand. "I can't do that with this much animosity coming from you *or* from your boyfriend. We don't have to like each other. We don't have to be friends. But we *have* to be our sons' dads."

Bryan winced, and I prayed like hell I'd hit the mark I was aiming for. After a long, silent moment, he quietly said, "You're right."

It took all I had not to blink in actual surprise and ask, "*I am?*" That would only set him off.

"I'm sorry, Trev," he said softly. "I... no, we don't have to be friends. But you're right. We've driven enough wedges between us without someone else making it worse."

I had to fight hard not to snap back that *"we"* hadn't driven the enormous wedge that broke us up. "I just want us to be able to raise the boys as best we can. Ideally without one of us getting shipped off to the other side of the country or something, which is still on the table if the club decides to trade me."

He grimaced. "I'm sorry."

"I know. And what you decide to do going forward with Chats—that's up to you. But there have to be some boundaries between him and me." I hardened my voice a little. "And about what he says in front of our children."

Defensiveness flared in Bryan's expression, but it quickly died away. Anger surged in me; here I'd tried to believe Chats *hadn't* talked shit about me in front of our boys. Or that my ex-husband *wouldn't* allow it.

A pair of familiar thoughts drifted to the front of my mind, laced with more disgust than sadness this time.

What happened *to us?*

What the fuck did I ever see *in you?*

"I'm sorry," Bryan said again. "We'll work on it. I'll talk to Tim. And we'll..." He swallowed again, refusing to look at me. "You're right that I need to do better. That we—me and Tim—need to do better."

Somehow, it seemed like it should be more satisfying to hear him say that. If anything, it just made me feel like I could finally release my breath. Like a hard-fought battle was over. "Okay. That's all I ask."

He nodded silently.

"I'm, uh... I'm going to head home."

Another nod.

I turned to go, already mentally shifting gears toward the conversation I needed to have once I got there.

"Trev."

I faced my ex-husband again, and I was surprised to see an even more contrite and exhausted version of him. "Hmm?"

He glanced over his shoulder as if to check on the boys. Then he faced me again, took a deep breath, and set his shoulders back, though that didn't do much for his wilted posture. "Maybe... Maybe we should look into some counseling again. As a family. It won't bring us back together, but co-parenting... navigating things with the boys and whoever we're dating..."

The suggestion almost sent me back a step. "You'd be willing to do that?"

Bryan nodded. "I, um... I think we should've stuck with it before." He hesitated, then whispered, "I'm sorry, Trev. I really am."

I pressed my lips together. After a moment, I said, "If you're willing to set something up, I'm willing to go."

There was a flash of irritation in his eyes—probably at the idea that he had to do the legwork. Quite frankly, I thought that was a fair trade. I'd made plenty of mistakes with him, but the mess we were in right now was the result of his choices. Seemed like the least he could do was find us a counselor and get the ball rolling.

Evidently, he either agreed or didn't want to argue anymore, because he sighed and nodded. "Okay. I'll look around online and text you."

"All right. Do you need the team's schedule?"

"No. I have it." He shifted his weight, not meeting my eyes. "And I'll make sure there's some flexibility."

"Okay. Thanks."

After that, I left, and he let me go this time. In the parking lot, I started the engine, but just sat there for a moment. That had probably been the most productive conversation we'd had since long before the divorce. I was wrung out and exhausted, but I also felt like we'd finally gotten somewhere. Not enough to reconcile—that ship had sailed—but enough that maybe we could function like civil adults while we raised our boys.

It was a big step in the right direction. I'd take it.

With a heavy sigh, I started out of the condo parking lot. This day had taken a lot out of me, but it wasn't over yet.

I'd made some serious headway with my ex-husband.

Was it too much to ask to get somewhere with my ex-boyfriend, too?

Cam was only going to put up with this tension for so long. I could feel it. Every time he texted me, which wasn't nearly as often as before, I expected him to be telling me he'd landed a job elsewhere and was moving out. The surge of panic his text tone brought was driving me out of my head. I was terrified of losing him, and though I felt guilty about it, I was also terrified of losing the childcare he provided.

Which... no wonder he'd tapped out. Our relationship, his presence in the house—it all looped back to his job taking care of my kids. He didn't want to risk a relationship because he could lose his job. I was scared to have tough conversations with him or even acknowledge the elephant in the room for fear that he'd leave.

He was right that we couldn't separate us from his job. I didn't know what the solution was for that, but... he was right.

I needed to talk to him, and it couldn't wait.

But I also needed to do this in person. This wasn't a conversation we could have over FaceTime, never mind text.

I exhaled into the stillness of my car. I didn't want to wait another minute, but he deserved to hear it face to face.

I just hoped he was still there when I got home.

Cam was home.

Thank God, he was still here.

Guilt needled at me for being happy that Zach and Zane weren't here, but I reminded myself it wasn't glee that I was free or anything like that. I just didn't want them to hear this go down, especially because it might not go well. And I wanted Cam and me to be able to focus on this conversation and not worry about our words carrying to the ears of my kids.

Still... guilt. The next time they were here, we'd do something special, if only to alleviate my conscience for this.

First things first, I needed to have this conversation with Cam, and it couldn't wait.

I found him in the kitchen, cleaning up from making his lunch. When I walked in, he tensed; he didn't bristle or glare at me, and his hackles didn't go up, but the discomfort was palpable.

He was probably hoping I'd leave without saying anything.

I felt guilty, because I knew it wouldn't be comfortable at first, but I hoped like hell I was doing the right thing and the outcome would be worth it.

"Hey." I slid my hands into my pockets as I leaned against the counter. "Can we talk? Please?"

He chewed his lip, but as he closed the dishwasher, he nodded. "Okay. Yeah. We can talk."

Well, that was progress.

"To cut right to the chase..." I hesitated, my guilt intensifying along with his obvious uneasiness.

Come on, Trev. Just fucking do it.

I took a deep breath. "Look, I don't want you to be trapped with me, or to feel like your job and your stability are something I would hold over your head. *I* know I would never do that, but you don't, and I get that. People change during breakups, and they do shit you never thought they would."

Cam sighed. "Yeah. They definitely do." He stared down at his hands. "For the record, I don't think you would. It's not you. I'm just... I still don't feel like the ground is solid under my feet after what Daniel did. And everything he did..." Cam laughed bitterly. "It was on-brand for him. Someone that controlling and vindictive—I should've known. And I think I did know." He paused, then met my gaze. "I know you're nothing like him. But..."

"But once bitten."

"Exactly. I'm sorry."

"Don't apologize." It was so damn hard in that moment not to reach for his hand. "You're right to worry about it, especially after what you've been through. I get it." I swallowed, and as my heart pounded, I went on, "If things were different—if you didn't have to be afraid that you'd be out of a job and a place to live if things didn't work out between us —would you want to be with me?"

I hated myself for the pain that crossed his expression.

"Trev," he whispered. "We can't—what's the point of torturing ourselves like this?"

"I don't want to torture ourselves. But I think that's what we've *been* doing. And I can't help but wonder if maybe we're doing this all wrong."

He met my eyes. "There's no way around it, though." He gestured at our surroundings. "I live with you. I work for you. If you decide you can't stand me anymore... what do I do? I've managed to save some money since I've been here, but it isn't like I can just waltz out the door and pick up someplace else." He blew out a breath. "Whether we like it or not, breakups do happen, and they can get ugly. But breaking up with you isn't *just* a breakup for me. My job and my place to live are gone." He set his jaw. "We've been through this, Trev."

"I know we have," I said softly. "But what if there was a safety net?"

"A safety—what?"

I shifted a little, trying like hell to get comfortable while every muscle in my body was this tense. "An account. One that you have sole access to, with enough money in it to keep you going until you've landed a job and found a place."

He grimaced. "I don't have that kind of money."

"No, but I do."

Cam blinked. "You—wait, are you suggesting you're going to... You want to create an escape fund for me?"

I half-shrugged. "You could call it that, I guess? What I want is to give you whatever you need to feel safe and secure. And to keep things separate. Yeah, you're working for me and living here, but I don't want you to feel like you're stuck in any of those things—the job, the house, or a relationship." I had to clear my throat because it was getting harder to keep my voice steady. "I can hire someone else to watch the kids, too, if that makes the lines clearer. Whatever you need. Whatever makes you feel safe, and like you're here because we both *want* you to be, not because you have to be."

I had never seen so much shock on Cam's face before.

After a moment, he asked, "But... why?" He shook his

head slowly. "You could have literally any man you wanted. You don't have to settle for me. Why would you—why are you doing all of this just to be with me?"

It was so hard not to laugh out loud at that. The idea was just so absurd. *Settling* for him? *Just* being with him? There was no man in this world I wanted more than him.

"Cam..." I hesitated, then reached for his hand. "I don't want any other men. Just you."

He stared at me incredulously, as if he barely comprehended what I'd said, and what little he did understand, he couldn't believe.

I gripped his hand tighter. "I love you, Cam. I'm in love with you. I..." I shook my head. "I can't imagine being in love with anyone *but* you."

His lips parted, eyes wide with disbelief.

"I mean it," I whispered. "The truth is..." I had to fight back my emotions, and my voice came out unsteady, but I managed to finish, "The truth is that I've loved you since we were kids who didn't know who we were."

"Are you..." Cam swiped away some tears that had begun welling up. "Are you serious?"

"Yes," I said shakily. "There is nothing I won't do to make sure you're happy and safe. If that's a bank account with enough money to leave if you want to—done. If that's hiring someone else to watch the kids so this feels less like a transaction—fine. If it's—whatever you need. Whatever you want." I swallowed hard, and I fought to hold his gaze as my eyes stung. "That includes *not* doing this. Not being together. I want you happy and safe. Full stop."

"But you do want us to be together." His voice was full of wonder.

"Yes," I said. "There's no one else for me."

Cam stared at me for long seconds, his eyes wide and

lips apart. I was sure I should've been saying more, but I was out of words. I'd put every single card I had on the table, and all I could do now was wait for him to say something.

When he finally broke the standoff, he didn't say a word.

He pulled me in closer by the hand I was holding. Then, just like he had that first time in my gym, he curved his other behind my neck, and...

Oh. God, yes. Finally.

Cam's kiss had never made me break down before, but this time, there was a good chance it would. The softness of his lips, the firmness of his grasp on the back of my neck, the way all this tension just fell away—it was all so damn perfect, I wouldn't have been surprised or ashamed if I'd fallen apart right there in his arms.

Still holding onto my neck, he broke the kiss. His breath was warm and ragged across my lips, and his voice shook as he murmured, "I love you, Trev. So much."

The words almost sent me to my knees, and when I spoke, my voice cracked. "I love you, too."

"I'm sorry," he murmured. "I never meant to put you in a position where—"

My lips silenced his. Then I kissed his forehead and pulled him in tight. "It's not your fault. The situation was what it was." Stroking his hair, I added, "I never wanted you to feel like you were trapped or things were going to get yanked out from under you."

He sighed, relaxing against me and holding me tighter. "I know. That's not you."

"But I get that the circumstances—even if it was never my intention, that doesn't mean you won't feel trapped." I ran a hand up and down his back. "I want to be with you, but more than anything else in the world, I want you to feel safe. I want you to *be* safe."

Though he didn't let me go, the lessening tension was impossible to miss.

Holy fuck. It was like my entire life—my entire world—had been leading to this. That I'd spent the last decade flailing around and trying to find my way to this, and now that I was wrapped up in Cam's arms...

I was home.

I was right where I'd always needed to be.

"God, I love you," I whispered shakily, stroking his hair and just holding on as if he might vanish if I loosened my embrace.

"Me too," he breathed. "Ever since we broke up..."

"It's been awful."

"It has." He lifted his head and met my gaze, a few tears clinging to his lashes. "I think I missed you more when you were home than when you were on the road."

Jesus. Did he want me to break down sobbing? Because that was where this was headed.

I cradled his face in both hands and kissed his forehead again. "We are going to make up for so much lost time when the season is over. I promise."

He smiled. "I can't wait."

"Neither can I." I pressed a soft kiss to his mouth, and we let it linger for a moment as the whole world seemed to... settle. As if, for the first time, everything was exactly the way it needed to be.

I'd wondered a few times if I'd ever meet someone who'd be worthy of being a stepfather to my sons. I wasn't even a little bit surprised that when he'd shown up, it was the friend I'd been missing and the man I'd loved for most of my life.

Cam drew back a little. "You know, I've never had makeup sex before." His lips curved into a devilish grin that weakened my knees. "Want to go find out if it's as good as everyone says it is?"

I returned the grin. "It's sex with you. I *know* it's going to be good."

"Still, we should find out." He tugged me toward the stairs. "For science."

Laughing, I followed him. "For science."

CHAPTER 34

CAM

I'd been missing Trev so bad I was losing my mind, but I hadn't realized just how much until I landed in bed with him. Naked with his hips between my thighs and my hands all over his powerful back, I was overwhelmed by how amazing it was to be in his arms again. To be holding him close while we kissed like our lives depended on it. Yes, every inch of him was hot as hell, and I was so turned on I could barely breathe, but this was also coming home. Returning to a place that leaving had never felt right, not even for a second.

Everything was right again.

Trev pushed himself up on his forearms and gazed down at me with smoldering eyes. "Tell me what you want. Anything."

Immediately, my head was full of every imaginable thing we could do. Some from fantasies, most from the scorching hot reality of being with him. I saw us sixty-nining, or making out while we got each other off with our hands, or fucking in every position imaginable until we couldn't move. I wanted it all right the hell now, but the urgency also ticked down a few notches because... I didn't *have* to have it all right now. We had time. We were back to where we'd always belonged, and we had all the time in the world to explore all the ways we could drive each other wild.

There was no rush.

At the same time, though, the thing I was hungriest for was Trev's orgasm. The sounds he made, the way his whole body shook with his surrender, the indescribable bliss of knowing I could make him feel that good.

"Let me ride you," I panted.

He shivered. "You know it'll be quick if you do, right?"

I grinned. "Uh-huh. And we've got all day, so plenty of time to go a few rounds and take our time?"

"God, Cam..." He bent to kiss my neck. "You're going to kill me. You know that, right?"

"I mean, not on purpose."

Trev huffed a warm laugh against my throat, then lifted his head to kiss my mouth again. I couldn't help whimpering into his deep, needy kiss, and when he rubbed his hard cock against my hip, I almost came unglued. I fucking *needed* him. Like *now*.

Before I could say anything, though, he rolled onto his back and took me with him. I straddled him as we kept making out, and when I pressed against his cock, the helpless sound he made had the whole room spinning.

"Let me fuck you," he pleaded, his voice strained with need. "I want to make you scream."

I was suddenly out of breath, but I managed, "You always do."

"Uh-huh." He nipped my lower lip. "Get some lube. I can't wait."

The hunger in his shaky voice made my spine tingle. Get some lube? Didn't have to tell me twice.

I handed him the bottle, and... Christ, he was gorgeous like this. He was gorgeous anyway, but lying back with those abs on full display, stroking lube onto his dick as he raked his eyes up and down my body—he was mind-blowingly sexy.

I hadn't been the least bit horny since we'd stopped fooling around. Now, I couldn't get enough of him, and I couldn't get him into me fast enough.

And that low purr he gave as I sank down on top of him? Fuck, he wasn't the only one who was going to come fast, and not only because every move either of us made meant *just* the right amount of friction.

"Oh my God..." He slid his hands up my thighs. "That feels so... He squeezed his eyes shut and arched under me, driving himself deeper. "Fuck, Cam..."

I fought to hold on to my rhythm. Every thrust, every stroke—I was ready to lose it, but Trev was teetering so perfectly on the edge, and I wanted him to come. I loved it when he was too keyed up to hold back.

"Cam," he panted. "Jesus Christ, I'm—"

He sucked in a breath and thrust up so hard he knocked me off-balance. He kept me in place with his strong hands on my hips, though, and he fucked up into me as he cried out with the force of his orgasm. Watching and feeling him fall apart like that—when he was frenzied with the need to get as deep as I could take him—I damn near came with him.

With a shudder, he relaxed back onto the bed, and his iron grip on my hips relaxed as he closed his eyes and exhaled.

That was a sight I'd be remembering the next time I got

myself off while he was on the road. Sweaty, flushed, shaking Trev, every muscle standing out as he trembled through the last few aftershocks of his orgasm. He was gorgeous anyway, and he was never hotter than in that moment after he'd come, when he was an utter mess who probably couldn't even remember where he was.

Knowing I could do that to him was the sexiest thing *ever*.

His eyelids fluttered open, and when his gaze landed on me, it sharpened as if he were coming back to earth. He swept his tongue across his lips and whispered, "My turn."

Oh, hell yeah.

I eased myself up off him and onto my back beside him. Before I'd even settled onto the pillows, Trev's lips were on mine and his magic fingers were between my thighs. I moaned into his mouth as he slipped his fingers into me, and —oh, God, I loved his hands. The way he finger-fucked me while the heel of his hand rubbed *just* right to melt my damn spine. His touch was light but insistent—enough to send me into the stratosphere without making me too sensitive.

A memory flickered through my mind of fantasizing about Trev to get myself over the edge, but I didn't need to do that anymore. Trev was here. He was holding me close, driving me wild, and kissing me while he tried to catch his breath from his own orgasm. That reality took me higher than any fantasy ever could, and I gripped his shoulders tighter as I rutted against his hand.

He started kissing my neck, pausing just long enough to breathlessly murmur, "You gonna come?"

"Uh-huh." I arched, squeezing my eyes shut. "God, baby, keep..." I shuddered hard. "Keep doing that."

He growled softly against my throat, and he kept doing

that, and... fuck, I was almost there. So damn close. Right on the brink. I wanted to come so bad I was on the verge of tears, but I also fought it back just because I loved what he was doing. This felt so goddamned good—his magic fingers, his lips on my neck, his purred encouragement, his hot, powerful body against mine—that I wanted to enjoy it and savor it.

Finally, though, I let him carry me over the edge, my spine lifting off the bed as my orgasm drove a cry of "fuu-uck!" out of me. Trev kept me going, lightening his touch just enough that I wouldn't get too sensitive, but still teasing me enough that I kept coming... and coming... and—

"S-stop," I panted.

He did, lifting his hand away and gathering me in his arms as I trembled and gasped for air.

"I love making you come," he growled into my hair.

All I could manage was a wordless whimper, which I hope he took to mean that I, too, loved when he made me come.

We lay like that for a while, just holding each other. Once I caught my breath, there was some lazy kissing, and I was in heaven.

It wasn't just bliss because Trev had made me come hard enough to see stars, either. We were here. Together. We'd found a way to make things work, and by some mira-cle, I was in the arms of the man I'd loved for most of my life.

Except it *wasn't* a miracle or divine intervention. It was Trev refusing to give up and figuring out a way to make sure the financial side of things didn't muddy the romantic side.

It was Trev wanting this enough to fight for us. It was him loving me the way I'd always loved him.

"The truth is that I've loved you since we were kids who didn't know who we were."

God, it was like he'd said out loud what I hadn't been able to put into words. Because I had loved him since then, and by some miracle... he had too.

And it wasn't just words or lip service. Not when he was offering to put things into motion to make sure I was more secure than I'd thought possible.

I carded my fingers through his hair as I gazed into his beautiful eyes. "What you said about a bank account—were you serious about that?"

Trev nodded. "Completely."

Apparently taking my silence for disbelief—which it kind of was, because holy shit—he rolled over and leaned down to pick up something off the floor. When he came back, he had his phone in his hand, which he must've dug out of his pants pocket. Without a word, he tapped the screen a few times, then showed it to me.

There was an open banking app on the screen, which showed a newly created account. The only activity so far was a deposit made a few days ago.

A deposit of $100,000.

It took a second to process everything he was showing me. When I did, I shook myself and met his gaze. "That's an insane amount of money, Trev."

"It's enough that you won't have to worry about anything for a while." He signed out of the app and put the phone on the nightstand. Then he turned onto his side and rested his hand on my waist. "It's in my name right now, but they told me it won't take more than a ten-minute visit to the branch to transfer it to you. Completely."

I stared at him. The bank balance again. Then him.

"You... already set this up? Even before you knew we'd..." I gestured at us.

Cheeks coloring a little, he said, "I wanted you to know I was serious. Because I am."

"What if..." I hesitated. "What if I'd said no?"

He half-shrugged. "I still would've kept the money aside for you. In case you wanted to leave the job and needed something to help you get on your feet."

I blinked. "I... You... You were going to let me take a hundred grand as severance?"

Trev pursed his lips, then shrugged again. "I guess you could call it that?" He trailed his fingers down my cheek. "I saw it more as making sure my friend didn't end up out on his ass. Even if we're not together, I still care about you. I always have."

I had to work to swallow. "You really are more than I deserve."

"No, I'm not." He leaned in for a soft kiss. "I love you, Cam. I always have. I want you to be happy and secure, and that doesn't hinge on you being with me."

"I kind of do want to be with you, though."

His eyebrow flicked up, as did one corner of his mouth. "Kind of?"

"Well. You know." I half-shrugged as I fought a grin. "I could be persuaded. Maybe."

He tsked and rolled his eyes. "Shut up."

I laughed, which he cut off with a long, perfect kiss. I held him close as the moment lingered, and his words continued to echo in my mind. I really didn't deserve him. He'd always been an amazing friend, even during our young and stupid days, and now—somehow—I had the best version of him as more than a friend. Where my ex had loved to keep me destabilized as much as possible so he'd always have the upper hand, Trev was willing to do whatever it took to make sure the ground was solid beneath my feet. And none of that was contingent on me being his boyfriend.

As if anyone on this planet existed who I could possibly want as a partner more than I wanted Trev.

I broke the kiss and touched my forehead to his. "I love you, Trev."

He ran his fingers through my hair. "I love you, too."

I kissed him lightly. Then I drew back a little to meet his gaze. "Thank you, by the way. You don't have to give me money or—I mean, I appreciate it, but you don't have to."

"I know," he murmured. "But it'll keep the lines clearer. And you won't feel like you're trapped with me if things go south."

I wanted to insist that would never happen. For all I'd been afraid it could, Trev wasn't Daniel; he wouldn't do shit to make me feel unsafe, and he wouldn't leave me out in the cold. But after Daniel, I couldn't take that for granted. Not even with Trev. I hated that.

I moistened my lips. "I, um... I think I might look for a job locally. At a gym or something. Not even because of the financial side of things—I want to have my own income and all, but also... I miss it. I love looking after the boys, but I miss training, you know?"

Trev nodded. "I get that. And there's tons of gyms around here, so I'm sure you could find something. Or—" He hesitated.

"What?"

He chewed his lip, then looked at me through his lashes. "I don't want more of your life to be tangled up with me— more than you're comfortable with, I mean. But there are always people at the team's training center who are looking for trainers. Especially strength trainers. And I'm pretty sure the team has an open position for one too."

I straightened. "Oh. That could be interesting."

"I can get you in touch with the right people if you want to talk to them." He carded his fingers through my hair. "If you're good with a job that's with my team."

"I wouldn't be working directly for you, though. I can live with that."

Some interest sparked in his eyes. "Yeah?"

"Sure. But what if you don't stay in Pittsburgh?"

"It's always a possibility. If that happens, we can do the long-distance thing during the season, and I'll come back here during the off-season." He gestured around us. "You're welcome to stay here, too."

I had no idea what I'd done to deserve this man, but whatever it was, I'd do it all again in a heartbeat.

I curled closer to him. "You're amazing. You know that?"

He stroked a hand down my back. "I know. I've seen my stats."

I snorted and bumped him with my knee.

Chuckling, Trev kissed my forehead and held me to him.

Eyes closed, I sighed into his embrace. Everything about this was perfect. Even all the messiness that had apparently had to happen for us to get here. I'd never wish the aftermath of my breakup with Daniel on my worst enemy, but for the first time, I was genuinely glad it had happened. All of it. Though there'd been a lot of hell and fear during those weeks, that shitstorm was the tornado that had miraculously deposited me here. In Pittsburgh. In this house. In Trev's arms. In love with my best friend.

We'd lost a lot of years, and I hated that we'd missed so

much of each other's lives, but maybe that had been a blessing too. Immaturity and figuring ourselves out had stood in the way of us connecting when we were younger. Maybe we'd needed to go our separate ways for a while, grow up, and become the people who could give this relationship the chance it deserved.

One way or the other, we'd made it back to each other.

And I hoped we never let each other go again.

EPILOGUE
TREV

A YEAR AND A HALF LATER

"Oh, hey! He does clean up!"

I turned around to see Mike, Don, and Jake, my old friends from back home, walking into the room where I'd been getting ready. "Hey, guys! And what do you mean I clean up? I wear bespoke suits all the damn time!"

"Yeah," Don said, "but you don't usually go *this* fancy."

He had a point. While I wore suits regularly, tuxes were reserved for very special occasions. The League awards banquet. The team's casino night.

My wedding.

As I exchanged hugs and handshakes with my friends, I asked, "How does Cam look?"

"Pfft." Mike smacked my arm. "You know we don't do spoilers."

"Oh come on. Does he look good?"

In unison, they all rolled their eyes.

"Dude." Jake shook his head. "It doesn't matter what

we think. Cam could rock up in sweatpants and a jersey from your biggest rival, and you'd still think he looked hot."

My face burned. "I mean... maybe not a *rival's* jersey, but—"

"Bullshit," they all said.

Eh, okay. They once again had a point.

"Anyway," Jake said. "We just wanted to stop in and say congrats before everything got rolling."

"Thanks," I said with a smile. "I still can't believe we're getting married."

"I can't believe it took you this long," Don said.

"No shit," Mike said. "We always knew you two would end up together."

That brought me up short. "You... You did?"

"Well, yeah." Beside him, Don shrugged. "We all did."

"Really?"

"Uh, yeah?" Jake said. "You guys were inseparable in high school. When you started dating, we were all like, 'okay, yeah, Cam and Trev, that makes sense.'"

Mike nodded. "Yep. Now that you guys got rid of the dickbags you were with, I mean—no shit, you're together. Who *else* would you have ended up with?"

I eyed all three of them. "None of you guys ended up with anyone from high school."

"No," Don acknowledged, "and I can barely remember some of my high school girlfriends' names. You two, though? You were it. You always were."

Jake and Mike nodded.

My mouth went a little dry, and my throat got tight. Truth be told, I was pretty sure I'd subconsciously known it too. It was just mind-blowing to realize that three of our closest friends from back then—our *straight* friends, no less

—had clocked us as the real thing even when we were stupid kids.

"Well," I finally croaked. "We got here eventually."

"Yeah, you did." Mike clapped my shoulder. "Congrats, man."

They each hugged me one more time, and then left to join the rest of our guests.

Alone in the room, I faced myself in the mirror again and fussed with my bowtie for the millionth time.

My friends' words kept rolling around in my head. It had taken Cam and me a while to get here, and we'd taken some unfortunate detours over time, but we'd made it. And maybe those detours had been necessary to get us here. We'd needed to grow up. If I hadn't married Bryan, I wouldn't have Zach and Zane. If Cam hadn't needed a job when I'd needed a nanny, we wouldn't have been thrown into the same house with our simmering attraction.

Maybe we still would've made it here if things had happened differently. Maybe we needed all those bumps and switchbacks. All I knew was that we were here, and there was no other man I wanted but him. Of course our relationship wasn't all sunshine and roses, and we could argue and snipe as much as anyone, but it was perfect for me. I loved him. I loved coming home to him. I loved watching him bonding with my twins. I loved the boring evenings we spent watching TV in our sweats.

I couldn't have asked for anything better.

The past year and a half had been good for both of us individually, too. I'd re-signed with the Pittsburgh Rebels for four more years. Though I hadn't made any noise about wanting Chats gone, I wasn't sad in the least when he was traded to San Jose. I still didn't know if Eric had decided Chats was too toxic to keep, or if San Jose had wanted him in exchange for the *dynamite* goalie we'd acquired. I didn't ask. Either way, he was no longer on my team or even in my division or conference. And we had a kickass goalie, so... seemed like a win all around for me!

Getting Cam in touch with our team's fitness managers had worked out *very* well. They'd been super impressed with him, and they hadn't been bothered by his disclosure about why he'd been fired from his previous gym. This was especially true after one of them had called the gym to verify the information, and she found out that Cam's ex had been fired as well. Turned out he'd been caught on camera harassing both male and female gym goers. Oh, and he'd tried to badger a younger trainer who'd just been hired into sucking him off in his office, only to find out that younger trainer was the son of the gym's owner.

In fact, the person our trainer spoke to said they'd been trying to get in touch with Cam to hire him back now that they'd discovered he'd been fired over false allegations from a predator. They were out of luck, though—the Rebels were offering Cam significantly more money to come work for them.

"Well," the person had apparently said, *"tell him we wish him the best of luck, and our door is always open if he comes back to Portland."*

Cam was relieved to hear that, but he didn't seem interested in going back to the West Coast any time soon. Not just because we were together, either—the job had been a perfect fit for him. He was now training several of my teammates, plus numerous prospects and youth hockey players, and literally *half* of my teammates' spouses and partners. He was thriving, all his clients loved him—even if they did complain sometimes that he worked them hard—and he was making money hand over fist.

It worked out well for childcare, too. His schedule was mostly during the boys' school hours, and his evening and weekend clients were usually when I was home or Bryan had custody.

And speaking of Bryan, things had evened out with him, too. Ever since we'd had our come-to-Jesus conversation, the dynamic between us had shifted a *lot*. He'd mellowed considerably, especially the more he'd realized how much Chats was adding to our antagonistic relationship. It didn't hurt that the two of them had broken up shortly after that, either. Without Chats in the picture to add to the tension, we were finding some much more comfortable footing than we'd had before. Bryan still hadn't confirmed or denied if his relationship with Chats had overlapped with ours, but given the change in his attitude after they'd split up, I was pretty sure I had my answer. I left it alone, though; we were making progress, and that felt like a wound that didn't need reopening.

We weren't best friends or anything, but we were cordial, and he'd also worked out a fairly comfortable dynamic with Cam. The family counselor he'd suggested had been seriously helpful, and we'd gone both together and separately. The boys joined us for some sessions. So did Cam. Bryan's new boyfriend, Rick, had also started coming once it became clear that he was sticking around and Bryan wanted him to meet the boys.

Our family had spent a lot of hours in that office (and I'd spent a lot of hours doing televisits when I was on the road), and it had paid off in spades. During custody swaps, we'd sometimes even linger to talk beyond coordinating things with the twins.

It helped a lot that Bryan had also started going to a therapist on his own. I wasn't privy to what they'd talked about, but I could see the shift in Bryan over time. Some of that was probably from being away from Chats. Some of it, though, seemed more introspective. More like he was making a genuine effort to work on himself. That was especially apparent when he'd pulled me aside one night for a long heart-to-heart. He'd apologized for the things he'd done that had been the catalyst for our divorce. I had too—though I hadn't been the one to cheat, I'd learned through our counseling that I'd neglected other issues in our relationship. Bryan openly accepted the blame for cheating, but we both owned our parts in our marriage unraveling.

After that, I'd confided in Cam that maybe it was time for me to get a therapist too. My first appointment was a couple of weeks later, and it had helped a lot. My sessions with him made a huge difference with my relationship with Bryan, my confidence as a father, and even my otherwise rock-solid relationship with Cam. Why the hell didn't I start going to him sooner?

Bryan had also apologized to Cam for the obnoxious things he'd said, and they were getting along better than I'd ever imagined they would. They could communicate about the kids' schedules, homework, sports, and any issues without the slightest tension. When they'd had a disagreement a few months ago over who should handle driving to and from a doctor's appointment scheduled for our custody swap time, they'd sorted it out before I'd ever known there was a problem. Bryan had even gone to a cake-decorating class with Cam and the boys one night when I'd had to cancel due to a media obligation; by all accounts, everyone had had a good time.

I think that was better for the boys, too. Though we'd all endeavored to keep the animosity out of their sight, even while Chats had still been in the picture, they weren't stupid. They could pick up on the uncomfortable vibe whenever we were in the same room.

Now that that vibe was gone, and we could all act like adults around each other, the boys were more relaxed too.

I felt guilty about that. I hated that we hadn't been able to put our differences aside for so long, and that they'd felt it. But I was glad things were looking up now. Hopefully over time, we could all make it up to them.

Just before last season's training camp, Bryan admitted he missed going to games, so I'd hooked him and Rick up with season tickets. A few games in, Cam had invited them up to the partners' and spouses' box so they could be with the kids and Bryan's friends. Cam had, of course, consulted with the others to make sure that was all right. Bryan and Rick didn't join them for every game, but once in a while they did, and everyone got along fine. The kids loved it, too.

I had no desire to return to being with Bryan. I was blissfully happy with Cam, and Bryan was finding his own joy with Rick. But now we could share things like Christmas morning, the twin's birthday, and school events. Neither of us had to miss out on important moments in our sons' lives. Well, no more than hockey demanded, anyway. I think that was what I was most grateful for through all of this—that I'd found enough peace with my ex-husband to reclaim what precious moments I wasn't already missing because of my job.

And now, a year and a half after we'd found our way back to each other, Cam and I were doing this. We were tying the knot.

Nothing left to do but get my ass out there and say my vows.

I held my own gaze in the mirror, took a deep breath, and let it out. This was it. We were doing this. Zach and

Zane were excited to take part in our ceremony, and they were undoubtedly already seated with Bryan. All our friends and family were here, along with teammates past and present (minus Chats). Nothing left to do now but go join the man I loved so we could walk up to the altar together.

The butterflies were as calm as they'd ever be, so I stepped out of the room.

When I came down the stairs to the foyer outside the banquet hall where the ceremony would be held, there was only one person standing outside the closed doors.

And I halted.

And I stared.

Seeing Cam in that tux took me back to both our winter formal dance and that home opener after he'd first come to Pittsburgh. Back to those moments when I'd fallen in love with him all over again. We wore white tuxes this time, not black, but the look was still the same. His short, sandy blond hair was perfectly styled, and he had a rose boutonnière that matched mine.

Back then, when I'd seen him standing on his parents' front porch in that tux, we'd both been confused about who we were. Today, I knew exactly who I was, and I knew exactly who I loved, and seeing him like this almost had me breaking down in tears before our wedding even started.

Cam grinned up at me. "You ready for this?"

I laughed and tried to be as subtle as possible about wiping my eyes as I closed the last bit of distance between us. "I think I've been ready for this since before we could drink."

His laugh was a little damp around the edges, too, and when I stopped in front of him, he had tears in his eyes.

I chuckled and made a more conspicuous gesture of wiping at mine. "So it's not just me?"

"No." He sniffed. "No, it's not just you."

Our eyes met, and we both laughed. Then I wrapped my arms around him and pulled him in tight.

"I'm so glad we got here," I whispered.

"Me too." He paused. "Otherwise we'd have lost our deposit and—"

I burst out laughing and playfully shoved him back. "Oh my God."

He snickered, but his eyes were still wet and full of the same love and disbelief I was feeling.

We were doing this. We were really, really doing this.

Sobering, I touched his face, brushing away a tear with my thumb. "You ready?"

He smiled and pushed himself up to kiss me softly. "When you are."

We held each other's gazes for a moment. Then we shared one last, soft kiss as boyfriends.

And started up the aisle to start our life as husbands.

MORE HOCKEY ROMANCES BY L.A. WITT

The Gentlemen of the Emerald City Series

The Pucks & Rainbows Trilogy

Rookie Mistake (written with Anna Zabo)

Scoreless Game (written with Anna Zabo)

Injured Reserve

Name From a Hat Trick

Brick Walls

Interference

Aftermath

Red Line

Own Goal

Burner Account

Writing as Ann Gallagher

Even Strength (co-written with Cari Z)

Writing as Lauren Gallagher

Playmaker

TRANS ROMANCES BY L.A. WITT

Static

Adrift

Ashore

Afloat (coming soon)

Writing as Ann Gallagher

Having Her Back

The Left Hand of Calvus

Romances by L.A. Witt

The Anchor Point Series

The Husband Gambit

After December

Leave

Romantic Suspense by L.A. Witt

The Hitman vs. Hitman Series (written with Cari Z)

The Bad Behavior Series (written with Cari Z)

The Venetian and the Rum Runner

If The Seas Catch Fire

The Truth in My Lies

...and many, *many* more!

For more books by L.A. Witt,

or to subscribe to my newsletter, please visit

http://www.gallagherwitt.com

Newsletter perks:

- Exclusive discounts & giveaways
- Access to ARCs
- All the latest news about pre-orders, collaborations, and more!

Romance * Suspense

Contemporary * Historical * Sports * Military

ABOUT THE AUTHOR

L.A. Witt is a romance and suspense author who has at last given up the exciting nomadic lifestyle of the military spouse (read: her husband finally retired). She now resides in Pittsburgh, where the potholes are determined to eat her car and her cats are endlessly taunted by a disrespectful squirrel named Moose. In her spare time, she can be found painting in her art room or destroying her voice at a Pittsburgh Penguins game.

Website: www.gallagherwitt.com
Email: gallagherwitt@gmail.com
Twitter, Instagram, & Threads: @GallagherWitt